Theophilus North

A 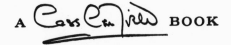 BOOK

BOOKS BY THORNTON WILDER

NOVELS
The Cabala
The Bridge of San Luis Rey
The Woman of Andros
Heaven's My Destination
The Ides of March
The Eighth Day
Theophilus North

COLLECTIONS OF SHORT PLAYS
The Angel That Troubled the Waters
The Long Christmas Dinner

PLAYS
Our Town
The Merchant of Yonkers
The Skin of Our Teeth
Three Plays:
Our Town
The Skin of Our Teeth
The Matchmaker

THORNTON WILDER

Theophilus North

HARPER & ROW, PUBLISHERS
New York, Evanston, San Francisco, London

FIRST EDITION

Designed by Patricia Dunbar

Library of Congress Cataloging in Publication Data

Wilder, Thornton Niven, 1897-
 Theophilus North.
 (A Cass Canfield book)
 I. Title.
PZ3.W6468Tf   813'.5'2   73-4165
ISBN 0-06-014636-2
ISBN 0-06-014637-0 (lim. ed.)

For Robert Maynard Hutchins

Contents

The Nine Ambitions

In the spring of 1926 I resigned from my job.

The first days following such a decision are like the release from a hospital after a protracted illness. One slowly learns how to walk again; slowly and wonderingly one raises one's head.

I was in the best of health, but I was innerly exhausted. I had been teaching for four and a half years in a boys' preparatory school in New Jersey and tutoring three summers at a camp connected with the school. I was to all appearance cheerful and dutiful, but within I was cynical and almost totally bereft of sympathy for any other human being except the members of my family. I was twenty-nine years old, about to turn thirty. I had saved two thousand dollars—set aside, not to be touched—for either a return to Europe (I had spent a year in Italy and France in 1920–1921) or for my expenses as a graduate student in some university. It was not clear to me what I wanted to do in life. I did not want to teach, though I knew I had a talent for it; the teaching profession is often a safety-net for just such indeterminate natures. I did not want to be a writer in the sense of one who earns his living by his pen; I wanted to be far more immersed in life than that. If I were to do any so-called "writing," it would not be before I had reached the age of fifty. If I were destined to die before that, I wanted to be sure that I had encompassed as varied a range of experience as I could—that I had not narrowed my focus to that noble but largely sedentary pursuit that is covered by the word "art."

Professions. Life careers. It is well to be attentive to successive ambitions that flood the growing boy's and girl's imagination. They leave profound traces behind them. During those years when the first sap is rising the future tree is foreshadowing its contour. We are shaped by the promises of the imagination.

At various times I had been afire with NINE LIFE AMBITIONS— not necessarily successive, sometimes concurrent, sometimes dropped and later revived, sometimes very lively but under a different form and only recognized, with astonishment, after the events which had invoked them from the submerged depths of consciousness.

The FIRST, the earliest, made its appearance during my twelfth to my fourteenth years. I record it with shame. I resolved to become a saint. I saw myself as a missionary among primitive peoples. I had never met a saint but I had read and heard a great deal about them. I was attending a school in North China and the parents of all my fellow-students (and my teachers in their way) were missionaries. My first shock came when I became aware that (perhaps covertly) they regarded the Chinese as a primitive people. I knew better than that. But I clung to the notion that I would be a missionary to a really primitive tribe. I would lead an exemplary life and perhaps rise to the crown of martyrdom. Gradually during the next ten years I became aware of the obstacles in my path. All I knew about sainthood was that the candidate must be totally absorbed in a relationship with God, in pleasing Him, and in serving His creatures here on earth. Unfortunately I had ceased to believe in the existence of God in 1914 (my seventeenth year), my view of the intrinsic divinity in my fellow-men (and in myself) had deteriorated, and I knew that I was incapable of meeting the strictest demands of selflessness, truthfulness, and celibacy.

Perhaps as a consequence of this brief aspiration I retained through life an intermittent childishness. I had no aggression and no competitive drive. I could amuse myself with simple things, like a child playing on the seashore with shells. I often appeared to be vacant or "absent." This irritated some; even valued friends, both men and women (perhaps including my father), broke with me charging me with "not being serious" or calling me a "simpleton."

The SECOND—a secularization of the first—was to be an anthropologist among primitive peoples and all my life I have returned to that interest. The past and the future are always *present* within us. Readers may observe that the anthropologist and his off-shoot ✳ the sociologist continue to hover about this book.

The THIRD, the archaeologist.

The FOURTH, the detective. In my third year at college I planned to become an amazing detective. I read widely in the literature, not only in its fictional treatment, but in technical works dealing with its refined scientific methods. Chief Inspector North would play a leading role among those who shield our lives from the intrusions of evil and madness lurking about the orderly workshop and home.

The FIFTH, the actor, an amazing actor. This delusion could have been guessed at after a consideration of the other eight ambitions.

The SIXTH, the magician. This aim was not of my seeking and I have difficulty in giving it a name. It had nothing to do with stage-performance. I early discovered that I had a certain gift for soothing, for something approaching mesmerism—dare I say for "driving out demons"? I understood what a *shaman* or a medicine-man probably relies upon. I was not comfortable with it and resorted to it seldom, but as the reader will see it was occasionally ✳ thrust upon me. It is inseparable from a certain amount of imposture and quackery. The less said about it the better.

The SEVENTH, the lover. What kind of a lover? An omnivorous

lover like Casanova? No. A lover of all that is lofty and sublime in women, like the Provençal Troubadours? No.

Years later I found in very knowledgeable company a description of the type to which I belonged. Dr. Sigmund Freud spent his summers in a suburb of Vienna called Grinzing. I was spending a summer in Grinzing and without any overtures on my part I was invited to call at his villa on Sunday afternoons for what he called *Plaudereien*—desultory conversations. At one of these delightful occasions the conversation turned upon the distinction between "loving" and "falling in love."

"Herr Doktor," he asked, "do you know an old English comedy —I forget its name—in which the hero suffers from a certain impediment [*Hemmung*]? In the presence of 'ladies' and of genteel well-brought-up girls he is shy and tongue-tied, he is scarcely able to raise his eyes from the ground; but in the presence of servant girls and barmaids and what they are calling 'emancipated women' he is all boldness and impudence. Do you know the name of that comedy?"

"Yes, *Herr Professor.* That is *She Stoops to Conquer.*"

"And who is its author?"

"Oliver Goldsmith."

"Thank you. We doctors have found that Oliver Goldsmith has made an exemplary picture of a problem that we frequently discover among our patients. *Ach, die Dichter haben alles gekannt!"* ("The poet-natures have always known everything.")

He then went on to point out to me the relation of the problem to the Oedipus complex and to the incest-tabu under which "respectable" women are associated with a man's mother and sisters— "out of bounds."

"Do you remember the name of that young man?"

"Charles Marlow."

He repeated the name with smiling satisfaction. I leaned forward and said, *"Herr Professor,* can we call that situation the 'Charles Marlow Complex'?"

"Yes, that would do very well. I have long looked for an appropriate name for it."

Theophilus suffered, as they say (though there was no suffering about it), from that *Hemmung*. Well, let other fellows court and coax, month after month, the stately Swan and the self-engrossed Lily. Let them leave to Theophilus the pert magpie and the nodding daisy.

The EIGHTH, the rascal. Here I must resort to a foreign language, *el pícaro*. My curiosities throw a wide net. I have always been fascinated by the character who represents the opposite of my New England and Scottish inheritance—the man who lives by his wits, "one step ahead of the sheriff," without plan, without ambition, at the margin of decorous living, delighted to outwit the clods, the prudent, the money-obsessed, the censorious, the complacent. I dreamt of covering the entire world, of looking into a million faces, light of foot, light of purse and baggage, extricating myself from the predicaments of hunger, cold, and oppression by quickness of mind. These are not only the rogues, but the adventurers. I had read, enviously, the lives of many and had observed that they were often, justly or unjustly, in prison. My instinct had warned me and my occasional nightmares had warned me that the supreme suffering for me would be that of being caged and incarcerated. I have occasionally approached the verge of downright rascality, but not without carefully weighing the risk. This eighth ambition leads me into my last and overriding one:

The NINTH, to be a free man. Notice all the projects I did not entertain: I did not want to be a banker, a merchant, a lawyer, nor to join any of those life-careers that are closely bound up with directorates and boards of governors—politicians, publishers, world reformers. I wanted no boss over me, or only the lightest of supervisions. All these aims, moreover, had to do with people—but with people as individuals.

As the reader will see, all these aspirations continued to make ✳ claims on me. As they were conflicting they got me into trouble; as they were deep-lodged their fulfillment often brought me inner satisfaction.

I was now free after four and a half years of relative confinement. Since my trip abroad, six years earlier, I had kept a voluminous Journal (from which the present book is largely an extract, covering four and a half months). Most of the entries in this Journal were characterizations of men and women I knew, together with as much of the life-story of each as I could learn. Myself was present for the most part only as witness—though occasionally an entry was devoted to an ill-digested bit of self-examination. I might almost say that for the last two years the center of my life had become that gallery of portraits. Only years later did I come to see that it was a form of introspection via extrospection. It's wonderful the way nature strives to create harmony within ourselves.

From the moment I resigned, two days before leaving the school, I discovered that several things were happening to me in my new state of freedom. I was recapturing the spirit of play—not the play of youth which is games (aggression under the restraint of rules), but the play of childhood which is all imagination, which improvises. I became light-headed. The spirit of play swept away the cynicism and indifference into which I had fallen. Moreover, a readiness for adventure reawoke in me—for risk, for intruding myself into the lives of others, for extracting fun from danger.

It happened that in 1926 it became possible for me to enter upon my new liberty earlier than I expected. Six weeks before the school's term-end an epidemic of influenza declared itself in central New Jersey. The infirmary filled up and overflowed. Beds were installed in the gymnasium which soon looked like a lazaret. Parents drove down and took their sons home. Classes came to an end and we masters were free to leave and I set out at once. I did not even return to my home in Connecticut since I had so recently enjoyed the Easter vacation there. I had bought a car from a fellow-master, Eddie Linley, on the condition that I take possession of it at his home in Providence, Rhode Island, after he'd driven it there from our school in New Jersey. I had known the car well for some time. It had belonged to the tutoring camp in New Hampshire where Eddie was also on the staff. Like all the masters we had taken turns in driving the students—usually in the larger vehicles—to church or to dances or to the motion pictures. This smaller car, known as "Hannah"—from the then popular song "Hard-hearted Hannah"—was used for short routine trips into the nearest village to the post office, to the grocery store, to the doctor, and occasionally to carry a few masters to a little applejack sociable. Hannah had known long service and was breaking up. Two years before, the directors of the camp had sold it to Eddie for fifty dollars. Eddie was a born mechanic. Poor Hannah asked only to lie down in a New Hampshire gully, but Eddie kept resuscitating her. He knew her "ways"; he "favored" her. She carried him to and from New Hampshire, Rhode Island, and New Jersey. I offered him twenty-five dollars for her on condition that he would give me some superficial instruction against emergencies. He agreed to this and I drove him to Trenton and back, Hannah responding admirably. He invited me to join him on his trip to Providence, but I told him that I wanted to spend a night in New York and would call at his home the next day. He consented to transport two suitcases and some books of mine—the inconsiderable possessions I had accumulated during my years at the school. These included the last two volumes of my precious Journal. I went to New York carrying a light handbag. From that Tuesday noon I was *all* free.

I felt then that New York was the most wonderful city in the world and now, about fifty years later, I am of the same opinion. I already knew and loved many others: Rome and Paris, Hong Kong and Shanghai, where I had passed a part of my boyhood; I was later to feel no stranger in London, Berlin, Rome, and Vienna. But none have equaled New York in its diversity, its richness in surprises, and in its climate.

Its extraordinary climate contains not only those extremes of hot and cold, but those radiant days of sunlight in the intense cold and those delightful days of temperate weather with which it is blessed in July and August. Moreover I believed (and still believe) in the theory, published from time to time by so-called authorities, that there is a sort of magnetic band about a hundred miles wide and a thousand miles long extending under the soil from New York to Chicago. Persons living in that area are animated by a galvanic force; they are alert, resourceful, optimistic, and short-lived. The diseases of an overtaxed heart abound. They are offered and must accept the choice of Achilles: a brief but buoyant life as against a bland and uneventful one. Men, women, and children are aware of this force rising from the pavements of New York and Chicago—and the cities between them—particularly in spring and autumn. It has been reported by entomologists that even ants walk more quickly in this area.

I had planned to spend the night—as so often—in the national clubhouse of the fraternity to which I had belonged during my student days at Yale University and I had tried to plan an engagement for the evening. I had telephoned certain friends in New York from my school in New Jersey:

"Good morning, this is Dr. Caldwell of Montreal speaking. May I speak to Mrs. Denham?"

The butler answered. "Mrs. Denham is in North Carolina, sir."

"Oh, thank you. I shall call when I'm next in New York."

"Thank you, sir."

"Good morning, this is Dr. Caldwell of Montreal speaking. May I speak to Miss LaVigna?"

"W'ich'a Miss'a LaVigna, Anna or Grazia?"

"Miss Grazia, please."

"Grazia no live here no more. She have a job in Newark. The 'Aurora Beauty Parlor'—in the telephone book."

"Thank you, Mrs. LaVigna. I'll call her there."

These disappointments were so acute that I altered my plan. I changed trains in New York and proceeded immediately to

Providence. I put up at a hotel and called for my car at Eddie Linley's house the next afternoon.

I had no very clear idea of how I would pass the summer. I had been told that one could live inexpensively in the province of Quebec. I would stop a short time in the Boston area which I scarcely knew, look at Concord, Walden Pond, Salem; then drive north through Maine, write a postcard to my father from his birthplace . . . something like that.

It was enough that I was to be at the wheel of my own car with the roads of the northern hemisphere before me . . . and four months without a single engagement to be met.

The Nine Cities of Newport

So in the early afternoon I called at Eddie Linley's home to pick up Hannah and my possessions that were stored in her. I asked him to sit beside me as I drove about the city and to instruct me again in the old car's idiosyncrasies.

Suddenly I saw a sign: "NEWPORT, 30 MILES."

Newport! I would revisit Newport where seven and eight years earlier I had served—modestly enough, from private to corporal—in the Coast Artillery defending Narragansett Bay. During my free hours I had taken many long walks over the region. I had come to love the town, the bay, the sea, the weather, the night sky. I knew only one family there, hospitable friends who had heeded the injunction to "Invite a Serviceman to Sunday Dinner," and I had received a favorable impression of the townspeople. There had been little to see of the much-publicized resort of the very wealthy; their residences were boarded up and under gas-rationing few wheels were turning on Bellevue Avenue. On seeing the sign an idea occurred to me as to how I might earn my daily expenses with a part-time activity without drawing on my savings. I then returned Eddie to his door, shook hands with the members of his family, paid him the twenty-five dollars, and drove off to Newport on the island of Aquidneck.

Oh, what a day! What promises of a still-retarded spring! What intimations that I was approaching the salt sea!

Hannah behaved pretty well until we got within the city limits when she started coughing and staggering. We persevered and reached Washington Square, where I stopped to inquire the location of the Young Men's Christian Association—not the "Army and Navy Y," right before me, but the civilian "Y." I entered a store selling newspapers, postcards, etc. (The family that ran it will reappear in this history in the chapter entitled "Mino.") I telephoned the "Y" asking if there was a room available. I added buoyantly that I was under thirty, had been christened in the First Congregational Church in Madison, Wisconsin, and that I was fairly sociable. A weary voice replied, "That's all right, buddy—calm down! Fifty cents a night." Hannah objected to going further, but was persuaded to enter Thames Street. I brought her to a stop at "Josiah Dexter's Garage. Repairs." A mechanic examined her long and thoughtfully and uttered some words that were unintelligible to me.

"How much would that cost?"

"Fifteen dollars, looks like."

"Do you buy old cars?"

"My brother does. Josiah! Josiah! Jalopy for sale!"

This was in 1926 when all mechanics, electricians, and plumbers were not only reliable but were held in high esteem as props of the self-respecting household. Josiah Dexter was much older than his brother. He had one of those faces one sees now only in daguerreotypes of judges and parsons. He too examined the car. They conferred together.

I said, "I'll sell you the car for twenty dollars, if you drive me and my luggage to the 'Y.' "

Josiah Dexter said, "Agreed."

We transferred my luggage into his car and I was about to climb in when I said, "Wait a minute!" The air made me giddy. I was about a mile from where I had spent a part of my twentieth and twenty-first years. I turned back to Hannah and stroked her hood. "Goodbye, Hannah," I said. "No hard feelings on either side— see what I mean?" Then I whispered into her nearest headlight: "Old age and death come to all. Even the weariest river winds its way to sea. As Goethe said, '*Balde ruhest du auch.*' "

Then I took my place beside Mr. Dexter. He drove a block slowly and then said, "Had that car long?"

"I have been the owner of that car for one hour and twenty minutes."

Another block, "Do you get worked up about everything you own?"

"Mr. Dexter, I was stationed at Fort Adams during the War. I'm back here. I've now been in Newport for a quarter of an hour. It's a beautiful day. It's a beautiful place. I'm a little light-headed. Sadness is just around the corner from happiness."

"May I ask what it was you said to the car?"

I repeated what I had said, translating the German ending, " 'Soon, you too will rest.' Those are commonplace remarks, Mr. Dexter, but I have come to see lately that if we shrink from platitudes, platitudes will shrink from us. I never sneer at the poems of Henry Wadsworth Longfellow who spent so many happy weeks in and near Newport."

"I know that."

"Can you give me the address of an establishment that rents bicycles?"

"I do."

"Then I shall be at your garage in an hour to hire one. . . . Mr. Dexter, I hope that my light-headedness has not offended you?"

"We New Englanders don't go in for light-headedness much, but I've heard nothing to be offended at. . . . What were the words that German said again?"

"In a poem he was talking to himself, late at night, in a tower-room, a deep forest all around him. He wrote them with a diamond on a windowpane. They are the last words of the most famous poem in the German language. He was in his twenties. He got his rest at eighty-three."

We had reached the entrance to the "Y." He stopped the car and remained still a moment, his hands on the wheel, then said, "I lost my wife five weeks ago tomorrow. . . . She thought a lot of Longfellow's poetry."

He helped me carry my baggage into the hall. He put a twenty-dollar bill in my hand, nodded slightly, saying "Good day to you," and left the building.

Mr. Josiah Dexter was not in his garage an hour later, but his brother helped me select a "wheel," as we generally called them in those days. I continued down Thames Street and set out on the "ten-mile drive." I rode past the entrance of Fort Adams ("Corporal North, T.!" "Present, sir!"), past the Agassiz House ("Seldom has so great a wealth of learning been so lightly borne!"), and drew up at the sea wall before the Budlong House. The wind in my face, I gazed across the glittering sea toward Portugal.

Not longer than six months before—in my exhaustion—I had been haranguing a fellow-master at the school: "Drive all those ideas out of your head! The sea is neither cruel nor kind. It is as mindless as the sky. It's merely a large accumulation of H_2O . . . and even the words 'large' and 'small,' 'beautiful' and 'hideous' are measures and valuations projected from the mind of a human being of average height, and the colors and forms which have taken on characteristics from what is agreeable or harmful, edible or inedible, sexually attractive, tactually pleasing, and so on. All the physical world is a blank page on which we write or erase our ever-shifting attempts to explain our consciousness of existing. Restrict your sense of wonder to a glass of water or a drop of dew— begin there: you'll get no further." But on this afternoon in late

April all I could do was to choke on the words: "Oh, sea! . . .
Oh, mighty ocean!"

I did not complete the ten miles of the famous drive, but returned to town by a short cut. I wanted to walk some of the streets
I had walked so often during my first stay in the city. In particular
I wanted to see again the buildings of my favorite age—the eighteenth century—church, town hall, and mansions; and to gaze again
at the glorious trees of Newport—lofty, sheltering, and varied.
The climate, but not the soil, of eastern Rhode Island was favorable to the growth of large and exotic trees. It was explained that
a whole generation of learned scientists had derived pleasure from
planting foreign trees on this Aquidneck Island and that thereafter
a generation of yachtsmen had vied with one another in bringing
here examples from far places. Much labor had been involved,
caravans of wagons bringing soil from the interior. I was to discover later that many residents did not know the names of the
trees that beautified their property: "We think that's a banyan or
. . . or a betel nut tree," "I think Grandfather said that one was
from Patagonia . . . Ceylon . . . Japan."

One of my discarded ambitions had been to be an archaeologist;
I had even spent the large part of a year in Rome studying its
methods and progress there. But long before, like many other boys,
I had been enthralled by the great Schliemann's discovery of the
site of ancient Troy—those nine cities one on top of the other.
In the four and a half months that I am about to describe I found
—or thought I found—that Newport, Rhode Island, presented
nine cities, some superimposed, some having very little relation
with the others—variously beautiful, impressive, absurd, commonplace, and one very nearly squalid.

The First City exhibits the vestiges of the earliest settlers, a
seventeenth-century village, containing the famous stone round-
tower, the subject of Longfellow's poem "The Skeleton in Armor,"
long believed to have been a relic of the roving Vikings, now gen-

erally thought to have been a mill built by the father or grandfather of Benedict Arnold.

The SECOND CITY is the eighteenth-century town, containing some of the most beautiful public and private edifices in America. It was this town which played so important a part in the War of Independence, and from which the enthusiastic and generous French friends of our revolt, under Rochambeau and Washington, launched a sea-campaign that successfully turned the course of the War.

The THIRD CITY contains what remains of one of New England's most prosperous seaports, surviving into the twentieth century on the bay side of Thames Street, with its wharfs and docks and chandlers' establishments, redolent of tar and oakum, with glimpses of drying nets and sails under repair—now largely dependent on the yachts and pleasure boats moored in the harbor; recalled above all by a series of bars and taverns of a particular squalor dear to seamen, into which a landlubber seldom ventured twice.

The FOURTH CITY belongs to the Army and the Navy. There has long been a system of forts defending Narragansett Bay. The Naval Base and Training Station had grown to a great size during the War, a world apart.

The FIFTH CITY was inhabited since early in the nineteenth century by a small number of highly intellectual families from New York and Cambridge and Providence, who had discovered the beauties of Newport as a summer resort. (Few Bostonians visited it; they had their North Shore and South Shore resorts.) Henry James, the Swedenborgian philosopher, brought his family here, including the young philosopher and the young novelist. In his last, unfinished novel, Henry James, Jr., returns in memory and sets the scene of *The Ivory Tower* among the houses and lawns edged by the Cliff Walk. Here lived to a great age Julia Ward Howe, author of "The Battle Hymn of the Republic." There was a cluster of Harvard professors. The house of John Louis Rudolph Agassiz that I had just passed was converted into a hotel, and is still one in 1972. At a later visit I was able to engage the pentagonal room in a turret above the house; from that magical room I could see at night the beacons of six lighthouses and hear the booming or chiming of as many sea buoys.

Then to make the SIXTH CITY came the very rich, the empire-builders, many of them from their castles on the Hudson and their villas at Saratoga Springs, suddenly awakened to the realization that inland New York State is crushingly hot in summer. With them came fashion, competitive display, and the warming satisfaction of exclusion. This so-called "great age" was long over, but much remained.

In a great city the vast army of servants merges into the population, but on a small island and a small part of that island, the servants constitute a SEVENTH CITY. Those who never enter the front door of the house in which they live except to wash it become conscious of their indispensable role and develop a sort of underground solidarity.

The EIGHTH CITY (dependent like the Seventh on the Sixth) contains the population of camp-followers and parasites—prying journalists, detectives, fortune-hunters, "crashers," half-cracked aspirants to social prominence, seers, healers, equivocal protégés and protégées—wonderful material for my Journal.

Finally there was, and is, and long will be the NINTH CITY, the American middle-class town, buying and selling, raising its children and burying its dead, with little attention to spare for the eight cities so close to it.

I watched and recorded them: I came to think of myself as Gulliver on the island of Aquidneck.

On the morning following my arrival I called for advice on a person with whom I dared to presume I had a remote connection —William Wentworth, superintendent at the Casino. Ten years before this my brother, while still an undergraduate at Yale, had played there in the New England Tennis Championship Tournament and had won high place. He had told me of Mr. Wentworth's congeniality and ever-ready helpfulness. I first strolled through the entrance and surveyed the playing area and the arrangements for spectators. The building was designed—as were other edifices in Newport—by the brilliant and ill-fated Stanford White. As in every work from his hand it was marked by distinguished design and a free play of fancy. Although it was early in the spring the famous lawn courts were already a carpet of green.

I knocked on the superintendent's door and was bidden to enter by a hale man of fifty who put out his hand, saying, "Good morning, sir. Sit down. What can I do for you?"

I told him of my brother's past in the Tournament.

"Let me see, now. Nineteen-sixteen. Here's his picture. And here's his name on the annual cup. I remember him well, a fine fellow and a top-ranking player. Where's he now?"

"He's in the ministry."

"Fine!" he said.

I told him of my military service at Fort Adams. I told him of my four years of uninterrupted teaching, of my need of a change, and of a less demanding teaching schedule. I showed him the sketch for an advertisement I planned to put in the newspaper and asked him if he'd be kind enough to tack a copy on the Casino's bulletin board. He read it and nodded.

"Mr. North, it's early in the season, but we always have young people, home for one reason or another, who need tutoring. Generally, they call on the masters from the nearby schools, but those masters don't like to give the time as their term-end approaches. You'll get some of their pupils, I hope. But we have another group that might be eager for your services. Would you be ready to read aloud to older people with poor eyesight?"

"Yes, I would, Mr. Wentworth."

"Everybody calls me 'Bill.' I call every man over sixteen 'Mister.' —Do you play tennis too?"

"Not as well as my brother, of course, but I passed a lot of my boyhood in California and everybody plays it there."

"Do you think you could coach children between eight and fifteen?"

"I was coached pretty intensively myself."

"Until ten-thirty three courts are reserved for children. The professional coach won't arrive until the middle of June. I'll start collecting a class for you. One dollar an hour for each youngster. You can ask two dollars an hour for the reading aloud.—Did you bring any tennis gear with you?"

"I can get some."

"There's a room back there filled with the stuff—discarded, lost, forgotten, and so on. I even keep a pile of flannels dry-cleaned so they won't foul up. Shoes and racquets of all sizes. I'll take you back there later.—Can you typewrite?"

"Yes, Bill, I can."

"Well, you sit down at this desk here and run up your advertisement for the paper. Better rent a box at the Post Office to receive your mail. Give them the 'Y' for phone calls. I've got to go and see what my carpenters are doing."

Kindness is not uncommon, but imaginative kindness can give a man a shock. I could occasionally be altruistic myself—but as a form of play. It's easier to give than to receive. I wrote:

T. THEOPHILUS NORTH

Yale, 1920. Master at the Raritan School in New Jersey, 1922–1926. Tutoring for school and college examinations in English, French, German, Latin, and Algebra. Mr. North is available for reading aloud in the above languages and in Italian. Terms: two dollars an hour. Address, Newport Post Office Box No. ——. Temporary Telephone, Room 41, the Young Men's Christian Association.

I ran the advertisement in only three successive issues of the paper.

Within four days I had pupils on the tennis courts and very enjoyable work it was. (I had played the game without much interest. At the Casino I found some dog-eared manuals. "Improve

Your Tennis," "Tennis for Beginners." More respected callings than was mine are supported by an element of bluff.) Within a week telephone calls and letters were arriving daily. Among the first of the letters was a summons to be interviewed at "Nine Gables," an engagement which led to complications related hereafter; another, to read aloud from the works of Edith Wharton to an old lady who had known her when Mrs. Wharton resided in Newport; and others. The responses on the telephone were more varied in character. I learned for the first time that anyone who presents himself to the general public is exposed to contacts with what is too frivolously called "the lunatic fringe." An angry voice informed me that I was a German spy and that "we have our eyes on you." A woman urged me to learn and teach Globo and so prepare the world for international and perpetual peace.

Others were more challenging.

"Mr. North? . . . This is Mrs. Denby's secretary speaking. Mrs. Denby wishes to know if you would be able to read aloud to her children between the hours of three-thirty and six-thirty on Thursday afternoons?"

I saw at once that this was the governess's "afternoon off." I was still subject to "light-headedness." For some reason I am more outspoken and even rude over the telephone than in personal confrontations. I suspect that it has something to do with being unable to look into the speaker's eyes.

"May I ask the age of Mrs. Denby's children?"

"Why . . . why, they are six, eight, and eleven."

"What book does Mrs. Denby recommend that I read to them?"

"She would leave that to you, Mr. North."

"Thank Mrs. Denby and tell her that it is impossible to hold *one* child's attention on a book for longer than forty minutes. I suggest they be encouraged to play with matches."

"Oh!"

Click.

"Mr. North? This is Mrs. Hugh Cowperthwaite speaking. I am the daughter of Mr. Eldon Craig."

She paused to let me savor the richness of my privilege. I was never able to remember the sources of my employers' wealth. I cannot now recall whether Mr. Craig was reputed to receive a half-dollar every time a refrigerator car locked its door or to receive a dime every time a butcher installed a roll of brown paper.

"Yes, ma'am."

"My father would like to discuss with you the possibility of your reading the Bible to him. . . . Yes, the entire Bible. He has read it eleven times and he wishes to know if you are able to read rapidly. . . . You see, he would like to break his record which is, I believe, eighty-four hours."

"I am thinking it over, Mrs. Cowperthwaite."

"If you are interested, he would like to know if you would be able to make special terms for . . . for such a reading."

"Special terms?"

"Well, yes—reduced terms, so to speak."

"I see. At my rate that would be over one hundred and fifty dollars. That's certainly a considerable sum of money."

"Yes. My father wondered if you could—"

"May I make a suggestion, ma'am? . . . I could read the Old Testament in Hebrew. There are no vowels in Hebrew; there are simply what they call 'breathings.' That would reduce the time by about seven hours. *Fourteen dollars less!*"

"But he wouldn't understand it, Mr. North!"

"What has understanding got to do with it, Mrs. Cowperthwaite? Mr. Craig has already heard it eleven times. Hearing it in Hebrew he would be hearing God's own words as He dictated them to Moses and the prophets. Moreover I could read the New Testament in Greek. Greek is full of silent digammas and enclitics and prolegomena. Not a word would be lost and my price would be reduced to one hundred and forty dollars."

"But my father—"

"Moreover in the New Testament I could read Our Lord's words in His own language, Aramaic! Very terse, very condensed. I've been able to read the Sermon on the Mount in four minutes, sixty-one seconds, and nothing over."

"But would it count in making a record?"

"I'm sorry you don't see it as I do, Mrs. Cowperthwaite. Your respected father's intention is to please his maker. I am offering you a budget plan: *one hundred and forty dollars!*"

"I must close this conversation, Mr. North."

"Let's say ONE HUNDRED AND THIRTY!"

Click.

So before long I was cycling up and down the Avenue like a delivery boy. Lessons. Readings. I enjoyed the work (the *Fables* of La Fontaine at "Deer Park," the works of Bishop Berkeley at "Nine Gables"), but I soon ran up against the well-known truth that the rich never pay—or only occasionally. I sent bills every two weeks, but even the friendliest employers somehow overlooked them. I drew on my capital and waited; but my dream of renting my own apartment (a dream fostering other dreams, of course) seemed indefinitely postponed. Except for a few engagements to read aloud after dark, my evenings were free and I became restless. I looked into the taverns on Thames Street and on the Long Wharf, but I had no wish to join those dim-lit and boisterous gatherings. Card-playing was permitted in the social rooms at the "Y" on condition that no money changed hands and I lose interest in card games without the incentive of gain. Finally I came upon Herman's Billiard Parlor—two long rooms containing seven tables under powerful hanging lights and a bar dispensing licit beverages, for these were "Prohibition" days. Any strong liquor you brought in your own pocket was winked at, but most of the players and myself were contented with orders of Bevo. It was a congenial place. The walls were lined with benches on two levels for onlookers and for players awaiting their turn. The game principally played at that time was pool. Pool is a concentrated rather than a convivial sport, conducted in grunts, muted oaths, and prayers, intermittently punctuated by cries of triumph or despair. The habitués at Herman's were handymen on the estates, chauffeurs, a few store clerks, but mostly servants of one kind or another. I was occasionally invited to take a cue. I established my identity as one who taught tennis to the beginners at the Casino. I play fairly well (long hours—in Alpha Delta Phi), but I became aware of an increasing coolness toward me. I was about to go seek another poolroom when I was rescued from ostracism by being adopted by Henry Simmons.

What a lot I came to owe to Henry: his friendship, the introductions to his fiancée, to Edweena, the incomparable Edweena, and to Mrs. Cranston and her boardinghouse; and to all that followed from that. Henry was a lean English valet of forty. His face—long, red, and pockmarked—was brightened by dark observant eyes. His speech had been chastened by seven years in this country, but often reverted in high spirits to that of his earlier years—a speech which delighted me with its evocation of those characters of a similar background in the pages of Dickens and Thackeray. He served a well-known yachtsman and racing enthusiast whom he much admired and whom I shall call Timothy Forrester. Mr. Forrester, like others of his class and generation, lent his boat to scientific expeditions and explorations (and participated in them) where the presence of a "gentleman's gentleman" would have seemed frivolous. So Henry was left behind in Newport for months at a time. This arrangement agreed well with him because the woman he planned to marry spent the greater part of the year there. Henry was always dressed in beautifully cut black suits; only his brightly colored vests expressed his individual taste. He was a favorite at Herman's, to which his low-voiced banter brought an element of extravagant and exotic fancy.

He must have been observing me for some time and connecting me with my advertisement in the newspaper, because one evening when I had been sitting overlong on the sidelines he suddenly approached me and said, "You there, professor! How about three sets at two bits each, eh? . . . What's your name, cully? . . . Ted North? Mine's Henry Simmons."

At this time of our first encounter Henry was a very unhappy man. His master was helping a team to photograph the birds of Tierra del Fuego and Henry hated idleness; his fiancée was away on another voyage and he missed her painfully. We played in relative silence. I had a run of luck or perhaps Henry disguised his greater proficiency. When the game came to an end the rooms were emptying. He invited me to a drink. The house reserved some cases of Bass's Ale for his use; I ordered the usual near-beer.

"Now who are you, Ted, and are you happy and well? I'll tell you who I am. I'm from London—I never went to school after I was twelve. I was a bootblack and swept the barber's shop. I raised my eyes a bit and learned the trade. Then I went into domestic service and became a 'gentleman's gentleman.' " He had accompanied his gentleman to this country and finally was engaged as Mr. Forrester's valet. He told me about his Edweena, absent as lady's maid to a group of ladies on a famous yacht. He showed me some bright postcards he had received from Jamaica and Trinidad and the Bahamas—meager consolations.

In turn I told him the story of my life—Wisconsin, China, California, schools and jobs, Europe, the War, ending up with my reasons for being in Newport. When I concluded my story we struck our glasses together and it was understood that we were friends. This was the first of many pool games and conversations. At the second or third of these I asked him why the players were so slow to invite me to join the game. Was it because I was a newcomer?

"Cully, there's a lot of suspicion of newcomers in Newport. Distrust, do you see what I mean? There are a number of types we don't want around here. Let's pretend that I didn't know that you're all right. See? I'll ask you some questions. Mr. North, were you planted in Newport?"

"How do you mean?"

"Do you belong to any organization? Were you sent here on a job?"

"I told you why I came here."

"I'm asking you these questions, like it was a game. Are you a flicker?"

"A what?"

"Are you a detective?"

I take pleasure in the modifications that words undergo as they pass from country to country and descend from century to century. "Flicker" was a bird and in 1926 it was a motion-picture. But in France a "*flic*" is a police detective; the word must have crossed the Channel, entered the slang of the English underworld, and had probably been imported to Newport by Henry himself. I raised my hand as though I were taking an oath. "I swear to God, Henry, I've never had anything to do with such things."

"When I saw in the newspaper that you were ready to teach Latin—that did it. There's no flicker ever been known that can handle Latin.—It's this way: there's nothing wrong with the job; there's lots of ways of earning a living. Once the season's begun there'll be scores of them here. Some weeks there's a big ball every night. For visiting celebrities and consumptive children, like that. Diamond necklaces. Insurance companies send up their men. Dress them up as waiters. Some hostesses even invite them as guests. Keep their eyes glued on the sparklers. Some families are so nervous, they have a flicker stay up all night sitting by the safe. Some jealous husbands have flickers watching their wives. A man like you comes to town—doesn't know anybody—no serious reason for being here. Maybe he's a flicker—or a thief. The first thing a regular flicker does is to call on the Chief of Police and get it straight with him. But many don't; they like to be very secret. You can be certain that you weren't three days in town before the Chief was fixing his eyes on you. It's a good thing you went to the Casino and found that old record about yourself—"

"It was about my brother, really."

"Probably Bill Wentworth called up the Chief and told him he had confidence in you."

"Thanks for telling me, Henry. But it's your confidence in me that's made all the difference here at Herman's."

"There are some flickers in the crowd at Herman's, but what we can't have there is a flicker who pretends he isn't. Time after time flickers have been known to steal the emeralds."

"What are some of the other types I was suspected of being?"

"I'll tell you about them, gradual. You talk for a while."

I told about what I had found out and "put together" about the glorious trees of Newport. I told him about my theory of "The Nine Cities of Newport" (and of Schliemann's Troy).

"Oh, Edweena should hear this! Edweena loves facts and pulling ideas out of facts. She's always saying that the only thing people in Newport talk about is one another. Oh, she'd love that about the trees—and about the nine cities."

"I've only made out five so far."

"Well, maybe there are fifteen. You might talk it over with a friend of mine in town named Mrs. Cranston. I've told her about you. She's said she wants to meet you. That's a very special honor, professor, because she don't make many exceptions: she only likes to see servants in the house."

"But I'm a servant, Henry!"

"Let me ask you a question: all these houses where you've got students—do you go in the front door?"

"Well, yes . . ."

"Do they ever ask you to lunch or dinner?"

"Twice, but I've never—"

"You're not a servant." I was silent. "Mrs. Cranston knows a lot about you, but she says that she would be very happy, if I brought you to call."

"Mrs. Cranston's" was a large establishment within the shadow of Trinity Church, consisting of three houses that had been so adjoined that it had required merely making openings in the walls to unite them into one. The summer colony at Newport was upborne by almost a thousand servants most of whom "lived in" at their places of employment; Mrs. Cranston's was a temporary boardinghouse for many and a permanent residence for a few. At the time of my first visit most of the great houses (always referred to as "cottages") had not yet been opened, but servants had been sent on in advance to prepare for the season. In a number of cases female domestics refused to pass the night "alone" in the remoter houses along the Ocean Drive. In addition Mrs. Cranston harbored a considerable number of "extra help," a sort of labor pool for special occasions, though she made it perfectly clear that she did not run an employment agency. The house was indeed a blessing to the Seventh City—to the superannuated, to the temporarily idle, to the suddenly dismissed—justly or more often unjustly dismissed—to the convalescent. The large parlor and adjacent sitting rooms by the entrance hall furnished a sort of meeting place and were naturally filled to overflowing on Thursday and Sunday evenings. There was a smoking room off the front parlor where legalized beer and fruit drinks were served and where trusted friends of the house—men servants, coachmen, and even chefs—gathered. The dining room was reserved for residents only; even Henry had never entered it.

Mrs. Cranston ran her establishment with great decorum; no guest ever ventured to utter an inelegant word and even gossip about one's employers was kept within bounds. I was surprised to discover that stories of the legendary Newport—the flamboyant days before the War—were not often recalled—the wars between social leaders, the rudeness of celebrated hostesses, the Babylonian extravagance of fancy-dress balls; everyone had heard them. More recent summers had not been without great occasions, eccentricity, drama and melodrama, but such events were alluded to in confidence. Mrs. Cranston conveyed that it was unprofessional to discuss the private lives of those who fed us. She herself was present every evening, but she did not choose to sit enthroned governing the conversation. She sat at one or other of the many small tables preferring that her friends join her singly or by twos or threes. She had a handsome head, nobly coiffured, an impressive figure, perfect vision, and perfect hearing. She dressed in the manner of the ladies in whose service she had passed her younger days—corseted, jet-bugled, and rustling in half a dozen petticoats. Nothing gave her greater pleasure than to be consulted on some complicated problem requiring diplomacy and thoroughly disillusioned worldly wisdom. I can well believe that she had saved many a drowning soul. She had risen through the ranks from scullery maid and slop-carrier to upstairs maid and to downstairs maid. Rumor had it—I only venture to repeat it so many decades later—that there had never been a "Mr. Cranston" (Cranston is a town a mere crow's flight from Newport) and that she had been set up in business by a very well-known investment-banker. Mrs. Cranston's best friend was the incomparable Edweena who retained in perpetuity the first-floor "garden apartment." Edweena was awaiting the long-overdue break-up and death of her alcoholic husband in distant London in order to celebrate her marriage to Henry Simmons. An advantage inherent in her possession of the "garden apartment" was apparent to a few observers; Henry could enter and depart as he chose without causing scandal.

It was a rule of the house that all the ladies—with the exception of Mrs. Cranston and Edweena—withdrew for the night at a quarter before eleven, either to their rooms upstairs or to their domiciles in the city. Gentlemen retired at midnight. Henry was a great favorite of the lady of the house to whom he paid an old-world deference. It was this last hour and a quarter that Henry (and our hostess) most enjoyed. The majority of the men remained in the bar, but occasionally, Mrs. Cranston was joined by a very old and cadaverous Mr. Danforth, also an Englishman, who had served—no doubt majestically—as butler in great houses in Baltimore and Newport. His memory was failing but he was still called in from time to time to grace a sideboard or an entrance hall.

It was during this closing hour that Henry presented me to

Mrs. Cranston. "Mrs. Cranston, I should like you to make the acquaintance of my friend Teddie North. He works at the Casino and has some jobs reading aloud to some ladies and gentlemen whose eyesight is not what it used to be."

"I'm very pleased to make your acquaintance, Mr. North."

"Thank you, ma'am, I feel privileged."

"Teddie has only one fault, ma'am, as far as I know, he minds his own business."

"That recommends him to me, Mr. Simmons."

"Henry does me too much credit, Mrs. Cranston. That has been my aim, but even in the short time I've been in Newport I've discovered how difficult it is not to get involved in situations beyond one's control."

"Like a certain elopement recently, perhaps."

I was thunderstruck. How could word of that brief adventure have leaked out? This was my first warning of how difficult it was to keep a secret in Newport, things that could easily escape notice in a big city. (After all servants are praised for "fore-seeing every wish" of their employers; that requires close and constant attention. Aquidneck is not a large island, and the heart of its Sixth City is not of wide extent.)

"Ma'am, I can be forgiven for trying to be of assistance to my friend and employer at the Casino."

She lowered her head with a slight but benevolent smile. "Mr. Simmons, you'll excuse me if I ask you to go into the bar for two minutes while I tell Mr. North something he should know."

"Yes, indeed, gracious lady," said Henry, very pleased, and left the room.

"Mr. North, this town has an excellent police force and a very intelligent Chief of Police. It needs them not only to protect the valuables of some of the citizens but to protect some of the citizens from themselves; and to protect them from undesirable publicity. Whatever it was that you were called upon to do two and a half weeks ago, you did it very well. But you know yourself that it might have ended in disaster. If some such complication should present itself to you again, I hope you will get in touch with me. I have done some helpful things for the Chief of Police and he has been kind and helpful to me and to some of the guests in my house." She put her hand briefly on mine and added, "Will you remember that?"

"Yes, indeed, Mrs. Cranston. I thank you for letting me know that I can trouble you, if the occasion arises."

"Mr. Simmons! Mr. Simmons!"

"Yes, ma'am."

"Please rejoin us and let us break the law a little bit." She tapped a handbell and gave a coded order to the bar boy. As a sign of good fellowship we were served what I remember as gin-fizzes. "Mr. Simmons tells me that you have some ideas of your own about the trees of Newport and about the various parts of the town. I would like to hear them in your own words."

I did so—Schliemann and Troy and all. My partition of Newport was, of course, still incomplete.

"Well! Well! Thank you. How Edweena will enjoy hearing that. Mr. North, I spent twenty years in the Bellevue Avenue City, as most of my guests upstairs have; but now I am a boarding-house keeper in the last of your cities and proud of it. . . . Henry Simmons tells me that the gentlemen in Herman's Billiard Parlor thought that you might be some kind of detective."

"Yes, ma'am, and some other undesirable types that he was not ready to tell me."

"Ma'am, I didn't want to put too heavy a burden on the chap in his first weeks. Do you think he's strong enough now to be told that he was suspected of being a *jiggala,* maybe, or a *smearer?*"

"Oh, Henry Simmons, you have your own language! The word is '*gigolo.*' Yes, I think he should be told everything. It may help him in the long run."

"A *smearer,* Teddie, is a newspaperman after dirt—a scandal hound. During the season they're thick as flies. They try to bribe the servants to tell what's going on. If they can't find any muck they invent some. It's the same in England—millions and millions read about the wicked rich and love it. 'Duke's daughter found in Opium Den—Read all about it!' And now it's Hollywood and the fillum stars. Most of the smearers are women, but there's plenty of men, too. We won't have anything to do with them, will we, Mrs. Cranston?"

She sighed. "They aren't entirely to blame."

"Now that Teddie's wheeling up and down the Avenue he'll begin to get feelers. Have you been approached yet, old man?"

"No," I said sincerely. A minute later, I caught my breath; I had indeed been "approached" without realizing what lay behind it. Flora Deland! I shall give an account of that later. It occurred to me that I should keep my Journal locked up—it already contained material not elsewhere obtainable.

"And the *gigolo,* Mr. Simmons?"

"Just as you wish, ma'am. I know you'll forgive me if I call our young friend by one nickname or another. It's a way I've got."

"And what are you going to call Mr. North now?"

"It's those teeth, ma'am. They blind me. Every now and then I've got to call him 'Choppers.' "

There was nothing remarkable about my teeth. I explained that I had spent my first nine years in Wisconsin, a great dairy state, and that one of its gifts to its children was excellent teeth. Henry had good reason to envy them. Children reared in the center of London often missed this advantage; his caused him constant pain.

"Choppers, old fellow, the men at Herman's thought for a while that you might be one of these—?"

"*Gigolos.*"

"Thank you, ma'am. That's French for dancing partners with ambitions. Next month they'll be here like a plague of grasshoppers—fortune-hunters. You see, there are dozens of heiresses here with no young men of their own class. These days the young men from the big houses go off to Labrador with Dr. Grenfell to carry condensed milk to the Eskimos; or they go off, like my master, to photograph birds at the South Pole; or they go to ranches in Wyoming to break their legs. Some go off to Long Island where they hear there's lots of fun to be had. No young man wants to enjoy himself under the eyes of his parents and his relatives. Except during Yacht Race Week and the Tennis Tournament no man under thirty would be seen here."

"No single man under forty, Henry."

"Thank you, ma'am. So when the hostesses want to give a dance for their beautiful daughters they call up their dear friend the Admiral at the Naval Station and ask him to send over forty young men that can waltz and one-step without stumbling. They've learned from experience, the old ladies, to put a lot of pure spring water in the punch. Another thing they do is to invite house-guests for a month at a time from the embassies in Washington—young counts and marquesses and barons that are climbing up the first steps in the diplomatic career. That's the stuff! I came over to this country of yours, Choppers, as a 'gentleman' to an Honourable six removes from an earldom. He got engaged to a daughter of Dr. Bosworth at 'Nine Gables'—nicest fellow you could hope to meet but he couldn't get up before noon. Fell asleep at dinner parties; loved the meal but couldn't stand the waits between courses. Even with my tactful persuasion he was an hour late for every appointment. His wife, who was as energetic as a beehive, divorced him with a cool million— that's what they say. . . . All that an ambitious young man's got to have is a pleasant way of talking, a pair of dancing pumps, and *one* little respectable letter of introduction and all the doors are open to him, including a card to the Casino. So at first we thought you were one of them."

"Thank you, Henry."

"Nevertheless, Mrs. Cranston, we wouldn't think the worse of Mr. North here, if he found a sweet little thing in copper mines or railroads, would we?"

"I advise against it, Mr. North."

"I have no intention of doing so, Mrs. Cranston, but may I ask your reasons against it?"

"The partner who owns the money owns the whip and a girl brought up to great wealth thinks she has great brains too. I'll say no more. By the end of the summer you will have made your own observations."

I greatly enjoyed these pre-midnight conversations. If at times I thought of myself as Captain Lemuel Gulliver shipwrecked on the island of Aquidneck and preparing to study the customs and manners there I could scarcely have fallen on better luck. Telescopes are generally mounted on tripods. One leg of mine was grounded on my daily visits on the Avenue; another rested on the experience and wisdom available to me at Mrs. Cranston's; a third was still to seek.

I was not sincere in promising Mrs. Cranston to call on her aid whenever a complicated and even dangerous situation arose. By nature I like to tend to my own business, to keep my mouth shut, and to scramble out of my own mistakes. Probably Mrs. Cranston soon knew that I was engaged eight or nine hours a week at "Nine Gables"—a "cottage" where something peculiar was certainly going on; she may have suspected that I was getting involved beyond my depths at the George F. Granberrys' in a situation that might at any moment burst into a lurid conflagration of "yellow journalism."

In the matter that turned on my reading at "Wyckoff House" I did call on her for help and got it handsomely.

Diana Bell

So there I was, bicycling my way up and down the Avenue and not only earning my living but saving money toward renting a small apartment. One morning in the middle of my third week, having come to the end of my children's class at the Casino and preparing to take a shower and change my clothes before entering on my day's academic program, I was stopped by Bill Wentworth. "Mr. North, can I see you here some time at the end of the day?"

"Yes, of course, Bill. Will six-fifteen be all right for you?"

I had come to know Bill well and with increasing admiration. He had invited me to Sunday dinner in his home with his wife and with a married daughter and her husband—sound Rhode Islanders, every one of them. I was aware that something was worrying him. He looked at me narrowly and said, "When you were at my house you told us of some adventures you'd had. Would you like to try a little expedition that's not in the regular run of things? You can turn it down flat, if you don't like the sound of it, and it won't change things between you and me. It'll call for some sharp wits, but it'll be well paid."

"Yes, I would, especially if it would be of any service to you, Bill. Send me to the North Pole."

"That might attract attention, likely. This is what they call a 'confidential mission.' "

"Just what I like."

At six-fifteen I entered his office of cups and trophies. Bill sat at his desk, passing his hand despondently over his close-cropped gray hair. He came at once to the point. "A problem has been dropped on my lap. The chairman of our Board of Governors here has been for some time a Mr. Augustus Bell. He's a New York businessman, but his wife and daughters live here a large part of the year. They go to New York for a few months in the winter. His older daughter Diana is about twenty-six; that's old for a girl in her set. They have a saying here: 'She's worn out a lot of dancing shoes.' She's high-spirited and restless. Everybody knows that in New York she started going around with some undesirable company. She got written up in the papers—and you know the kind of papers I mean. Then something worse happened. About two and a half years ago one of those undesirable characters followed her up here. Her family wouldn't receive him. So they eloped. She was brought back before she got very far— police, private detectives, and all that. The newspapers went wild. . . . The trouble is that Newport's no longer a summer resort for young men of her own class. Newport's for the middle-aged and upward." Bill struggled with himself a moment. "Now it's happening again. Her mother found in her room a letter from a man making arrangements to go off with her day-after-tomorrow night. Going to Maryland to get married. Now, Mr. North, it's very difficult to deal with the rich. Mr. Bell thinks it's my obvious duty to drop everything and pursue two adults and somehow *block* them. He doesn't want anything more to do with the police and with private detectives. I will not do it and probably my job is at stake."

"Of course, I'll do it, Bill. I'll try my best." Bill sat silent, mastering his emotion. "Who's the man?"

"Mr. Hilary Jones, head of the athletic staffs in the school system here. He's about thirty-two, he's been divorced and has a daughter. He's well thought of by everybody, including his former wife." He picked up a large envelope. "Here are some newspaper photographs of Miss Bell and Mr. Jones and some clippings about them. Do you drive?"

"Yes, for four summers at the camp in New Hampshire I've driven every kind of car. Here's my driver's license; it has three weeks to go."

"Mr. North, I took a great liberty for which I hope you will forgive me. I told Mr. Bell I knew someone who was young, who got on well with everybody, and who I thought was level-headed and resourceful. I didn't tell him your name, but I said you were a Yale man. Mr. Bell's a Yale man, too. But I don't want you to do this for me. You're free to tell me it's a nauseating underhand business and that you'll have nothing to do with it."

"Bill, I intend to enjoy it. I like demands on what you call my resourcefulness. I would like to hear the whole project from Mr. Bell's own mouth."

"He will reward you well—"

"Stop! I'll go into that with him. When can I see him?"

"Could you be in my office at six tomorrow evening? That'll leave another day for further plans."

I shall now have to repeat a good deal of the above material, but I want the reader to hear it from another angle. At six o'clock on the following evening Bill was sitting in his office. A gentleman of about fifty whom I suspected of having "touched up" his hair and mustache was striding about the room kicking chairs.

"Mr. North, this is Mr. Bell. Mr. Bell, Mr. North. Sit down, Mr. North." Mr. Bell does not shake hands with tennis coaches. "Mr. Bell, I suggest that you let me start the story. If I get anything wrong, you can correct me." Mr. Bell grunted unhappily and continued his prowling. "Mr. Bell is also a Yale man, where he had a notable athletic career. He has served at intervals on the Board of the Casino for almost twenty years which shows in what high esteem he is held. Mr. Bell has a daughter Miss Diana who's played excellent tennis on these courts since she was a child. She's a most attractive young woman with a host of friends . . . perhaps a little self-willed. Can I say that, Mr. Bell?"

Mr. Bell slashed at the window-curtains and overturned a championship cup or two.

"Mr. Bell and Mrs. Bell have discovered by chance that Miss Diana is planning to run away from home. She ran away from home once before, but she didn't get very far. The police were alerted in three or four states and she was brought home. That's quite a humiliation for a proud girl."

"Oh, God, Bill! Get on with it!"

"The Bells are, on the whole, year-round residents of Newport, but they keep an apartment in New York and spend some months there in the winter. Mr. Bell won't mind my saying that Miss Diana is a high-spirited girl, and some of those newspapermen got in the way of reporting that she was seen in public places with certain undesirable acquaintances—including the very man she was with when that pursuit was set up." I kept looking Bill in the eye. I could see that he had regained a large measure of his New England spunk and that he did not intend to let Mr. Bell off easily. "Now Mrs. Bell happened to come across a letter hidden in her daughter's lingeray. A man in Newport whom I know slightly sent her the arrangements for their meeting tomorrow night. It contained plans for a trip to Maryland where they planned to be married as soon as possible."

"Oh, God, Bill, I can't stand this!"

"Whose car are they driving, Bill?" I asked.

"Her car. His car is the school truck in which he carries his teams to athletic meets. They're driving off the island on the ten P.M. ferry to Jamestown, then the ferry to Narragansett Pier. You can well understand that Mr. Bell doesn't wish to call in the police a second time. Above all, the family wishes to avoid any more of that Sunday-supplement publicity—what they call the 'scandal sheets.' "

Mr. Bell advanced on Bill angrily: "That's enough of that, Bill!"

"These are facts, Mr. Bell," he replied firmly. "We've got to put the facts on the table. Mr. North must know what we're asking him to do." Mr. Bell clenched his fists and shook them before him. "The idea, Mr. North, is that you might intercept them somewhere—somewhere, somehow—and bring Miss Diana back. —You're a free man. There's no compulsion on you whatever. Miss Diana's a mature woman; she may refuse absolutely to return to her father's home. All Mr. Bell is asking you, as a favor —as one Yale man to another—is to try. Would you be willing to see what you could do?"

I looked down at the floor.

I didn't believe in any sense in the universe. I thought I didn't believe in loyalty or friendship—but there was Bill Wentworth, maybe with his life-long job at stake. And there was that apoplectic bully; there was Mrs. Bell who ransacked the bureau drawers of a twenty-six-year-old daughter for private letters—and read them.

Of course I would do it and I would succeed. But I wasn't going to make it easy for Mr. Bell, either.

"What's your idea that I should do, Mr. Bell?"

"Why, follow them. Better follow them beyond Narragansett Pier so that whatever you decide to do won't happen too near Newport. Wait to see where they stop to eat or spend the night. Put their car out of order. Beat down their door if necessary. Point out to her what an idiot she is. The disgrace of it! She'll break her mother's heart."

"Do you know anything disreputable about this man?"

"What?"

"This Mr. Jones—do you know him?"

"God, no! He's a nobody. He's a goddam fortune hunter. He's trash."

"Have you Mr. Jones's letter on you, Mr. Bell?"

"Yes, here it is, and to hell with it!" He pulled it from his pocket and threw it on the carpet between us. Bill and I were also "nobodies" and "trash."

Bill rose and picked it up from the floor. "Mr. Bell, we are asking Mr. North to help us in a matter of strict confidence. We hope that he will be successful and that you and Mrs. Bell will wish to thank him."

Mr. Bell struggled with himself. In a choked voice he said, "I am in a very disturbed state. I apologize for throwing the letter on the floor."

I said to Bill, "We're putting this in a large envelope and sealing it with wax. Address it to Miss Bell and write: 'Received from Mr. Augustus Bell, sealed, unread, by William Wentworth and Theophilus North.'—Mr. Bell, may I ask where your daughter met Mr. Jones?"

"We live in Newport most of the year. My daughter and a number of her friends belong to a group of voluntary assistants at the hospital. Diana is crazy about children. She met this Mr. Jones when he was calling on his three-year-old daughter who was a patient there. He's a vulgar unscrupulous fortune hunter, just like the others. We've had to cope with these bastards over and over again. It's obvious."

The only thing to do with a man like that is to continue looking at him expectantly, as though he were about to say something completely convincing. Without agreement and applause such men deflate; they gasp for air.

After a pause I began again. "Mr. Bell, I must propose a few reasonable conditions. There shall be no mention of any remuneration to me whatever. I shall send a bill for the exact amount I lose for canceling my engagements here. That's compensation, not payment for a job. I want a car placed at my disposal, dark blue to black in color—one that can hold three persons in the front seat if possible. I would like a good revolver."

"Why?" asked Mr. Bell angrily.

"I won't be using conventional ammunition; I can make my own. If your daughter's car were to be found by the police at the

side of a Rhode Island or Connecticut highway punctured by a
bullet, it might be reported in the newspapers. I can puncture it,
as you might say, naturally. I would like a sealed envelope containing ten ten-dollar bills to cover certain expenditures that might
arise. I think I shall not need them; in that case I shall return the
envelope unopened to Mr. Wentworth. But most important of
all, if I succeed or fail, I shall say nothing about this matter to
anyone outside your family. Do you agree to those conditions?"

He growled, "Yes, I do."

"I have brought a memorandum of these five conditions. Will
you sign it, please."

He read the list and began signing his name. Suddenly, he
looked up. "But, of course, I shall *pay* you for this. I am ready to
pay you a thousand dollars."

"In that case, Mr. Bell, you must *hire* someone to kidnap Miss
Bell. No amount of money could hire me to do that. I see my
mission as one merely of persuasion."

He looked dazed, as though he were being led into a trap. He
looked inquiringly at Bill.

"I had not heard those conditions before, Mr. Bell. I think
they are reasonable."

Mr. Bell finished signing the document and laid it on the
table. I shook hands with Bill, saying, "Will you keep that signed
agreement, Bill? I'll be here tomorrow night at six to pick up the
car." I bowed to Mr. Bell and went out.

The clerk at the reception desk of the "Y" lent me road maps
of Rhode Island and Connecticut. I studied them closely at intervals during the next day. That about making my own ammunition was just bluff and swagger. In revolver practice at Fort
Adams we had used cork bullets with a pin in them that pene-
trates the target board; I assumed that they could puncture a tire
and I bought a package of them.

The car was a beauty. I crossed on an early ferry to Jamestown
and waited at the dock before the second ferry until I saw Miss

Bell's car enter the ferry boat. She was driving. I followed them into the vast dimly lit hull. Soon after the boat started she got out of the car and walking between the cars examined the faces of the occupants. She saw me from some distance and walked straight toward me. Mr. Jones followed her in a bewildered manner. I got out of my car and stood waiting for her, not without admiration; she was a tall handsome young woman, dark-haired and high-colored.

"I know who you are, Mr. North. You run the kindergarten at the Casino. You have been paid by my father to spy on me. You are beneath contempt. You are the lowest form of human life. I could spit on you. . . . Well, haven't you got anything to say for yourself?"

"I am here in one capacity, Miss Bell. I am here to represent common sense."

"You!"

"What you are doing now will call down a world of ridicule in the newspapers; you will ruin Mr. Jones's career as a teacher—"

"Rubbish! Nonsense!"

"I hope that you'll marry Mr. Jones—and with your family sitting in the front pew, as is fitting in a woman of your class and distinction."

"I can't stand it! I can't stand being hounded and dragged about by snooping policemen and detectives. I'm going crazy. I want to be free to do what I want."

Mr. Jones touched her elbow lightly: "Diana, let's hear what he has to say."

"Hear him? Hear him?—that yellow-bellied spy?"

"Diana! *Listen to me!*"

"How dare you give orders to me?" and she slapped his face resoundingly.

I never saw a man more astonished, then humiliated. He lowered his head. She continued shouting at me: "I won't be followed! I'll never go back to that house again. Someone stole my letter. *Why can't I live like other people?* Why can't I live my life in my own way?"

I repeated in an even voice, "Miss Bell, I am here to represent common sense. I want to spare you and Mr. Jones a great deal of mortification in the future."

Mr. Jones found his voice. "Diana, you're not the girl I met in the hospital."

She put her hand to his reddened cheek. "But, Hilary, can't you see what nonsense he talks? He's trying to cage us in; he's trying to block us."

I continued. "This crossing will take about half an hour. Will you permit Mr. Jones and myself to go to the upper deck and talk this matter over reasonably?"

He said, "Any conversation we have, I want Miss Bell to be there too. Diana, I ask you again: will you listen to what he has to say?"

"Let's go upstairs, then," she said, despairingly.

The big hall upstairs looked like a cheap dance hall, ten years abandoned. It had a sandwich and coffee counter, closed at this early season. The tables and chairs were rusty and stained. The lamps gave off a steel-blue light, such as would serve to photograph criminals. Even Diana and Hilary—fine-looking persons, both—looked hideous.

"Will you speak first, Miss Bell?"

"How could you take this nasty job, Mr. North? Some children pointed you out to me at the Casino. They *said* they like you."

"I'll tell you anything you want to know about me later. I'd like to hear you talk about yourselves first."

"I met Hilary at the hospital where I do volunteer work. He was sitting by his daughter's bed. It was wonderful the way they were talking together. I fell in love with him, just watching them. Most fathers bring a box of candy or a doll and they act as though they wished they were a thousand miles away. I love you, Hilary, and I want you to forgive me for slapping your face. I'll never *think* of doing it again." He put his hand on hers. "Mr. North, I lose control of myself every now and then. My whole life has been mixed up and full of mistakes. I was sent home from three schools. If *you*—and my father—somehow pull me back to Newport this time I'll put an end to myself—as my Aunt Jeannine did. I never want to put foot in Newport again as long as I live. Hilary's cousin, who lives in Maryland where we're going to be married, says that there are schools and colleges all over where he can go on with his work. I have a little money of my own, left me by Aunt Jeannine in her will. It will help to pay for the operations that Hilary's daughter will need next year. Now, Mr. North, what has this common sense you keep boasting about to say about that?"

There was a silence.

"Thank you, Miss Bell. Can I ask Mr. Jones to speak now?"

"I guess that you don't know I'm a divorced man. My wife's Italian. Her lawyer told her to tell the judge that we weren't compatible, but I still think she's a very fine woman. . . . She works in a bank now and . . . she says she's happy. We both contribute from our salaries to pay Linda's hospital bills. When I met Diana she was in a sort of blue-striped uniform. When I saw her leaning over Linda's bed, I thought she was the most beautiful person I'd ever seen. I didn't know that she came from one of the big families. For lunch hours we used to meet in a corner table at the Scottish Tea Room. . . . I wanted to call on her father and mother, like most men would, but Diana thought that that wouldn't do any good . . . that the only thing to do is what we're doing tonight."

Silence. It was my turn.

"Miss Bell, I'm going to say something. I have no intention of offending you. And I'm not trying to put any obstacles in the way of your marrying Mr. Jones. I'm still talking in the name of common sense. There's no need for you to elope. You are a very conspicuous young woman. Everything you do stirs up a lot of publicity. You've run out of your allowance of elopements. I hate to say it, but do you know that you have a nickname known in millions of homes where they read those Sunday papers?"

She stared at me furiously. "What is it?"

"I'm not going to tell you. . . . It's not nasty or vulgar, but it's undignified."

"What is it?"

"I beg your pardon, but I'm not going to be part of cheap journalists' chatter."

I was lying. It was maybe half-true. Besides, I wasn't breaking any bones.

"Hilary, I didn't come here to be insulted!"

She rose from her chair. She walked about the room. She clutched her throat as though she were strangling. But she got the point. Again she cried, "Why can't I live as other people live?" Finally, she returned to the table and said scornfully, "Well, what have you got to suggest, Doctor Nosey Commonsense?"

"I suggest that when we reach Narragansett Pier we return to Newport by the same ferries. You return to your home as though you'd merely been out for an evening ride. Later, I shall have some suggestions as to how you may marry Mr. Jones in simplicity and dignity. Your father will give you away and your mother will sit duly weeping in the front pew. As many as possible of the children you have befriended will be brought to the church. Dozens of Mr. Jones's young athletic teams will also be there. The newspapers will say, 'Newport's most beloved friend of children has married Newport's most popular teacher.'"

There was no doubt that she was dazzled by this picture, but she had had a hard life. "How could that be done?"

"You fight bad publicity with good publicity. I have some newspaper friends there, and in Providence and in New Bedford. The world we live in swims in publicity. Articles will appear about the remarkable Mr. Jones. He will be proposed for 'TEACHER OF

THE YEAR IN RHODE ISLAND.' The Mayor will have to take notice of it. 'WHO IS DOING MOST TO BUILD THE NEWPORT OF THE FUTURE?' There'll be a medal. Who would be most suitable to present the medal? Why, Mr. Augustus Bell, Chairman of the Board of the Newport Casino. Bellevue Avenue loves to think that it's democratic, patriotic, philanthropic, big-hearted. That'll break the ice."

I knew this was just folderol, but I had a job to do for Bill Wentworth, and I knew that a marriage between these two would be disastrous. My low strategy worked.

They looked at one another.

"I don't want my name in the papers," said Hilary Jones.

I looked Diana straight in the eye and said, "Mr. Jones doesn't want his name in the papers." She got it. She looked me straight in the eye and murmured, "You devil!"

Hilary had gained assurance. "Diana," he said, "don't you think it's best that we go back?"

"Just as you wish, Hilary," she answered and burst into tears.

Arriving at the ferry slip we learned that the boat tied up there for the night. If we wished to return to Newport, we must drive the forty miles to Providence and then the thirty miles to Newport. It was Hilary's suggestion and mine that we drive in one car and that we send for the other in the morning. Diana was still weeping profusely—she saw her life as one spiteful frustration after another—and mumbled that she couldn't drive, she didn't want to drive. So they transferred their luggage into mine. I took my place at the wheel. She pointed at me saying, "I don't want to sit by *that man.*" She sat by the window and fell asleep, or seemed to.

Hilary was not only field-games director of the High School, but supervisor in all the public schools. I asked him about the prospects of the teams as we approached the crucial games of the year. He picked up animation.

"Please call me Hill."

"All right. You call me Ted."

I heard about the teams' hopes and fears—about promising pitchers who got strained tendons and great runners who got charley horses. About the possibility of winning the pennant from Fall River or the All Rhode Island School Cup. About the Rogers High School team. And the Cranston School's. And the Calvert School's. Very detailed. Very interesting. It began to rain, so it was necessary to awake Diana and to close the window. Nothing stopped Hill's flow of information. As we reached the working-class periphery of Providence it was nearly midnight. Diana opened her handbag, pulled out a package of cigarettes, and lit one. Hill turned to stone: his bride-to-be smoked!

A gas station was about to close. I drove up and filled the tank. To the attendant I said, "Joe, is there any place around here where you can get a cup of Irish tea at this hour?"

"Well, there's a club around the corner that sometimes stays open. If you see a green light over the side door, they'll let you in."

The light was on. "There's still an hour's drive," I said to my companions. "I need a little drink to keep me awake."

"Me too," said Diana.

"You don't drink, do you, Hill? Well, you can come along and be our bodyguard, if we get into any trouble."

I forget now what club it was—"The Polish-American Friendship Society" or "Les Copains Canadiens" or the "Club Sportivo Vittorio Emanuele"—dark, cordial, and well-attended. Everybody shook hands all around. We weren't even allowed to pay for our beverages.

Diana came to life. She was surrounded.

"Gee, lady, you're gorgeous."

"You're gorgeous yourself, brother."

She was invited to dance and consented. Hill and I sat at a remote table. He appeared stricken. We had to shout to be heard above the din.

"Ted?"

"Yes, Hill?"

"Is that the way she was brought up?"

"It's all perfectly innocent, Hill."

"I never knew a girl that would smoke and drink—least of all with strangers."

We looked straight before us—into the future. At the next pause in the music I said, "Hill?"

"Yes."

"You have a contract with the Board of Education or the school system, haven't you?"

"Yes."

"You're not running out on it, are you?"

Our elbows were on the table, our heads were low over our folded hands. He turned scarlet. His teeth bit into the knuckles of his right hand.

"Does Miss Bell know that?" Behind my question lay others. "Does she know that you couldn't get another job like your own in the whole country? That the only jobs you could get would be in private athletic clubs—weight-reducing institutes for middle-aged men?"

He slowly raised his eyes to mine in agony. "No."

"Have you sent in your letter of resignation yet?"

"No."

He perhaps saw clearly for the first time that his honor was at stake. "Don't you see? We loved each other so much. It all looked so easy."

The loud music began again. We averted our eyes from the sight of the young woman being snatched from one dancing partner to another. Finally he struck my elbow sharply. "Ted, I want you to help me break this up."

"You mean tonight's party?"

"No, I mean the whole thing."

"I think it's broken up already, Hill. Listen, on the way to

Newport I want you to talk without stopping about your teams' football chances. Tell us what you told us before and then tell us some more. Give every fellow's weight and record. Don't let anything stop you. If you run short, give us the college teams; you'll be coaching a college team yourself one of these days."

I arose and approached Diana. "I guess we'd better get on the road, Miss Bell."

We made a big exit—renewed handshakes and thanks all round. It had stopped raining; the night air felt wonderful.

"Gentlemen, I haven't had such a good time in years. My shoes are ruined—the big brutes!"

We drove off. Hilary couldn't find his voice so I took over.

"Hill, it seems to me that you must get home pretty late every afternoon?"

"Yes."

"I'll bet your wife used to complain that she didn't see you from seven o'clock in the morning until eight o'clock at night."

"I felt terrible about that, but I couldn't help it."

"And, of course, Saturdays must have been the worst day of all. You'd come back from Woonsocket or Tiverton, dog-tired. You could go to the moving-pictures once in a while?"

"There are no moving-pictures on Sunday."

We got back to the subject of football. I nudged him and he picked up animation a little. . . . "Wendell Fusco at Washington's a real comer. You should see that boy lower his head and crash through the line. He's going to Brown University year after next. Newport will be proud of him one of these days."

"Which sport do you like coaching most, Hill?"

"Well, track, I guess. I was a track man myself."

"Which event do you like best?"

"I'll confess to you that for me the most exciting event of the year is the All-Newport relay race. You have no idea how different the men are from one another—I call them 'men'; it does something for their morale. They're all fifteen to seventeen. Each does three laps around the course, then passes on the stick to the next man. Take Bylinsky, he's captain of the blue team. He's not as fast as some of the others, but he's the thinker. He likes to run second. He knows the good and bad points of each of his men and every inch of the course. Brains, see what I mean? Then there's Bobby Neuthaler, son of a gardener up on Bellevue Avenue. Determined, dogged—kind of excitable, though. You know, he bursts into tears at the end of every race, win or lose. The other men respect it, though; they pretend they don't see it. Ciccolino— lives down at the Point, not far from where I lived when I was married—he's the clown of the red team. Very fast. Loves running, but he's always laughing. Interesting thing, Ted; his mother and older sister go to the all-night chapel at Sacred Heart at midnight before the race and pray for him until they have to go home and make breakfast. Imagine that!"

I didn't need anyone to tell me to imagine that. I felt I was listening to Homer, blind and a beggar, singing his story at a banquet: "*Then the fair-tressed Thetis raised her eyes to Zeus the thunderer and prayed for her son, even for Achilles, goodliest of men whom she bore to Peleus, King of the Myrmidons; grief filled her heart, for she knew that to him had been allotted a short life, yet she prayed that glory be his portion this day on the plains before wide-wayed Troy.*"

"Golly, I wish you could see Roger Thompson pick up that stick—just a little runt but he puts his whole soul into it. His father runs that ice-cream parlor down at the end of the public beach. Our doctor at the gym says he's not going to let him run next year; he's only just fourteen and it's not good for his heart when he's growing so fast. . . ."

On went the catalogue. I glanced at Diana, neglected, forgotten. Her eyes were open, seemingly lost in deep thought. . . . What had they talked about during those rapturous hours at the Scottish Tea Room?

Hill directed me to the door of his rooming house. While we

extracted his suitcases from the back of the car Diana descended
and looked about the deserted street in the Ninth City where she
had so seldom put down her foot. It was well after one o'clock.
Apparently Hill had not notified his landlady of his departure for
he drew the front door key from his pocket.

Diana approached him. "Hilary, I slapped your face. Will you
please slap mine so that we'll be quits, fair and even?"

He stepped back, shaking his head. "No, Diana. No!"

"Please."

"No . . . No, I want to thank you for the happy weeks we had.
And for your kindness to Linda. Will you give me a kiss so that
I can tell her you sent her a kiss?"

Diana kissed him on the cheek and—uncertain of foot and hand
—she took her place in the car. Hill and I shook hands in silence
and I returned to the wheel. She directed me to her home. As we
drove through the great gates we saw that there was some kind of
party going on. There were cars drawn up before the house with
chauffeurs sleeping at the wheel. She murmured, "Everybody's
mad about mahjong. It's tournament night. Please drive around
to the back door. I don't want anyone to see me returning with
luggage."

Even the back door had a great sandstone porte-cochère. I
carried her suitcases up to the darkened entrance.

She said, "Hold me a minute."

I put my arms around her. It was not an embrace; our faces did
not touch. She wanted to cling for a moment to something less
frozen than the lofty structure under which we stood; she was
trembling after the freezing realization of the repetitions in her
life.

There were servants moving about in the kitchen. She had only
to ring the bell and she rang it.

"Good night," she said.

"Good night, Miss Bell."

The Wyckoff Place

Among the first replies to my advertisement was a note in a delicate old-world penmanship from a Miss Norine Wyckoff, such and such a number on Bellevue Avenue, asking me to call between three and four on any day at my convenience. She wished to discuss arrangements for my reading aloud to her. I might find the work tedious, and in addition she would be obliged to submit to me certain conditions which I might feel free to accept or reject.

The next evening I met Henry Simmons for a game of pool. Toward the end of the game I asked him offhandedly, "Henry, do you know anything about the Wyckoff family?" He stopped in mid-aim, stood up, and looked at me hard.

"Funny, your asking me that."

Then he bent over and completed his shot. We finished the set. At a wink from him we hung up our cues, ordered something to drink, and strolled over to the remotest table in the bar. When Tom had placed our steins before us and departed, Henry looked about him, lowered his voice, and said, "The 'ouse is 'aunted. Skeletons going up and down the chimneys like bloody butterflies."

I had learned never to hurry Henry.

"To my knowledge, cully, there have been four haunted houses among the big places in Newport. Very bad situation. Maids won't take service there; refuse to spend the night. They see things in corridors. They hear things in cupboards. There's nothing contagious like hysterics. Twelve guests to dinner. Maids drop trays. Fainting all over the place. Cook puts on her hat and coat and leaves the house. Gives the house a bad name—see what I mean? Can't even get a night watchman who'll swear to do the rounds of the *whole house* at night. . . . The Hepworth place—sold it to the Coast Guard. The Chivers cottage—it was said that the master strangled the French maid—nothing proved. They got in a procession of priests, candles and incense, the whole works . . . drove the spirits out and sold it to a convent school. The Colby cottage— deserted for years, burned down one night in December. You can go out and see the place yourself—only thistles grow there. Used to be famous for wild roses.

"Now your Wyckoff place, beautiful house—nobody knows what happened. No body, no trial, nobody disappeared, nothing, just rumors, just talk—but it got a bad name. Old family, most respected family. Rich!—Like Edweena says, could buy and sell the State of Texas without noticing it. In the old days before the War—great dinner parties, concerts, Paderewski; very musical they were—then the rumors started. Miss Wyckoff's father and mother used to charter ships and go off on scientific expeditions— collector, he was—shells and heathen idols. Be gone for half a year at a time. Then in about 1911 he came back and closed the whole place up. Went to live in their New York house. During the War both Mr. Wyckoff and his wife died decently in New York hospitals leaving Miss Norine alone—the last of the line. What can she do? She's got a lot of spirit. She comes back to Newport to open her family house—her girlhood home; but she can't get any help *after dark*. For eight years she's taken an apartment at the La Forge Cottages, but she goes every day to the Wyckoff place, gives lunches, asks people in to tea—but when the sun starts to set her maids and butler and housemen say, 'We've got to go now,

Miss Wyckoff,' and they go. And she and her personal maid drive
off in their carriage to the La Forge Cottages, leaving lights on all
over the house."

Silence.

"Henry, you swear you don't know of anything that might have
started the rumors? Mrs. Cranston knows everything. Do you suppose she has a theory?"

"Never heard her say so; and Edweena, who's the sharpest
girl on Aquidneck Island—*she* don't know anything."

I arrived at the Wyckoff place the next day at three-thirty. I had
long admired the house. I used to dismount from my bicycle just
to rest my eyes on it, the most beautiful cottage in Newport. I had
never been in or near Venice, but I recognized it as being "Pal-
ladian," as resembling those famous villas on the Brenta. Later I
came to know the ground floor well. The central hall was large
without being ponderous. The ceiling was supported by columns
and arches decorated in fresco. The wide doorways, framed in
marble, opened in all directions—noble, but airy and hospitable.
An elderly maid opened the great bronze front door to me and
led me to the library where Miss Wyckoff was sitting at a tea-table
before an open fire. The table was set for a considerable company
but the urn was still unlit. Miss Wyckoff, whom I judged to be
about sixty, was dressed in black lace; it fell from a cap about
her ears and continued in flounces and panels to the floor. Her
face was still that of an unusually pretty woman and her expression was candid and gracious and—as Henry said—"spirited."

"Thank you so much for coming to see me, Mr. North," she
said extending her hand; then turning to the maid, "Perhaps Mr.
North will have a cup of tea before he must go. If anyone calls
on the telephone, take the name and number; I shall call them
back later." When the maid had gone she whispered to me, "May
I ask you to close the door? Thank you . . . I know you are busy
so let us talk at once about my reason for asking you to call. My old
friend Dr. Bosworth has spoken to me warmly in your favor."

A sign had been exchanged. The wealthy are like members of the Masonic Order; they pass commendations and disapprobations to one another by passwords and secret codes.

"Moreover, I knew that I could trust you when I read that you were a Yale man. My dear father was a Yale man as was his father before him. My brother, had he lived, would have been a Yale man. I have always found that Yale men are honorable; they are truly Christian gentlemen!" She was moved; I was moved; Elihu Yale revolved in his grave. "Do you see those two ugly old trunks there? I have had them brought down from the attic. They are filled with family letters, some of them dating back sixty and seventy years. I am the last in my line, Mr. North. The greater number of these letters have lost their interest by now. I have long wished to make a rapid inspection of most of them . . . and destroy them. My eyesight is no longer able to read handwritten material, particularly in cases where the ink has begun to fade. Is your eyesight in good condition, Mr. North?"

"Yes, ma'am."

"Often it will be merely necessary to glance at the beginning and the ending. My father's serious correspondence—he was an eminent scientist, a conchologist—it has gone, with his collections, to Yale University where both are safe. Would you be willing to undertake this task with me?"

"Yes, Miss Wyckoff."

"In reading old letters there is always the possibility that intimate matters might be revealed. May I ask your promise as a Yale man and a Christian that these matters will remain confidential between us?"

"Yes, Miss Wyckoff."

"There is, however, another matter about which I must ask your confidence. Mr. North, my situation in Newport is very strange. Has anyone spoken to you about it—about me?"

"No, ma'am."

"A malediction rests upon this house."

"A *malediction?*"

"Yes, this house is believed by many people to be haunted."

"I do not believe there are haunted houses, Miss Wyckoff."

"Nor do I!"

From that moment we were friends. More than that, we were conspirators and fighters. She described the difficulty of engaging domestic servants who would stay in the house after dark. "It is humiliating to be unable to ask my friends to dinner although they continue to invite me to their homes. It is humiliating to be an object of pity . . . and to feel perhaps that they hold my dear parents in some sort of suspicion. Many a woman, I think, would give up and abandon the place altogether. But it is my childhood home, Mr. North! I was happy here! Besides, many people agree with me that it's the most beautiful house in Newport. I shall never give it up. I shall fight for it as long as I live."

I was looking at her gravely. "How do you mean—fight for it?"

"Clear its name! Lift its shadow!"

"We are reading these letters, Miss Wyckoff, to find some clue to that unjust suspicion?"

"Exactly!—Do you think you could help me?"

Between one breath and another I became Chief Inspector North of Scotland Yard. "In what year did you first notice that domestic servants were refusing to work here after dark?"

"My father and mother went away on long expeditions. I couldn't go with them because the motion of the ship made me dreadfully ill. I stayed with cousins in New York and studied music. My father returned here in 1911. We meant to live here, but suddenly he changed his mind. He closed the house, dismissed the servants, and we all lived in New York. We went to Saratoga Springs for the summer. I begged him to return to Newport, but he didn't wish to. He never explained why. During the War both my parents died. In 1919 I was alone in the world. I decided to return to Newport and live in this house the whole year round. It was then that I discovered that no servants would consent to live here."

Did Miss Wyckoff have any ideas that would throw light on the matter? None. Did her father have any enemies? Oh, none at all! Did the matter come to the attention of the police? What was there to bring except the reluctance of servants and the vague rumor about a house being haunted?

"When your father was away on these expeditions who was left in charge of the house?"

"Oh, it was left fully staffed. My father liked the idea that he could return to it at a moment's notice. It was in charge of a butler or majordomo whom we'd had in the family for years."

"Miss Wyckoff, we shall begin reading the letters surrounding the years 1909 to 1912. When shall I come?"

"Oh, come every day at three. My friends don't drop in for tea before five."

"I can come alternate days at three. I shall be here tomorrow."

"Thank you, thank you. I shall sort out the letters covering those years."

The great man had the last word: "There are no haunted houses, Miss Wyckoff!—there are only excitable imaginations, perhaps malicious ones. We shall try to find out how this matter all started."

When I arrived the next afternoon the letters that might concern us were laid out in packets bound in red cord: her letters to her parents 1909 to 1912; her parents' letters to her; six letters of her father to her mother (they were seldom apart for a day); her father's letters to his brother (returned to him) and his brother's replies; letters from the majordomo at Newport (Mr. Harland) to her father; letters to and from her father's lawyers in New York and Newport; letters from friends and relatives to Mrs. Wyckoff. The reading of the domestic letters was a painful experience for Miss Wyckoff, but she stout-heartedly set many aside for destruction. Weather, storms off Borneo, blizzards in New York; health (excellent); marriages and death of Wyckoffs and relatives; plans for the following year and alterations to plans; "love and kisses to our darling girl." Miss Wyckoff and I had begun to divide the task. She found that her eyesight was able to sustain reading letters written to her by her parents and she preferred to read those to herself. So we were soon working on separate lots. I read those from Mr. Harland: leak in the roof repaired; requests from strangers to "view the house" rejected; damage to conservatory by Halloween merrymakers repaired, and so on. I began reading the letters from Mr. Wyckoff to his brother: discovery of rare shells, sent to the Smithsonian for identification, narrow escape in the Sunda Strait, financial transactions agreed upon, "delighted with news of our Norine's progress in music." . . . Finally I came upon a clue to the whole unhappy matter. The letter was written from Newport on March 11, 1911:

I trust that you have destroyed the letter written to you yesterday. I wish the whole thing to be forgotten and never mentioned again. It was fortunate that I left Milly and Norine in New York. I wish them to retain only happy memories of this house. I have dismissed the entire staff, paid their wages and given each a generous bonus. I did not even bring the matter to the attention of Mr. Mullins [his lawyer in Newport]. I have engaged a new caretaker and some helpers who come in by the day. We shall perhaps return and reopen the house after a number of years when I shall have begun to forget the whole wretched business.

I slipped this letter into an envelope that I had prepared "For later rereading."

I had an idea of what probably took place.

While I was an undergraduate at college I had written and printed in the *Yale Literary Magazine* a callow play called *The Trumpet Shall Sound*. It was based upon a theme borrowed from Ben Jonson's *The Alchemist*: Master departs on a journey of indefinite length, leaving his house in charge of faithful servants; servants gradually assume the mentality of masters; liberty leads to license; Master returns unannounced and puts an end to their riotous existence. Lively writer, Ben Jonson.

Mr. Wyckoff had returned to discover filth and disorder, perhaps had broken in on some kind of orgy.

But how could that have given rise to a reputation of being "haunted"—a word associated with murder? I decided that I must break my oath to Miss Wyckoff and make inquiries in another quarter. Besides, I did not want our readings to come to an end too soon; I needed the money. At the end of each week her maid, showing me out of the house, placed in my hand an envelope containing a check for twelve dollars.

I called on Mrs. Cranston soon after ten-thirty when the ladies gathered about her were beginning to withdraw for the night. I bowed to her, murmuring that there was a matter which I wished to discuss with her. Until the field was clear I sat in a corner of the bar over a glass of near-beer. In due time I received a signal to approach and I drew up a chair beside her. We temporized for a few minutes, discussing our state of health, the weather, my plan to rent a small apartment, the increasing number of my engagements, and so on. Then I said, "Mrs. Cranston, I want your advice and guidance on a very confidential matter that has come up."

I told her about the project at Wyckoff House, but made no mention of the significant letter I had discovered.

"A sad story! A sad story!" she said with ill-disguised relish, striking a handbell on the table before us. In the late evening she often partook of a tall glass of what I took to be white wine. When Jerry had served her and retired she repeated, "A sad story. One of the oldest and most respected families. Did Miss Wyckoff tell you anything?"

"Oh, not everything, Mrs. Cranston. She did not tell me what had happened to give the house a bad reputation. She assured me solemnly that she didn't know what it could be."

"She doesn't know, Mr. North. You're reading all those family letters up to the years just before the War?"

"Yes, ma'am."

"Have you come upon anything . . . sensational yet?"

"No, ma'am."

"You may."

The word "sensational" is a very sensitive word in Newport. The Sixth City lived under the white light—I should say the "yellow" light—of an immense publicity. It was bad enough to be thought frivolous, even scandalous, but it also dreaded being regarded as ridiculous.

Mrs. Cranston deliberated a moment, then picked up the telephone before her and called a number—that of the Chief of Police.

"Good evening, Mr. Diefendorf. This is Amelia Cranston . . . good evening. How's Bertha? . . . How are the children? . . . I'm very well, thank you. Thursday's my hard night, as you know. . . . Mr. Diefendorf, there is a young man here who has been engaged by a certain very respected lady in the city to make inquiries into some unhappy events in her family history. . . . No, oh, no! He has no connection with anything like that. He's merely been asked to read aloud to her from old family letters that have been stored in the attic. I think it's something that you'd like to know about. It's something that has officially never come to your attention, that needs very confidential handling. There's always the possibility that he might run across something that might get into the papers. I have full confidence in this young man, but of course he hasn't got your experience and your judgment. . . . Is there some evening when you could drop in here and see him or should I ask him to call on you in your office? . . . Oh! That would be very kind of you. Yes, he's here now. His name is North. . . . Yes, the same." (Probably the "same" who was involved in the Diana Bell elopement matter.)

It is evidence of the congeniality of our relationship that Mrs. Cranston (who seldom permitted herself to make a caustic remark about anyone) glanced at me and said dryly: "I have noticed that the Chief never refuses an excuse to leave the bosom of his family."

We did not have long to wait. I received permission to order another beer. The Chief was tall and wide. He gave the impression of being at once genial and uncomfortable. This, I was to learn, was the result of a long experience of being browbeaten by the

wealthy who tend to assume that the less fortunate are unbelievably dim-witted. His defense was to assume an air of doubting the
truth of any word spoken to him. He shook hands cordially with
Mrs. Cranston and guardedly with me. She told him the whole
story and again expressed her confidence in me.

"Mr. Diefendorf, I think that while reading those old letters the
story may come to light and that maybe it *should* come to light.
After all, there's nothing really damaging about it all; it doesn't
reflect on the character of anybody in the family. You told me all
you knew about it and I've kept my promise: I haven't breathed a
word about it to a soul. If Mr. North finds something definite
about it in a letter, I know he can be trusted to tell *you* about
it first. Then you can decide whether Miss Wyckoff should be
told."

The Chief's eyes rested on me deliberatingly: "What brought
you to Newport, Mr. North?"

"Chief, I was stationed at Fort Adams during the last year of
the War and I got to like it here."

"Who was the Commanding Officer then?"

"General Kalb or DeKalb."

"Did you ever go to church in town here?"

"Yes, to Emmanuel Church. Dr. Walter Lowrie was the rector."

"Did Mr. Augustus Bell pay you a large sum for handling
that matter of his daughter's elopement?"

"I told him beforehand I only wanted reimbursement for the
time I'd lost from my usual jobs. I've sent him a bill twice and
he hasn't paid it yet."

"What were you and your bicycle doing out at Brenton's Point
very early a few mornings ago?"

"Chief, I'm crazy about sunrises. I saw one of the finest I've
ever seen in my life."

This caused him a little difficulty. He examined the tabletop
for a few moments. He probably put my behavior down to one
of the idiosyncrasies consequent on a college education.

"How much do you know about the Wyckoff House story?"

"Only that it's supposed to be haunted."

He outlined the situation as I already knew it—"Somehow the rumor had gotten round that there were ghosts in the house. . . . Now, Mr. North, just after the War our waterfront life used to be much more active than it is now. Many more yachts and pleasure boats, the Fall River Line, fishing business, a certain amount of merchant shipping. Sea-going men drink. We used to collect them every night—stark, staring mad, delirium tremens. Those taverns on Thames Street used to be out-of-bounds to the men at the Naval Training Station—too many fights. One night in 1918 we had to lock up a man named Bill Owens, a merchant seaman about twenty-one years old, born and raised in Newport. He'd get very drunk, night after night, and start telling stories about the awful things he'd seen at the Wyckoff place. We couldn't have that. And we'd try to piece together what he was roaring and raving about in his cell."

Here the Chief made us wait while he lit a cigar. (There was no smoking in Mrs. Cranston's front rooms.)

"Mr. Wyckoff used to be away six and eight months at a time. He was a collector. What was it, Mrs. Cranston—sharks' teeth?"

"Shells and Chinese things, Chief. He left them to that big museum in New York." (No information was ever accurate in Newport, a matter of intellectual climate.)

"All that time he kept a kind of super-butler in charge, named Harland. Harland picked his own staff."

"Girls he found in New York, Chief. I never had anything to do with them."

"The front of the house was brightly lighted until midnight. Everything seemed to be in perfect order. Owens was a boy of about twelve, hired to empty the slops and carry the coals up to the fireplaces—odd jobs. I think Mrs. Cranston will agree with me that servants are like schoolchildren; they need a strict hand over them. When the teacher's out of the classroom they begin to raise the Old Nick."

"I'm sorry to say there's some truth in it, Chief," said Mrs.

Cranston, shaking her head. "I've seen it over and over again."

"Mr. Wyckoff was a bad judge of men. His butler Harland was
as crazy as they come. . . . Bill Owens said he was sent home every
night at six o'clock when he'd finished his chores. But a few times
he crept back to the house. The front rooms were brightly lighted,
but the doors and windows of the dining room were hung with felt
curtains—thick felt curtains. They couldn't have their unholy
goings-on down in the kitchen—oh, no! They were masters and
had to use the master's dining room. Owens said he used to hide
in the cupboards and peek through the felt curtain. And he saw
awful things. He'd been telling the crowds down on Thames
Street that he'd seen banquets and people taking their clothes off
and what he called 'cannibals.' "

"Chief! You never used that word before!"

"Well, he said it. I'm sure he didn't see it, but he thought
he did."

"Oh, Lord in Heaven!" said Mrs. Cranston crossing herself.

"When you see half-cooked meat eaten *with their own hands,*
that's what a boy of twelve would think he saw."

"God save us all!" said Mrs. Cranston.

"I've no idea what Mr. Wyckoff saw, but he saw the felt curtains and the raw meat stains all over the floor and beastliness in
the faces of the servants, very likely. . . . Now pardon my language,
but rumor is like a stink. It took about three years for Bill Owens's
stories to pass from Thames Street to Mrs. Turberville's Employment Agency. And rumor always gets blacker and blacker. What
do you think of it, Mr. North?"

"Well, Chief, I think that there was no murder, and not even
mayhem; there was just brutishness and somehow it got mixed up
in the popular imagination with spooks."

"And now there's nothing we can do about it. Remember, it
never reached the police desk. The ravings of a man in delirium
tremens are not a deposition. Owens shipped out of town and has
not been heard from since. I'm glad to have met you, Mr. North."

I had got what I wanted. We parted with my usual dishonest

assurances that I would share with him any further information that came to light. As far as I was concerned that problem was solved, but my imagination had been occupied for some time with a far more difficult problem: What way could be found to dispel the "malediction" that rested on the Wyckoff House? Explanations and appeals to reason have no power to efface deeply ingrained and even cherished dreads.

I had glimpsed an idea.

One afternoon when I had presented myself at the door for the accustomed reading, I found a barouche, a coachman, and a pair of what used to be called "spanking" horses waiting in the driveway. Miss Wyckoff met me in the hall, dressed to go out. She begged my pardon, saying that she had been called to visit an invalid friend; she would be back within half an hour. Her maid was standing beside her.

"Miss Wyckoff, may I have permission to visit the rooms on the first floor? I greatly admire what I have seen of the house and would like to see some of the other rooms."

"Oh, yes, indeed, Mr. North. Make yourself completely at home. Mrs. Delafield will be glad to answer any questions, I'm sure."

It was a beautiful spring afternoon. All the doors were open. I viewed the great hall from all sides; I saw the dining room and the library for the first time. Everywhere I was arrested by some felicity of detail, but above all I was held by the harmony of the entire structure. "This is Palladio," I thought. "He himself was the heir of great masters and this is one of his descendants, just as Versailles is; but this is nearer the Italian source." When I was returning through the great hall to my work table Mrs. Delafield said, "Years ago before the master started going on expeditions, they used to give musical parties here. Have you heard of Padderooski, Mr. North? . . . He played here, and Ole Bull, the Norwegian violinist. And Madame Nellie Melba—have you heard of her? Very fine, she was. Those were lovely days. Just think of it now! It's a shame, isn't it?"

"You haven't seen or heard anything that made you uncomfortable, have you, Mrs. Delafield?"

"Oh, no, sir—not a thing!"

"Would you be willing to spend the night here?"

"Well, sir, I'd rather not. I know that maybe it's all foolishness, but we're not always in control of our feelings, if you know what I mean."

"What do people think took place here?"

"I don't like to talk about it or *think* about it, sir. Some people say one thing and some people say another. I think it's best to leave things as they are."

The readings continued. Miss Wyckoff seemed relieved that no intimation of a sinister nature came to our attention. We read on for the pleasure of reading, for the Wyckoffs were admirable letter writers. But all the time the idea of what was possible was growing in my head.

I have told of the various aspirations that had successively absorbed me when I was a very young man. A journalist's life was not among them. My father was a newspaper editor both before and after he was sent on consular missions to China. He brought a dedication to it that I was never able to share. To me it smacked too much of the manipulation of public opinion, however sincerely prompted. The idea that was developing in my head for the rehabilitation of Wyckoff House involved precisely that, but I didn't know how to go about it.

Chance opened the way to me.

The account of my relation to Wyckoff House falls into two parts. The second part led me into the Eighth City—that of campfollowers and parasites to whom I had so close an affinity. It led me to Flora Deland.

By the fifth week in Newport my schedule had begun to be exacting. The professional coach returned to the Casino and I was relieved of the second hour of instructing children, but all day I was busy with French or Latin or arithmetic in one house or another. I searched for somewhere to have lunch in as quiet a place as the town afforded. I found the Misses Laughlins' Scottish Tea Room—where Diana Bell and Hilary Jones had done their courting—in the heart of the Ninth City. It was frequented by girls from offices, some schoolteachers of both sexes, some housewives "downtown shopping"—a subdued company. The food was simple, well-cooked, and cheap. I had noticed a strange apparition there and hoped to see it again—a tall woman sitting alone, dressed in what I took to be the height of fashion. One day she reappeared. She wore a hat resembling a nest on which an exotic bird was resting, and an elaborate dress of what I think used to be called "changeable satin," blues and greens of a peacock's feathers intermingling. Before eating it was necessary that she remove her gloves and raise her veil with gestures of apparently uncalculated grace. Zounds! What was this? As before, when she entered or rose to take her departure the room was filled with the rustle of a hundred petticoats. Not only *what* was she, but *why* should she visit our humble board?

Her face was not strictly beautiful. Norms of feminine beauty change from century to century and sometimes oftener. Her face was long, thin, pale, and bony. You will later hear Henry Simmons describe it as "horsy." It can be seen in Flemish and French paintings of the fifteenth and sixteenth centuries. The kindest thing that could be said of it in 1926 was that it was "aristocratic," a designation more apologetic than kind. What was sensational about her was what we lustful soldiers at Fort Adams used to call her "build," her "altogether," her "figger."

You can imagine my surprise when on leaving she approached me with extended hand and said: "You are Mr. North, I believe. I've long wanted to introduce myself. I am Mrs. Edward Darley.— Might I sit down for a moment?"

She took her time, seating herself, her eyes resting on mine in happy recognition of something. I remembered hearing that the first thing a young actress is taught in dramatic school is to sit down without lowering her eyes.

"Perhaps you might know me better under my *nom de plume*. I am Flora Deland."

I had lived a sheltered academic life. I was one of the meager thirty million Americans who had never heard of Flora Deland. Most of the others in this thirty million had never been taught to read anything. I made appreciative noises, however.

"Are you enjoying life in Newport, Mr. North?"

"Yes—very much indeed."

"You certainly *do* get about! You are everywhere—reading aloud to Dr. Bosworth all those fascinating things about Bishop Berkeley; and reading the *Fables* of La Fontaine with the Skeel gairl. What a learned man you must be at your age! And so very clever, too—I mean resourceful. The way you managed the foolish elopement of Diana Bell—think of that! Diana is a sort of cousin of mine through the Haverlys. Such a headstrong gairl. It must have been perfectly marvelous the way you persuaded her not to make a fool of herself. Do tell me *how* you did it."

Now I have never been a handsome man. All I've got is what was bequeathed to me by my ancestors, together with that Scottish jaw and those Wisconsin teeth. Elegant women have never crossed a room to strike up an acquaintance with me. I wondered what was behind these amiabilities—then, suddenly, it struck me: Flora Deland was a smearer, a newspaper chatterbox. With her I was in the Eighth City—the parasitic camp-followers.

I said, "Mrs. Darley—how do you like to be called, ma'am?"

"Oh, call me Miss Deland," adding lightly, "You may call me Flora—I'm a working woman."

"Flora, I have not a word to say about Miss Bell. I have given my promise."

"Oh, Mr. North, I didn't mean for *publication!* I'm simply interested in cleverness and resourcefulness. I like people who use their wits. I'm a frustrated novelist, I suppose. Do let's say that we're friends. May we?" I nodded. "I lead a whole other life that has nothing to do with the newspapers. I have a cottage at Narragansett Pier where I love to entertain at the weekend. I have a guest cottage and can put you up. We all need a change from time to time, don't we?" She rose and again extended her hand. "Can I call you up at the Y.M.C.A.?"

"Yes . . . yes."

"And what may I call you—Theophilus?"

"Teddie. I prefer being called Teddie."

"You must tell me about Dr. Bosworth and Bishop Berkeley, Teddie. What a household that is at the 'Nine Gables'! Goodbye again, Teddie, and do accept an invitation to come to my dear little 'Sandpiper' for swimming and tennis and cards."

A working girl with a hundred and twenty million readers and a figure like Nita Naldi's and a speaking voice of smoked velvet like Ethel Barrymore's. . . . Oh, my Journal!

This was not a matter to submit to Mrs. Cranston. This was for a man among men. "Henry," I said, as we were chalking our cues at Herman's, "who are some of the smearers that hang around town?"

"Funny, you asked me that," he said and went on with the game. When we'd finished the set he beckoned me to the remotest table and ordered our usual.

"Funny, you asked me that. I saw Flora Deland on the street yesterday."

"Who's she?"

In all barbershops and billiard parlors there are tables and shelves bearing old and new reading matter for the customers to glance at while waiting to be called. Henry went to a pile and unerringly pulled out the Sunday supplement of a Boston paper. He opened it and spread it wide before me: "NEW YORK JUDGE BLAMES MOTHERS FOR INCREASING DIVORCE RATE AMONG THE FOUR HUNDRED, *By our special correspondent Flora Deland.*"

I read it. Terrible situation. No names mentioned; certain hints that would be clearer to more experienced readers than myself.

"Cowboy," he continued (Henry presumed that Wisconsin was in the center of the Wild West), "Flora Deland comes from the oldest and most respected families of New York and Newport. None of that railroad and mining stuff—the real Old Guard. Related to everybody. Very high-spirited—'fast,' like they say. Made a few mistakes. It's all right to break up a family or two, but don't break up a family where the money's broken up, too. She ran out of her allowance of *pardonable* mistakes. Got a man disinherited. Flora's relations wouldn't see her. Are you following me, old cully? What's the poor girl to do? Can't even borrow money from Aunt Henrietta. She'd 'ad it. So she takes to pen and paper; becomes a smearer—real stuff from the inside. Like . . . like . . . many wives overspend their allowance; don't dare tell their husbands; where do you pawn your diamond tiara? In Wisconsin they eat it up. Now the stuff she writes under the name of Deland is fairly under control; but *we* know that she writes under other names too. She's got a feature called 'What Suzanne Whispered to Me,' signed 'Belinda.' Makes your eyes pop. Must make a lot of money, one way or another. Goes on lecture tours, too; 'A Newport Girlhood.' Funny stories about how we're all monkeys here."

"Does she spend the whole summer in Newport, Henry?"

"Where'd she go? The La Forge Cottages wouldn't consider it. The Muenchinger-King makes it a rule—or says it's a rule—that no guest can stay over three nights. She has a place at Narragansett Pier. The Pier is livelier than Newport—better beaches, younger set, better hideaways, clubs where you can play—all that."

"Where does she get her information from?"

"Nobody knows. Probably has plants—nurses in hospitals, for example. Patients will talk. Lots of talk goes on in beauty parlors. Servants, almost never."

"Is she beautiful, Henry?"

"Beautiful? Beautiful! She's got a face like a horse."

My invitation to visit "The Sandpiper" came through. Saturday for dinner until Monday morning: "I have plenty of swimsuits for you here. You'd only need one in the day. We often go in *au naturel* at midnight to cool off." To freeze, I suppose; the New England waters are not even tolerable until August.

I was going on the trip to enlist Flora Deland in my PLAN relative to the Wyckoff House; Flora Deland had invited me because she wished to obtain some information from me. I foresaw some form of negotiation. I had a service to ask of her. I did not take seriously the possibility that there might be a little romancing involved; I had never been in that kind of business with a woman almost fifteen years older than myself, but as the old hymn says: "Where duty call or danger, Be never lacking there."

It was on my mind that I wished to get off the island with my bicycle without being observed by the police and others. Luck came to my aid. As I waited at the first of the two ferry slips (in those days it required two ferry rides to get to Narragansett, as the reader may recall) I heard my name called from a standing car.

"*Herr North!*"

"*Herr Baron!*"

"Can I carry you anywhere? I'm going to Narragansett Pier."

"So am I. Have you room for my bicycle, too?"

"Naturally."

This was the Baron Egon Bodo von Stams whom I had met many times at the Casino and who used to enjoy conversations in my enthusiastic hit-and-miss German. He was known as "Bodo" to everyone except Bill Wentworth and myself. He was an attaché at the Austrian Embassy in Washington on early leave for his second summer at Newport; a house-guest of the Venables at "Surf Point," even in the absence of the owners. He was the most likable fellow in the world. Two years older than I, endowed with a forthrightness and candor that approached naïveté. I climbed in and we shook hands.

He said, "I've been invited for the weekend by Miss Flora Deland—do you know her?"

"I've been invited there too."

"That's fine! I didn't know who I'd meet there."

We talked of this and that. On the second ferry boat, I asked: "Where did you meet Miss Deland, *Herr Baron?*"

He laughed, "Well, she came up to me and introduced herself at that bazaar for crippled children at the church on Spring Street."

I held my tongue for half an hour. When we approached the driveway of our hostess's cottage I said, *"Herr Baron,* stop the car a moment. I want to be sure that you understand where you're going."

He stopped the car and looked at me questioningly.

"You are a diplomat and a diplomat should always know exactly what is going on around him. What do you know about Miss Deland and what she's interested in?"

"Why, nothing much, old man" (Bodo had been to Eton), "but that she's a cousin of the Venables and she's a writer, too—novels and things like that."

I paused, then said, "The Venables haven't asked her to their house for at least fifteen years. They might be deeply offended if they knew you had visited hers. She was born into their class and circle; but she lost it. Do not ask me how; I don't know. She earns her living by writing thousands of words every week about what is called 'society.' Have you such journalists in Vienna?"

"Oh, in politics we have! They are very rude."

"Well, Miss Deland is very rude about the private lives of men and women."

"Will she write rude things about me?"

"I think not, but she will say that you were a guest in her home and that will give an air of authenticity to stories she tells about other people—the Venables, for instance."

"But that is terrible! . . . Thank you, thank you for telling me. I think I should drop you at her house and go back to Newport and telephone her that I have the influenza."

"*Herr Baron*, I think that would be wise. You represent your country."

He turned about in his seat and said to me directly: "Then why do *you* come to her house? If what she does is as bad as that, why do *you* come here?"

"Oh, *Herr Baron*—"

"Don't call me *Herr Baron!* Call me Bodo. If you are kind enough to open my eyes to this mistake, you can be kind enough to call me Bodo."

"Thank you. I shall call you Bodo *only* in this car. I am an employee at the Casino. I am a schoolmaster on a bicycle who gets paid by the hour."

"But we are in *America,* Theophilus. (What a beautiful name that is!) Here everybody calls everybody else by their given names after five minutes."

"No, we are not in America. We are in a little extraterritorial province that is more class-conscious than Versailles."

He laughed, then again solemnly asked, "Why are *you* here?"

"Well, I'll tell you another time." I pointed to the house before us. "This is a part of Newport's *demimonde.* Miss Deland is what you would call a *déclassée.* She has been ostracized, but during the summer all she thinks about is Newport—her Paradise Lost. I do not know what other guests will be at her house tonight, but the outcasts huddle together, just as you toffs do."

"I'm coming with you. I don't care what she writes about me." He started the engine, but I stopped him.

"I am interested in Flora Deland. She is a real pariah. She knows that she's engaged in a degrading business, but she has a kind of bravery about it. Do you think she's beautiful?"

"Very beautiful. She's like a Flemish ivory madonna. We own one. Theophilus, damn it, I've got to see this, too. You're quite right: I live in a little arena, like a dancing horse. I ought to know some outcasts too. If the Venables hear about it, I'll apologize to them. I'll apologize to them before they hear about it. I'll say I'm a foreigner and I didn't know any better."

"But, Bodo, your ambassador might hear about it. Tonight the guests will certainly get drunk; they'll break glass. Anything might happen. Flora intimated that we all might go swimming *mutter-nackt*. The neighbors would report it and the police would haul us off to the hoosegow. That would be a black mark for you, *Herr Baron*—Bodo, I mean."

He sat silent a minute. "But I've got to see it. Theophilus, let me come to dinner. Then I'll tell her I'm expecting a call from Washington and must return to Newport."

"All right, tell her the minute you go in the door. On Saturday night the last ferry boat leaves at twelve."

He slapped my back joyously. *"Du bist ein ganzer Kerl! Vorwärts."*

"The Sandpiper" was a pretty little seaside cottage from one's grandmother's time—Gothic gingerbread scrollwork, pointed window frames—a jewel. A butler directed us to the guest house where a maid welcomed us and showed us to our rooms. Bodo whistled: silver-backed hairbrushes, kimonos and Japanese sandals for bathing. Toulouse-Lautrec posters on the walls, copies of the *Social Register* and *The Great Gatsby* on the bedside tables. The maid said, "Cocktails at seven, sirs."

He appeared at the door. "Theophilus—"

"Herr Baron, just because we are where we are I want to be called Mr. North. What is it you want to know?"

"Tell me again whom we may be meeting at dinner."

"Some Newport men install their mistresses over here for the summer—let's hope there'll be one or two of them. There'll be no jewel thieves, but there may be some detectives who've been placed here by insurance companies to catch them. There are always some young men about who are trying to get one foot in the door of 'society'—fortune hunters, in other words."

"Oh!"

"We're all adventurers, outsiders, shady, *louches*."

He groaned. "And I have to go home at eleven!—But are you safe?"

"I'll tell you one more reason why I'm here. I'm working on a carefully thought out PLAN for which I need Flora Deland's assistance. It's one that won't do anyone any harm. If all goes well, I'll tell you the whole story at the end of the season."

"I can't wait that long."

"During dinner I'm going to grab hold of the table conversation for a short time; if you listen carefully you can get a glimpse of the first steps in my strategy."

We had been told not to dress, but Flora greeted us in a most wonderful gown—it was of yellow silk with little tabs of yellow velvet and little this-and-thats of yellow lace, each a slightly different shade of yellow. My face expressed my admiration.

"It is nice, isn't it?" she said lightly. "It's by Worth, 1910—belonged to my mother.—Baron, I'm delighted to see you. Will you have a cocktail or champagne? I drink only champagne. We must talk about Austria at dinner. My parents were presented to your Emperor when I was a gairl. I was too young, of course, but I used to see him taking his walk every day at Ischl."

Bodo made his deeply felt excuses that he must return to Newport for an important telephone call from his embassy on Sunday morning. "My Chief uses Sunday for his most important business and I have received notice that he will call me."

"What a pity, Baron! You must come some other weekend when you know you'll be free."

There were ten at the table, of whom only four were women. There was an exquisite French girl, Mlle. Desmoulins, who sat beside Bodo and who (he told me later) kept giving him little pinches to which he gallantly responded. Her chauffeur—who much resembled a bodyguard—called for her at ten-thirty and she took a tender leave of her *"bon petit Baron Miche-Miche"* (Bodo was six feet tall). There was a stout old lady—Flora whispered that she had been a famous actress in musical comedy—heavily bejeweled, who scarcely said a word, but ate and ate double portions of whatever was served. There was a young couple named Jameson from New Orleans, who had taken a cottage nearby for the summer, extremely sedate and increasingly bewildered. I sat at Flora's left and beside Mrs. Jameson. I asked Mrs. Jameson where she had met Miss Deland. "We met her by chance in the village here. She helped my husband out of some difficulty with a traffic policeman, and she invited us to dinner. Mr. North, who are these people?"

"I cannot discuss them under this roof. I leave that question to your perspicacity."

"My perspicacity is very uneasy."

"You're on the right track."

"Thank you. We shall leave as soon as it's decent. But you're all right?"

"Oh, Mrs. Jameson, I'm a salamander. I can live in air, fire, or water."

And then there were the three young men, all beautifully dressed (what to wear at an informal dinner at a famous resort), all increasingly drunk, and all very much at ease.

The conversation turned on the life at Newport during the previous season—the parties and balls to which they had or had not been invited, the famous hostesses who were too idiotic to be believed, the abysmal boredom of "all that life."

Finally the moment came when I spoke up:

"Flora, I think the wonderful thing about Newport is the trees."

"The trees?" Everyone stared at me.

I described the importations by Harvard scientists and by world travelers. I deplored the poverty of the soil and gave them a picture of long caravans of wagons bringing soil from Massachusetts (my improvisation but probable). I gave the cedars of Lebanon and the Buddha's bo tree ("If you sleep under it you'll dream of *nirvana*; I'm getting permission to do so next week"), the tara-tara tree of Chile that no bird will ever approach; the eucalyptus of Australia whose gum cures asthma; the ash tree of Yggdrasill, "the tree of life," whose berries drive away melancholy and thoughts of suicide in the young ("There's one in the garden of the Venables' house where the Baron is staying").

Bodo looked startled.

"Why, Teddie," cried Flora, "you're an angel! I could write a piece about all that!"

"Oh, there are some extraordinary subjects in Newport. There's a house that a famous Italian architect, Dr. Lorenzo Latta, has called the most beautiful house in New England—and the healthiest. Built in the nineteenth century, too. He called it 'The House that Breathes,' 'The House with Lungs.' "

" 'The House with *Lungs*'! Which one is it?"

"I don't think you know it. There's a house in Newport whose great hall has such perfect acoustics that when Paderewski played in it he burst into tears; he apologized to the audience, saying that he had never played so well."

"Which house is it?"

"I'm pretty sure you don't know it. When the great Norwegian violinist Ole Bull gave a concert there he played on his Stradivarius, of course; but he said afterwards that the room itself was the best Stradivarius in the world."

"Teddie! Where do you find out these things?"

"There's a house in Newport where a simple woman lived for a while as a sort of nursing nun—Sister Colomba. She'll probably be canonized one of these days, St. Colomba of Newport. After dark, people from the working classes go and kneel before the house gates. The police don't know what to do about it. Can you arrest kneeling people for loitering?"

Flora was spellbound. The old lady stopped eating. The *jiggalas,* the crashers, and the flickers looked about wildly for strong drink.

"Flora, if you could write up these stories—"

"Why don't *you* write them?"

"Oh, I can't write, Flora. You're one of the most famous writers in the country. You've written reams and reams about Newport, but most of it has been satirical. If you began to write some pieces about the attractive things in Newport, all those cousins of yours would be very pleased—very pleased, indeed."

This sank in. She looked dazed. Then under the tablecloth she pinched me in what I suppose is called the thigh.

As we rose from table, she whispered, "You're a duck! You're a darling! *And*, I think, just a little bit, a devil!—Gentlemen, go to the smoking room. And, Baron, don't let them drink too much. We're all going in swimming later. I don't want any of you to get cramps and drown. That's happened *too* often."

Bodo and I stepped into the garden. "Teddie, give me a hint of what that was all about—I mean as a stratagem. Give me something to think about on the drive back to Newport."

"All right, I'll give you a hint. Have you a castle?"

"Yes."

"An old one?"

"Yes."

"Is it said to have ghosts?"

"Yes."

"Have you ever seen one?"

"Teddie, what do you think I am! There are no ghosts. The servants like to give themselves a thrill by talking about them."

"Do your servants stay with you?"

"Generation after generation."

"Well, I'm engaged in exorcising a supposedly haunted house where servants refuse to stay in the house after dark. All those three houses that I want Flora to write about are one house. Superstition is black magic; the only way to fight it is with white magic. Think that over."

He looked up at the stars; he looked down at the ground; he laughed. Then he put his hand on my shoulder and said, "Teddie, you're a humbug, you know."

"How do you mean?"

"You pretend that you have no aim in life."

He shook his head, smiling. Then he became very serious; I

had never seen Bodo very serious: "I may have to ask you to advise me again before long. I have a real problem to face."

"In Newport?"

"Yes, in Newport."

"Can it wait?"

His gravity had become a sadness. "Yes, it can wait."

I couldn't imagine Bodo with "a real problem to face." Except for that touch of naïveté (which was really his innocence and his clear-hearted goodness) that had brought him to "The Sandpiper" he seemed to be completely endowed for the world into which he had been born. What could it be?

"I'll give you a hint. Theophilus, I'm a fortune hunter; but I'm really in love with the heiress, *really* in love—and she won't look at me."

"Do I know her?"

"Oh, yes."

"Who is it?"

"I'll tell you at the end of the season.—Now I'll say good night to Flora and catch that last boat. Remember everything to tell me later. *Gute Nacht, alter Freund.*"

"Gute Nacht, Herr Baron."

I saw him off from the guest house. When I returned to "The Sandpiper," the Jamesons and Mlle. Desmoulins had left. The old lady had been helped upstairs. The three young men were singing and breaking glass.

"Is your head better?" asked Flora tenderly. I had made no mention of a headache, but I said, "I need a drink to pull me together. May I pour myself a whiskey, Flora?"

"You go and lie down in your room. I'll send you a drink. Then I'll call on you and we'll have a little talk. . . . I'll send the boys home. They're getting disorderly and it's much too cold to go in swimming. . . . No, they're staying at the Rod and Gun Club just down the road. . . . I shall change into something more comfortable. We shall talk about all those extraordinary houses— *if they do really exist, Teddie.*"

I said good night to the members of the Rod and Gun Club.
Returning to my lodgings I put on the kimono and Japanese slippers and waited. I had brought with me pages and pages of notes
about the three aspects of Wyckoff House. There was some truth
in the first two; some outrageous invention in the second; the
third was pure fantastication. They were in the form of jottings
which she could consult while writing her articles. A Philippine
houseboy arrived bearing a tray of bottles and ice. I poured myself
a drink and went on writing. At last my hostess arrived wearing
something light and comfortable under a long dark-blue cape.

"I see you have made yourself a drink. Be an angel and pour
me a little champagne. The boys were beginning to be noisy and
I have to be so careful of the neighbors. They make complaints
when the boys fire off guns and scramble over the roof. . . . Thank
you, I only drink still champagne. . . . Now tell me: who owns
those houses you talked about?"

I made a long pause, then said, "They are all one house. It
is the Wyckoff House."

She sat up straight. "But it is haunted. It is full of ghosts."

"I am ashamed of you, Flora. You are not an ignorant servant
girl. You know that there are no such things."

"But I have so much Irish blood. I believe all ghost stories! Tell
me more about it."

I brought out the sheaf of my notes. "Here's some material
you might want to use in some articles sometime—articles that
will *endear* you to Newport."

"Sometime! Sometime! I'll start them tomorrow morning. Show
them to me."

"Flora, I'm in no mood to talk about houses now. I can only
think of one thing at a time." I arose and stood above her, locking
her knees between mine. "When a beautiful lady pinches a man
in his thigh he is permitted to hope for other marks of her . . .
good will and"—leaning over I kissed her—"her kindness."

"Oh! You men are so *exigeants!*" She pushed me away, rose,
kissed me on the ear, and moved toward the bedroom.

There was no literary composition that night.

Work began the next morning at eleven.

"Read me the notes you've written," she said, laying out a pile of journalists' yellow work-paper and half a dozen pencils.

"No, I want to tell it to you first, so that I can keep looking into your beautiful eyes while I talk."

"You men!"

"First, the House with Lungs. I'm going to start a long way off the subject. Do you know New Haven, Connecticut?"

"I used to go to dances at Yale. I had glorious times."

"Where did you stay?"

"A cousin and I stayed at the Hotel Taft and another cousin came along as chaperon."

"Then you remember that corner on the New Haven Green. One day I was crossing the street with a lady under the windows of the Hotel Taft. It was cold. A wind was blowing the lady's skirts and her hat in every direction. She suddenly said something very surprising for she was a most sedate professor's wife. She said, 'Damn Vitruvius!' All I knew about Vitruvius was that he was an ancient Roman who'd written a famous book about architecture and city planning. 'Why Vitruvius?' I asked. 'Don't you know that many New England cities were laid out according to his rules? Build your city like a great gridiron. Make a study of the prevailing winds, cross currents, and so on. Let the city breathe; give the city lungs. Paris and London awoke to his advice too late. Boston has a "green" but the streets were laid out to follow old cow-paths. Naturally Vitruvius's study reflected the Italian world which can be pretty cold, but not as cold as New Haven. Now listen to this: that corner by the Hotel Taft is the only cool refreshing spot in New Haven during the dreadful hot summer days. The very pigeons know it and gather there by the hundreds; the very bums and hoboes know it. The wisdom of Vitruvius!' "

"Really, Teddie, why are we talking about pigeons and hoboes?"

"This house was built in the style of Palladio who was a de-

voted student of Vitruvius. Now I'm getting to the point. An
eminent Italian architect toured New England and said this was
the most beautiful and most *healthful* house he saw. New England
houses were built of wood and built around a chimney in the
center to heat the house in winter; but they're dreadful in summer.
The corridors are in the wrong places. The first and second floors
are cut up into rooms that surround it and the doors and windows
are in the wrong places. The air doesn't circulate; the stale air has
nowhere to go. But the builders of the Wyckoff House had the
money and the good sense to build fireplaces all over the house;
so the center of the house is a great high hall. It can inhale and
exhale. Miss Wyckoff told me herself that she never knew anyone
to have a cold there—the great American common cold! It was
built in 1871 by an Italian architect who brought over a group
of decorators and painters and stone-workers. Flora, it's a dream
of serenity and peace—healthy lungs and a healthy heart!"

"I'll write it up! You just wait and see!"

"But that's not all. Are you fond of music, Flora?"

"I adore music—all music except those crashing bores, Bach
and Beethoven. And that other fellow, Mozetti."

"What's the matter with him?"

"Mozetti? He had just *one* tune in his head and he wrote it
over and over again."

I wiped my forehead.

"Well, I told you how Paderewski burst into tears at the perfection of the acoustics in the great hall. He also asked the
Wyckoffs if it would disturb the family if he stayed on an hour
after the guests had gone home just to play to himself. After
Dame Nellie Melba sang there she persuaded Thomas Alva
Edison to come up to Newport and supervise the gramophone
records she made in that hall. 'The Last Rose of Summer'—it
outsold all the records ever made until Caruso came along. Madame
Schumann-Heink sang 'The Rosary' in that hall and had to
repeat it three times. Everybody was sobbing like babies. Your first
article could be called 'The House of Perfect Well-Being'; your

second article you could call 'The House of Heavenly Music.' Newport will *love* you.''

"Have you all those names down in these notes, Teddie?"

"But the third article is the best. Many years ago there was a sort of saint in this town. She was never admitted into any religious order because she couldn't read or write. She was only a lay-sister, but the working people called her 'Sister Colomba.' All her days and nights were spent with the sick and the aged and the dying. She calmed the feverish, she visited the sickrooms of those with the worst contagious diseases and never caught a single one of them. A small boy in the Wyckoff home had diphtheria. She nursed him daily and he recovered—*miraculously* they believed. She lived in a little room across the hall from him. When her end approached, at a very great age, she asked that she be allowed to die in her old room. As I told you at dinner throngs silently kneel before the gates of the house—before Sister Colomba's room."

Deeply moved, Flora put her hand on mine. "I'll have the sound of angel voices dimly heard by the faithful at midnight. I'll have perfumes. . . . Bellevue Avenue . . . What was her real name?"

"Mary Colomba O'Flaherty."

"Wait until you see what I do with that!—Great Heavens! It's a quarter of one—my guests will be arriving for lunch. Give me those notes. I'm going to start working on them at once."

Whatever one might think of Flora Deland, she was a diligent hard-working woman. Bees and ants could have taken lessons from her. My reading sessions with Miss Wyckoff were interrupted for two weeks during which she paid a visit to some old friends at their rustic camp on Squam Lake in New Hampshire. When she returned she invited me to tea at once. I made it a rule to accept no social invitations, but no rule could stand in the way of what I wished to learn about the progress of my PLAN.

Miss Wyckoff received me in a state of considerable agitation. "Mr. North, the most extraordinary thing has happened. I'm at my wit's end. A newspaper woman has been publishing a series of articles about this house! Look at the piles of letters I've been getting! Architects want to visit the house and bring their students. Musicians want to see the house. People from all over the country want appointments when they may see the house. Droves of strangers are ringing the doorbell all day. . . ."

"What have you done about it, Miss Wyckoff?"

"I haven't answered a single letter. Mrs. Delafield had orders not to admit strangers. What do *you* think I should do?"

"Have you read that newspaper woman's articles?"

"Dozens of people have sent them to me."

"Did they make you very angry?"

"I don't know where she got all that information. There's nothing horrid in them; but there are hundreds of things about this house that I never knew before and . . . this is my home. I spent a large part of my life here. I don't know if they're true or not."

"Miss Wyckoff, I confess I read the articles and I was very surprised. But you can't deny that it's a very beautiful house. Fame is one of the consequences of excellence, Miss Wyckoff. The possession of a thing of exceptional beauty carries certain responsibilities. Have you ever visited Mount Vernon?"

"Yes. Mrs. Tucker asked us to tea."

"Did you know that certain portions of the house were open to the public on certain hours of the week? I suggest that you engage a secretary to handle this matter. Have an entrance card engraved and let the secretary send it to all those who seem to be seriously interested, stating the hours at which they may view the Wyckoff House."

"It frightens me, Mr. North. I wouldn't know how to answer the questions they might ask."

"Oh, you won't be there. Your secretary will show them about and answer their questions only in a very superficial way."

"Thank you. Thank you. I guess that's what I *must* do. But, Mr. North, there's something far more serious." She lowered her voice: "People want to bring the sick here. . . . Whole companies from religious schools want to come and pray here! I never heard of this Sister Colomba. My dear brother I told you about was a very sickly child and I think I remember that we did have some nurses from the religious orders; but I don't remember *one* of them."

"Miss Wyckoff, there's an old Greek saying, *'Reject not the gifts of the gods.'* You said that a 'malediction' hung over this house. It appears to me that that malediction is lifting. . . . I can tell you that all Newport is talking about the beauty and healthfulness of this house, and about the blessing that dwells here."

"Oh, Mr. North, I'm frightened. I've done a wicked thing. Even my old friends who've come to tea with me for years now want to see the room where Sister Colomba died. What could I do? I told a lie. I chose a room near my poor brother's where a night nurse *probably* slept."

"You foresee the next step, don't you, Miss Wyckoff?"

"Oh, dear! Oh, dear! What's the next step?"

"Servants will be clamoring to *live* in this house."

She put her hand over her mouth and stared at me. "I never thought of that!"

I leaned forward and said in a low but very distinct voice: *"Miss Wyckoff requests the pleasure of your company for dinner on such-and-such a day. At the conclusion of dinner the Kneisel Quartet with an assisting guest violist will perform the last two string quintets of Wolfgang Amadeus Mozart."*

She stared at me. She rose and clasped her hands, saying, "My childhood! My beautiful childhood!"

"Nine Gables"

One of my first summonses to be interviewed came in the form of a note from Sarah Bosworth (Mrs. McHenry Bosworth), "Nine Gables," such and such a number, Bellevue Avenue. The writer's father, Dr. James McHenry Bosworth, it said, had employed many readers, a number of whom had proved to be unsatisfactory. Could Mr. North present himself at the above address at eleven o'clock on Friday morning to be interviewed by Mrs. Bosworth on this matter? Kindly confirm the appointment by telephone, et cetera, et cetera! I telephoned my compliance and promptly visited the "People's Library" (as it was then called) to consult various reference books about this family.

The Honorable Dr. James McHenry Bosworth was seventy-four years old, a widower, father of six and grandfather of many. He had served his country as attaché, first secretary, minister, and ambassador to several countries on three continents. In addition he had published books on early American architecture, notably Newport's. Further inquiry revealed that he lived the year round in Newport and that several of his children maintained summer

homes in the vicinity—in Portsmouth and Jamestown. Mrs. Mc-
Henry Bosworth was his daughter, divorced and childless, who
had resumed her maiden name under this form.

On that Friday morning in late April—the first radiantly spring-
like day of the year—I drove my bicycle to the door and rang the
bell. The house was neither a French château nor a Greek temple
nor a Norman fortress but a long rambling cottage, under weather-
silvered shingles, adorned with wide verandahs, turrets, and gables.
It stood in extensive grounds ennobled by mighty and far-sought
trees. Within the house there was nothing rustic whatever. Through
the open but latched screen door I saw a platoon of men servants
in striped waistcoats and maids in uniform with flying white
sashes waxing the floors and polishing the furniture. I was to learn
later that the furniture well rewarded this care; here was the largest
collection outside a museum of Newport's notable eighteenth-
century cabinetmakers.

A formidable butler in a red striped vest and a green apron
appeared at the door. I announced my business. His eyes rested
with a kind of outrage on my bicycle. "Err . . . You are Mr.
North?" I waited. "In general, sir, this door is not used in the
morning. You will find the garden door around the corner of the
house at your left."

I was willing to enter the house by the chimney or the coal
cellar, but I didn't like the butler, his protruding eyes, his super-
fluous chins, and his tone of contempt. It was a beautiful morning.
I felt fine. I didn't need the job as badly as that. I brushed my
sleeve slowly and took my time. "Mrs. Bosworth asked me to
call at this address at this hour."

"*This* door is not generally used . . ."

I had learned from my youth up—and in the Army—that when
you are confronted with self-important authority and browbeating
the procedure is as follows: smile amiably, even deferentially,
lower your voice, affect a partial deafness, and talk steadily, dragging in red herrings and bushy-tailed squirrels. The result is that

Sir Pompous raises his voice, becomes distraught, and (above all) attracts others to the scene.

"Thank you, Mr. Gammage . . . Mr. Kammage. I assume that you are expecting the piano-tuner, or—"

"What?"

"Or the chiropodist. What a lovely day, Mr. Gammage! Kindly tell Mrs. Bosworth that I have called as she requested."

"*My name is not* . . . Sir, take your bicycle to the door I have indicated."

"Good morning. I shall write Mrs. Bosworth that I called. *Irasci celerem tamen ut placabilis essem.*"

"Sir, are you deaf or insane?"

"Dr. Bosworth—I knew him well in Singapore—Raffles Hotel, you know. We used to play fan-tan." I lowered my voice still further—"Temple bells and all that. Punkahs swaying from the ceiling—"

"I've . . . I've . . . 'ad enough of you. *Go away!*"

It always works. Indeed, others had been drawn to the scene. The platoon of servants gazed open-mouthed. A handsome woman of middle age appeared in the distance. A young woman in a pale green linen dress (Persis, Persis herself!) had descended the great staircase. I came to think of "Nine Gables" as the house of hidden listening ears.

The lady in the distance called, "Willis, I am expecting Mr. North. . . . Persis, this is none of your affair. . . . Mr. North, will you follow me into my sitting room?"

The divine Persis glided between Mr. Willis and myself, lifted the latch without glancing to right or left, and disappeared. I thanked Mr. Willis (who had lost the power of speech) and advanced slowly down the long hall. Through an open door I saw in one of the sitting rooms a large painting, "The Three Bosworth Sisters," perhaps by John Singer Sargent—three lovely girls, seated nonchalantly on a sofa, endowed with everything, including angelic dispositions. It was painted in 1899. Those sisters were Sarah,

who had been briefly married to the Honorable Algernon De
Bailly-Lewyss and was now Mrs. McHenry Bosworth; Mary, Mrs.
Cassius Marcellus Leffingwell; and Theodora, Mrs. Terence On-
slowe, long resident in Italy. Mrs. Bosworth, the eldest of the
three, was in a rage also. "I am Mrs. Bosworth. Will you sit
down, please."

Gazing about I admired both the room and the lady. I noticed
that a door at my left was ajar; every other door in sight was wide
open. I suspected that the eminent Dr. Bosworth was probably
overhearing this interview. Mrs. Bosworth had arranged three
books beside her, each with a colorful book-marker between the
pages. I suspected that *one* marked the page selected to eliminate
the applicant.

"My father's eyes are easily tired. For one reason or another
his readers have proved unsatisfactory. I know his tastes. In order
to save your time, might I ask you to commence reading at the
top of this page?"

"Certainly, Mrs. Bosworth."

I kept her waiting. Well, well! It was the history by my old
friend Mr. Gibbon. Things were going badly in the eastern Mediterranean, a mess of court intrigues, dozens of Byzantine names,
jaw-breakers of all kinds; but bloodwarming. I read slowly and
enjoyed myself.

"Thank you," she finally said, interrupting me in an assassina-
tion. She rose and apparently without design closed the door
beside me. "Your reading has much to recommend it. I am sorry
to have to tell you that my father finds a reading with intermittent
emphasis very tiring. I don't think I should waste your time any
longer."

From behind the closed door an old man's voice could be heard
calling, "Sarah! Sarah!" She put out her hand to me and said,
"Thank you, Mr. North. Good morning!"

"Sarah! Sarah!" In the next room a handbell rang; a hurled
object smote the door. It opened revealing a trained nurse. I

looked about the floor as though I had lost something. Willis appeared. Persis appeared.

"Willis, go about your work. Persis, this is none of your affair!"

Whereupon the old man himself appeared. He was wearing a quilted dressing-gown; his pince-nez danced on his nose; his Van-dyke beard pointed toward the horizon.

"Send that young man in to me, Sarah. Finally we have found someone who can read. The only readers you've ever found are retired librarians with mice in their throats, God help us!"

"Father, I *will* send Mr. North in to you directly. You go back to your desk at once. You're an ill man. You mustn't get excited. Nurse, take my father's arm."

For the second time I had introduced discord into "Nine Gables." I must change my ways. When the bystanders had withdrawn, Mrs. Bosworth resumed her seat and asked me to sit down. How she hated me!

"In the event that Dr. Bosworth approves of you as a reader there are some things you should know. My father is an old man; he is seventy-four. He is not a well man. His health has caused us great concern. In addition, he has a number of idiosyncrasies to which you must pay *no* attention. He tends to make large promises and to enter into extravagant projects. Any interest in them on your part could only lead you into serious difficulties."

"Sarah! Sarah!"

She rose. "I want you to remember what I have said. Have you heard me?"

I looked her in the eye and said amiably, "Thank you, Mrs. Bosworth."

That was not the answer she expected nor the tone to which she was accustomed. She replied sharply, "Any further trouble from you and you go out of this house at once." She opened the door. "Father, this is Mr. North."

Dr. Bosworth was sitting in a heavily cushioned chair before a great table. "Please sit down, Mr. North. I am Dr. Bosworth.

You may have heard my name. I have been able to be of some service to my country."

"Indeed, I know of your distinguished career, Dr. Bosworth."

"Hm . . . very good . . . May I ask where you were born?"

"In Madison, Wisconsin, sir."

"What was your father's occupation?"

"He owned and edited a newspaper."

"Indeed! Did your father also attend a university?"

"He graduated from Yale and obtained a doctorate there."

"Did he? . . . *Vous parlez français, monsieur?*"

"*J'ai passé une année en France.*"

There followed: what occupation had I been engaged in since leaving school? . . . my age? . . . my marital status? . . . what plans I entertained for later life, et cetera, et cetera.

I rose. "Dr. Bosworth, I came to this house to apply for a position as a reader. I was told that you have had many unsatisfactory readers. I foresee that I shall disappoint you also. Good morning."

"What? What?"

"Good morning, sir."

He appeared to be highly astonished. I left the room. As I progressed down the great hall, he called after me: "Mr. North! Mr. North! Kindly let me explain myself." I returned to the door of his study. "Please sit down, sir. I did not intend to be intrusive. I ask your apology. I have not left this house for seven years except to visit the hospital. We who are shut in tend to develop an excessive curiosity about those who attend us. Will you accept my apology?"

"Yes, sir. Thank you."

"Thank you . . . Are you free to read to me this morning until twelve-thirty?"

I was. He placed before me an early work of George Berkeley. When a variety of bells struck the half hour before one I finished a paragraph and rose. He said, "We have been reading from a first edition of this work. You may be interested in seeing the inscription on the title page." I reopened the book and saw that it had been inscribed by the author to his esteemed friend Dean Jonathan Swift. It took me some time to recover from my astonishment and veneration. Dr. Bosworth asked me if I had heard of Bishop Berkeley previously. I told him that at Yale University I had roomed in Berkeley Hall, that all Yale men were proud that the philosopher had left a part of his library to enrich our own—the books had been transported by bullock cart from Rhode Island to Connecticut; that moreover I had spent much of my boyhood in Berkeley, California, where we were often reminded that the town was named after the Bishop. We were pronouncing the name differently but had no doubt that it was the same man.

"God bless my soul!" exclaimed Dr. Bosworth. It is difficult for a Harvard man to believe that sober scholarly interests are pursued elsewhere.

It was arranged that I was to read for two hours on four days of the week. George Berkeley is not easy reading and neither of us had been trained in rigorous philosophical discussion, but we allowed no paragraph to be left behind without thorough digestion.

Two days later he interrupted our reading to whisper to me conspiratorially; he rose and opened the door to the great hall abruptly and peered about as though to surprise eavesdroppers; he repeated this manoeuvre at the door leading into his bedroom. Then he returned to his table and, lowering his voice, asked me, "You know that Bishop Berkeley lived three years in Newport?" I nodded. "I am planning to buy his house 'Whitehall' and fifty surrounding acres. There are many difficulties about it. It is still a *great secret*. I plan to build an Academy of Philosophers here. I was hoping that you would help me draft the invitations to the leading philosophers in the world."

"To come and lecture here, Dr. Bosworth?"

"Sh! . . . Sh! . . . No, to come and live here. Each would have his own house. Alfred North Whitehead and Bertrand Russell. Bergson. Benedetto Croce, and Gentile. Wittgenstein—do you know if he is still alive?"

"I am not sure, sir."

"Unamuno and Ortega y Gasset. You must help me draft the letters. The Masters are to have full liberty. They may teach or not teach, lecture or not lecture. They would not even be required to meet one another. Newport would become like a great lighthouse on a hill—a Pharos of Mind, of elevated thought. There is so much planning to be done! Time! Time! They tell me I am not well."

He heard—or thought he heard—a step outside the door. He put his forefinger against his mouth warningly, and we returned to our reading. The subject of the Academy did not arise again for some time. He seemed to fear that we were surrounded by too many spies.

At the end of the second week he asked if I was averse to late hours; he enjoyed a long siesta in the afternoon and felt no need to retire before midnight. This suited me very well as there were increasing requests for my time in the morning. The Bosworths gave several dinner parties a week, but it was the host's custom to rise from the table at ten-thirty—having partaken of some invalid's diet—and to join me in the library. As the season advanced these occasions became more frequent and more elaborate. It was a childish vanity on the part of the former diplomat to commemorate at these meals the national holidays of the countries where he had served; he was thus enabled to wear the decorations that had been conferred upon him. Neither our Independence Day nor the Fall of the Bastille happened to coincide with my visits to the house, but often enough he arrived resplendent in the study, murmuring modestly that "Poland had had a tragic but gallant history" or that "one could not overestimate the contributions of Garibaldi," or of Bolívar or of Gustavus Adolphus.

We continued our studies relative to *Dean* Berkeley's visit to the western hemisphere. He could see that my interest was almost equal to his own. Imagine our delight when, reading *The Analyst,* we discovered that "our boy"—now *Bishop Berkeley*—had *smashed* and *pulverized* Sir Isaac Newton and the mighty Leibnitz on the matter of infinitesimals. Both Dr. Bosworth and I were babes-in-arms in the realm of cosmological physics, but we got the point. Newton's friend Edmund Halley (of the comet) had mockingly spoken of the "inconceivability of the doctrines of Christianity" as held by Bishop Berkeley, and the Bishop replied that Newton's infinitesimal "fluxions" were as "obscure, repugnant and precarious" as any point they could call attention to in divinity, adding, "What are these fluxions . . . these velocities of evanescent increments? They are neither finite quantities, nor quantities infinitely small, nor yet nothing. May we call them the ghosts of departed quantities?" Crash! Bang! The structure of the universe, like the principles of the Christian faith—according to the Bishop—were perceived only by the intuition. It could not be said that Dr. Bosworth and I danced about his study, but the spies listening at the doors must have reported that something strange was going on—at midnight! These were giants indeed! Including Swift—my patron since I had begun to think of myself as Gulliver. We were in the heart of the Second City, in the eighteenth century.

At our first interview I had rebuked Dr. Bosworth's excessive curiosity about myself; our intermittent conversations were limited to historical subjects, but I was aware that he continued to be "consumed with curiosity" about me. When the very wealthy take a liking to any one of us belonging to the less fortunate orders they are filled with a pitying wonder as to how we "make out" in those conditions of squalor and deprivation to which we are condemned—to put it briefly they try to figure out *how much money we make*. Do we get enough to eat? I was to meet this concern over and over again during the summer. Plates of sandwiches, bowls of fruit, were constantly placed before me. Only once (at another house) did I consent to take as much as a cup of tea in any of my employers' homes or in their friends' homes, though invitations to luncheons, dinners, and parties began to arrive in considerable numbers.

I was uneasily aware that I had become an object of exaggerated curiosity on the Avenue by reason of the indefatigable pen of Flora Deland. As I have related, she lost no time in endearing herself to Newport. Her nation-wide (and local) audience had been enthralled by her account of the nine cities and the glorious trees on Aquidneck Island, and of the wonders of the Wyckoff House. I had revisited "The Sandpiper" a number of times, but the flower of friendship had lost its bloom; she nagged at me and then quarreled with me. She could not understand why I did not strain every nerve to become a social success among the "cottages," presumably with herself on my arm. I told her firmly that I had never accepted an invitation and that I never would. But before we parted company she had published a sixth article—a glowing picture of the cultural renaissance that had taken place in this earthly paradise. This had been sent to me, but I failed to read it until long after. Without naming me she wrote of an unbelievably learned young man who had become the "rage" of the summer colony and was reading Homer, Goethe, Dante, and Shakespeare with young and old. He had revived the Browning Club and his French *matinées* were depopulating Bailey's Beach. Her article opened with a scornful repudiation of a witticism twenty years old to the effect that "the ladies of Newport had never heard the first act of an opera nor read the last half of a book." Newport was—and always has been—she affirmed, one of the most enlightened communities in the country, the foster home of George Bancroft, Longfellow, Lowell, Henry James, Edith Wharton, and of Mrs. Edward Venable, author of that moving volume of verse, *Dreams in an Aquidneck Garden.*

Nor did I know at the time that there was a less flattering reason why I had become in those circles an object of almost morbid curiosity.

It was a custom of the house that toward midnight Dr. Bosworth's guests would file into the study to take a second leave of their distinguished host. I stood against the wall in that self-effacement that became my station. Mrs. Bosworth did not accompany them, but Dr. Bosworth and Persis saw to it that I was presented to them all. Among them were some who were, or had been, my employers: I received from Miss Wyckoff a radiant smile, from Bodo (a frequent guest) a fraternal and inelegant greeting in German. Ladies whom I had never met told me of their children's progress:

"My Michael's set his heart on becoming a tennis champion, thanks to you, Mr. North."

Mrs. Venable: "Bodo tells me that you're reading Bishop Berkeley—how fascinating!"

Another: "Mr. North, Mr. Weller and I are giving a small dance on Saturday week. To what address may I send a card?"

"That's very kind of you, Mrs. Weller, but my days are so filled that I'm unable to accept any invitations."

"No parties *at all?*"

"No—thank you very much—no parties."

Another: "Mr. North, is it too late for me to join your Robert Browning Society. I've always loved the Brownings."

"Ma'am, I don't know of any Browning Society in Newport."

"Oh? . . . Oh? . . . Perhaps I was misinformed."

The Fenwicks, whom you will meet later, were very cordial with a smile of complicity. I was presented to the parents of Diana Bell who did not acknowledge the introduction. I leaned forward to Mrs. Bell and said in a low voice but very distinctly: "I have twice sent my bill to Mr. Bell for services which he agreed upon. If he does not pay my bill, I shall tell the whole story to Miss Flora Deland and sixty million Americans will learn of that purloined letter. Good evening, Mrs. Bell."

That was low; that was unworthy of a Yale man. She stared straight ahead of her, but the bill was paid. Let him who will be a gentleman!

Among the guests I met more and more members of the family clan: Mr. and Mrs. Cassius Marcellus Leffingwell, and their older children; the Edward Bosworths and their older children; the Newton Bosworths and a child or two. All these ladies put out their hands and declared that they were delighted to meet me; these gentlemen not only refused their hands but either stared at me stonily or turned their backs. When I had been the object of hostility on repeated occasions I became aware that Gulliver was encountering some example of the *mores* on Aquidneck Island that deserved a closer study.

I was not comfortable at "Nine Gables." I had come to Newport to observe without becoming deeply involved. Among the Bosworths I felt obscurely that I was in danger of becoming extremely involved in some imbroglio out of late Elizabethan drama. I had already made two enemies in the house: Willis loathed me; when I passed Mrs. Bosworth in the hall, she lowered her head slightly but her glance said, "Beware young man, we know what your game is. . . ." Day after day I planned to throw up the job. Yet I enjoyed the readings in Bishop Berkeley; I enjoyed Dr. Bosworth's constantly recalling the Newport of the eighteenth century half a mile from where we were working. I was deeply interested in Persis, Mrs. Tennyson, though I had never been presented to her. She seemed to regard me with puzzled distrust. I wondered how was she able to live the year round in a house governed by her vindictive "Aunt Sally." Above all I had been exalted by my employer's preposterous vision of gathering together here the greatest living thinkers—a vision he could only communicate in whispers. I had lived four and a half uneventful years in a New Jersey where there were no perils and no visions, no dragons and no madmen—and very little opportunity to exercise and explore any of those youthful ambitions that lay dormant within me. I did not resign.

It was I who unwittingly opened the next door into a deeper involvement. We had been reading aloud from Dr. Bosworth's own work *Some Eighteenth Century Houses in Rhode Island*. When we finished the chapter that contained a detailed description of Bishop

Berkeley's "Whitehall" I expressed my admiration for the art with which it was written; then I added, "Dr. Bosworth, I think it would be a great privilege to visit the house in your company. Would it be possible to drive out some afternoon and see the house together?"

There was a silence. I looked up and found him gazing at me searchingly, piteously. "Indeed, I wish we could. I thought you understood . . . I have this disability. I am unable to leave this house for more than a quarter of an hour. I can walk in the garden for a short time. I shall never leave this house. I shall die here."

I returned his gaze with that impassive expression I had learned to adopt in the Army where irrationality knows no bounds and where we underlings have no choice but to make a pretense of unfathomable stupidity. To myself I thought, "He's crazy. He's around the bend." We had often sat uninterruptedly in his study for almost three hours, after which he had accompanied me unhurriedly to his front door. All I knew at that moment was that I did not want to hear one more word about it. I wanted to have nothing to do with the appealing, longing, dependent expression on his face. I was no doctor. I didn't know what I was, but Dr. Bosworth was a bad judge of men. He had assumed that I was a sympathetic listener. A miserable man cannot hold his tongue in such company and soon I was to receive the whole damnable ludicrous story.

But I must interrupt my narrative here.

I must give the reasons—which I was soon to learn—why encounters with the guests at the close of the Bosworths' dinner parties were of so mixed a nature.

I continued to enjoy occasional late hours at Mrs. Cranston's boardinghouse now aglow with the expectation of Edweena's imminent return. Henry continued to share with us the postcards he received telling of whales, mighty storms, flying fishes, and picturing the beauties of the Leeward Islands. The conversation flowed on. For the most part I played the role of an appreciative listener. I gave them only a general idea of my activities, mentioning few names. After the retirement of the other ladies Mrs. Cranston intermittently relaxed her rule against the use of our Christian names. Generally Mr. Griffin sat with us, lost in deep thought or in vacancy, occasionally delighting us with some far-sought non-sequitur. My Journal was enriched by many of Mrs. Cranston's reflections.

"The Whitcombs!" cried Mrs. Cranston. "There's another case of the Death Watch, Henry. Oh, how I wish Edweena were here to tell Teddie about her theory of the Death Watch. You tell him, Henry. I'm tired tonight. Do now, I know it will interest him."

"Will you interrupt me, ma'am, if I get to sliding on the ice, as often happens? . . . Well, it's this way, old matey: in a dozen houses in Newport there's an aged party, male or female, sitting on a mountain of money. . . ."

"Twenty houses, Henry, at *least* twenty."

"Thank you, ma'am. Now let's call the aged party the Old Mogle—some call it Mogull, you can pronounce it either way. Newport's the only place in the country where rich old men live longer than rich old women. I've heard you make that observation, Mrs. Cranston."

"Yes, I think it's true. It's the social life that kills. The old men simply withdraw upstairs. No old woman has ever been known to withdraw from the social life of her own accord."

"And the Old Mogle has sons and daughters and grandchildren and flying nevvies and nieces, all waiting for the reading of the will. But the Old Party won't die. So what do you do? You gather around him every hour of the clock and ask him tenderly about his health—tenderly, sadly, lovingly. You call in doctors to ask him doubtfully, tenderly about his health. 'Well, Mr. Mogle, how are we today? God bless my soul, we look ten years younger! Splendid! Let me look again at that little inflammation. We don't like that one little bit, do we? Too near the brain. Is it sensitive to the touch, Mr. Mogle?' Oh, I wish Edweena were here; she does the doctor business glorious, doesn't she, Mrs. Cranston? She says that all men over seventy can be made to be high-pepper-condriacs in zero time with a little attention from the loved ones. She says all women are, anyway."

"I'm not, Henry."

"You're nowhere near that age, Mrs. Cranston—and God gave you the constitution and the figure of the Statue of Liberty."

"I'm above compliments, Henry. Go on with your story."

"Now the Death Watch has a lot to worry about, cully—see what I mean? For instance, *favoritism!* One son over another, one daughter over another, down to the new-born grandchild. Terrible thought! Then there's always the Old Man's Folly—falls in love with his nurse or secretary. Or a beautiful divorcée arrives from Europe, pulls his beard and strokes his hands right at the dinner table. An old lady falls in love with her chauffeur; we've seen it scores of times. The Death Watch goes frantic. Frantic—and starts to act. We've seen some terrible *action* around here. Expel 'em! Crush 'em!"

"You've forgotten something else, Henry."

"Thankee, and what's that, ma'am?"

"The callers, the confidential callers, with noble causes—"

"How could I forget them! Universal peace. Colleges *named after you!* Eskimos. Fallen women—very popular. Old men are very tender about fallen women."

"Dogs' cemeteries," said Mr. Griffin.

"How bright you are tonight, Mr. Griffin!—All these things taking the food out of the mouths of his nearest and dearest."

The room seemed to have become uncomfortably warm.

"What kind of action do they take, Henry?" I asked.

"Well, they've got two lines of action, haven't they? To get rid of the favorite they've got slander—they tell stories. Even if it's their nearest kith 'n' kin. That's easy. But their 'object all sublime' —as the poet said—is to take the pen out of the great Mogle's hand—to remove his power to write checks. To drive him dotty. To get him quivering and bursting into tears. Guardianship— soften him up for guardianship."

"Terrible!" said Mrs. Cranston, shaking her head.

"They've got their doctors and lawyers all lined up. Why, we know a Mogle in this town who hasn't left his front door for ten years—"

"Eight, Henry."

"You're always right, Mrs. Cranston."

"No names, Henry."

"He's just as well as you or me. They make him think that he's got cancer of the sofa cushion. The great specialist comes up from New York—you can't do these things without specialists—specialists are the Death Watchers' best friend. Dr. Thread-and-Needle comes up from New York and tells him it's about time for another of those little operations. So the Mogle is wheeled in and they take a little piece of skin off the area. The nurses near die of laughing. 'Ten thousand dollars, please.' "

"Henry, I'd say you were sliding on the ice a bit."

"I'll be forgiven if I exaggerate. Teddie's new to the town. You never can tell when he might come up against an example of things like this."

"Let's talk about something more cheerful, Henry. Teddie, who have you been reading aloud to lately?"

"Mostly I've been getting children ready to return to school, Mrs. Cranston. I've had to turn down a number of jobs. I think there's a craze on to trace a family's genealogy to William the Conqueror."

"That's always been true."

The conversation flowed on.

I returned to my room thoughtfully.

My next engagement at "Nine Gables" was on the following Sunday morning. Dr. McPherson had suddenly decided that the late-hour sessions were inadvisable. I was surprised to see Dr. Bosworth fully dressed to go out. He was arguing with his nurse. "We shall not need your company, Mrs. Turner."

"But, Dr. Bosworth, I must obey Dr. McPherson's orders. I must be near you at all times."

"Will you leave the room and close the door, Mrs. Turner?"

"Oh, dear! I don't know what to do!" she answered and left.

To me he whispered, "Listening! Always listening!" His eyes searched the ceiling. "Mr. North, will you climb up on that chair and see if there's some kind of gramophone up there listening to what's said here?"

"No, Dr. Bosworth," I said, raising my voice, "I was engaged to read aloud here. I am not an electrical engineer."

He put his ear to his bedroom door. "She's telephoning all over the house. . . . Come, follow me."

We started down the great hall to the front door. As we approached it Mrs. Leffingwell came floating down the staircase.

"Good morning, Papa dear. Good morning, Mr. North. We're all coming over to lunch. I came early to see if Sally wanted to go to church. She can't make up her mind. But I'd much rather listen to the reading. Mr. North, do persuade my father to let me join you. I'll be as quiet as a mouse."

Something in her voice astonished and pained him. He stared at her for a moment and said, "You too, Mary?" then added harshly, "Our discussion would not interest you. Run off to church and enjoy yourselves. . . . We are going to the beech grove, Mr. North."

It was a most beautiful morning. He had brought no book with him. We sat for some time in silence on a bench under the great trees. Suddenly I became aware that Dr. Bosworth's eyes were fixed on me with an expression of suffering—of despair.

"Mr. North, I think I should explain my disability to you. I suffer from a disorder of the kidneys which the doctors tell me may be related to a far more serious illness—to a fatal disease. I find this very strange because—apart from certain local irritations—I have experienced no pain. But I am not a medical man; I must rely on the word of certain specialists." His eyes now bored into mine. "As a side aspect of this wretched business, I suffer from a compulsion to urinate—or try to urinate—every ten to fifteen minutes."

I returned his gaze as solemnly as he could wish.

"Why, Dr. Bosworth, you and I have sat in your study for hours at a time without your leaving the room once."

"That's the ridiculous part about it. Perhaps it's all in the mind —as Bishop Berkeley is constantly insisting! As long as I'm in my own house—keeping quiet, so to speak—I am not inconvenienced. I am assured that it is not the usual old man's affliction; it is not prostate trouble. It's something far graver."

(Oh, hell! Oh, crimson tarnation! Resign right now!—Besides, every two weeks I'd sent my bill to Mrs. Bosworth, my ostensible employer, and she'd made no reply. This was my fifth week. She owed me over sixty dollars!)

The old man went on: "For many years I served my country in the diplomatic life. Public functions tend to be long drawn out. State funerals, weddings, christenings, openings of parliament, national holidays. Unforeseen delays! Snowstorms in Finland, hurricanes in Burma! . . . Waits at railway stations, waits on grandstands. I was the head of my delegation. . . . I have always been a healthy man, Mr. North, but I began to get a dread of that— that little necessity. Now I know that it's all in the mind. Bishop Berkeley! Doctors laugh at me, I know, behind my back. One doctor fitted me out with a sort of goat's udder." Here he covered his face with his hands, murmuring, "I shall die in this house or in their wretched hospital."

There was a silence. He lowered his hands and whispered, "The worst of it is that the idea is getting around that I'm crazy. Do *you* think I'm crazy?"

I raised my hand for silence and got it. I was as authoritative as a judge and solemn as an owl. "Dr. Bosworth, none of this is new to me—this kidney trouble. I know all about it."

"What's that you say?" He clutched my sleeve. "What's that you say, boy?"

"One summer I left Yale and went to Florida and got work as a swimming and sports director at a resort. One of the hurricanes came along. The tourists canceled their bookings. I was out of a job. So I became a truck driver. Long drives—Miami to Winston-Salem, Saint Petersburg to Dallas, Texas. Now the three things that truck drivers think about are: the bonus for speed of delivery, falling asleep at the wheel, and kidney trouble. There's something about sitting all day in that shaking truck that upsets a man's waterworks—irritates it. Driving is hell on the kidneys. Some men get the fear of retention—afraid that they'll never piss again. Others have what you have—the constant itch. Of course, they can get down when they want to, but nothing comes. Now I have an idea."

"An *idea?* What . . . what idea?"

"I have very few pupils tomorrow. I'll cancel them. I'll go to Providence to the truck drivers' stop. They sell stay-awake pills and a *certain gadget.* It's got a very vulgar name that I won't repeat to you. I'll bring it back to you and one of these days we'll drive to 'Whitehall' and try it out."

Tears were rolling down the old man's face. "If you do that, Mr. North, if you do that, I'll believe there's a God. I will. I will."

I had never been to Florida since the age of eight. I had never driven a truck farther than twenty miles—it was the summer school's carry-all. But in the Army barracks a man picks up a lot of desultory information, a great deal of it scatological.

"I have three pupils in the morning. I shall have to charge you for the canceled lessons, as well as for the cost of the trip to Providence and for the gadget I hope to find. I live on a strict budget, Dr. Bosworth. I think I can do the whole thing for twenty dollars. Maybe the gadget costs more. I shall submit an itemized account. Shall I send it to you or to Mrs. Bosworth?"

"What?"

I continued firmly. "I have sent Mrs. Bosworth a bill for our readings every two weeks, but so far I have received no payment whatever. She has the bills."

"What? I don't understand it!"

"I shall need some money to go to Providence."

"Come in the house. Come in the house at once. I am shocked. I am grieved, Mr. North."

He started for the house like a runaway horse. He met Willis at the door. "Willis, tell Mrs. Bosworth to bring my checkbook to my study and Mr. North's bills also!"

Long wait. He smote his handbell. Enter Persis.

"What is it, Grandfather?"

"I wish to speak to your Aunt Sarah."

"I think she may be at church."

"Hunt for her. If she's out of the house, go to her desk and bring me my checkbook or her checkbook. She has failed to pay Mr. North's bills."

"Grandfather, she has given strict orders that no one may open her desk. May I write a check for you?"

"It's *my* checkbook. *I* shall open her desk."

"I'll see if I can find her, Grandfather."

While we waited I filled in the time with further graphic accounts of the discomfitures of truck drivers. Presently there was a knock at the door and Willis entered, nobly bearing a bronze tray on which lay a checkbook and my two envelopes, opened. Dr. Bosworth asked me to state the total sum for my past and future services. He recalled my full name and wrote the check. I receipted the bills.

Mrs. Bosworth entered the room. "Father, you directed me to keep the accounts of this house."

"Then keep them! Pay them!"

"I assumed that a monthly payment for Mr. North would be sufficient."

"Here is your checkbook for the household accounts. I have paid Mr. North for our readings and for some errands he is doing for me. Kindly return to me my own checkbook for my own private use.—Mr. North, is it agreeable to you, if we return to our former evening schedule?"

"Yes, Dr. Bosworth."

"Father, Dr. McPherson is convinced that the late hours are harmful to you."

"My compliments to Dr. McPherson . . . Let me see you to the door, Mr. North. I am too agitated to continue our work this morning. May I expect you Tuesday evening?"

In the hall we passed Mrs. Bosworth. She said nothing, but our eyes met. I bowed slightly. In the Orient, they believe that hatred, in itself, kills; and I was brought up in China.

At the door her father whispered feverishly: "Perhaps I shall live again."

The next morning at the "Y" I fitted myself out, with the help of some acquaintances in the corridor, with a dirty sweater, some dirty pants, and a battered hat. I was a truck driver. At the truck drivers' stop in Providence I bought—as a pretext—some stay-awake pills and asked where was the nearest drugstore frequented by us road men. It was across the street, "O'Halloran's." I bought some more stay-awake pills and had an intimate conversation with Joe O'Halloran about some inconveniences I suffered on the road.

"Let me show you something, Jack. First they invented this for babies. Then they made 'm bigger for hospitals and insane asylums, see what I mean? Lots of incontinence in insane asylums."

I bought the medium size. "Mr. O'Halloran, I get a kind of ache in my wrists and forearms. Have you some mild—real mild—painkiller? Nothing potent, you know. I've gotta drive over four hundred miles a day."

He put a bottle of scarlet pills on the counter. "How many should I take?"

"Driving like you do, not more than one an hour."

Was I taking a great risk? I weighed the matter thoroughly. Medicine had never been among my youthful ambitions, but it had always been high among my curiosities. I had no doubt that Dr. Bosworth had been for years the victim of a carefully staged conspiracy that had taken advantage of an insecurity frequently found among diplomats, policemen on all-night guard duty, performing artists. Among my fellow-soldiers in the barracks I had heard ex-chauffeurs telling hilarious stories of the "perfect hell" of driving ladies out shopping in midtown where there was no place to park. When Dr. Bosworth and I were immersed in the eighteenth century it was apparent that he was as filled with well-being as with intellectual delight and as with self-esteem. It was only when the obsession descended upon him that he became a pitiable man. The risk I was taking was a risk for me, not for him. I was in a condition to assume a risk and to relish it.

I was back in Newport at four in the afternoon. I'd swallowed two of the red pills, very bitter with little effect—perhaps a slight numbness in the neck. I telephoned my employer.

"Yes, Mr. North? Yes, Mr. North?"

"I have a message for you. Can I give it to you on this line?"

"Wait a minute. I must think. . . . Tell me your number. I will call you back from the gardener's house."

He did. "Yes, Mr. North?"

"Dr. Bosworth, in a quarter of an hour a telegraph boy is going to call at your house with a parcel for your hands only and for your signature. Don't let anyone intercept it. I think you'll want to use what's inside. You take a walk around the garden at five, you told me. When you start out take one of those red pills. Thousands of men take them on the road every day. After about ten minutes you may feel a little itching, but it'll go away. Ignore it. The other thing is just a safeguard. You'll be able to throw it away after a week or two."

His voice was trembling. "I don't know what to say. . . . I'll be at the front door. . . . I'll report to you Tuesday night."

When I entered his study Tuesday night, he clutched at me excitedly, then closed both the doors. "First afternoon, half an hour! This morning, half an hour! This afternoon, forty-five minutes!"

"That's fine," I said calmly.

"*Fine?* FINE?" He wiped his eyes. "Mr. North, can you drive with me to 'Whitehall' next Sunday morning or afternoon?"

"I am sorry I am engaged with Colonel Vanwinkle on Sunday mornings. I would feel it to be a great privilege to go with you on Sunday afternoon."

"Yes, I shall take my granddaughter with me this Sunday."

There was a knock at the door. "Come in!"

Mrs. Bosworth entered. "Forgive me interrupting you, Father. I must discuss our dinner Tuesday week. The Thayers have been called to New York. Whom would you like in their place?" Her father muttered something agitatedly. "I'm sorry, Father, but I *must* know whether you prefer the Ewings or the Thorpes."

"Sarah, how many times must I tell you *not* to disturb me when I am at work?"

She stared at him. "Father, you have been behaving very strangely lately. I think these readings and those *walks* have overexcited you. Shouldn't you say good night to Mr. North and—?"

"Sarah, you have your car and driver. I do not wish to interfere with your life. Tomorrow I want you to arrange for the rental of a car and a driver for my use. I wish to go for a drive tomorrow after my nap—at four-thirty."

"You are not going to—?!"

"What you take for my *strange behavior* is an improvement in my health."

"A drive! Without Dr. McPherson's permission! Your doctor for thirty years!"

"Dr. McPherson is *your* doctor. I do not now feel the need of one. If I do, I shall call in that young Dr. What's-his-name that Forebaugh was telling me about. . . . I wish now to return to my studies."

"But the children . . . !"

"Edward? Mary? What have they to do with it?"

"We are all deeply concerned. We love you!"

"Then you'll be glad to hear that I feel much better. I would like to speak to Persis."

Persis appeared almost at once. This was "the house of listening ears."

"Persis, can you arrange to take a short drive with me in my car every afternoon after my nap?"

"I'd love to, Grandfather."

"The Sunday after next we will take Mr. North with us and show him 'Whitehall.' "

The roof had fallen down about Mrs. Bosworth's ears. She did not even glance at me. Her manner suggested that the time had come for stronger measures.

Our readings in the works of Bishop Berkeley continued, though with a relaxed concentration. Dr. Bosworth was filled with an irrepressible elation. They now were enjoying the famous "ten-mile drive" daily. He hoped soon to revisit Providence; they would put up for the night at the hotel "without Mrs. Turner." He was dreaming of going to New York in the fall—plans for the Academy . . .

A storm was gathering about my head.

I enjoyed the flashes of lightning.

Increasingly the Leffingwells were present at every dinner party at "Nine Gables" and on each occasion joined the late parade into Dr. Bosworth's study. Mrs. Leffingwell extended her hand to me in greeting; her husband stared into my face and seemed about to address me, but the war within him between rage and decorum silenced him. (I always thought of Cassius Marcellus as "Vercingetorix or The Dying Gaul"—the only mustached head known to me in ancient sculpture—probably straw-blond.) One evening there was—as in all parades—a halt in the line. The Leffingwells were marking time directly in front of me. Mrs. Leffingwell and I discussed the weather, the beauty of Newport, and her father's improved health until even her conversational resources were exhausted. She fanned herself with her handkerchief, smiling sweetly. Her husband growled, "Get on with it, Mary. Get on with it!"

"I can't, Cassius. Mrs. Venable is holding up the line."

At last Cassius found his tongue. He stretched his head toward me and said between his teeth (right out of *"The Curfew Shall Not Ring Tonight"*): "One of these days, North, I shall horsewhip you."

His wife overheard him. "Cassius! Cassius, we shall not wait to see my father any longer. We shall go upstairs."

But he balked; he wanted to drive his point home more forcefully. "Remember my words: horsewhip!"

I looked at him gravely. "Are they still horsewhipping in the South, Mr. Leffingwell? I thought that went out fifty years ago."

"Cassius, follow me!"

It was an order and he obeyed. The trouble with him was that he hadn't had enough to drink.

A few nights later I found a note waiting for me at the Y.M.C.A. *"Dear Mr. North, I have heard that a member of a family—where you read—has been talking wildly all over town—about doing you harm. A freind of mine—you met him—has arranged to have a car call for you at midnight Friday. Do not leave the house until you are told that a car and driver are waiting for you at the door."* It was signed *"A Freind on Spring Street."* Freinds indeed: Amelia Cranston—more for Newport's sake than for mine—had arranged with the Chief of Police to prevent the summer residents from getting into trouble.

There was no dinner party on Friday. Dr. Bosworth and I read Benedetto Croce on the subject of Giambattista Vico. My employer's knowledge of Italian was superior to mine and it gave him pleasure to help me over the difficult passages. It gave him pleasure, too, to believe that the author would soon be his guest and neighbor in the Academy of Philosophers. It gave me pleasure because author and subject were new, astonishing, and big. I forgot that I was to be called for.

At a quarter before twelve Persis Tennyson knocked at the door and was asked to enter. "Grandfather, I wish to drive Mr. North home in my car tonight. Please let him leave a little early because it's late."

"Yes, my dear. Do you mean *now?*"

"Yes, Grandfather, please."

As I was preparing to take my departure Mrs. Bosworth appeared at the door. She had overheard her niece's proposal. (At "Nine Gables" no one went to bed until that abominable Mr. North was out of the house.) "That will not be necessary, Persis. It is unsuitable that you drive about town at this hour. I've arranged for Dorsey to drive Mr. North home in my car."

"Well, my friend," said Dr. Bosworth in Italian, "everybody wants to see that you get home safely tonight."

Willis appeared at the door and announced that Mr. North's car was waiting. . . .

"What car is that, Willis—mine?"

"No, madam, a car called for by Mr. North."

"Well," said Persis, "let's all go and see Mr. North to the door . . . !"

We made quite a procession advancing down the hall. From the foot of the staircase Mrs. Leffingwell approached us agitatedly. "Sally, I can't find Cassius anywhere. I think he's out of the house. Please help me find him. If we can't find him I shall drive Mr. North home in my own car.—Willis, have you seen Mr. Leffingwell anywhere?"

"Yes, madam."

"*Where* is he?"

"Madam, he is in the bushes."

"Yes, Aunt Mary," said Persis. "I saw him lying in the bushes. That's why I asked to drive Mr. North home. He had something in his hand."

"Persis, that will do," said Mrs. Bosworth. "Hold your tongue. Go to your room."

Willis said to Mrs. Bosworth, "Madam, may I speak to you at one side for a moment?"

"Talk up, Willis," said Dr. Bosworth. "What are you trying to say. What is it that Mr. Leffingwell has in his hand?"

"A gun, sir."

Mrs. Leffingwell was too well brought up to shriek. She squeaked. "Cassius is playing with guns again. He will kill himself!"

The driver who had called for me stepped forward. "Not at present, madam. We have taken the gun from him." And he held it under our noses.

"And who are you?" asked Mrs. Bosworth grandly. The driver flipped his lapel and showed his badge.

"God bless my soul!" exclaimed Dr. Bosworth.

"*And,*" asked Mrs. Bosworth. who enjoyed beginning a question with "and," "what authority have you for trespassing on this property?"

"Mr. Loft . . . Mr. Left . . . the gentleman in the bushes . . . has been overheard in three places threatening to kill Mr. North. We can't have that, madam. Is Mr. Leveringwall a resident of Newport?"

"Mr. Leffingwell lives in Jamestown."

"The Chief told us not to press charges, if the gentleman lives outside Aquidneck County. But he must agree not to appear in this township for six months. Felix, call him in."

Mrs. Leffingwell said, "Officer, please do not call him in now. I am his wife and I will stand guarantee that he will not return here. We have a farm in Virginia, also, *where a man may carry a gun in self-defense wherever he goes.*"

That's what's called the last word. She delivered the line grandly and couldn't have looked handsomer.

My rescuer ("Joe") had had free ingress to all motion-pictures

and knew how to behave in great houses. "If Mr. North is ready
to go, the car is waiting for him. We have a call to the Daubigny
cottage. Good night, ladies and gentlemen, we are sorry to have
been an inconvenience to you."

I bowed in silence to the company and left.

Outside Joe said to his companion, "Let's see where the gook's
gone."

"He's knocking at the side door, Joe. Do you think he needs
any help, Joe?"

"They'll find him. . . . The Chief says to have as little to do
with these people as possible. They're crazy as coots, he says. Let
them wash their own sheets, he says."

If I'd had a grain of decent feeling in me, I'd have resigned
the next morning; but what's a little family unpleasantness com-
pared to discovering Bishop Berkeley, Croce, Vico, and letting
one's eyes rest on Persis Tennyson?

When the hour arrived for the Sunday drive to "Whitehall"
Dr. Bosworth and his granddaughter were waiting at the door. It
was a beautiful afternoon in August (but I remember no others;
on Aquidneck Island rain fell—considerately—only when the
inhabitants were sleeping).

Persis said, "I shall sit in front with Jeffries. Mr. North, will
you sit with Grandfather. He likes to drive slowly and I know
he wants to talk to you."

"Mrs. Tennyson, I have never had the pleasure of being introduced to you?"

"What!" said Dr. Bosworth.

"We have exchanged greetings," I said.

Persis laughed. "Let us shake hands, Mr. North."

Dr. Bosworth was bewildered. "Never met! Never introduced!
What a house I live in! Cassius lying in the bushes—policemen
passing around guns—Sarah and Mary behaving like . . ." He
began laughing. "Makes an old man feel like King Lear."

"Let's forget all about it, Grandfather."

"Yes." He began pointing out to me some eighteenth-century doors and fanlights. "There are some beautiful houses all over town—going to rack and ruin. Nobody appreciates them."

"Dr. Bosworth, I've discovered a resident in Newport who could have helped us with those metaphysical passages in Bishop Berkeley."

"Who's that?"

"Someone you know well—Baron Stams. He has a doctorate from Heidelberg in philosophy."

"Bodo? God bless my soul! Does Bodo know anything?"

"He also has a doctorate from Vienna in political history."

"Do you hear that, Persis? He's a pleasant fellow, but I thought he was just one of these dancing-partners that Mrs. Venable collects for her parties. You always found him rather empty-headed, didn't you, Persis?"

"Not empty-headed, Grandfather. Just difficult to talk to."

"Yes, I remember your saying that. Surprised me. He seems to be able to talk easily to everybody he sits by except you. A regular *gigolo*. Your Aunt Sally always seats him by you and Mrs. Venable always seats him by you, I hear."

Persis remained silent.

Dr. Bosworth again addressed me confidentially. "I always thought he was one of these fortune hunters, if you know what I mean—title, good looks, and nothing else."

I began laughing.

"Why are you laughing, Mr. North?"

I made him wait for it and laughed some more.

"You find something droll about it, Mr. North?"

"Well, Dr. Bosworth, it's Baron Stams who has the fortune."

"Oh? He has money, has he?"

I looked Dr. Bosworth in the eye and I didn't lower my voice. "A fortune: excellent brains, excellent character, a distinguished family, an assured career. He has been decorated by his country for bravery in battle and he almost died of his wounds. His castle at Stams is almost as beautiful as the famous monastery at Stams—

which you must know. In addition, he's lots of fun." Again I laughed. "That's what I call a fortune."

Persis had turned her profile toward us. She appeared to be annoyed and bewildered.

We arrived at "Whitehall." I had to hold my breath from awe. Bishop Berkeley was the author of the line "Westward the course of empire takes its way." There we were, pilgrims from the East.

In spite of kind invitations I never drove out in Dr. Bosworth's car again; though I was taken for a drive in Persis Tennyson's—an account of that starlit encounter I must defer. It will be found in a later chapter entitled "Bodo and Persis" whom it more closely concerns. Persis became her grandfather's constant companion—running head on into the danger from which I was escaping, "favoritism." Mrs. Bosworth's tone became increasingly sharp to her, but Persis held firm. One afternoon I called on Dr. Bosworth at his request for a short talk following his daily drive. While waiting in his study for him to change his clothes I overheard the following conversation in the hall.

"You must be able to see, Aunt Sally, that these drives agree with Grandfather."

"You are an ignorant girl, Persis. This activity will *kill* him."

"I asked Grandfather as a favor to me to submit to an examination by Dr. Tedeschi. Dr. Tedeschi recommended the drives."

"How could *you* take such a responsibility? Dr. Tedeschi is a puppy, and an Italian puppy at that."

Dr. Bosworth reentered his study. He was overflowing with ideas that had occurred to him. He was preparing to present the great project to a still unselected board of directors. There was to be an administration building with two lecture halls, a large and a small; a well-stocked library; at least nine separate residences; large annual grants to the Masters; a dormitory and dining hall for whatever students the Masters consented to accept. Further expenditures were added in pencil along the margins. . . . The project called for millions and millions. Very exhilarating.

Two evenings later I arrived at the usual hour. Persis was waiting outside the house. She put her fingers on her lips, raised her eyebrows, and pointed toward the hall. There was trepidation and a shade of amusement on her face. She spoke no word. I rang the bell and was admitted by Willis. Mrs. Bosworth met me in the hall at some distance from her father's study. She addressed me in a low voice but very distinctly. "Mr. North, since you entered this house you have been a constant source of confusion. I regard you as a foolish and dangerous man. Will you explain to me what you are trying to do to my father?"

I replied even more quietly. "I don't understand what you mean, Mrs. Bosworth."

It worked. Her voice rose. "Dr. Bosworth is a very sick man. These exertions may kill him."

"Your father invited me to accompany him to 'Whitehall.' I assumed that he had his doctor's permission."

"*Assumed!* It is not your business to assume anything."

I was now almost inaudible. "Dr. Bosworth spoke of his doctor's approval."

"*He refuses to see his doctor—the man who has been his physician for thirty years.* You are a trouble-maker. You are a vulgar intruder. Mr. North, it was I who engaged you to come to this house. Your engagement is terminated. Now! *Now!* Will you tell me what I owe you?"

"Thank you . . . Dr. Bosworth is expecting me. I shall go to his study to say goodbye to him."

"I forbid you to take one step further."

I had one more trick up my sleeve. Now I raised my voice. "Mrs. Bosworth, you are very pale. Are you unwell? Can I get you a glass of water?"

"I am perfectly well. Will you lower your voice, please?"

I started dashing about, shouting, "Mr. Willis! Mr. Willis! Is anybody there? Mrs. Turner! Nurse!"

"Stop this nonsense. I am perfectly well."

I ran the length of the hall, calling, "Smelling salts! Help! Asafoetida!"

I overturned a table. Persis appeared. Mrs. Turner appeared. Willis appeared. Maids emerged from the kitchen.

"Do be quiet! I am perfectly well!"

"Call a doctor. Mrs. Bosworth has fainted." I recalled a smashing phrase from eighteenth-century novels, "Unlace her!"

Willis pulled up a chair behind Mrs. Bosworth so abruptly that she sank into it, outraged. Persis knelt and patted her hands. Dr. Bosworth appeared at the door of his study and the room fell silent. "What's the matter, Sarah?"

"Nothing! This *oaf* has raised a great noise about nothing."

"Persis?"

"Grandfather, Aunt Sally suddenly felt unwell. Fortunately Mr. North was here and called for help."

Now it was like grand opera—that relief in the air *when things crack open*. Mrs. Bosworth rose and advanced toward her father— "Father, either that monster leaves this house or I do!"

"Willis, call Dr. McPherson. Sarah, you're tired. You're overworked. Mrs. Turner, will you kindly take Mrs. Bosworth up to her room. Go to bed, Sarah; go to bed! Persis, I want you to stay here. Willis!"

"Yes, sir."

"I will have a whiskey and soda. Bring one for Mr. North, too."

Whiskey! It was that request that made it clear to Mrs. Bosworth that her authority was at an end. After years of gruel, *whiskey*. She started for the stairs, brushing Mrs. Turner aside. "Don't touch me! I can walk perfectly well by myself."

"Dr. Bosworth," I said, "I have great respect for Mrs. Bosworth. I shall certainly discontinue my visits here since they are so unwelcome to her. May I remain a few minutes to thank you for the privilege it has been to meet with you here?"

"What? What? We must talk this over. Persis, will you please join us?"

"Yes, Grandfather."

"Mr. North feels that he must leave us. I hope he will be able to meet me from time to time at the 'Reading Rooms.' "

Willis entered with our drinks. Dr. Bosworth raised his glass, saying, "Dr. Tedeschi recommended today that I have a little whiskey in the evening."

Persis and I exchanged no glances, but I felt that we shared a sense of something accomplished.

That was my last engagement at "Nine Gables."

Both Mrs. Bosworth and I left the house—she to visit a dear friend in England, I to offer my services elsewhere. But, as I have already told the reader, I had not yet entirely terminated my relations with all the residents at "Nine Gables."

Toward the end of the summer I met Dr. Bosworth by chance. He was as cordial as ever. He confided to me that he was too old to cope with the numerous details involved in setting up an Academy of Philosophers; he had another project in mind—still a secret; he was planning to build and endow a clinic for that "excellent young physician Dr. Tedeschi."

Rip

Late in June I was surprised to discover that someone I had known fairly well at college was living in Newport's Sixth City. One late afternoon I was wheeling homewards along the Avenue when I was startled to hear a voice from a passing car calling "Theophilus! Theophilus! What the hell are you doing here?" I drew up beside the curb. The car which had passed me did so also. A man alighted and walked toward me laughing. Still laughing he slapped me on the back, punched me in the thorax, seized my shoulder, and shook me like a rat. It took me some minutes to recognize Nicholas Vanwinkle. All his life—through school, college, and military service—he had naturally been called "Rip." There was a legend in his family that Washington Irving had known his grandfather well and had written him one day asking permission to use the name Vanwinkle, applying it to a likeable old character in a story he was writing about the Dutchmen living in the Catskills. He was given cordial permission and the result became known around the world.

And once again the name "Rip Van Winkle" attained a wide

celebrity, for the man who was handling me roughly on Bellevue Avenue was the great ace in the War, one of the four most decorated veterans on "our side" and The Terror (and tacitly acknowledged admiration) of the Germans. He had been a member of the class of 1916, but the men who received their degrees in 1920 included many who had left school long before to take part in the War—some enlisting in Canada before our country was involved; some like my brother and Bob Hutchins joining ambulance units in France and the Balkans, then later transferring to our services. Many among the survivors of these dispersed students returned to Yale to complete their undergraduate education in 1919 and 1920. I had not known Rip well; he had moved in far more brilliant circles; he was the very flower of the *jeunesse dorée* and an international celebrity in addition; but I had conversed with him many times in the Elizabethan Club, where he could very well represent for us the figure of Sir Philip Sidney, the perfection of knighthood. Tall, handsome, wealthy, preeminent in all the sports he engaged in (though he did not play football or baseball), and endowed with a simplicity of manner far removed from the stiffness and condescension prevalent in his own *coterie,* sons of the great steel and investment banking houses.

[margin note: gilded youth]

By chance I ran into him in Paris one noon on the Avenue de l'Opéra in the late spring of 1921, soon after I had finished my year's study in Rome. We crossed near the entrance to the Café de Paris and he promptly asked me to lunch there. His simple spontaneity was unaltered. He was returning to America the next day, he said, to marry "the finest girl in the world." It was a delightful hour. Little could I perceive that the price of our meal was from the bottom of his pocket. I had not seen him nor heard anything about his private life in the intervening five years. Five years is a long time in one's late youth. He was now thirty-five, but looked well over forty. The buoyancy of his greeting soon gave way to an ill-concealed dejection or fatigue.

"What are you doing, Theo? Tell me about yourself. I've got to go out to dinner, but I have a whole hour before I have to dress. Can we sit down and have a drink somewhere?"

"I'm free, Rip."

"Come on—the Muenchinger-King! Put your bike in the back seat. Gee, I'm glad to see you. You've been teaching somewhere— is that right?"

I told him what I had been doing and what I was doing. I pulled out of my purse a clipping of the advertisement I had placed in the Newport paper. There was something refreshing and moving about the selflessness of his attention, but I was soon aware that it was precisely the relief of not talking or thinking about himself that he was enjoying. Finally I fell silent. His eyes kept returning to the clipping.

"You know all these languages?"

"Hit or miss and a bit of bluff, Rip."

"Have you a good number of students or listeners, or whatever you call them?"

"Just about as many as I can handle."

"You know German, too?"

"I went to German schools in China when I was a boy and have kept up my interest in it ever since."

"Theo?—"

"Call me Ted, will you, Rip? 'Theophilus' is unmanageable and 'Theo' is awkward. Everybody calls me Ted or Teddie, now."

"All right . . . listen, I have an idea. Next spring, in Berlin, there's going to be a banquet and two-day reunion for the men on both sides who fought in the air. Bury the hatchet, see what I mean? Hands across the sea. Gallant enemies. Toasts to the dead and all that. I want to go. I've got to go. And I want to get a little practice in the German language first. I had two years of German in prep school and I had a German grandmother. Now at that meeting I'd like to be able to show that I can at least stumble around in German. . . . Ted, could you find two two-hour lessons a week for me?"

"Yes. Early morning all right for you? Eight o'clock? I'm giving up some of those tennis coaching hours now that the pro's come back."

"Fine."

He looked down at the table a moment. "It won't go down well with my wife; but this is a thing I *want* to do, and, by Jesus, *I'll do it.*"

"Your wife doesn't like anything that has to do with Germany?"

"Oh, it isn't that! She has a hundred reasons against my going. Leaving her alone with the children in New York. She thinks that any recall of the War makes me nervous and high-strung. God damn it, this trip would make all that easier for me. And there's the *expense,* Ted—the useless *expense!* Mind you, I love my wife; she's a wonderful woman, but she hates useless expense. We have the New York house and we have this cottage. She thinks that's all she can manage. But, Ted, I've got to go. I've got to shake their hands. Bury the hatchet, see what I mean? They tell me I'm as well known over there as Richthofen is over here. Can you understand how I feel about it?"

"Yes, I do."

"Gee, it's great seeing you again. It gives me the strength I need to put this thing through. Don't you think I owe them the courtesy of making an attempt to speak German? You can start me picking it up again this summer; and I'll work like a fool on it for the rest of the year. God knows, I have nothing else to do."

"What do you mean by that, Rip?"

"I have an office. . . . The idea was that I was to manage my wife's property. But the money kept getting bigger and the advisers at the bank kept getting more and more important—so that there was less and less for me to do."

I got the idea and answered quickly, "What would you like to do?"

He rose and said, "Do? Do? Suggest something. I'd like to be a streetcar conductor. I'd like to be a telephone repairman!" He brushed his hand across his forehead and looked about him almost feverishly; then concluded with forced joviality, "I'd like to break my engagement tonight and go out to dinner with you, *but I can't,*" and he sat down again.

"Well," I said in German, "I'm not leaving town. We can have dinner some other night."

He pushed his glass backward and forward broodingly, as though that possibility was doubtful. "Ted, do you remember how Gulliver in the land of the little people—"

"In Lilliput—"

"In Lilliput was tied to the ground by thousands of small silk threads? That's me."

I rose and looked him straight in the eye: "You're going to that banquet in Germany."

He returned my seriousness, lowering his voice. "I don't see how. I don't see where I'll get the money."

"I always thought you came of a very well-to-do family."

"Didn't you know?" He named his birthplace. "In 1921, in my city three large companies and five prominent families went bankrupt."

"Did you have any inkling of that when I saw you in Paris?"

He pointed to his head. "Oh, more than an inkling. But fortunately I was engaged to a girl with considerable means. I told her that I had nothing but my severance pay. She laughed and said, 'Darling, of course, you have money. You're engaged to look after my property and you'll be very well paid for that.' . . . I spent my last hundred dollars getting to the church."

In 1919 and 1920 and in the years immediately following I came to know a large number of combat veterans—to say nothing, for the present, of those whom it was my duty to interrogate in a later war. (My part in "Rip's war," as has been said, had been safely passed among the defenders of Narragansett Bay.) As could be expected the marks left by that experience on the veteran varied from man to man; but in one group the aftereffects were particularly striking—the airmen. The fighting men on land and sea in early youth experienced what journalists called their "glorious hour"—the sense of weighty responsibility bound up with belonging to a "unit," exposure to extreme fatigue, to danger, and to death; many carried the inner burden of having killed human beings. But the "hour" of the first generation of combat aviators comprised all this and something in addition. Air combat was new; its rules and practice were improvised daily. The acquisition of technical accomplishment *above the earth* filled them with a particular kind of pride and elation. There were no gray-haired officers above them. They were pioneers and frontiersmen. Their relations with their fellow-fliers and even with their enemies partook of a high camaraderie. Unrebuked, they invented a code of chivalry with the German airmen. None would have stooped to attack a disabled enemy plane trying to return to its home base. Both sides recognized enemies with whom they had had encounters earlier, signaled to them in laughing challenge.

They lived "Homerically"; that was what the *Iliad* was largely about—young, brilliant, threatened lives. (Goethe said, "The *Iliad* teaches us that it is our task here on earth to enact hell daily.") Many survivors were broken by it and their later lives were a misery to themselves and to others. ("We didn't have the good fortune to die," as one of them said to me.) Others continued to live long and stoic lives. In some cases, if one looked closely, it was evident that a "spring had broken down" in them, a source of courage and gaiety had been depleted, had been spent. Such was Rip.

There was some discussion as to where Rip and I could meet for an eight o'clock class. "I'd like you to come over to my place, but the children would be having their breakfast and my wife would be running in and out to remind me of things I should do."

"I think Bill Wentworth would let us use one of those social rooms behind the gallery at the Casino. We might have to move from room to room while they're cleaning up. I've never seen you in the Casino, but I assume Your Honor is a member there."

He grinned and held his hand beside his mouth as though it were an unholy secret. "I'm a life-member. They don't let me pay any dues," and he poked me as though he'd stolen the cookie jar.

So the lessons began: an hour of vocabulary and grammar followed by an hour of conversation, in which I played the role of a German officer. Rip owned a collection of books in both languages describing those great days. No session passed without his being called to the telephone from which he returned with an enlarged list of the day's agenda, but he had a notable gift for immediately resuming his concentration. There was no doubt that he derived great enjoyment from the work; it touched some deep layer of self-recovery within him. He studied intensively between sessions; and so did I. ("Did his homework," as he called it.) My daily program permitted little time for desultory conversation at the close of the lesson, nor did his. When he rose he consulted the list of errands he must do: register certain letters at the Post Office; take the dog to the vet's; call for Miss So-and-so, his wife's part-time secretary; take Eileen to Mrs. Brandon's dancing class at eleven and call for her at twelve. . . . Apparently Mrs. Vanwinkle needed her car and chauffeur the greater part of the day. His appearance began to improve; he laughed more frequently, with some of the buoyancy of our first meeting on Bellevue Avenue. But there was no word that he had received permission to go to Germany.

One evening I paid my respects at Mrs. Cranston's.

"Good evening, Mr. North," Mrs. Cranston said graciously, eyeing a straw box I was carrying. It was lined with moss and contained some jack-in-the-pulpits, trilliums, and other flowers whose names I did not know. "Wild flowers! Oh, Mr. North, how could you know that I value wild flowers above all others!"

"I believe, ma'am, that it's against the law to dig some of these up, but at least I rode outside the city limits to gather them. I've also borrowed a trowel and a flashlight and am ready to replant them around your house at any point you indicate to me."

Henry Simmons happened at that moment to enter from the street.

"Henry, look at what Mr. North has brought me. Henry, help him replant them under Edweena's window where she will find them when she returns. A gift like that is a gift to us all and I thank you heartily for my share in it." She tapped her table bell. "Jerry will bring you a pitcher of water. That will make the flowers feel at home at once."

Neither Henry nor I was an experienced horticulturist, but we did our best. Then we washed our hands and returned to the parlor where some illicit refreshment was waiting for us.

"We have missed you lately," said Mrs. Cranston.

"We thought you had shifted your affections to Narragansett Pier, Teddie, I swear we did."

"And I missed you, ma'am, and you, Henry. I have some late-evening students now; and on some days my schedule is so crowded that I fall into bed at ten o'clock."

"Now you're not going to overwork and make a dull dog of yourself, are you, cully?"

"Money! Money!" I sighed. "I'm still hunting for that little apartment. I've looked at a dozen, but the rent is more than I'm ready to pay. A number of my older students have offered to make me a present of a very acceptable apartment in their former stable or an empty gardener's house, but I have learned the rule that the relations between landlord and tenant should be as impersonal as possible."

"It's a very good rule, but admits of an occasional exception," replied Mrs. Cranston, tacitly alluding to Edweena's possession of the "garden apartment" and probably to a number of her other lodgers.

"I think I've found the real right thing. It's not in an elegant neighborhood. The furnishings are modest but neat and clean; and it's within my means, after I've done a bit more haggling. I am not of a spendthrift nature, Mrs. Cranston, being wholly New

England on my father's side and almost wholly Scottish on my mother's. In fact, I am what New Englanders call 'near.' Schoolboys say 'chinchy.' "

Mrs. Cranston laughed. "In Rhode Island we often say 'close.' I am not ashamed to say that I am fairly 'close' in my dealings."

Henry was indignant. "Why, Mrs. Cranston, you are the most generous person I've ever known. You have a heart of gold!"

"I never liked that expression, Henry. I would not have been able to run this house and keep my head above water, if I had not been 'careful.' There's another word for you, Mr. North. I hate close-fisted stinginess, of course; but I certainly recommend a firm grasp on what money should and should not do." She sat back in her chair, warming up to the subject. "Now twenty and thirty years ago Newport was famous for reckless spending. You wouldn't believe the amount of money that could be thrown away in a single night—to say nothing of a single season. But also you wouldn't believe the stories of miserliness, penny-pinching, meannesses—what's the word that's the opposite of extravagance, Mr. North?"

"Parsimony?"

"That's it!"

"Avarice?"

"Listen to that, Henry: That's what comes of a college education; hitting the nail on the head. Edweena's fond of saying that extravagance—give me another word, Mr. North."

"Conspicuous waste."

"Oh, what a beauty!—that conspicuous waste and avarice are related; they're two sides of the same desperateness. 'Newport avarice,' she used to say, 'was of a special kind. They all had millions, but their behavior was like a fever-chart: it would go up and down.' There was one hostess who would send out invitations for a big party—two hundred on gold plate; catering and additional staff from Delmonico's or Sherry's. But four days before the party she'd come down with an attack of some kind and cancel the whole thing. When this had happened a number of times her dearest friends made plans for an 'emergency dinner' in case of another cancellation. She was the same lady who went through two seasons in two evening gowns; she appeared in the black or the purple one. She'd write orders for dresses to be sent up from New York, but she'd forget to mail the letter. These people think that no one notices! There's some demon inside them that robs them of the ability to look an expenditure in the face. It's a sickness, really."

Here followed some staggering examples of penuriousness and "trimming."

"Why," said Henry, "there's a woman in town now—a very young woman, too. She's married to a man as famous as General Pershing—"

"Almost, Henry."

"Thank you, ma'am. 'Almost as famous' as General Pershing."

"No names, remember! A rule of the house."

"She has one all-absorbing interest: cruelty to animals. She's given half a dozen shelters to communities around here and pays their upkeep. She's on the National Anti-carve-'em-up Society. She gets hysterical about feathers on hats. But the stories—"

Mrs. Cranston broke in: "Mr. North, she does much of her own shopping. She puts on a thick brown veil, gets in her car, and goes down to those shipping supply shops; sends her chauffeur inside to tell the butcher that 'Mrs. Edom' would like to speak to him outside. Mrs. Edom was the woman who *used* to be her housekeeper. She buys a whole side of beef from the salt-barrel. Takes two weeks to soak the salt out of it—*half*-soak the salt out. That's what the national hero and his children eat. She drives out to the Portuguese market and buys great milk cans of their kale soup with their *linguiça* sausages in it. When her servants protest and resign she scarcely gives them a civil letter of recommendation. She replaces them from those immigrant employment agencies in Boston and Providence. But she comes of an old Bellevue Avenue family and she must keep up her social position. About every ten days she gives a dinner party—catering from Providence; spends all the money she skimped for. Oh, it makes me boil—to think of that wonderful husband of hers and her children living on corned beef and kale soup while she spends thousands on dogs and cats!"

"Well, Mrs. Cranston, we have a saying in the Old Country: kind to animals, cruel to humans."

"It's a kind of sickness. Mr. North, let's talk about something pleasant."

I came to know the limits to which Mrs. Cranston could go in discussing any unfavorable aspect of the Newport she loved.

The lessons went on in fine shape, but the sweeping and dusting and the telephone calls from Rip's home were no small inconvenience. One day Rip asked me: "Do you ever take pupils on Sunday morning?"

"Yes, I have."

"Could you manage one of my sessions every Sunday morning about eleven? My wife goes to church then; I don't. . . . Would that be all right? . . . So I'll pick you up at the 'Y' next Sunday at a quarter before eleven. I'll take you to a classroom where we won't be disturbed. I belong to a club called the 'Monks' Club'; it's a sort of shooting, fishing, drinking, and dining club, with a little dice-rattling on the side now and then. It's just over the line in Massachusetts, beyond Tiverton. It belongs to a little group of the lively set. No ladies allowed, but every now and then you see some girls there—from New Bedford or Fall River. No one ever shows up before sunset, especially not on Sunday. The Monks have pretty much given up hunting." He added with his confidential grin, "Very expensive membership, but they made me an honorary member—*no dues!* . . . A great place for our work."

The thought of a quarter of an hour's drive disturbed me a little. I'd come to like and admire Rip more and more, but I didn't want to hear his "story"—how Gulliver came to be bound supine by a thousand small silk threads. It was a woeful situation, but there was nothing I could do about it. I felt in my bones that he was burning to tell me the story—the whole sorry business. So far I had never met Mrs. Vanwinkle and had no wish to. I have a ready interest in eccentrics and my Journal was filled with their "portraits," but I shrank from those borderline cases that approach madness—raging jealousy, despotic possessiveness, neurotic avarice. Rip's wife appeared to me to be stark staring mad. This view had been confirmed by a strange event that happened to intrude itself into my daily routine.

I had a pupil whom I was preparing for the college entrance examination in French, a girl of seventeen. Penelope Temple and I were working in the library when Mrs. Temple entered hurriedly:

"Mr. North, please forgive me, but the upstairs telephone is in use and I want to answer a call here. I think it will be very brief."

I rose. "Shall we go into another room, Mrs. Temple?"

"It's not necessary. . . . It's a woman I never met. . . . Yes, Mrs. Vanwinkle? This is Mrs. Temple speaking. I'm sorry to have made you wait, but Mr. Temple is expecting an urgent call on the other telephone. . . . Yes . . . Yes . . . It is true, those were egret feathers I was wearing at the ball when that photograph was taken. . . . Excuse me, let me interrupt. . . . Those feathers belonged to my mother. They are at least thirty years old. We have preserved them with great care. . . . Excuse me interrupting you: the feathers are now falling to pieces and I shall destroy them, as you request. . . . No, kindly do *not* send Mr. Vanwinkle to this house. Any home in America would be proud to receive Mr. Vanwinkle, but he is too distinguished a man to go about town picking up dilapidated feathers. . . . *No,* Mrs. Vanwinkle, I wish you to do me the credit of *believing* me when I tell you that I will destroy the wretched feathers *at once.* Good morning, Mrs. Vanwinkle, thank you for your call. . . . Excuse me again, Mr. North. Penelope, I think the woman's insane."

Twenty minutes later the front door bell rang and down the hall I heard Rip's voice in conversation with Mrs. Temple.

Naturally, I did not mention this episode to Rip.

Our first Sunday morning drive into Massachusetts was on a beautiful day in early July. Rip drove like Jehu, as all *retired* aviators do. Even in that aging car he exceeded the speed limits in city and country. The police never interfered; they were proud to receive a wave of his hand. In order to forefend any confidential communications about the enslaved Gulliver, I plunged into my overworked theory about the nine cities of Troy and of Newport. I made a considerable digression about the great Bishop Berkeley as we passed near his house ("I lived in Berkeley Oval in my freshman year at college," he said). I had just about come to the end of my exposition when we drove up to the door of the Monks' Club. He brought the car to a standstill but remained at the wheel gazing before him.

"Ted?"

"Yes, Rip?"

"You remember that you asked me what I'd like to *do?*"

"Yes."

"I'd like to be a historian. . . . Is it too late?"

"Why, Rip, you've got your niche in history. It isn't too late to pour out all you know about that—begin there and then broaden out."

His face clouded over. "Oh, I wouldn't want to write anything about that. It's what you were saying about the eighteenth century in Newport—Rochambeau and Washington and Berkeley— that reminded me that I'd always wanted to be a historian. . . . Besides, a historian works in a study where he can close the door, doesn't he? Or he can go to some library where there's a SILENCE sign on every table."

"Rip," I ventured, "in New York is your life much like this— a lot of errands during the day and dinners out every night?"

He lowered his voice. "Worse, worse. In New York I do most of the shopping."

"But you have a housekeeper!"

"We *had* a housekeeper—Mrs. Edom. Oh, I wish she were back. Capable, you know—quiet and capable. No arguments."

The Monks' Club had been an important roadside tavern before the Revolution. Many alterations had been made since. It had served as a storehouse, as a home, and as a school, but much of the original structure remained, built of hewn stone with high chimneys and a vast kitchen. The front room must have been originally designed for dancing; there was a fiddlers' gallery opposite the great fireplace. The "Monks" had furnished and adorned it as a luxurious hunting lodge, complete with some masterpieces of taxidermy. We worked upstairs in the library surrounded by maps, files of sporting magazines, law manuals of the Commonwealth of Massachusetts relative to shipping and game-hunting. The room overlooked the front entrance and was large enough for us to stride up and down in during our mock international dialogues. It was ideal for us. At one o'clock we used to collect our textbooks and reluctantly return to Rhode Island.

During our second Sunday morning session the telephone rang at the bottom of the stairs.

"I know who that is! Come along, Ted, I want you to hear this."

"I don't want to hear your private conversations, Rip."

"I *want* you to. You're a part of this—you're a part of my campaign.—Anyway, leave the door open. I swear to you, I *need* you to back me up! . . . Hello? Yes, this is the Monks' Club. . . . Oh, is that you, Pam? I thought you were at church. . . . I told you: I'm having a German lesson. . . . I know it's a sunny day. . . . We went over that before. The children are perfectly safe at Bailey's Beach. There are three lifeguards there—one on a scaffold and two in rowboats; and on the beach there are at least thirty nurses, nannies, governesses, *Fräulein, mademoiselles,* and *gouvernantes.* I cannot and will not sit there for three hours amid a hundred women. . . . Rogers can bring them back, can't he? . . .

Then arrange with Cynthia or Helen or the Winstons' chauffeur to bring them. Pamela, I have something to say to you: I shall never go to Bailey's Beach again. . . . No, the children will not drown. Both of them hate to go in the water. They say it 'thtinkth.' . . . No, I don't know where they picked up that word. They say that all the children say so. They want to go to the Public Beach where there's real surf. . . . I will not be disturbed in my lesson. . . . No, there's no one else in the building as far as I know; the staff have gone to church. . . . Pam, be yourself; talk like yourself; don't talk like your mother! . . . I don't want to discuss that over the telephone. . . . Pamela, be your sweet, reasonable self. . . . I have never said anything more disrespectful about your mother than you have said many times. . . . I will be back well before one-thirty. This long-distance call is costing a good deal of money. . . . Yes, I'll pick up some ice cream at the dairy. No, it's got to be at the dairy where I can charge it, because I haven't a penny in my pocket. . . . I have to go back to my lesson now, but I don't wish to hang up on my dear wife, so will you please hang up first? . . . Yes . . . Yes . . . No . . . Goodbye, see you soon."

He rejoined me with raised eyebrows, saying: "Gulliver and the hundreds of silk threads. Every day I cut a few of them."

I made no comment and we went on with our work. He seemed to be reinvigorated, or should I say, proud of himself.

I was getting caught up in a situation that was more than I could handle. What I needed was not advice—which I have seldom found profitable—but more facts; not gossip but facts. I thought I knew the reason why Rip was a diminished man. I wanted to know more about his wife. I wanted to be sure that I was being just to her; to be just you must seek out all the facts you can get. I felt that I had reached the end of what Mrs. Cranston and Henry Simmons could tell me.

Where could I go for solid facts about Pamela Vanwinkle?

Suddenly I thought of Bill Wentworth. I asked him for a half hour of his time. Again at the end of the day I found myself in his office among the shining trophies. I told him about the German lessons, the constant interruptions, and the sheer servitude to which my friend had been reduced. "Bill, how long have you known Colonel Vanwinkle?"

"Let me see. Pamela Newsome—as I knew her—brought him here in the summer of 1921 soon after they were married."

"Had you known her long?"

"Since she was a child. During the summer she was in here every day; since her marriage she scarcely appears here at all. Her parents are old Newporters."

"Are many Newporters aware of the tight reins she holds over him?"

"Mr. North, they're the laughing-stock of the town."

"How is it that she has so much money in her own name?"

"The Newsomes are not so much a family as a corporation. Every child on reaching twenty-one gets a large bundle of stock—well over a million, they say—and continues to get more annually. . . . She was a very difficult girl. She never got on with her parents. Perhaps that's the reason why—when she became engaged in the fall of 1920—they gave her their Newport cottage and themselves started going to Bar Harbor for the summer."

"Excuse my frankness, Bill, but is she as miserly and hard-driving as they say?"

"My wife was a long-time friend of their housekeeper, Mrs. Edom, a fine woman, a strong character. Mrs. Edom used to call on Mrs. Wentworth on an occasional Sunday morning. It broke her heart to see what Pamela was doing to the Colonel. You wouldn't believe what went on in that house. Mrs. Edom used to come to my wife for comfort."

"Bill, why has the Colonel so few friends?"

"Everybody likes him—not only admires him, but likes him. But both men and women are made uncomfortable by the picture they see. Mr. North, before the war there were many young men around here who did nothing—simply enjoyed themselves and nobody thought the worse of them. But times have changed. They have jobs, even if they don't need the money. Idleness is out of fashion; it's made fun of. And everybody can see the bad effects of it. We've seen it before—a poor man married to a very rich girl; she cracks the whip and he jumps through the hoop like a monkey."

I gave him my picture of the young man who had had his "glorious hour" too early in life and whose vitality or will-power had been broken by it. I went on to tell him how Rip was beginning to lean on me to help him get some freedom.

"Well, if you have any influence on him urge him to get a job. If what I've heard is right, he hasn't a penny. He has to crawl to her for an allowance which she can give or she can withhold. Now I'm going to tell you a story that I've never told to a soul, and I'm trusting you. The second summer he was here the Board of Governors made him an honorary member of the Casino. I asked him to call on me the day before so that I could explain to him how we were setting up the ceremony. I told him that perhaps his wife might want to come, but he telephoned me later that she would be present at the ceremony, but that on that rehearsal morning she was busy with one of her 'cruelty to animals' committees. Well, he arrived; it's always a pleasure to meet him—a fine fellow, and all that. I told him a photographer would be present; we wanted the picture to hang on our walls. There it is! We never give out publicity photos for the newspapers, except during the Tennis Championship Week. I told him the Governors would be pleased if he wore his uniform and his medals. He said he had his uniform and a few medals. He'd sat beside the Mayor on the grandstand at the Fourth of July parade. Which medals did they want? I told him they hoped he'd wear the American 'big three' and the French and English ones. 'I haven't got them, Bill.' Then he grinned. Do you know his grin?"

"Oh, yes, whenever he talks about his war record or his celebrity he grins."

"He said that he'd wanted to buy a birthday present for his wife on her first birthday since their marriage, and that he'd borrowed money on them as security from those medal and trophy dealers in New York. Now, I'll tell you one thing more: *she didn't come to the ceremony.* She hates his fame; she's afraid it may 'go to his head' and spoil him. Mr. North, urge him to get a job. He'll be a different man."

"Thanks, Bill. Has he been offered any?"

"Of course he has—with that famous name of his. Corporation directorships, things like that. She won't let him consider them. You know he comes from western New York State. The Governor wanted to create one for him, provided that he'd move to Albany. I heard it was about twenty thousand a year, State Marshal. His wife laughed at it. To her that's peanuts. She said it was degrading."

"Is it true that she feeds the family mostly salt beef and kale soup?"

"Oh. The town makes up stories about her. But she does buy canned goods by the gross."

So it is profitable to go to the right person for advice, after all.

The next Sunday morning we were up in the library at the Monks' Club having a breezy time, breaking irregular verbs. Rip had arrived at that borderline in learning a new language when words hitherto only recognized in print become vocables—an exhilarating feeling.

"*Na ja, Herr Major, ich kenne Sie.*"

"*Und ich kenne Sie, verehrter Herr Oberst. Sie sind der Herr Oberst Vanderwinkle, nicht wahr?*"

"*Jawohl. War das nicht ein Katzenjammer über dem Hügel Saint-Charles-les-Moulins? Dort haben Sie meinen linken Flügel kaputt gemacht. Sie waren ein Teufel, das kann man sagen.*"

Rip glanced out of the window. "Jesus! There's my wife." Sure enough, there was the car and the chauffeur was coming up the walk. The doorbell rang. "Go downstairs. Pretend you're the club steward or something. Say that I gave orders not to be disturbed until one o'clock."

I put on my blazer ("YALE 1920"). "I can't be a steward in this. I'll pretend I'm a member. I'll work something out." I descended the stairs slowly and opened the door.

"Sir, Mrs. Edom is calling and wishes to speak to Colonel Vanwinkle."

I caught a glimpse of "Mrs. Edom" in a deep brown veil sitting in the car. I said loudly, "I think he gave orders that he was not to be disturbed on any account. Has something serious happened in his home? Fire? Appendicitis? Mad dog bite?"

"I don't . . . think so."

"Wait. I'll see if he can be seen. Tell Mrs. Edom that his German professor is very strict about interruptions. He's a holy terror."

Rip was waiting for me on the stairs. "She says she's Mrs. Edom and she wishes to speak to you."

"She'll come in. Nothing can stop her."

"I'm going to lock the door leading upstairs. It's half-past twelve already. I'll stay down and keep her company."

"Damn it, I want to hear what you say. I'm going to stretch out on the floor of the fiddlers' gallery. She can't see me from there." I went down to the front room, locked the inner staircase door, put the key in my pocket, picked up a copy of *Yachting,* and sat down to read it. There was a noise up in the gallery. Rip had pulled a coverlet about himself and was lying down. The doorbell rang again. I opened the door and faced a determined woman. She had thrown the veil up about her hat—a very good-looking young woman, furious. She pushed the door open and passed me into the front room.

"Good morning."

"Good morning, madam. Forgive me if I say that it is a rule of the club that ladies are not admitted here. There is no reception room for women."

"Kindly tell Colonel Vanwinkle that Mrs. Edom wishes to speak to him."

"Madam, as the chauffeur told you . . ."

She sat down. "Excuse me, are you the steward of the club?"

"No," I said, deeply offended.

"Who is in authority here? . . . Are there no servants here?"

"The caretaker and his wife seem to have gone to church."

"Sir, will you kindly tell me whom I am addressing?"

I was amiability—dare I say: charm?—itself. "Mrs. Edom, surely you know something about men's clubs. It's a rule of the club that *no* member may be addressed by the name he bears in private life. We are addressed by the name given us by the Abbot. I am Brother Asmodius. The member to whom you have been referring is Brother Bellerophon."

"Childish nonsense!"

"Since the Middle Ages and the Crusaders' Orders. I happen to be a Mason and the member of a fraternity. In each club I have been assigned a name to be used in that club. You surely know that monks in a religious order do the same. My wife finds it hard to forgive me that I do not tell her every detail of our ceremonies. . . . I think I remember hearing that you are the housekeeper in Brother Bellerophon's home."

She glared at me in silence. Then she rose, saying, "I *will* speak to the Colonel." She went to the door leading upstairs and shook the knob.

I was cleaning my fingernails. "That German professor locked it, I expect. I wouldn't put anything beyond him."

"I shall sit here until the Colonel comes down."

"Would you like something to read, Mrs. Edom?"

"No, thank you."

I resumed my reading in silence. She looked about her. "I see that you monks—as you call yourselves—shoot deer, foxes, and birds. Contemptible sports!"

"There's less and less of that now. You can understand why." She stared at me in silence. "Out of respect for Brother Bellerophon's wife." Silence. "Surely, you know of her crusade for the prevention of cruelty to animals. . . . What a fine woman she must be! Saves the lives of dogs and cats and wild animals every year! A great heart! A big heart!"

I strolled across the room to straighten a picture. Nonchalantly I added, "Having heard what an intelligent woman she is—and what an excellent wife and mother—I have always been surprised that she permits her children to go to Bailey's Beach. My wife wouldn't let our children be seen dead there."

"What is unwise about that?"

"I am surprised you ask, Mrs. Edom. The transatlantic sea lane and the Gulf Channel both pass a few miles from that point. Hundreds of ships in each direction go by all day and night. And by some unfortunate combination of land, tides, and currents the rubbish thrown overboard finds its way to Bailey's Beach as to a magnet. Each morning the employees rake up baskets of trash: seamen's boots, decaying fruit, dead parrots, picture postcards unsuitable for children, and other things too distasteful to mention."

She stared at me appalled. "I do not believe that to be true."

"It is very discourteous of you to say that, Mrs. Edom. In this club gentlemen do not call one another liars."

"I beg your pardon. I meant to say that I find that difficult to believe."

"Thank you. . . I have also heard that the lady about whom we are talking is careful about the diet furnished to her family and staff. Do you know my wife and I think that kale soup is one of the most nutritious—and delicious—dishes that exist." (Pause.) "But a very experienced doctor advised us not to let children under twelve eat that highly spiced *linguiça* sausage that is cooked in it at the Portuguese market. . . . And beef and pork soaked in brine —excellent! The British Navy served it to their seamen for centuries and ruled the sea. The Battle of Trafalgar was said to have been won on corned beef. That same doctor advised my wife, however, that too much of that salted meat is not to be recommended for young children, even after weeks of soaking in clear water."

"Does Brother Bellerophon—as you call him—come often to this club?"

"Not as often as we'd like. I think I can say that he is the most beloved and admired member here. The club members, who are all very wealthy men, became aware that his family is less fortunately *provided* than themselves. They made him honorary member which requires no dues. Four of them, including myself, offered him high positions in their companies and enterprises. Brother Prudentius has offered him a vice-presidency in an insurance company in Hartford. Brother Candidus is developing resident areas in Florida. Brother Bellerophon's name on the letterhead, his presence, his famous probity, would bring the firm millions of dollars which they would be glad to share with him. And so the rest of us. Brother Bellerophon is too deeply attached to his family; his wife does not wish to move to Connecticut or to Miami. I am hoping that he will change his mind and join my company from sheer necessity."

"What business are you engaged in, sir?"

"I'd rather not say, Mrs. Edom. But considering his distinguished service to our country, the Federal Government would not be inclined to examine our operations too closely." I lowered my voice. "Do you think I can hope that he will?"

"Brother Asmodius, I have no desire to continue this conversation."

"A man must work. A man must stand up on his own feet, ma'am."

"I will pound on that door!"

"Oh, Mrs. Edom, don't do that! You would wake up the girls!"

"Girls! What girls?"

"Naturally on the weekends there are some convivial times here. A little drinking. And some pleasant company from New Bedford and Fall River. The members return to their homes at a very late hour. But we allow their charming friends to sleep later. They will be picked up in a limousine at two."

"Girls! Do you mean to tell me that the Colonel is upstairs now among a lot of Jezebels?"

I looked thoughtful. "I don't recognize the name. . . . I met an Anita, a Ruth, a Lilian, an Irene. And a Betty."

"I am leaving this minute.—No! I *will* pound on that door."

"Madam, as a member of this club I must restrain you from creating an unseemly disorder." I added bitingly, "I had always heard that Mrs. Edom conducted herself as a woman of distinction, which has not always been said of her mistress."

"What do you mean by *that?*"

I pointed to the clock. "You have only a quarter of an hour to wait."

"What did you mean by that unpleasant remark?"

"It was not an unpleasant remark. It was a tribute to yourself, Mrs. Edom."

"I am waiting—"

"If you sit down and stop abusing this club, I shall . . . give you a short explanation."

She sat down and glared at me, expectantly. I returned to polishing my nails, but I began to speak offhandedly: "My dear wife does not engage in gossip. I have never heard her repeat a malicious remark—but once. By the way, we took the doctor's advice. We no longer serve the children kale soup and beef in brine."

"You were about to tell me some remark about Mrs. Vanwinkle."

"Oh, yes." I lowered my voice and moved my chair toward hers. "There is a nickname that is going around about that otherwise *wonderful* woman."

"A nickname!"

"My wife heard it from Mrs. Delgarde who heard it from Lady Bracknell who heard it from Mrs. Venable herself."

"Mrs. Venable!"

I rose. "No! I don't circulate things like that. I've changed my mind."

"You're a very exasperating man, Brother Asmodius. You'd better finish what you began."

"All right," I sighed, "but promise not to repeat it—least of all to Mrs. Vanwinkle."

"I will *not* repeat it."

"Well, Mrs. Venable heard that Mrs. Vanwinkle sent her husband—that great man—to Mrs. Temple's house to pick up a thirty-year-old egret feather, because she refused to believe Mrs. Temple's promised word that she would destroy it herself. Mrs. Venable said, 'I shall not give another penny to those animal shelters until Mrs. Vanwinkle is locked up. She's a Delilah!' "

"Delilah!"

"You remember that Delilah cut short the mighty Samson's hair whereby he lost his strength—so that his enemies could rush into his tent and blind him. She beat on cymbals and tambourines and danced on his prostrate body. Scholars of the Old Testament know very well that the story means that she performed a far more serious operation on him."

Mrs. Vanwinkle had turned as white as a sheet. She was speechless.

"Shall I get you a drink of water?"

"Yes, please do."

When I returned from the kitchen, Rip had climbed out of the fiddlers' gallery, descended the stairs, and was pounding on the locked door. I opened it.

Husband and wife stared at one another in silence. She accepted the glass from my hand without taking her eyes off Rip. Finally she said, "Nicholas, will you ask this dreadful man to leave the room?"

"This is my German professor, Pam. I'm driving him back to Newport in a few minutes. Ted, will you go upstairs and wait until I call you?"

"I'll start walking into town, Rip. You can pick me up on the road. Good morning, ma'am."

And I went out the front door. As I passed the threshold I heard Mrs. Vanwinkle break into a convulsion of weeping.

It was a beautiful day. I walked for a quarter of an hour. Soon after I passed Tiverton I saw Mrs. Vanwinkle's car go by. She had lowered her veil but her head was held high. Not long after Rip stopped for me. I climbed into the car.

"You were very tough, Ted. . . . You were very tough." He started the car. After a few minutes he said, "You were very tough."

"I know I went too far, Rip, and I apologize."

We drove in silence for a while.

Ten miles in silence. Then he said, "I told her you were an old joker way back in college days and that all that about Mrs. Venable was just horse-feathers. . . . But how the hell did you know about Mrs. Temple's goddamned feather?"

"I won't tell."

He stopped the car and cracked my skull against his.

"Oh, you're an old son-of-a-bitch, Ted—*but I got a thousand dollars to go to Berlin!*"

"Well, you gave me a wonderful lunch at the Café de Paris—when you were low in funds, remember?"

At Mrs. Keefe's

The events that led to my obtaining an apartment occurred during my sixth week in Newport, perhaps later. I was living at the "Y," contentedly enough; my relations there were impersonal and left me time to prepare for my classes. I was on good terms with the superintendent—unjustly called "Holy Joe," for he was not at all sanctimonious. From time to time, for a change, I would descend to the "library" where card games of the family type, like hearts and three jacks, were permitted and desultory conversation tolerated.

It was in this library that I met a remarkable young man whose portrait and unhappy predicaments I find recorded in my Journal. Elbert Hughes was a reedy youth, barely twenty-five, belonging to that often wearisome category of human beings known as "sensitive." This adjective once meant intensely aware of aesthetic and spiritual values; then it took on a sense of someone quick to resent slights; recently it has become a euphemism for someone incapable of coping with even the smaller demands of our daily practical life. Elbert chiefly fulfilled the third description. He was short but delicately proportioned. His eyes were deeply set under a protruding forehead, lending an intensity to his gaze. His fingers were much occupied with a tentative mustache. He was something of a dandy and on cool evenings wore a black velveteen jacket and a flowing black tie, recalling the students I had seen near the Beaux-Arts Academy when I lived in Paris. Elbert gave me a partial account of his life and I presently discovered that he was a sort of genius—subdivision, calligraphic mimicry. He was a Bostonian and had followed courses in a technical high school there, devoting himself passionately to copperplate writing and to lettering, with a particular interest in tombstone inscriptions.

By the age of twenty he had secured a profitable job at a leading jeweler's establishment where he furnished the models for engraved inscriptions on presentation silver, for formal invitations and calling cards. For another firm he wrote diplomas on parchment and honorary tributes to retiring bank presidents. He made no claims to originality; he imitated scripts from standard "style books" or from admired early English and American "plate" in museums and private collections. But that was not all. He could copy any signature or individual penmanship after a moment's profound "absorption" in a model before him. He could furnish a receipt in the hand of almost any signer of the Declaration of Independence at a moment's notice. He was a wonder.

It was not new to me that these "sensitives" are an unhappy mixture of humility and boldness. One evening he asked me to write a sentiment and to sign it. I wrote (in French, of which he did not know a word) a *maxime* of the Duc de la Rochefoucauld and signed it with my own name. He studied it gravely for a few minutes and then wrote: *Mr. Theodore Theophilus North regrets that he will be unable to accept the kind invitation of the Governor of the Commonwealth of Massachusetts and of Mrs. So-and-so for such-and-such an evening."* It was in my own hand, staggeringly in my own hand. Then he wrote it again and passed it over to me, saying lightly, "That is how Edgar Allan Poe would have

written it. I like to do his handwriting best. When I do his handwriting I feel him moving my hand. People say I look like him. Can
you see that I look like him?"

"Yes. But I never heard that he was much of a draughtsman."

"We're a lot alike though. We were both born in Boston. . . .
The thing I like to draw best is the lettering on tombstones. There's
a lot about graves and tombs in Poe's writings. He's my favorite
writer that ever lived."

"What are you doing in Newport?" I asked.

"Much the same kind of work I did in Boston. A man named
Forsythe saw some presentation copies I had made on vellum of
a poem by Edgar A. Poe in Poe's handwriting, and some alphabets
I had drawn up in several styles. He said he was an architect and
building contractor with an office in Newport. He offered me a
pretty good salary to come down here and work for him. I do
lettering for the fronts of buildings—post offices, town halls,
things like that. I do gravestones for masons too. I like that best."

I had been staring at our (mine and Poe's) replies to the Governor.

"I'll show you something else," he said. He extracted from a
portfolio beside him a leaf of the Governor's personal stationery—
seal embossed—and wrote the invitation for which he had twice
written the reply.

"Is that the Governor's own handwriting?"

"I've done lots of work for both his office and his mansion. I've
worked for all the best stationers and I collect samples. I've got
a trunk full of the best stuff. There are collectors all over the
world, you know—they keep it secret. I trade duplicates." He laid
before me: "The White House," "L'Ambassade de France," "John
Pierpont Morgan," "The Foreign Office," Enrico Caruso's
cartoon of himself as a letterhead, a bookplate by Stanford
White. . . .

"Are you doing that kind of work for Forsythe here in Newport?"

"Not very much," he answered, evasively, returning the "samples" to their portfolio. "We do something like it."

He changed the subject.

Elbert Hughes might have been, *should* have been, good company, but he wasn't. He suffered like many of his kind from alternations of vitality and depletion. He would launch forth on a subject with enthusiasm only to fall silent in a short time like a deflated bellows. He was engaged to be married. Abigail was a wonderful woman; she was (he whispered) divorced; she was six years older than he was and had two children. He added, with abated enthusiasm, that he had saved up three thousand dollars to buy a house (where they would presumably live gloomily ever after). One couldn't help admiring and even liking Elbert, but I began losing interest in him; I tend to avoid the disconsolate. I am indebted to him, however, for awakening my interest in an aspect of Newport that I had neglected. Elbert took to bringing down to our little library the work he was doing; he said that the light was better than that provided in our rooms upstairs, as indeed it was. I would occasionally use the library for my own "homework," when it was not also occupied by a conversational gathering. One evening I asked permission to see what he was engaged upon. He answered confusedly that it was just "some nonsense he was doing for fun." It was a letter from the eminent historian George Bancroft inviting the equally eminent Louis Agassiz to an evening of "punch and good talk." Elbert seemed to have given himself the enjoyment of writing Agassiz's reply to this attractive invitation.

"Where are the originals of these letters?" I asked.

"Mr. Forsythe has a big collection. He says he advertises for them and buys them from the owners."

Entirely apart from Elbert's "fun" with such documents, I was delighted with them. That was Newport's Fifth City—the city that had disappeared leaving little trace behind it—the Newport of the mid-nineteenth-century intellectuals. My various jobs were nourishing my interest in the Second City, the Sixth City, and the

Seventh City; I was living in the Ninth City. In my early twenties I had fancied myself as an archaeologist. Here was a field for excavation. Dr. Schliemann had possessed a large private fortune; I had not a dollar to spare. I reminded myself of an old saying I had read somewhere: "To the impassioned will nothing is impossible."

There were still a few half-mornings and half-afternoons free in my schedule. I prepared myself by visiting the "People's Library," and "reading up" on the period. Then I visited the antiquaries and second-hand stores. I nursed the hope that I might come upon things that no one else had spotted. I concentrated on letters and manuscripts—diaries, correspondences, job-lots of books and papers from old houses, family photograph albums, the emptyings of attics. . . . The James family, the Agassiz families (the great father and the great son), the Bancrofts, Longfellow. Longfellow spent his summers at Nahant, but he often visited his friend George Washington Greene at West Greenwich near Narragansett Bay and Greene's parents who lived in Newport. Two of his best-known poems show his interest in our First City, "The Skeleton in Armor" and "The Jewish Cemetery at Newport."

The "antique shops" were still selling objects from the First and Second Cities. The vogue for taking a half-condescending pleasure in the furniture and decoration of the Victorian age was still twenty years in the future. Here and there I found collections of daguerreotypes, framed letters or poems signed by the notable men of the time; but these had already been discovered and were beyond my means. I descended to the second-hand stores and received permission to climb ladders with a flashlight, to poke in old barrels and open old dressers, the flotsam and jetsam of the years: here a clergyman's wife had sold a lifetime of her husband's sermons for rag paper, a thrifty merchant's family their father's account books, and so on.

Almost at once I made a small discovery. It was a schoolgirl's "memory book," bound in coral velvet, moth-eaten, mouldy. There were faded blue photographs of picnics and birthday parties, dance cards and autographs. On one page H. W. Longfellow had copied out "The Children's Hour," "for my dear young friend Faith Somerville." With a show of casual interest I bought the book for two dollars; the following autumn I sold it in New York for thirty. I found bundles of Somerville papers and bought them for forty cents a pound. My idea was that somehow I might penetrate that magic world (my father used to call it "plain living and high thinking") and glimpse those enchanted late afternoons in Newport when professors played croquet with their children until fireflies hovered over the wickets and a voice called, "Come in, children, and wash your hands before supper."

I knew that any first edition of a work by Edgar Allan Poe was among the greatest prizes in all American book-collecting and that any letter from his pen was eagerly sought. Poe had paid an extensive visit to Providence, only thirty miles away; but there was no record of his having visited Newport. If I could discover a bundle of Poe's letters—what a lively interest for me and, later, what an addition to my capital savings! (No biographer had yet drawn up the wide spectrum of *that* boyhood's ambitions: poet, detective, gentleman, actor perhaps [like his mother], metaphysician ["Eureka!"], cryptographer, landscape gardener, interior decorator, tormented lover—too great and diverse a load for any American to carry.)

I found no Poe letters, but his name was brought to my attention repeatedly. One evening I found under my door a copy of his poem "Ulalume," signed by the poet and a triumph of Elbert Hughes's art. Meeting Hughes by chance in the hall I thanked him; but I tore the counterfeit up.

There was no night watchman prowling the corridors of the "Y," but a night clerk, Maury Flynn, tended the front desk. Maury was a cheerless old man in poor health. Like many night attendants in hotels and clubs he was a retired policeman. One night toward three in the morning I was awakened by a knock at my door. It was Maury.

"Ted, are you a partickler friend of Hughes in 32?"

"I know him, Maury. What's the matter?"

"Fellow in the next room says he's been having nightmares. Groaning like. Falling out of bed. This fellow telephoned me. Would you go in and see if you could calm him down, sort of?"

I threw on a bathrobe and got into some slippers and went down to Room 32. Maury had left the door ajar and the light on. Elbert was sitting on the edge of his bed, his head bent over his knees.

"Elbert! Elbert! What's the matter?"

He raised his head, gazed at me vacantly, and resumed his former position. I shook him brusquely but he made no response. I looked about the room. On the center table lay an unfinished example of his accomplished art. It was the opening of "The Fall of the House of Usher." On the bedside table stood a half-empty bottle of "Dr. Quimby's Sleeping Syrup." I sat down and watched him for a while, repeating his name in a low insistent voice. Then I went to the washstand, dipped a washrag in cold water, and applied it to his face, the nape of his neck, and to his wrists— as I used to do to drunken companions in Paris in 1921. I now did this several times.

At last he raised his head again and mumbled, "Hello, Ted. Nothing . . . Bad dreams."

"Get up, Elbert. I'm going to walk you up and down the corridor a few times. Breathe, breathe deep."

He fell back on the bed and shut his eyes. More cold water. I slapped his face and struck his shoulder sharply. At last we were walking the corridor. We must have done a quarter of a mile. We returned to the room. "No! You remain standing. Take some more deep breaths. . . . Tell me about your dreams. . . . Yes, you can hold on to the wall."

"Buried alive. Can't get out. Nobody can hear me."

"Do you take this syrup all the time?"

"Don't sleep very good. Don't want to sleep because . . . *they* come. But I've got to sleep, because when I don't, I make mistakes in my work. They take it off my pay."

"Do you know Dr. Addison?"

"No."

"Why don't you? He's the 'Y's' doctor. He's in and out of the building all the time. I'm going to send him to see you tomorrow night. Talk to him; tell him everything. And don't drink any more of this stuff. Will you give me permission to take this bottle away? . . . And, Elbert, don't read any more Edgar Allan Poe. He's not right for you—all those crypts and vaults. Do you think you'll be able to sleep calmly now? . . . Do you want me to read aloud to you for ten minutes?"

"Yes, will you, Ted?"

"I'm going to read to you in a language you don't understand. All you have to know is that it's serene and beautiful like the printing of the Elzevirs."

So I read him from Ariosto and he went off like a baby.

I lost touch with Elbert for about ten days. Dr. Addison gave him some sleeping pills and some stern advice about his diet; he had been scarcely eating at all. I continued my search for the Fifth City. In another store—now down almost at the rags-bottles-and-sacks level—I had another stroke of luck: the rejected sketches of the elder Henry James's commentary on a work of Swedenborg. They were resting in a barrel together with bundles of old letters to the family. I separated the letters from the theology and bought them for very little. I had first become interested in the writing Jameses while reading (in my earliest phase), with mounting dissatisfaction, William James's *Varieties of Religious Experience;* more recently I had read a number of his brother's novels. The James family lived in Newport throughout the Civil War. The two eldest sons had left to join the Army. William, Henry, and their sister Alice all had had nervous breakdowns in 1860 and enlistment of those brothers was out of the question. The letters had little to tell me, but I felt I was on the trail.

Within two weeks my teaching schedule became so heavy that I had to give up those researches entirely. What little free time I had was devoted to hunting for an apartment. This was limited to opportunities within my means—among the jerry-built workmen's homes on the streets leading up the slope from the further reach of Thames Street. I rang every doorbell whether there was an advertisement of lodging or not. I had a clear idea of what I wanted: two rooms or one large room, a bath, a cooking facility however simple. I wanted the rooms to be on the second story, entered by an outside stairway so that (yet not the only reason) I would not be required to come and go through the landlord's residence and family. I did not object to crying babies, boisterous children, a location above a kitchen, a sloping roof, proximity to a firehouse or to a convivial fraternal organization or to church bells. This requirement of a separate entrance was not as uncommon as might appear. These old houses were beginning to be subdivided into family apartments; elderly lodgers were increasingly afraid of fires, frequent enough in this run-down area. I was shown many apartments and derived considerable enjoyment from the encounters this search involved.

One morning I found my apartment. I had surveyed the premises and seen the exterior stairway. The mailbox said "Keefe." The door was opened by a thin distrustful woman in her middle fifties. Her face was lined but retained the high coloring characteristic of those living by a northern sea. I learned later that on the death of her husband over twenty years ago she had opened a rooming house and raised two sturdy sons to become merchant seamen. In spite of many disappointments she had never been able to free herself of the idea that a rooming house should have the character of a home. She was distrustful but eager to trust.

"Good morning, Mrs. Keefe. Have you an apartment to let?"

She paused a moment. "I have and I haven't. How long would you want it?"

"All summer, ma'am, if it suited me."

"Are you alone? . . . What is your work?"

"I'm a tennis instructor at the Casino. My name is Theodore North."

"Do you attend any church regularly?"

"I've only been a short time in Newport. During the War I was stationed at Fort Adams. I used to walk into town to attend the evening service at Emmanuel Church."

"Come in and sit down. Excuse my dress; it's early and I'm housecleaning."

She led me into a sitting room that should have been preserved in a museum for generations yet unborn.

"What exactly were you looking for, Mr. North?"

"One large room or two small ones; a bath and some simple kitchen facility; some housecleaning and a change of linen once a week. And I'd like it to be on the second floor with an exterior stairway."

She had been looking me up and down. "How much would you be willing to pay, Mr. North?"

"I was thinking of twenty-five dollars a month, ma'am."

She sighed and examined the floor in silence. I remained silent too. With each of us every penny counted; but she had a weightier anxiety on her mind. "It is occupied at present, but I have told the men there that they must be prepared to give it up on two weeks' notice. They agreed to that."

"You don't find them satisfactory, Mrs. Keefe?"

"I don't know what to think. They don't sleep there. They had me take the beds away. They used it like it was a business office. They brought in a big table to work on. They say they're architects, working on some problem, some prize-contest they want to win. Like a plan for a perfect town, something like that."

"Do they give you any trouble?"

"I don't see them or hear them for a week at a time, except sometimes when they come and go up their back stairs. I never see any of them face to face except when he pays the rent. They keep the doors locked all day and night. They do their own cleaning up. Never any letters; never any telephone calls. Mr. North, they're like ghosts in the house. Never say good morning; never exchange the time of day. I don't call that *roomers*."

She was looking at me with a first sign of confidence, even of appeal.

"Did they give any kind of reference in town when they came? Any other address?".

"The oldest one, I guess he's the head of 'em, gave me the number of his postbox at the Post Office—Number 308. One Sunday noon I saw them all eating at the Thames Street Blue Star Restaurant."

"Have you taken other people up to inspect the apartment?"

"Yes, two married couples. They didn't like it—no beds, hardly any chairs. I guess it didn't look like an apartment to them. Besides, there's the smell."

"Smell!"

"Yes, it's getting all through the house. Some chemical they use."

"Mrs. Keefe, I think you have reason to be worried."

"How do you mean?"

"I don't know yet. Can you take me up there now?"

"Yes . . . Yes, I'd *like* to."

That amazing detective Chief Inspector Theophilus North had sprung to life again. I followed her up the stairs and when she had knocked loudly at the door I gestured to her, smiling, to stand at one side. I put my ear to the crack in the door. I heard a muffled oath, whispered commands, rapid motions, a falling object. Finally the door was unlocked and a tall man with a southern colonel's mustache and goatee, very angry, faced us. He was wearing a white linen coat that I associate with surgeons.

"I'm sorry to disturb you, Mr. Forsythe, but there's a gentleman here who'd like to look at the apartment."

"I asked you to arrange these interruptions at the noon hour, Mrs. Keefe."

"My visitors have to make these calls at their own time. They visit five and six apartments every morning. I'm sorry; that's the way it is."

It was a large room filled with the sunlight that I would seldom be able to enjoy—seeming all the larger because of the sparseness of the furniture. A long trestle-like table ran the length of the room. On one end of it rested what I think would be called a "mock-up" of an ideal village in miniature, a delightful piece of work. The four men stood against the wall as though they were undergoing a military inspection.

To my great surprise the youngest of the men was Elbert Hughes. He was as astonished as I was, and extremely frightened. In my role as detective I knew that it was my task to appear as unsuspicious as possible. I strolled over to Elbert and shook his hand. "Good morning, Hughes. Too bad to be indoors on a fine morning like this. We'll get you out on the tennis courts yet." I gave him a blow on the shoulder. "You look kind of thin and peaked to me, Hughes. *Tennis,* man, that's what you need!— What! Making children's toys? Awfully pretty village that. Excuse me, gentlemen, while I see if there'd be room in these cupboards for my collection of tennis cups." There was a row of china cupboards, faced with glass and lined with silk. I grasped at their handles, but they were locked. "Locked?—Well, don't take the trouble to unlock them now." I strolled into the bathroom and kitchen. "Just right for me," I said to Mrs. Keefe. "Funny smell, though. I also have a collection of rocks—an old hobby of mine, semiprecious stones. I'd like a good deal of cupboard space for them, too." Returning into the main room I looked about me genially. It appeared as unlike an architect's *atelier* as possible. *There were no wastepaper baskets!* It was as neat and uncluttered as a business office in a department store window—except for one thing: across the open windows were strung sheets of paper, delicately fastened together; they were damp and had been hung out to dry. They had been dyed the color of blond tobacco.

I smiled to Mr. Forsythe and said, "Laundry day, eh?"

"Mrs. Keefe," he said, "I think the gentleman has had time enough to inspect the apartment. We must get back to our work."

I assumed that the making of counterfeit money and the engravers' and etchers' art would require a bulky press and pots of blue and green ink, but nothing of the kind was to be seen. The sheets of paper in the window were certainly being "aged." But I was getting "hot."

"There are some more cupboards for my collections up in that corner," I cried eagerly. They were not furnished with locks. I could hardly reach their handles, but I made two jumps for them. They swung open. To break my fall I clutched at the stacks of paper they contained, bringing down cascades of leaves that covered the floor—yes, "Thick as autumnal leaves that strew the brooks in Vallombrosa." All four men rushed forward to pick them up, but not before I saw that they were copies in a delicate old-fashioned calligraphy of "The Battle Hymn of the Republic," signed by Julia Ward Howe, once resident in Newport. As I lay flat on the floor over them I could see that each was inscribed to a different recipient —"For my dear friend . . . ," "For the Honorable Judge So-and-so . . ." I showed no sign of finding anything remarkable. "Gee, gentlemen, I'm sorry about this," I said, picking myself up. "I hope I haven't sprained my ankle!—I'm ready to go now, Mrs. Keefe. Thank you very much for your patience, gentlemen."

As I started limping out of the door, Mr. Forsythe said, "Mrs. Keefe, I hope you'll allow us to retain the rooms until the end of August—without interruptions. I was about to propose an arrangement of this matter."

"We'll talk that over at another time, Mr. Forsythe. Now I'll leave you to your work."

At the bottom of the stairs I asked, "Can we talk somewhere else—in the kitchen, maybe?"

She nodded and started down the corridor. I turned back and opened the front door, saying loudly: "I'm sorry, Mrs. Keefe, I can't consider it. It would take weeks to get rid of that unpleasant

odor. Thank you for your trouble. Good morning, Mrs. Keefe!"
I then slammed the front door loudly and followed her on tiptoe
to the kitchen.

She watched me open-eyed. "You think they're undesirable
roomers, Mr. North?"

"They're forgers."

"*Forgers,* God bless my soul! *Forgers!*"

"They don't make counterfeit money. They make antiques."

"Forgers! I've never had them before. Oh, Mr. North, the
father of the Chief of Police was a good friend of my husband's.
Shouldn't I go to him?"

"I wouldn't make a big thing of it. They're not harming anybody. Even if they sold a hundred fake letters of George Washington only fools would buy them."

"I don't want them in the house. *Forgers!* What should I do,
Mr. North?"

"When is their month up?"

"Like I said, they've agreed to go any time on two weeks'
notice."

"You shouldn't let them suspect that you know what they're
doing. They're ugly customers. Let everything go on for a few
days just as usual. I'll think of something."

"Oh, Mr. North, help me get them out. They pay thirty dollars
a month. I'll give it to you for twenty-five. I'll put the beds back
and some nice furniture." Suddenly she burst out, "My sister said
I should have gone back to Providence when my husband died.
She said I wouldn't be happy here. There's an element in this
town, she said, that's riff-raff and that attracts riff-raff, and I've
seen it over and over again."

I knew her answer, but I asked, "You mean the other side of
Thames Street?"

"No! No!" She tossed her head toward the north. "I mean up
there: Bellevue Avenue. No fear of God. *Filthy money, that's
what I mean!*"

I comforted her as best I could and drove off on my bicycle to a hard day's schedule, whistling. I'd found my apartment and I'd heard the voice of the Ninth City.

At about nine that evening as I sat brushing up my New Testament Greek for one of my students there was a knock at my door. I opened it to Elbert Hughes. He wore the look of the unhappiest man in the world.

"What can I do for you, Elbert? Nightmares again? . . . Well, what is it? Sit down."

He sat down and burst into tears. I waited.

"For God's sake, stop crying and tell me what's the matter."

Sobbing he said, "You know. You saw it all."

"What do I know?"

"They said if I told anyone, they'd crush my hand." He extended his right hand.

"Elbert! Elbert! How did a decent American boy like you get mixed up with a gang like that? . . . What would your mother think, if she knew what you were doing?"

It was a shot in the dark, but it went home. Heavy precipitation. I got up and opened the door: "Stop crying or leave this room!"

"I'll . . . I'll tell you."

"Take this towel and clean up. Drink a glass of water at the washstand and begin at the beginning."

When he'd pulled himself together, he began, "I told you how Mr. Forsythe offered me the job to work for him. Then I found out it wasn't lettering they wanted, but . . . that other thing. They'd bought a lot of first and second editions of *Hiawatha* and *Evangeline* and made me inscribe them to the writer's friends. At first I thought it was a kind of stunt. Then I copied the poems and did the same thing. And short letters by a lot of people. He keeps thinking up new things, like Edgar Allan Poe. Lots of people collect the signatures of the Presidents of the United States."

"Where do they sell these?"

"They don't talk much about it in front of me. By mail, mostly. They have a stamp that says 'John Forsythe, Dealer in Historical Documents and Autographs.' They get a lot of letters every day from Texas and places like that."

For two months he had been working at this, eight hours a day, five and a half days a week. The men wanted him under their eyes every day and night. They lived in a commercial hotel on Washington Square. He was not a man of strong will, but Elbert had won a small battle; he had insisted on living at the Y.M.C.A. They surrounded him as in a cocoon. He couldn't go out for a meal or to a lecture without one or other of them in amiable attendance. When he announced that he was going to Boston for a weekend to see his mother and his fiancée, Mr. Forsythe said, "We're all taking a vacation in September." He pulled from his pocket the lengthy contract that Elbert had signed in which he agreed to a *"continuous residence in Newport, Rhode Island."* Mr. Forsythe added, kindly, that if Elbert broke that contract he could be sued in court for all the salary that had been paid him. "A team is a team, Elbert; a job is a job." I had long noticed that one or other of the team spent a large part of the evening in the lobby of the "Y" reading or playing checkers *and watching the stairs.*

No wonder that he dreamed of being buried alive, of walls closing in.

"What does the curly-haired one do?"

"He makes the watermarks, and ages the paper. He makes stains on the paper and sometimes he makes burns on it."

"And the other one?"

"He frames the writing and puts glass over them. Then he takes the boxes to the Post Office."

"I see. . . . What's this about smashing your hand?"

"Well, he said it just as a joke, of course. One day I said that I was really interested in lettering—and that's what they hired me for—and that I wanted to go down to Washington, D.C., for two weeks to study the lettering on the public buildings there, like the Supreme Court and the Lincoln Memorial. He said he wanted me right here. He said, 'You wouldn't want anything to happen to your right hand, would you?' and he pushed my fingers way back, like this. . . . He said it with a smile, but I didn't like it."

"I see. . . . Do you want to break away from them, Elbert?"

"Oh, Ted, I wish I'd never seen them. Help me! Help me!"

I looked at him for a few minutes. Damn it, I was caught. I was caught in a trap. It looked as though I were the sole person responsible for the welfare of this helpless incapable half-genius. If we called in the police, these men, sooner or later, would retaliate on Elbert or on me, or on Mrs. Keefe, or on all three of us. I had a busy schedule; I could not drop what I was doing to extricate this unhappy maladept from his predicament. I must throw the baby on someone else's lap—and I had an idea.

"Now, Elbert, things are going to change for you. You go back to work just as usual—and continue working so for a few days. Don't you give any sign that there's going to be a change or you'll ruin the whole plan."

"I won't. I won't."

"Now you go back to your room and go to sleep. Did Dr. Addison give you something to help you about that? Are you getting some sound sleep?"

"Yes," he said, unconvincingly. "He gave me some pills."

"Now you've got all wrought up. I can't read to you tonight. Take one of Dr. Addison's pills, and what have you got to think about to calm you down?"

He looked up at me with a confidential smile. "I think about designing a good gravestone for Edgar Allan Poe."

"No! No!—Forget Poe! Think about what's ahead for you— freedom, your marriage, Abigail. Get a good rest now. Good night."

"Good night, Ted."

There was a telephone at the end of the corridor. I called up Dr. Addison. "Doc, this is Ted North. Can I drop in and see you in about ten minutes?"

"Sure! Sure! Always ready for a little prayer-meeting."

As I have said the "Y" had its own doctor, Winthrop Addison, M.D., a tall trunk of walnut, over seventy. His professional notice was still attached to the post of his verandah, but he told all strangers that he had retired; no patient he had ever served, however, was turned away. He cut his own hair, cooked his own meals, tended his own garden, and, as the ranks of his former patients were thinning, he had plenty of free time. He liked to linger in the front room of our building and talk with any resident who chose to approach him. I greatly enjoyed his company and was assembling a portrait of him for my Journal. He had a fund of stories not always suitable for his younger listeners.

I ran down to Thames Street and bought a flask of the best, then came back up our street and rang his doorbell.

"Come in, professor. What is it now?"

I offered my present to him. As he knew I didn't drink hard liquor, he put the bottle to his lips murmuring, "Heaven, sheer Heaven!"

"Now, Doc, I've got a problem. You're under the oath of Hippocrates not to say a word about it for six months."

"Agreed, lad. Agreed! I can clean you up in two months. I should have warned you about going to 'Hattie's Hammock.' "

"I don't need a doctor. Listen: I need smart, experienced grade-A advice."

"I'm listening."

"What did you think of Elbert Hughes?"

"He needs rest; he needs food; he needs backbone. Maybe he needs a mother. He's got some load of misery. He won't talk."

I told him about the forgery ring, about Elbert's extraordinary gift; about his condition of slavery. Doc loved it and took a deep swig. "Elbert wants to get away from them without their suspecting that he'll talk to the police or to anyone. They're very ugly types, Doc. They've already threatened to maim him, to *smash his right hand.* Could you give him some disease that would put him to bed for six weeks? That would put them out of business and they'd leave town. He's all they've got. He's their pot of gold."

Doc laughed long and loud. "That reminds me of a case that I had twenty-five years ago—"

"Save it! Save it!"

"This man's wife had hives—cruel! What I call 'thistle-patch hives.' He told me he wanted an excuse not to sleep in the same bed with her. She said she couldn't sleep a wink without his being by her side."

"Doc, save it. Please save it. I want the *whole* story another time. Remember we're writing a book together." (It was to be called *Coughing Up the Diamonds: The Memoirs of a Newport Doctor;* the best of it is in my Journal.) "Get your mind back to Elbert Hughes. What's that disease that makes your hand tremble? Or could you sort of make out that he's blind for a while?"

Dr. Addison held up his hand to stop me. He was deep in thought.

"I've got it!" he cried.

"I knew you'd think of something, Doc."

"Last month Bill Hinkle was doing his laundry down in the basement. He got his hand caught in the mangle—get the picture? His hand came out as flat as a playing card. Well, I pushed the knuckles back in place and separated the fingers. He'll be playing poker by Christmas. I'll give Elbert a plaster cast as big as a wasps' nest."

"You're a wonder, Doc. Now you've got to say 'No Visitors Admitted' because those gangsters will want to call on him. They're so furious they'll tear off the plaster cast and wreck his hand. He's fouled up their game. They'd follow him to China. Doc, could you write a letter to 'Holy Joe' to make sure that no visitors could be admitted to his room?"

"When do you want me to put the cast on?"

"Today's Tuesday. I want him to go to work a few days as usual. Say Saturday morning.—Doc, does your daughter like poetry?"

"She writes it—hymns mostly."

"I'll see she gets a copy of 'A Psalm of Life,' framed in glass, practically signed by the author."

"She'd appreciate that. 'Life is real! Life is earnest! And the grave is not its goal.' Eyewash, but talented." Here he fell into deep thought again. "Wait a minute! 'Holy Joe's' not got spunk enough to prevent gangsters moving about his house. Elbert's not safe there."

"Oh, Doc, if you could hide him in your house. Elbert's saved up a lot of money. He could pay for a husky male nurse to watch him when you were out."

"Out or in, I'm too old to rassle with thugs. I might kill one of them, unintentional. Hide him in New Hampshire or Vermont."

"You don't know Elbert yet. He can't cope with anything except the alphabet. He'd get in touch with his mother and his fiancée and these fellows know their addresses. Somebody's got to do his thinking for him. He's not all there. He's a genius; he's a little bit crazy. He thinks he's Edgar Allan Poe."

"Great Jehoshaphat! I've got it. We'll give out that he's crazy. A friend of mine has a mental hospital twenty miles away that's as hard to get into as a Turkish harem."

"Wouldn't that be complicated? Couldn't you think of a simpler idea?"

"Hell! You're only young once. Let's make it as complicated as possible. Saturday morning we kidnap him. We'll call it brain fever."

"That's great, Doc. I knew I'd come to the right place. Now we've got Elbert out of the way of mayhem. But we have another problem and I want your ideas. Take a swig; you'll need inspiration—real inspiration. We want *them* out of town quick. We don't want to call in the police. We want to scare them out."

"I've got it," said Doc. "The only way these men can be charged and indicted is by the Post Office Department. They're shipping fraudulent goods through the mail. No wonder they don't get letters or telephone calls at Mrs. Keefe's. They had to give a local address to rent that post office box. So they probably gave the Union Hotel on Washington Square, where they're staying. This Forsythe isn't there at any time during the working day, is he? Well, tomorrow morning I'm going to drop in there and ask in a heavy manner for Mr. Forsythe. 'Not in.' 'Tell him a representative of the United States Post Office Department called on him and will call again.' "

"Wouldn't the hotel know you, Doc?"

"I haven't answered a call from that hotel for twenty years. Then *you* find time in the afternoon before five to do the same thing. Then I'll ask a patient of mine to do the same thing—a retired gardener, solemn as a judge. That'll get them rattled. I'll tell Mrs. Keefe to tell him that a representative of the P.O. Department called on him in the evening. That'll put a bur under his tail."

"Good!—Now I've been cooking up another idea to add to yours. Let me read you a letter from the Governor of Massachusetts that I've got ready for Elbert to forge on the Governor's own stationery. Take a swig. '*Mr. John Forsythe, Dealer in Historical Documents and Autographs, Newport, Rhode Island. Dear Mr. Forsythe, As you may know, my office in The State House is hung with portraits of worthies in our history. Those belong to the Commonwealth. I have a smaller reception room, however, on whose walls I have hung autographed letters from my own collection. A mimeographed sheet of your very interesting offers for the autumn of 1926 has just been brought to my attention by a friend who found it in a hotel room in Tulsa, Oklahoma. There are some lacunae in my collection that I would like to fill, particularly letters from Thoreau, Margaret Fuller, and Louisa May Alcott. In addition I would like to replace a number that I own—those of Emerson, Lowell, and Bowditch—with letters of more significant content. Would you kindly send me the address of your office or showroom in Newport, so that I may send an expert to report to me about the properties you have in stock. This is an unofficial letter and I request that you regard it as confidential. Faithfully yours,"* et cetera, et cetera.

"That'll smoke 'em out."

"I'll wake Elbert at six o'clock tomorrow morning so that he can copy it out before he goes to work. How'll I get it mailed in Boston?"

"My daughter'll mail it. Leave it at my door as soon as it's finished. Tomorrow's Wednesday; they'll get it Friday morning. Elbert must be out of the way before they read it."

"Anything else occur to you, Doc?"

"Yes. Do you think Elbert can afford to pay about thirty dollars for his rescue?"

"Sure of it."

"I'll have a friend of mine walk up and down in front of Mrs. Keefe's house. He needs the money and he'll love the work. He's a former actor. When that messenger of theirs goes to the P.O. carrying all those boxes Nick will follow him and stick his nose into everything this fella does. Then he goes back to Mrs. Keefe's house and when the forgers quit work, he'll give them the Hawkshaw eye and they'll see him writing all their comings and goings in a notebook—see what I mean?"

"Beautiful!"

"You telephone Mrs. Keefe that he's out there protecting her. They'll order a van and get out of there Saturday morning or I'm a Chinaman. Tell Mrs. Keefe to telephone me the minute they announce they're leaving and I'll go down and sit in the hall to see that they don't do any damage. Nick and I could take turns sitting up all night, if need be."

And that's the way it happened. I moved in the next week. The stink didn't last long.

The Fenwicks

My favorite among the pupils in the early morning tennis classes at the Casino was Eloise Fenwick. She was fourteen—that is, as the spirit moved her—of any age between ten and sixteen. Some days when I approached the courts she seized my left elbow with both hands and required me to drag her to the back line; some days she preceded me, the only female world's champion who was also a lady, Countess of Aquidneck and the Adjacent Isles. In addition, she was intelligent with breathtaking surprises; she was deep and kept her counsel; she was as beautiful as the morning and showed no sign that she was aware of it. At first we had few opportunities for desultory conversation, but we were acknowledged friends without that. Friendship between one of Shakespeare's heroines at the age of fourteen and a man of thirty is one of life's fairest gifts, only occasionally available to parents.

Eloise bore a burden on her shoulders.

One day she said, "I wish my brother Charles would take lessons with you, Mr. North." She surreptitiously indicated a young man who was practicing his tennis shots against a wall reserved

for such exercise at the farthest end of the courts. I had observed
him for some time. He was, I assumed, about sixteen; he was
always alone. There was something defensively arrogant about
him. His face was covered with the pimples and discolorations
usually associated with late puberty.

"Tennis lessons, Eloise? Mr. Dobbs teaches students of that
age."

"He doesn't like Mr. Dobbs. And he wouldn't take lessons
from you because you teach children. He doesn't like anybody.
No—I just wish you would teach him something."

"Well, I can't until I'm asked, can I?"

"Mama's going to ask you."

I glanced down at her. The tone of her voice and the carriage
of her head said as plain as words that she, Eloise, had arranged
it as she probably arranged many things that came to her notice.

At the conclusion of the next lesson two days later, Eloise said,
"Mama wants to talk to you about Charles." Her eyes indicated
a lady sitting in the spectators' gallery. I had already remarked
Charles back at the practice board. I followed Eloise who introduced me to her mother and withdrew.

She was indeed Eloise's mother. She had come to take her
children home after their strenuous exercise and was heavily
veiled for motoring. She put out her hand.

"Mr. North, may I speak with you for a few moments? Please
sit down. Your name is well known in our house and in the houses
of a number of my friends with whom you read. Eloise admires
you very much."

I smiled and said, "I had not dared to hope so."

She laughed softly and our reciprocal confidence was sealed.

"I wanted to talk to you about my son Charles. Eloise tells me
that you know him by sight. I was hoping that you could find
time to coach him in French. He has been accepted for school in
the fall." She mentioned a highly esteemed school for Roman
Catholic students in the vicinity of Newport. "He has lived in
France and speaks the language, after a fashion, but he needs to

apply himself to the grammatical constructions. He has a *bloc* against learning the genders of nouns and the tenses of verbs. He admires everything that is French and I have the impression that he really wishes to bring it up to a higher standard." She lowered her voice slightly. "It embarrasses him that Eloise speaks much more correctly than he does."

I paused a moment. "Mrs. Fenwick, for four years and three summers I have taught French to students most of whom would prefer to do anything else. It is like dragging loads of stones up-hill. During this summer I resolved not to work so hard. I have already rejected a number of students who are required to im-prove their French, German, and Latin. I must have the student's own expression of readiness to study French and to work on it with me. I would like to have a short talk with your son and hear him make such a commitment."

She lowered her eyes a moment, then rested them on her son in the distance. She finally said, sadly but directly: "That is a good deal to ask of Charles Fenwick. . . . I find it difficult to say what I must. I'm not a bashful woman, I'm not a bashful-minded woman at all, but I find it very hard to describe certain tendencies —or traits—in Charles."

"Perhaps I can help you, Mrs. Fenwick. In the school where I've been teaching the Headmaster has got into the way of calling my attention to any boys who don't fit into the pattern of the 'All-American Boy' he wants in the school—boys who seem to have what he calls 'problems.' My telephone will ring: 'North, I want you to have some talk with Frederick Powell; his housemaster says that he's been walking and groaning in his sleep. He's in *your* parish.' My parish comprises sleepwalkers, bed-wetters, boys who are so homesick that they cry all night and can't hold down their food; a boy who seemed to be preparing to hang himself because he failed in two subjects and foresaw that his father would not address a word to him throughout the whole Easter vacation—and so on."

"Thank you, Mr. North . . . I wish you had room in your parish for Charles. He has none of those problems. Perhaps he has a worse one: he has a disdain, almost a contempt, for everyone he has come into contact with, except perhaps Eloise, and several priests whom he has come to know in his religious duties. . . . He is far closer to Eloise than to his parents."

"What are the grounds for Charles's low opinion of the rest of us?"

"Some posture of superiority . . . I have found the courage to give it a name: he is a snob, an unbounded snob. He has never said 'Thank you' to a servant, or even raised his eyes to one. If he has thanked his father or myself when we have taken some pains to please him, the thanks are barely audible. At mealtimes when the family is alone (for he refuses to come downstairs when there are guests) he sits in silence. He takes no interest in any subject but one: our social standing. Neither his father nor I care one iota about that. We have our friends and enjoy them—here and in Baltimore. Charles is intensely anxious as to whether we are invited to what he regards as important occasions; whether the clubs his father belongs to are the best clubs; whether I am what the papers call a 'social leader.' He is driving his father mad with questions about whether we have more means than the So-and-sos. Charles has a low opinion of us because we don't stretch every nerve to—oh, I can't go on with this—"

She was blushing intensely under her veils. She put her hands to her cheeks.

I said quickly, "Please go on a moment more about this, Mrs. Fenwick."

"As I said we are Roman Catholics. Charles is serious about his religious life. Father Walsh, who is in our home quite often, is fond of Charles and pleased with him. I have talked over with him this . . . this preposterous worldliness. He does not see it as of much importance; he thinks Charles will outgrow it soon."

"Will you tell me something of Charles's education?"

"Oh!—At the age of nine Charles developed a form of heart trouble. Baltimore and Johns Hopkins Medical School is a center for many distinguished doctors. They treated him and cured him; they tell me he is completely well. But at that time we took him out of school and ever since his education has been entirely in the hands of private tutors."

"Does that explain why he has so few friends, why he seems to be always alone?"

"Somewhat—but there is always his disdainful manner too. The boys don't like him and he thinks the boys are coarse and vulgar."

"Do the blemishes in his complexion have a part in this self-isolation?"

"That condition has only developed in the last ten months. He has been under treatment by the best dermatologists. His attitude to us is of long standing."

I smiled at her. "Do you think he can be persuaded to come over here and talk to me?"

"Eloise can persuade him to do anything. You can imagine our gratitude to God that that little girl of fourteen is so helpful and so wise."

"Then I will go inside and cancel my next appointment. Please ask Eloise to persuade him to come to this table and talk with me. Could you and Eloise leave us alone together for half an hour on some pretext?"

"Yes, we have shopping to do." She beckoned to Eloise and told her of this plan. Eloise and I exchanged a glance fraught with meaning and I went off to telephone. When I returned Charles was seated in the chair his mother had left; he had turned it about so that only his profile was presented to me. In the school I had attended and the school where I had taught students rose when a master entered the room. Charles, without a glance at me, merely lowered his head in acknowledgment of my presence. He had good features, but the cheek he presented to me was marred by a number of cones and craters.

I sat down. There was no possibility of his shaking hands with the lowest menial at the Newport Casino.

"Mr. Fenwick—I shall call you that at the beginning of our

conversation, then I shall call you Charles—Eloise tells me that you have spent much time in France and have had several years of tutoring. Probably all you need is a few weeks putting some polish on the irregular verbs. Eloise certainly surprised me. She could get an invitation tomorrow to one of those châteaux for a weekend and pass the test with flying colors. As you probably know, French people of real distinction refuse to have anything to do with Americans who speak their language incorrectly. They think we're savages. In a few moments I am going to ask you if you would like to work with me on this matter, but first I think we should know each other a little better. Eloise and your mother have told me a number of things about you: aren't there some questions you'd like to put to me about myself?"

Silence. I held the silence so long that presently he spoke. His manner was offhand and freighted with condescension. "Did you go to Yale . . . is it true that you went to Yale?"

"Yes."

Same prolonged pause.

"If you went to Yale, why are you working at the Casino?"

"To make some money."

"You don't look . . . *poor.*"

I laughed. "Oh, yes, I'm very poor, Charles—but cheerful."

"Did you belong to any of those fraternities . . . and clubs they have there?"

"I was a member of the Alpha Delta Phi fraternity and of the Elizabethan Club. I was not a member of any one of the Senior Societies."

For the first time he glanced at me. "Did you try to get into one?"

"Trying has nothing to do with it. They did not invite me."

Another glance. "Did you feel very badly about it?"

"Maybe they were wise not to take me in. Maybe I wouldn't have suited them at all. Clubs are meant for men who have a lot in common. What kind of clubs would you like to be a member of, Charles?" Silence. "The best clubs are built around hobbies.

For instance there's a club in your own town Baltimore—a hundred years old—that I think must be the most delightful in the world and the hardest to get into."

"What club is that?"

"It's called the 'Catgut Club.' " He couldn't believe his ears. "It's always been known that there's a close affinity between medicine and music. In Berlin there's a symphony orchestra made up of physicians alone. Around your Johns Hopkins Medical School there are more great doctors than in any place of its size in the world. Only the most eminent professors belong to the 'Catgut,' but they're also pianists, violinists, violists, cellists, and possibly a clarinetist. Every Tuesday night they sit down and play chamber music."

"What?"

"Chamber music. Do you know what that is?"

A strange thing was happening. Charles's face already a mottled red and white had turned scarlet. He was blushing furiously.

Suddenly I remembered—with a bang—that to very young Americans the word "chamber," through association with chamber pots, was invested with the horror and excitement and ecstasy of the "forbidden"—of things not said openly; and every "forbidden" word belongs to a network of words far more devastating than "chamber." Charles Fenwick at sixteen was going through a phase that he should have outgrown by the age of twelve. Of course! He had had tutors all his life; he had little association with boys of his own age who "aerate" that suppressed matter in giggles and whispers and horseplay and shouting. In one area of his development he was "arrested."

I explained what chamber music was and then I laid another trap for him to see if my conjecture was right.

"There's another club, also very select, at Saratoga Springs, whose members own racehorses and bet on races, but seldom ride them. There's an old joke about them; some people call it the 'Horses and Asses Club'—the members don't sit on their horses, they sit on their asses."

It worked. The crimson flag went up. At chapel services in the school where I had taught, the Bible readings occasionally reminded us that Abraham or Saul or Job had lost a large number of asses. The air in the auditorium would become tense; in the seats reserved for the smaller boys there would be agonies of suppressed laughter, convulsion, and desperate coughing. I went on serenely. "Which club would you rather belong to?"

"What?"

"The Baltimore doctors wouldn't give a pin to get into the millionaires' club at Saratoga Springs and the horse-owners wouldn't be caught dead listening to a lot of chamber music. . . . But I'm wasting your time. Are you ready to say that you'd be willing to work with me on the finer points of the French language? Be perfectly frank, Charles."

He swallowed and said, "Yes, sir."

"Fine! When next you're in France you and Eloise may be asked to some noble's country house for a pleasant weekend and you'll want to feel secure about the conversation and all that . . . . I'll sit here and wait until your mother returns. I don't want to interrupt your practice any longer." I put out my hand; he shook it and rose. I grinned. "Don't tell that little story about Saratoga Springs where it might cause any embarrassment; it's all right just among men." And I nodded in dismissal.

Mrs. Fenwick returned followed by Eloise.

"Charles feels that he'd like to try a little coaching, Mrs. Fenwick."

"Oh, I'm so relieved!"

"I think Eloise had a large part in it."

"Can I come to the classes, too?"

"Eloise, your French is quite good enough. Charles wouldn't open his mouth if you were there. But you can be sure that *I'll* miss you. Now I want to discuss some details with your mother." Eloise sighed and drifted off.

"Mrs. Fenwick, have you ten minutes? I want to lay a plan before you."

"Oh, yes, Mr. North."

"Ma'am, are you fond of music?"

"As a girl I seriously hoped to become a concert pianist."

"Who are your favorite composers?"

"It used to be Bach, then it was Beethoven, but for some time I have become fonder and fonder of Mozart. Why do you ask?"

"Because a little-known aspect of Mozart's life may help you to understand what is making life difficult for Charles."

"Charles and Mozart!"

"Both suffered from an unfortunate deprivation in their adolescence."

"Mr. North, are you in your senses?"

(I must now interrupt this account for a brief declaration. The reader has not failed to notice that I, Theophilus, did not hesitate to invent fabulous information for my own amusement or for the convenience of others. I am not given to telling either lies or the truth to another's disadvantage. The passage that follows concerning Mozart's letters is the easily verifiable truth.)

"Ma'am, half an hour ago you assured me that you were not a bashful-minded woman. What I am about to say requires my discussing what many people would regard as vulgar and even distasteful matters. Of course, you may draw this conversation to a close at any moment you wish, but I think it will throw some light on why Charles is a closed-in and unhappy young man."

She stared at me in silence for a moment, then clutched the arms of her chair and said, "Go on."

"Readers of Mozart's letters have long known of a few that he addressed to a cousin living in Augsburg. Those that have been published contain many asterisks indicating that deletions have been made. No editor or biographer would print the whole, feeling that they would distress the reader and leave a stain on the image of the composer. These letters to his *Bäsle*—a German and Austrian diminutive for a female cousin—are one long chain of childish indecencies. Not long ago the famous author Stefan Zweig bought them and printed them, with a preface, for private dis-

tribution among his friends. I have not seen the brochure, but a
musicologist I know, living in Princeton, gave me a detailed account of them and of Stefan Zweig's introduction. They are what
is called scatological—having to do with the bodily functions. As
I was told, there is little or no allusion to sexual matters; it is all
'bathroom humor.' They were written in the composer's middle
and late teens. How can one explain that Mozart who matured so
early could descend to such infantile jokes? The beautiful letters
to his father, preparing him for the news of his mother's death in
Paris, were written not long after. Herr Zweig points out that
Mozart never had a normal boyhood. Before he was ten he was
composing and performing music all day and far into the night. His
father was exhibiting him about Europe as a wonderchild. You
remember that he climbed on Queen Marie Antoinette's lap. I have
not only been a teacher at a boys' school, I have earned my living
during the summers as counselor at camps and have had to sleep in
the same tent with seven to ten urchins. Boys pass through a phase
when all these 'forbidden' matters obsess them—are excruciatingly
funny and exciting and, of course, alarming. Girls are supposed to
be given to giggling, but I assure you boys between nine and
twelve will giggle for an entire half hour if some little physio-
logical accident takes place. They give vent to the anxiety surrounding the tabu by sharing it in the herd. But Mozart—if I
may put it figuratively—never played baseball in a corner lot, never
went swimming on a boy scout picnic." I paused. "Your son
Charles was cut off from his contemporaries and all this perfectly
natural childish adjustment to our bodily nature was driven underground; and has festered."

She addressed me coldly, "My son Charles has never uttered
a vulgar word."

"Mrs. Fenwick, that's the point!"

"How do you know that something is *festering*?" There was a
sneer in her voice. She was a very nice woman, but she was being
hard pushed.

"By sheer accident. In our conversation he gave me pretty hard treatment. He asked me if I had belonged to certain extremely exclusive clubs at Yale, and when I told him I had not, he tried to humiliate me. But I have had a lot of experience. I was beginning to think very well of him; but I could see that he was living in a capsule of anxiety."

She put her hands over her face. After a moment she regained possession of herself and said in a low voice, "Go on, please!" I told her about the musical club in Baltimore and about Charles's crimson reaction. I told her that I had made an experiment and invented a club for card-players which offered rewards for the best and the worst players called the "Tops and Bottoms Club" and aroused the same response. I explained that for boys—and probably girls—during certain years the English language was a mine-field sown with explosives—words, dynamite; I said that I had remembered Mozart's letters and that Charles had been brought up by tutors, cut off from the life usually led by boys. I said that he was entrapped in a stage of development which he should have outgrown years before and that the trap was *fear* and that what she had called his snobbery was his escape into a world where no shattering word was ever spoken. I had asked him if he would like to work with me in the hope of bringing his French up to Eloise's standard—and that he had agreed to it and that before he left he had shaken my hand and had looked me in the eye.

"Mrs. Fenwick, you may remember Macbeth's question to the doctor concerning Lady Macbeth's sleepwalking: 'Canst thou not . . . Cleanse the stuffed bosom of that perilous stuff Which weighs upon the heart?' "

With no tone of reproach she said, "But you are not a doctor, Mr. North."

"No. What Charles needs is a friend with a certain experience in these matters. You cannot be sure that doctors are also potential friends."

"You believe that Mozart outgrew his 'childishness'?"

"No. No man does. He outgrows most of his anxiety; the rest he turns into laughter. I doubt that Charles even knows what it is to smile."

"Oh, Mr. North, I've hated every word you've said. But I think I can see that you are probably right. Will you accept Charles as a pupil?"

"I must make a proviso. You must discuss it with Mr. Fenwick and Father Walsh. I could teach French syntax to Tom, Dick, and Harry, but now that I have glimpsed Charles's predicament, I cannot spend all those hours without trying to help. I couldn't teach algebra—as a friend of mine was paid to do—to a girl who was suffering from religious mania; she was secretly wearing hair shirts and sticking nails into her body. I want your permission to do a thing that I would not dream of doing without your permission. I want to introduce into each lesson a 'dynamite word' or two. If I had a student whose mind and heart was absorbed by birds, I would build French lessons about ostriches and starlings. Learning takes wings when it's related to what's passing in the student's inner life. Charles's inner life is related to a despairing effort to grow up into a man's world. His snobbery is related to this knot inside him. He won't realize it, but my lessons would be based on these fantasies of his—of social grandeur and of the frightening world of the tabu."

She had shut her eyes, but opened them again—"Excuse me; what is it you want?"

"A message from you that I may occasionally use low earthy images in the lessons. I want you to trust me not to resort to the prurient and the salacious. I don't know Charles. He may develop an antagonism against me and report to you and to Father Walsh that I have a vulgar mind. You probably know that ailing patients *also* cling to their illnesses."

She rose. "Mr. North, this has been a painful conversation for me. I must think it all over. You will hear from me. . . . Good morning."

She extended her hand tentatively. I bowed saying, "If you agree to my proviso, I can meet Charles in the blue tea room behind us for an hour every Monday, Wednesday, and Friday at eight-thirty."

She looked about confusedly for her children, but Eloise and Charles had been watching us and hurried forward. Eloise said, "Mr. North won't let me come to the classes, too; but I forgive him." Then she turned and threw her arms about her brother's stomach and said, "I'm so glad Charles is going to have them."

Charles, standing very straight above his sister's shining head, said, "*Au revoir, monsieur le professeur!*"

Mrs. Fenwick stared at her children with a distraught air and said, "Are you ready to go to the car, dears?" and led them off.

Two days later Eloise approached me at the close of the last of my tennis classes and gave me a note from her mother. I put it in my pocket.

"Aren't you going to read it?"

"I'll wait. Just now I'd rather take you to the La Forge Tea Rooms for a hot fudge sundae. . . . Do you think this note engages me or dismisses me?"

Eloise possessed three forms of laughter. I now heard the long low dove's ripple. "I shan't tell you," she said, having told me. This morning she had chosen to be all of twenty years old but she slipped her hand into mine—in full view of Bellevue Avenue, astonishing the horses, shocking the old ladies in their electric phaetons, and very definitely opening the summer season.

"Oh, Mr. North, is this really our last class? Shall I never see you again?"

We didn't sit on high stools before the soda fountain, as once before, but at a table in the furthest corner. "I was hoping that you'd have a hot fudge sundae with me every Friday morning at exactly this time—just when I finish my lesson with Charles." We were hungry after all that exercise and addressed ourselves to our sundaes with a will.

"You really do know a lot about what's been going on, don't you, Eloise?"

"Well, no one ever tells a young girl anything so she has to be a sort of witch. She has to learn to read people's thoughts, doesn't she? When I was a little girl I used to listen at doors, but I don't do that any more. . . . You grown-ups suddenly woke up about Charles. You saw that he was all caught in . . . a sort of spider's web; he was afraid of everything. You must have told Mother something that made her frightened, too. Did you tell her to ask Father Walsh to dinner?" I remained silent. "He came to dinner last night and after dinner Charles and I were sent upstairs, and they went into the library and had a council of war. And way upstairs, miles away, we could hear Father Walsh laughing. Mother's voice sounded as though she had been crying, but Father Walsh kept shouting with laughter.—Please read the letter, Mr. North—not to *me*, of course, but to yourself."

I read: *"Dear Mr. North, Reverend Father says to tell you that when he was young he had worked as a counselor at a boys' camp, too. He told me to tell you to go ahead—that he'll do the praying and you do the work. It comforts me to think of the lady in Salzburg for whom things worked out so well. Sincerely, Millicent Fenwick."*

I don't believe in unnecessarily hiding things from young people. "Eloise, read the letter, but don't ask me to explain it to you yet."

She read it. "Thank you," she said and thought a moment. "Wasn't Beethoven born in Salzburg? We went there when I was about ten and visited his house."

"Is it hard to be a witch, Eloise? I mean: does it make living harder?"

"No! It keeps you so busy. You have to be on your toes. . . . It keeps you from growing stale."

"Oh, is that one of your worries?"

"Well, isn't it everybody's?"

"Not when you're around.—Eloise, I always like to ask my young friends what they've been reading lately. And you?"

"Well, I've been reading the *Encyclopaedia Britannica*—I discovered it when I wanted to read about Héloïse and Abelard. Then I read about George Eliot and Jane Austen and Florence Nightingale."

"Some day turn to *B* and read about Bishop Berkeley, who lived in Newport, and go and visit his house. Turn to *M* and read about Mozart, who was born in Salzburg."

She slapped her hand to her mouth. "Oh, how boring it must be for you to talk to young girls who are so ignorant!"

I burst out laughing. "Let me be the judge of that, Eloise. Please go on about the *Encyclopaedia*."

"For another reason I read about Buddhism and glaciers and lots of other things."

"Forgive me asking so many questions, but why do you read about Buddhism and glaciers?"

She blushed a little, glancing at me shyly. "So that I'll have something to talk about at table. When Papa and Mama give luncheons or dinner parties Charles and I eat upstairs. When relatives or old friends are invited we are invited, too; but Charles *never* comes to table if anyone else is there—except Father Walsh, of course. When just the four of us are there he comes to table but he scarcely says a word. . . . Mr. North, I'm going to tell you a secret: Charles thinks he's an orphan; he thinks Papa and Mama adopted him. I don't think he really believes that, but that's what he says." She lowered her voice. "He thinks he is a prince from another country—like Poland or Hungary or even France."

"And you're the only one who knows that?"

She nodded. "So you see how hard it is for Papa and Mama to make conversation—and in front of the servants!—with a person who acts as though he were so far away from them."

"Does he think that you are of royal birth also?"

She answered sharply. "I don't let him."

"So at mealtimes you fill in about Buddhism and glaciers and Florence Nightingale?"

"Yes . . . and I tell them the things you've told me. About the

school you went to in China. That filled a whole lunchtime—I
embroidered it a little. Do you always tell the truth, Mr. North?"

"I do to you. It's so boring to tell the truth to people who'd
rather hear the other thing."

"I told how in Naples the girls thought you had the Evil Eye. I
made it funny and Mario had to leave the room he was laughing
so."

"Now I'm going to tell you something. Dear Eloise, if you see
that Charles is cutting his way out of that spider's web a little, you
can tell yourself that it's all due to you." She looked at me in
wonder. "Because when you love someone you communicate your
love of life; you keep the faith; you scare away dragons."

"Why, Mr. North—there are tears in your eyes!"

"Happy tears."

So I met Charles at eight-thirty on the following Monday. In
the intervening time he had relapsed somewhat into his haughty
distrust; but he deigned to sit in his chair facing me. He was like
a fox watching a hunter from behind a screen of foliage.

My Journal does not contain an account of our successive lessons, but I find, pinned into it, an almost illegible schema of our
progress—the day's syntactical problem and the "dynamite words"
at my disposal: auxiliary verbs, the subjunctive, the four past
tenses, and so on; *derrière, coucher, cabinet,* and so on. I find no
notations for my campaign against snobbery, but it was never long
absent from my mind. The day usually began with a little shocker,
then went on to forty minutes of pure grammatical grind, con-
cluding with free practice in conversational French. The entire
lesson was conducted in French which—for the most part—I
shall translate here. (Every now and then I'll give the reader a
little run for his money.)

In the earlier lessons, I used restraint in upsetting his modesty
during those conversational twenty minutes—though I became
increasingly exacting during the grammatical grind—to which he
responded admirably.

"Charles, what are these odd-looking kiosks in the streets called —these constructions for the convenience of men only?"

He had some difficulty in recalling the word *"pissoirs."*

"Yes, they also go by a more elegant and more interesting name *vespasiennes*, after the Roman emperor to whom we are indebted for the happy idea. Now that you're older and will be circulating more with maturer persons over there you will be astonished at the lack of embarrassment with which ladies and gentlemen of even the most refined sort refer to such matters. So be prepared for that, will you?"

"Yes, sir." . . .

"Charles, I hope that you will be a student in Paris in your twenties, as I was. We were all poor, but we had a lot of fun. Be sure that you live on the Left Bank, and *pretend* that you're poor. Don't drink too much Pernod; the only time that I was ever beastly drunk was on Pernod—watch that, will you? What times we had! I'll tell you a story—it's a little risqué, but you don't mind a bit of that when it's not disgusting, do you? . . . To save money we used to press our pants by putting them under our mattresses; that gave them a razor-edge crease, see? Well, my roommate was a music student and one afternoon his professor invited us both to his home for tea with his wife and daughter—delightful people. And Madame Bergeron commented on the elegance of his clothing and especially that brilliant crease. 'Thank you, madame,' he said, 'Monsieur North and I have a secret about that. Every night we put our trousers under our *maîtresses*.' Madame Bergeron, laughing heartily, waved her hands in the air, and then politely and smilingly corrected him." MATELAS

That was a dynamite word. Charles was so stunned that it took him ten minutes to think it over. Maybe it was on that occasion that for the first time I saw the ghost of a smile on his face.

One morning Charles brought me a message from his mother. She invited me to an informal Sunday supper with the family at the end of the week.

"Charles, that is very kind of your mother and of you all. I

shall write her a note. I shall have to explain that I'd made a rule
to accept no invitation whatever. I want you to read the note I
shall write to her and I know you both will understand. But it's
very hard to refuse this kindness from your mother. May I tell you
in confidence, Charles, that my work carries me into many cottages
in Newport and I've met a number of the admired hostesses in
this town. *In confidence,* not *one* can hold a candle to your mother
for distinction and charm and what the French call *race.* I'd always
heard that the ladies of Baltimore belonged to a class apart and
now I know it to be true." I struck his elbow. "You're a lucky man,
Charles. I hope you live up to that privilege. I like to think of you
finding a hundred delicate ways of expressing not only your
affection, but your admiration and gratitude to so remarkable a
mother—as all French sons do, and—I'm sorry to say—all American sons don't. You do, don't you, Charles?"

"*Oui . . . oui, monsieur le professeur.*"

"I must say I'm glad that this kind invitation wasn't brought
to me—face to face—by Eloise. The man hasn't been born who
could refuse a request from Eloise." I added in English, "Do you
understand what I mean?"

He returned my deep glance into his eyes—"Yes," he said, and
for the first time he laughed deeply. He understood.

But there was still much work to be done.

"*Bonjour, Charles.*"
"*Bonjour, monsieur le professeur.*"

"Today we're going to work with the conditional mood, with
verbs ending in *ir,* and with the second person singular *tu.* You
use *tu* to children, to your very old friends, and to members of
your family, though I've been told that until about 1914 even
husbands and wives addressed one another as *vous.* You notice
that I always address you as *vous*; if we haven't quarreled in the
meantime, I might address you as *tu* five years from now. Often
in French, and always in Spanish, God is addressed as *Tu,* capital

T. Of course, lovers call each other *tu;* all such conversations in bed are in this second person singular."

Up ran the scarlet flag.

Forty minutes of grammar drill.

Then at ten minutes past nine: "Now for some practice in conversation. Today we're going to have some man-to-man conversation. We'd better move to that table in the corner where we won't be overheard."

He looked at me in alarm and we moved to the corner. "Charles, you've been in Paris. After dark you must have often seen certain women of the street strolling singly or in couples. Or you've heard them addressing passing gentlemen in a low voice from doorways and alleys—what do they usually say?"

The scarlet flag was high on the mast. I waited. At last he murmured, strangulatedly, *"Voulez-vous coucher avec moi?"*

"Good! Since you're very young, they may say, *'Tu es seul, mon petit? Veux-tu que je t'accompagne?'* Or you're sitting alone at a bar and one of these *petites dames* slides up beside you and puts her arm through yours: *'Tu veux m'offrir un verre?'* How do you answer these questions, Charles? You're an American and a gentleman and you've had some experience with these encounters."

Charles was in a crimson agony. I waited. Finally he ventured, *"Non, mademoiselle . . . merci."* Then added generously, *"Pas ce soir."*

"Très bien, Charles! Could you make it a little more easy and charming? These poor souls are earning their living. They're not exactly beggars, are they? They have something to sell. They're not contemptible—not in France, they aren't. Can you try again?"

"I . . . I don't know."

"At the school where I've been teaching there's a master who teaches French. He loves France and goes to France every summer. He hates women and is afraid of them. He prides himself on his virtue and righteousness and he's a really dreadful man. In Paris he goes for strolls in the evening just so that he can humiliate these women. He told the story to us fellow-masters to illustrate what a tower of Christian morality he was. When he's spoken to by one of these women he turns on her and says, '*Vous me faites ch——!*' That's a very vulgar expression; it's far worse than saying 'You make me vomit.' He told us that the girl or girls sprang back from him aghast crying, '*Pourquoi? Pourquoi?*' He'd had his little triumph. What do you think of that?''

"It's . . . awful."

"One of the most attractive aspects of France is the universal respect for women at every level of society. At home and in public restaurants a Frenchman smiles at the waitress who's serving him, looks her right in the eye when he thanks her. There's an undertone of respectful flirtation between every man and woman in France—even when she's a woman of ninety, even when she's a prostitute.—Now let's act a little one-act play. You go out of the room and come in the door as though you were strolling in one of those streets behind the Opéra. I'm going to pretend I'm one of those girls."

He did as he was told. He approached me as though he were entering a cage of tigers.

"*Bonsoir, mon chou.*"

"*Bonsoir, mademoiselle.*"

"*Tu es seul? Veux-tu t'amuser un peu?*"

"*Je suis occupé ce soir. . . . Merci!*"

He threw a wild glance in my direction and added, "*Peut-être une autre fois. Tu es charmante.*"

"*A-o-o! A-o-o! . . . Dis donc: une demi-heure, chéri. J'ai une jolie chambre avec tout confort américain. On s'amusera à la folie!*"

He turned to me and asked in English, "How do I get out of this?"

"I suggest you make your departure quick, short, but cordial: '*Mademoiselle, je suis en retard. Il faut que je file. Mais au revoir.*' And here you pat her elbow or shoulder, smile, and say, '*Bonne chance, chère amie!*'"

He repeated this several times, elaborating on it. Presently he was laughing.

Make-believe is like dreams—escape, release.

I came to notice that on the days when the lessons began with heavy skirmishing in the "mine-field" area my pupil's memory and resource were quicker. He could laugh; he could skate over depth-bombs, and he could make conversation from recollections of his own past. Besides, he was working hard on his grammar exercises between classes—and his complexion was clearing up.

Another session from the following week, after we'd had a smart run-through of the gender and plural of three hundred nouns in frequent use:

"Now we're going to have another one-act play. The scene is laid in one of the great restaurants of Paris, *Le Grand-Véfour*. Charles, France is a republic. What became of the royal and imperial families—the Bourbons and the Bonapartes? . . . Oh, yes, they're around still. . . . What name do they give to the real King of France who is not permitted to use that title and to wear his crown?—He is called the Pretender, the *Prétendant.* In English that means an impostor; not in France, where it means merely claimant. He calls himself the *Comte de Paris.* In this play you are he. You are addressed as *Monseigneur* or as *Votre Altesse.* In your veins flows the blood of Saint Louis, king and saint, and of Charlemagne—your own name Carolus Magnus—and of all those Louis's and those Henris."

His face was getting very red.

"Your secretary has made a reservation for dinner. You arrive exactly on time—punctuality is called 'the courtesy of kings.' Your three guests have arrived before you—that is etiquette and woe to the guest who's late. You're very handsome and you carry yourself with extraordinary ease. Naturally the staff of the restaurant is at the highest pitch of excitement. I shall play the proprietor—let's call him Monsieur Véfour. I am waiting at the door. The porter is standing in the street and gives a secret signal when your car is seen approaching at exactly eight o'clock. Now you go out the door and come in."

He did. He was like a person dazed.

I bowed and murmured, *"Bonsoir, Monseigneur. Vous nous faites un très grand honneur."*

Charles, alarmed, was at his loftiest. He responded with a slight nod. *"Bonsoir, monsieur . . . merci."*

"One moment, Charles. The greatest noblemen and many of the kings have long established a tone of easy familiarity that would surprise even the President of the United States. Over there the greater the social status, the greater the democratic manner. The French have a word for cold, condescending self-importance: *morgue.* You would be horrified if you thought your subjects, the great French people, attributed that quality to you. Now let's do it again." Like a stage director I whispered some suggestions to him—some business, some lines. Then we did it again. He began to add some ideas of his own.

"Do you want to try it again? Let's go! Do anything that occurs to you, as long as you remember that you're the King of France. By the way when you meet me, you don't shake hands, you pat me on the shoulder; but when you meet my son you shake his hand. *Allons!"*

He entered the restaurant, wreathed in smiles; he handed his imaginary cape and top hat to an imaginary attendant, saying, *"Bonsoir, mademoiselle. Tout va bien?"*

I bowed and said, *"Bonsoir, Monseigneur. Votre Altesse nous fait un très grand honneur."*

"Ah, Henri-Paul, comment allez-vous?"

"Très bien, Monseigneur, merci."

"Et madame votre femme, comment va-t-elle?"

"Très bien, Monseigneur, elle vous remercie."

"Et les chers enfants?"

"Très bien, Monseigneur, merci."

"Tiens! C'est votre fils? . . . Comment vous appelez-vous, mon-

sieur? Frédéric? Comme votre grand-père! Mon grand-père aimait bien votre grand-père.—Dites, Henri-Paul, j'ai démandé des couverts pour trois personnes. Serait-ce encore possible d'ajouter un quatrième? J'ai invité Monsieur de Montmorency. Ça vous gênerait beaucoup?"

"Pas du tout, Monseigneur. Monsieur le Duc est arrivé et Vous attend. Si Votre Altesse aura la bonté de me suivre."

Charles was agitated; he was blushing but with a different kind of blush. *"Monsieur le professeur . . .* can we ask Eloise over to see it? She's sitting there, waiting to go home."

"Yes, indeed! Let me invite her.—Give it the works, Charles! Hoke it up! . . . Eloise, we're doing a little one-act play. Would you like to be our audience?"

I explained the scene, the plot, and the characters.

Charles surpassed himself. With his hand on my shoulder he told me how his mother had first brought him to this restaurant at the age of twelve. Was it true that I served a dish named after his mother? On his way to the table he recognized a friend (Eloise) among the guests. *"Ah, Madame la Marquise . . . chère cousine!"*

Eloise made a deep curtsy, murmuring, *"Mon Prince!"* He raised her up and kissed her hand.

At his table he apologized to his guests for being late. *"Mes amis, les rues sont si bondées; c'est la fin du monde."*

The Duc de Montmorency (myself) assured him that he had arrived exactly on time. And so our entertainment came to an end. Eloise had watched it in open-eyed wonder. To her there was nothing funny about it. She rose slowly, the tears pouring down her face. She threw her arms around her brother and kissed him with poignant intensity. All I got was a look from her, over his shoulder, but what a look! She couldn't see me, but I could see her.

"Charles," I said, "at our next class I'm going to give you the examination for those who have completed three years of French. I'm sure you'll pass it splendidly and our lessons will be over."

"Over!"

"Yes. Teachers are like birds. The moment comes when they must push the young out of the nest. Now you must give your time to American history and physics which I can't teach you."

On the following Friday I met Eloise for our visit to the tea room. On this morning she was neither the ten-year-old nor the Countess of Aquidneck and the Adjacent Isles. She was dressed all in white, not the white of the tennis courts but the white of snow. She was someone else—not Juliet, not Viola, not Beatrice—perhaps Imogen, perhaps Isabella. She did not put her hand in mine but she left no doubt that we were true friends. She walked with lowered eyes. We sat down at our removed table.

She murmured, "I'll have tea this morning."

I ordered tea for her and coffee for myself. Silence with Eloise was as rewarding as conversation. I left it to her.

"Last night there were no guests. At table Charles brushed away Mario and held the chair for Mother. He kissed her on the forehead." She looked at me with a deep smile. "When he sat down he said, 'Papa, tell me about your father and mother and about when you were a boy.' "

"Eloise! And you were all ready to tell them about the Eskimos."

"No, I was all ready to ask them about the Fenwicks and the Conovers."

We both burst out laughing.

"Oh, Eloise, you are a child of Heaven!"

She looked at me wide-eyed. "Why did you say that?"

"It just sprang to my lips."

We drank our tea and coffee in silence for a few minutes and then I asked, "Eloise, how do you see your life as it lies before you?"

Again she looked at me wonderingly. "You're very strange this morning, Mr. North."

"Oh no, I'm not. I'm the same old friend."

She reflected a moment and then said, "I'm going to answer your question. But you must promise not to say one word about it to anyone."

"I promise, Eloise Fenwick."

She put her arms on the table and, looking straight into my eyes, said: "I want to be a religious, a nun."

I held my breath.

She answered my unspoken question. "I'm so grateful to God for my father and mother . . . and brother, for the sun and the sea, and for Newport, that I want to give my life to Him. He will show me what I must do."

I returned her solemn gaze.

"Eloise, I'm just an old Protestant on both sides of my family. Forgive me if I ask you this: couldn't you express your gratitude to God while living a life outside the religious orders?"

"I love my parents so much . . . and I love Charles so much, that I feel that those loves would come between me and God. I want to love Him above all and I want to love everybody on earth as much as I love my family. I love them *too much*."

And the tears rolled down her cheeks.

I did not stir.

"Father Walsh knows. He tells me to wait; in fact I must wait for three years. Mr. North, this is the last time we'll meet here. I am learning how to pray and wherever I am in the world I shall be praying for Papa and Mama and Charles and for you and"— she pointed to the guests in the tea room—"for as many of the children of Heaven as I can hold in my mind and heart."

During the rest of the summer our paths crossed frequently. She was disattaching herself from love of her family—and naturally from friendship—in order to encompass us all in a great offering that I could not understand.

Myra

One day toward the middle of July—shortly before I was able to take possession of my apartment—I was called to the telephone at the "Y."

"Mr. North?"

"This is Mr. North speaking."

"My name is George Granberry. I should say George Francis Granberry because I have a cousin in town named George Herbert Granberry."

"Yes, Mr. Granberry."

"I'm told that you read aloud in English—English literature and all that."

"Yes, I do."

"I'd like to make an appointment with you to discuss reading aloud some books to my wife. My wife's a sort of invalid this summer, and it would . . . sort of . . . help her pass the time. Where could we meet and talk about it?"

"I suggest tonight or tomorrow night at the bar of the Muenchinger-King at six-fifteen."

"Good!—Tonight at the 'M-K' at six-fifteen."

Mr. Granberry was about thirty-five, young for Newport. He belonged to the category that journalists like Flora Deland call "sportsmen and men-about-town." Like many others of his kind he had a face that was handsome but wrinkled, even strangely ridged. I first thought this condition was the result of exposure to wind and wave in early youth—yacht races, Bermuda Cup trials, and so on; but later decided it was acquired on dry land and indoors. He had been designed to be a likable fellow, but idleness and aimlessness are erosive too. I received the impression that this interview with a "professor" was discomfiting, perhaps intimidating, and that he had been drinking. He offered me a drink. I accepted Bevo and we withdrew to the window-seat overlooking Bellevue Avenue and the Reading Rooms.

"Mr. North, my wife Myra is the brightest girl in the world. Quick as a whip. She can talk rings about anybody, see what I mean? But when she was a young girl she had an accident. Fell off a horse. She missed some years of schooling. Schoolteachers came to the house and taught her—terrible bores; you know what schoolteachers are like.—Where was I? Oh, yes: as a result of all this she hates reading a book. The way she puts it, she can't stand nonsense—*The Three Musketeers* and Shakespeare and all that. She's a very realistic girl. But she likes being read to, for a while. I've tried to read aloud to her, and her nurse, Mrs. Cummings, reads aloud to her, but after ten minutes she says she'd rather talk instead. Well—where was I? One of the results of this interruption in her education is that sometimes in general conversation she doesn't do credit to herself. You know that 'I-hate-Shakespeare' stuff and 'Poetry is for sheep.' . . . Newport's full of us Granberrys who think all that's just bad education and middle-western yap. It's a little embarrassing for me and my mother and all those cousins I have around. . . . As I told you, just now she's something of an invalid. She's pretty well got over that fall from the horse, but she's had two miscarriages. We're expecting a child again in about six months. The doctors have ordered her to get a little exercise in the morning and she's allowed to go out to dinner several evenings in the week, but all the afternoon she's got to spend resting on a sofa. Naturally she gets pretty bored. She has a bridge teacher twice a week, but she doesn't enjoy that . . . and a French teacher."

There was a pause. I asked, "Friends come to call?"

"In New York they do; not here. She's a great talker, but she says that in Newport people just talk *at* her. She told the doctor to give orders that she's not to receive callers—except me. I love Myra, but I can't spend all my afternoons just listening to her. It's those afternoons she finds hard. . . . Besides, I'm a sort of inventor. I have a laboratory in Portsmouth. That takes up a good deal of my time."

"An inventor, Mr. Granberry!"

"Oh, I tinker at some ideas I have. I hope to come on something important some day. . . . Until then I keep it pretty secret. So . . . uh . . . would you be willing to read aloud to her, say three afternoons a week from four to six?"

I took my time. "Mr. Granberry, may I ask you a question?"

"Oh, sure. Go ahead."

"I never take a student unless there is some assurance that the student wants to work with me. I can't get anywhere with an indifferent or an antagonistic student. Do you think she'll resent me as she does the bridge teacher?"

"I tell you frankly, it's a risk. But my wife's older now. She's twenty-seven. She knows that she's missed something . . . and that some of those ladies think she's a little . . . unfinished. Myra's not stupid—oh, no!—but she's strong-minded and very sincere. If you put her before a firing-squad and asked her to name five plays by Shakespeare, she'd say, 'Go ahead and shoot!' She's got a skunner against Shakespeare. She thinks he's piffle. So do I, rather, but I know enough to keep my mouth shut about it. She was born in Wisconsin and up there they don't allow anybody to tell them anything."

"I was born in Wisconsin."

"*You were born in Wisconsin?*"

"Yes."

"You're a Badger!"

"Yes."

All the states have their totems, but the middle-western states are particularly conscious of the animals with which they identify themselves.

"Oh, that'll be a big recommendation. Myra's very proud of being a Badger. . . . Oh, that's fine! Well, do you think you could try it, Mr. North?"

"Yes, but under one condition: the minute that Mrs. Granberry loses interest or becomes impatient, I must resign."

"I'd be awfully grateful if you'd give it a try. You may have to be a little patient with her at the beginning."

"I will."

We arranged a schedule. I thought the interview was over, but he had something further on his mind.

"Have another Bevo, Mr. North. Have something stronger. Have anything you want. I'm part owner of this hotel."

"Thank you, I'll have another Bevo."

We were served.

"I think I ought to tell you that one reason I've asked you to help me about Myra's reading is the way you behaved in that Diana Bell matter." I showed no sign of having heard him. "I mean that you made an agreement to say nothing about it and wild horses haven't been able to drag a word out of you about it. In Newport all they do is talk and talk—gossip, damned gossip. Can I make the same agreement with you?"

"Certainly. I never talk about my employers."

"I mean: you may be meeting me here and at the house. You met a friend of mine out at dinner, a very charming girl. She enjoyed talking French with you."

"Sir, I haven't been out to dinner *once* in Newport—except at Bill Wentworth's home."

"It wasn't here. It was at Narragansett Pier, at Flora Deland's."

"Oh, yes. Miss Desmoulins, a very charming young lady."

"You may be meeting her again over there. I just happen to have missed you twice at Flora Deland's. I'd appreciate it if you didn't mention it . . . in certain quarters—you see what I mean?"

"I'd like to return to the subject of Wisconsin again. Did you meet Mrs. Granberry there?"

"Lord, no! She lived way up in the north near Wausau. Only been there once in my life, the days before the wedding. Met her at parties in Chicago—she has cousins there and so have I."

The conversation floundered about like a rudderless ship. As I rose to go, he took one more look out of the window and said, "Ah! There she is!" A car had drawn up to the curb; the chauffeur had alighted and opened the door to a lady. Except for her white straw hat she was all in rose from the veils that covered her head to the tips of her shoes.

He muttered to me, "You go first!" and I opened the front door. French women are taught from the cradle to express delighted surprise at meeting any man—from twelve to ninety—whom they have met before.

"*Ah, Monsieur Nort', quel plaisir de vous revoir! Je suis Denise Desmoulins . . .*" et cetera. I expressed my moved admiration of what I saw before me, et cetera, and we parted with expansive hopes of meeting again soon at Narragansett Pier.

At the appointed afternoon I wheeled up to the door of "Sea Ledges," was received and led into Mrs. Granberry's "afternoon room." That lady, as beautiful as the morning but not as shy as the dawn, was lying on a chaise-longue. A stout pleasant-looking nurse sat near her knitting.

"Good afternoon, Mrs. Granberry. I am Mr. North. Mr. Granberry has engaged me to read aloud to you."

The lady glared at me in astonishment and silence, probably rage. I was carrying two volumes which I put down on the table beside me. "Will you kindly introduce me to your companion?"

This was another surprise. She murmured, "Mrs. Cummings, Mr. North."

I crossed and shook hands with Mrs. Cummings. "Are you from Wisconsin too, ma'am?" I asked.

"Oh, no, sir. I'm from Boston."

"Are you also fond of reading?"

"Oh, I love reading, but I don't get much time for it, you know."

"Surely some of your patients—as soon as they begin to feel better—like a bit of reading? Something light and amusing?"

"We have to be careful, sir. When I was in training the Mother Directress told us about a Sister who had read aloud *Mrs. Wiggs of the Cabbage Patch* to a surgical case. Had to restitch him, they did. She tells that story to every graduating class."

"It's a lovely book. I know it well."

Perhaps it was time that I gave my attention to the lady of the house. "Mrs. Granberry, I don't want to read anything that's boring and certainly you don't want to hear anything that's boring, so I suggest that we draw up some rules—"

She interrupted me curtly. "What exactly did Mr. Granberry say when he asked you to come and read to me?"

"He said that you were a very intelligent young woman who had lost a year or two of education because of an accident in your childhood; that you had routine teachers during your convalescence who had given you a prejudice against poetry and some of the standard classics."

"What else did he say?"

"I don't remember anything else, except his distress that you had to pass these afternoon hours without any interest or occupation."

The expression on her face was strong. "What are these rules that you propose?"

"I suggest that I start reading a book and that you let me read it for a quarter of an hour without interruption. Then I look at you and you give me a sign that I may go on for another quarter of an hour, or a sign that I start some other book. Does that rule seem unreasonable to you, ma'am?"

"Don't call me 'ma'am.' Let me make it clear to you, Mr. West, that there's something behind all this that I don't like. I don't like being treated as an idiot child."

"Oh, then," I said, rising quickly, "there's been some misunderstanding. I'll say good afternoon. Mr. Granberry gave me the impression that you might take some pleasure in being read aloud to." I went over to Mrs. Cummings and shook her hand. "Good afternoon, Mrs. Cummings. I hope I may meet you at another time. Please recall me as Mr. North, not Mr. West."

The lady of the house said sharply, "Mr. North, it's not your fault that I don't like the whole idea. Mr. Granberry asked you to come here and read to me, so please sit down and begin. I agree to your rules."

"Thank you, Mrs. Granberry."

I sat down and began reading: *"Emma Woodhouse, handsome, clever, and rich, with a comfortable home and happy disposition, seemed to unite some of the best blessings of existence; and had lived nearly twenty-one years in the world with very little to distress or vex her."*

"Excuse me, Mr. North. Will you read that again, please."

I did.

"Who wrote that?"

"Jane Austen."

"Jane Austen. She doesn't know anything about life."

"You find it hard to believe, Mrs. Granberry?"

"Twenty-one!—I wasn't ugly; I wasn't stupid; my father was the richest man in Wisconsin. I had a comfortable home and the disposition of an angel. I lived to the age of twenty-three and *most* of the time was sheer hell. Excuse my language, Mrs. Cummings. The only time when I felt happy was when I was out riding my horse and the four days when I ran away to join the circus. Ask any woman who's honest and she'll tell you the same thing. . . . But I agreed to let you read for a quarter of an hour. I keep my bargains. What comes next?"

I was a little uncomfortable. I remembered that Jane Austen lets us know that any girl with a grain of sense has a rough time in life. I read on. My listener was certainly attentive. When we made the acquaintance of Miss Bates and her mother, she murmured, "Why do people write about old fools? It's a waste of time!" At four thirty-five I looked up and received permission to continue. At six I closed the book and rose.

"Thank you," she said. "Next time start some other book. It's *starting* a book that kills me. Once it's started I can go on by myself. Is it a long book?"

"In this edition, it's in two volumes."

"Leave them here and bring another book next time."

"I'll say good evening, Mrs. Granberry."

I took leave of Mrs. Cummings also, who said in a low voice, "You read lovely. I had to laugh. Was that wrong?"

At the next session Mrs. Granberry was more amiable. For the first time she gave me her hand. "Are all those Austen books about the feeble-minded?"

"It has often been said that she had a fairly low opinion of men and women."

"She should know some people I know.—What's this new one called?"

"*Daisy Miller*. It was written by a man who lived in Newport when he was young."

"In Newport? In *Newport?*"

"Not far from this very house."

"Then why did he write books?"

"I beg your pardon?"

"If he was so rich why did he take the trouble to write books?"

I didn't answer at once. I looked her straight in the eye. She blushed slightly. "Well," I said slowly, "I think he got tired of buying and selling railroads, and building hotels and naming them after his family, and gambling at Saratoga Springs and betting on horses, and sailing his yacht into the same old ports, and going out to dinner and balls, meeting the same people every night. So he said to himself 'Before I die I want some real enjoyment. . . . Damn it!' He said—excuse my language, Mrs. Cummings—'I'm going to write it all down—how people behave in the world. The fat and the thin, the happy and the unhappy.' He wrote and wrote—over forty solid volumes about men, women, and children. When he died the last book—still unfinished on his desk—was a novel laid in Newport, called *The Ivory Tower,* about the emptiness and waste of the life here."

She looked at me, caught between anger and puzzlement. "Mr. North, are you trying to make me look ridiculous?"

"No, ma'am. Mr. Granberry told me that you don't always do justice to yourself—that sometimes out of sheer boredom you say the first thing that comes into your head. As we used to say in Wisconsin, I was just waving a feather under your nose."

She struggled with herself a moment, then directed me to begin. After listening for an hour she said, "Excuse me, but I'm tired today. I'll finish that by myself. I've finished *Emma* so you can take that back. Does it cost much when you take a book from the library?"

"No. They're free."

"*Anybody* can go in and take books home? Don't people steal a lot of them?"

"In winter almost three thousand books go in and out every week. Maybe they miss a few from time to time."

"In *winter!* But there's nobody here in winter."

"Mrs. Granberry, you do not always do yourself justice."

By the end of the second week we had read the openings of *Ethan Frome* (written by a lady who had lived three summers in a cottage nearby), *Jane Eyre, The House of the Seven Gables,* and *David Copperfield.* She made few comments, but the sufferings of young David dismayed her. She was thinking of the son she was expecting. "Of course, they were very poor," she added, as though dismissing the matter. I looked at her fixedly a moment. Again she blushed, recalling that the early years of the daughter of the richest man in Wisconsin had been described as "sheer hell." She stared me down, refusing to concede a fractured logic. I was somewhat in doubt as to whether she had read all those books to the end. I found a moment alone to ask Mrs. Cummings.

"Oh, Mr. North, she reads all the time. She'll ruin her eyes."

"But *you* never learn how the stories turn out."

"She tells me, sir; it's as good as a moving-picture! Jane Eyre! What happened to her! Tell me, sir, was that a true story?"

"You know more about life than I do, Mrs. Cummings. *Could* it be a true story?"

She shook her head sadly. "Oh, Mr. North, I've known worse things."

One day as we were entering upon the long reaches of *Tom Jones,* there was a knock at the door. For the first time we received a call from Mr. Granberry.

"Can I come in?" He kissed his wife, shook hands with me, and greeted Mrs. Cummings. "Well, Myra, how are things going?"

"Very well, darling."

"What are you reading, dear?"

"It's called *Tom Jones.*"

Vague memories of his college education returned to him. He turned to Mrs. Cummings. "Er . . . er . . . is that always suitable for—I mean—a lady's reading?"

"Oh, sir," said Mrs. Cummings from an unshakable professional authority, "if anything unsuitable happened in a book, I'd ask Mr. North to return it to the library at once. The important thing is that Mrs. Granberry is really interested, isn't it? When she's read aloud to she never gets fretful. I don't like it when she gets fretful."

"Well, I'll just sit here for ten minutes. Don't pay any attention to me. Forgive my interrupting you, Mr. North." So Mr. Granberry took a chair in a corner of the room, crossed his long legs, and laid his cheek on his hand, as though he were listening to a burdensome lecture on philosophy back at Dartmouth College. He stayed for a quarter of an hour. Finally he rose with his fingers on his lips and took his leave. Thereafter he returned about once a week, not always able to keep his eyes open. Myra read the whole of *Tom Jones* over a long weekend, but could not be drawn into any comment on it.

On another day, I arrived with *Walden* under my arm.

"Good afternoon, Mr. North. . . . Thank you, I'm very well. . . . Mr. North, you made a rule—the fifteen-minute rule. I want to make a rule too. My rule is that after the first forty-five minutes we take half an hour off for talk."

"As you wish, Mrs. Granberry."

There was an ormolu clock on the table beside her. At a quarter of five she interrupted me. "It is now talking time. What did you mean two weeks ago when you said something about 'the emptiness and waste' of life at Newport?"

"Those were not my words. I was reporting to you what Henry James said."

"In Wisconsin we don't quibble. You said it and you meant it."

"I don't know Newport life well enough to make any judgment about it. I have been here only a few weeks. I have no part in Newport life. I come and go on a bicycle. Most of my students are children."

"Don't quibble with me. You must be twenty-eight years old. You've been to college. You've been in dozens of Newport cottages. You sit up half the night at 'Nine Gables.' You get drunk at the Muenchinger-King bar. Stop running away from my questions."

"Mrs. Granberry—!"

"Don't call me 'ma'am' again and don't call me 'Mrs. Granberry.' Call me 'Myra.' "

I raised my voice. "Mrs. Granberry, I make it a rule that in all the houses where I *work* I use only family names and I wish to be called by my own."

"You and your rules! *We're from Wisconsin.* Don't be an Easterner. Don't be a stuffed owl."

We glared at each other.

Mrs. Cummings said, "Oh, Mr. North, I wish you would make an exception in this case—seeing"—and she gave me a significant glance—"that you are both Badgerers."

"Of course, I shall obey any request from Mrs. Cummings—but in this room only and in her presence only. I have a great admiration for Mrs. Cummings. She is an Easterner and I wish you would apologize to her for having called her a stuffed owl."

"Oh, Mr. North, Mrs. Granberry was just joking. I don't mind at all."

I looked sternly at Myra and waited.

"Cora, I admire you and am deeply indebted to you and I apologize if I have hurt your feelings in any way."

Mrs. Cummings covered her face with her knitting.

"Theophilus, I promise not to interrupt you if you tell us about your life in Newport—your friends, your good times, your enemies, and if you're making any money."

"This is not in my contract and I don't like it, but I shall obey. If I mention any names they will be 'made up' names. I live at the Young Men's Christian Association and am saving up money to rent a small apartment. I do not make friends easily, but to my surprise I have already made several in Newport whom I highly value." I told them about the superintendent at the Casino, about an unoccupied valet named "Eddie" ("who talks just like some of the characters in *David Copperfield*"), about some of my tennis pupils—including a girl named "Anemone" who was just like some of the girls in Shakespeare's plays—and about "Mrs. Willoughby's" boardinghouse for domestic servants. I did full justice to "Mrs. Willoughby's" decorum and generosity. When I came to a close there were tears in Myra's eyes. There was a pause.

"Oh, Cora, I wish I were a maid. I wish I lived at Mrs. Willoughby's. I'd be happy. My baby would be born as simply and sweetly as a . . . as a lamb. Theophilus, couldn't you take Cora and me to Mrs. Willoughby's some night?"

"Oh, Mrs. Granberry," said Cora righteously, "I'm a registered nurse. I'm not allowed to do anything like that."

"You go out to dinner parties with me."

"Yes, I sit upstairs until you are ready to go home."

"Myra," I said quietly, "it wouldn't be possible. Everybody likes to be with his or her own kind."

"I wouldn't talk. I know that just to look at it would be good for my baby."

I nodded and smiled and said, "Conversation time is up."

At the following session's conversation break I asked Myra to give me an account of her friends, her good times, and her enemies. She thought a moment. Her face took on a somber cast.

"Well, I grow older. I wait for my baby. I eat breakfast. Then the doctor calls and asks if I've been good. He gets ten dollars for that. Then if it's a sunny day Cora and I go to Bailey's Beach. We sit well wrapped up in a sheltered corner so as not to have to talk to people. We sit and watch the old boots and orange crates drift by."

"I beg your pardon?"

"My father owns hundreds of lakes. If any one were as dirty as Bailey's Beach he'd drain it and plant it with trees. What do we do then, Cora?"

"You go to luncheon parties, Mrs. Granberry."

"Yes, I go to luncheon parties. Ladies. There are men there only on Sundays, all named Granberry. During the week the ladies stay on and play cards. I'm allowed to go home early for my nap because I'm in an 'interesting condition,' as the lady in *Jane Eyre* was. Then my tutors arrive. Several evenings a week I go out to dinner and see the same people—as your Henry James said. Again I come home early and I read as long as Cora lets me. And I can't think of anything else to tell you."

I turned to Mrs. Cummings. "May we ask what you do in your free time?"

She glanced at me for reassurance. I nodded and maybe I winked at her.

"Well, I have an old friend in Newport. She went through training with me—Miss O'Shaughnessy. She's assistant director of nursing at the hospital. At six o'clock on Thursdays Mrs. Granberry kindly has me driven to the hospital in her car. And Miss O'Shaughnessy and I—and sometimes some friends of hers—go to dinner at a restaurant near the beginning of the Cliff Walk. We tell stories of our training days and, Mr. North—being off duty—we have a little bit of the Old Irish and we laugh. I don't know why it is but mostly nurses laugh when they're off duty. And Sunday mornings four of us go to Mass together. Rain or shine—we like the walk too. But I'm always glad to get back to this house, Mrs. Granberry."

Myra was staring at her. "I know Miss O'Shaughnessy. During my second summer here George let me join the Ladies Volunteer Workers at the hospital. I loved it. I couldn't do it the other summers because the doctor wouldn't let me. I hope Miss O'Shaughnessy remembers me; I hope she liked me. Couldn't I come with you some Thursday night?" There was a silence. "I never see anybody that's fun. I never see anybody I like. I never laugh, do I, Cora?"

"Oh, Mrs. Granberry, you forget! You laugh and you make me laugh. When I go to the kitchen they sometimes ask me, 'What do Mrs. Granberry and you laugh about all the time?' "

"Myra," I said, with a shade of severity, "it wouldn't be any holiday for Mrs. Cummings to have dinner with you on Thursday nights. You have dinner together on many evenings."

"It doesn't have to be Thursday nights. I still have my Volunteer's uniform. Mr. North, will you be so kind as to ring that bell?" A servant appeared. "Please ask Madeleine to bring down my Hospital Volunteer's uniform—and to lay it out in the dressing room down here. I won't want the shoes and stockings, but tell her not to forget the cap. Thank you. You've never seen me in my uniform, Cora.—It wouldn't have to be on a Thursday night. We could go on some other night and have a bit of the Old Irish and laugh. The doctor says that a little whiskey wouldn't be bad for me at all.—Besides, I love being in disguise. Cora, you could call me 'Mrs. Nielson.' Can't we go? Maybe Miss O'Shaughnessy could get an extra leave on another night. My husband's on the Hospital Board; he can do *anything.*"

We talked reassuringly about the project. Myra murmured meditatively, "When you're in disguise you feel more free."

There was a knock at the inner door and a voice said, "The uniform is ready, Mrs. Granberry."

Myra rose saying "I'll only be a minute," and left the room.

Mrs. Cummings confided to me. "The doctor says we're to let her do anything she wants within reason. Poor child! Poor child!"

We waited. Presently she returned smiling, downright radiant, *free,* in that uniform, in that cap. We clapped our hands.

"I am *Miss* Nielson," she said. She leaned over Mrs. Cummings and asked soothingly, "Where does it hurt, dear? . . . Oh, that's just wind. You must expect that after an operation. It's a sign that all's going well. Your appendix will never trouble you again." She resumed her place on the chaise-longue. "I'd have been happy as a nurse, I know I would.—Mr. North, let's not read any more today. Let's just talk."

"Very well. What shall we talk about?"

"Anything."

"Myra, why do you never make any comment on these novels we've been reading?"

She blushed slightly. "Because . . . you'd make fun of me. You wouldn't understand. They're all so new to me—*those lives, those people.* Sometimes they're more real than life. I don't want to talk about them. Please talk about something else."

"Very well. Are you fond of music, Myra?"

"Concerts? Heaven help us! In New York we go Thursday nights to the opera. The German ones are the longest."

"The theater?"

"No. I went a few times. It's all 'made up.' It's not at all like the novels; *they're* real. Why are you asking me these questions?"

I paused a moment. What was I doing in that house? I told my-self that I was earning twelve dollars a week (though my fort-nightly bills had not yet been paid); that I derived some satisfaction from introducing a bright but inadequately educated young woman to good reading—a pastime to render less painful her husband's neglect. But I was discouraged—as I was with others I worked with on the Avenue—by association with those who had more than their share of the disadvantages of their advantages.

She had asked me why I asked her those questions.

"Because, Myra, there is a theory that expectant mothers can prepare themselves to bear beautiful well-conditioned children by listening to beautiful music and gazing at beautiful objects."

"Who says that?"

"It's widely held. Italian mothers believe it especially, and everyone can see that their boys and girls look as though they had stepped out of those famous Italian paintings."

"Are there any in Newport—those paintings?"

"Not that I know of—except in books."

She was sitting up straight and looking at me fixedly. "Cora, have you ever heard of such an idea?"

"Oh, Mrs. Granberry! Doctors are always urging ladies in this condition to have lovely thoughts—oh, yes."

Myra continued to stare at me almost angrily. "Well, don't just sit there like a stick. Tell me what I can do."

"Please lie down and shut your eyes and let me talk to you." She looked about her as though annoyed and then did as I re-quested. "Myra, Newport is often said to be one of the most beautiful towns in this country. You drive up and down Bellevue Avenue and pay visits in the cottages of your friends. You go to Bailey's Beach and you have told me what you think of it. Do you often take the ten-mile drive?"

"It's too long. If you've seen one mile you've seen them all."

"The architecture of the so-called cottages is the laughing-stock of the nation. They are preposterous. There are only three that can be said to be truly beautiful. . . . Now let me tell you my idea of Newport." So I told her about the trees and—at considerable length—about the Nine Cities of Troy and the Nine Cities of Newport. Mrs. Cummings let her knitting fall to her lap, motionless. "Moreover, the view of the sea and the bay from the Budlong place, five miles from here, is one of which you could never grow tired—at dawn, at noon, at dusk, under the stars, and not least, in wind and rain. There you can see the circling beams of six lighthouses that give security to sailors and hear the voice of many buoys saying, 'Steer clear of these rocks and you will have a safe journey.' All of Newport is interesting in one way or another; the least so is the Sixth City."

"You mean *here?*"

"And the most interesting and beautiful is the Second."

"I forget which that is."

"That of the eighteenth century. I'll leave a marked map for your driver. Now can we go back to *Walden?*"

She put her hand to her forehead. "I'm tired today. Will you excuse me, if I ask you to leave now? I want to think. We'll pay you just the same. . . . But stop! Before you go write down the names of those painters in Italy that help make beautiful children, and some pieces of music that are good for that too."

I wrote down: "Raphael. Da Vinci. Fra Angelico," and added an address in New York where the best prints could be obtained. Then: "Gramophone records by Mozart: *Eine Kleine Nachtmusik. Ave, verum corpus.*"

There was a knock at the door. Mr. Granberry entered. Greetings.

"How's my dear little squirrel today?"

"Very well, thank you."

"What are you reading now?"

"*Walden.*"

"*Walden,* oh, yes—*Walden.* Well, that wouldn't interest us much, I think."

"Why not, George?"

He pinched her cheek. "We wouldn't be happy on thirty cents a day."

"I like it. It's the first book I want to read all through in class. George, this is a list of all the books I've read. I want you to buy every one of them for me. Mr. North has to go and get them at the People's Library. They're not very clean and people have written silly things in the margins. I want my own books so that I can write my own silly things in the margins."

"I'll see to that, Myra. My secretary will send for them tomorrow morning. Is there anything else I can do for you?"

"Here are the names of some painters who lived in Italy. If you want to be an angel, you can buy me some pictures by them."

He gasped. "Why, Myra, any pictures by one of these men would cost a hundred thousand dollars."

"Well, you pay more than that for those boats you never use, don't you? You can buy me one and Papa will buy me another. Here's the name of a man who wrote some good music. Please buy me the best gramophone that you can find and those records. . . . I'm a little tired today and I've just asked Mr. North to cut short the reading. I told him we'd pay him just the same . . . but don't *you* go."

Then something very painful happened.

Two days later I was met at the door, as usual, by the butler, Carel, a Czech—as distinguished in appearance as an ambassador but as self-effacing as an ambassador's personal secretary. He bent his head and whispered, "Mrs. Cummings wishes to speak to you here, sir, before you enter the morning room."

"I'll wait here, Carel."

Carel and Mrs. Cummings must have arranged some system of coded signals, for she appeared in the hall. She spoke hurriedly. "Mrs. Granberry received two letters this morning which have upset her *badly*. I think she wants to tell you about them. She wouldn't go for a drive. She has scarcely said a dozen words to me. When you leave, please tell Carel anything I should know. Wait three minutes before you knock on the door." She pressed my hand and returned to the morning room.

I waited three minutes and knocked on the door. It was opened by Mrs. Cummings.

"Good afternoon, ladies," I said buoyantly.

Myra's face was very stern. "Cora, I have something that I must discuss with Mr. North and I must ask you to leave the room for five minutes."

"Oh, Mrs. Granberry, you mustn't ask me to do that. I'm an R.N. and I must obey every word of the doctor's orders."

"All I ask is that you go out on the verandah. You can leave the door ajar, but you must not try to hear a single word."

"I don't like it at all; oh, I don't like it at all."

"Mrs. Cummings," I said, "since this seems to be an important matter to Mrs. Granberry I shall stand by the verandah door where you can see me every minute. If any subject arises that has to do with medical matters I shall *insist* on repeating it to you."

When Mrs. Cummings had withdrawn to a distance I stood waiting like a sentry.

"Theophilus, Badgers always tell the truth to Badgers."

"Myra, I am my own judge of what truths I shall tell. The truth can do just as much harm as a lie."

"I need help."

"Ask me some questions and I shall try to help you so far as I am able."

"Do you know a woman named Flora Deland?"

"I have dined at her house at Narragansett Pier three times."

"Do you know a woman named Desmoulins?"

"I have met her at dinner there once and I have met her by chance on the street in Newport once."

"Is she a harlot and a strumpet and that other thing in *Tom Jones*—a doxy?"

"No, indeed. She is a woman of some refinement. She is what some people would call an 'emancipated' woman. I would never think of applying those ugly words to her."

" 'Emancipate' means to free the slaves. Was she a slave?"

I laughed as cheerily as I could. "Oh, no.—Now stop this nonsense and tell me what you are trying to get at."

"Is she better-looking than I am?"

"No."

"Badger?"

"Badger!"

"BADGER?"

"BADGER!—She is a very pretty woman. You are a very beautiful woman. I'll go and call Mrs. Cummings."

"Stop!—Have you had dinner almost every Thursday night with my husband and Miss Desmoulins at the Muenchinger-King?"

"No. *Never.* Please get to the point."

"I have received two an-anonny-mous letters."

"Myra! You tore them up at once."

"No." She lifted a book on the table and revealed two envelopes.

"I'm ashamed of you. . . . In the world—and especially in a place like Newport—we are surrounded by people whose heads are filled with hate and envy and nastiness. Once in a while one of them takes to writing anonymous letters. They say it comes and goes in epidemics, like influenza. You should have torn them into small pieces—unread—and put them out of your mind. Do they say that I had dinner with those two persons at the M-K?"

"Yes."

"Well, that's a sample of the lies that fill anonymous letters."

"Read them. Please read them."

I debated with myself: "Hell, I'm resigning from this job tonight anyway."

I studied the envelopes carefully. Then I glanced through the contents; I can read fast. When I came to the end of the second

I burst out laughing. "Myra, all anonymous letters are signed either by 'A Friend' or 'Your Well-Wisher.' " She burst into tears. "Myra, no Badger cries after the age of eleven."

"I'm sorry."

"Years ago, Badger, I planned to make my life-career that of being a detective. When boys are ambitious they really are ambitious. I read all the professional handbooks about it—hard, tough books of instruction. And I remember that the tracing down of anonymous letter writers was an important section. We were taught that there are twenty-one 'give-away' clues to every anonymous letter. Give me these letters and in two weeks I'll find the writer and drive him—or her—out of town."

"But, Theophilus, maybe *him* or *her* is right. Maybe my husband loves Miss Desmoulins. Maybe my baby has no father any more. Then I might as well die. Because I love my husband more than anything else in the world."

"Badgers don't cry, Myra—they fight. They're smart, they're brave, and they defend what they've got. They also have something that I find missing in you."

She looked at me, appalled. "What?"

"They're like otters. They have a sense of fun and laughter and *wicked tricks.*"

"But, Theophilus, I've always had them too. But lately I've had so much illness and lonesomeness and boredom. Believe me, my father used to call me his 'little devil.' Oh, Theophilus, put your arm around me one minute."

Laughingly I squeezed her hand hard and said, "Not one second! —Now promise me that you'll put this whole wretched business out of your head for a week. . . . Badgers always catch the snake. Can I call Mrs. Cummings now? . . . Mrs. Cummings, it's school time. Mrs. Cummings, you're a wonderful friend and you should know what we talked about. Mrs. Granberry heard an ugly bit of gossip. I told her that no one who's intelligent and beautiful and rich has ever escaped gossip. Aren't I right?"

"Oh, Mr. North, you're very right."

Naturally that about the twenty-one clues was sheer kite-flying. In my hasty glance at the letter I read that Mr. Granberry entertained Mlle. Desmoulins at dinner in one of the small dining rooms at the Muenchinger-King every Thursday night. It went on to tell of Flora Deland's dinners, mentioned myself, bloodwarmingly, as an "odious person," then rambled on in a grieved self-righteous way. I judged that they had been written by a woman, some former friend of George Granberry, that unoccupied planless inventor— perhaps by a Granberry. I returned to our classroom work as though nothing had intervened to upset it. We read *Walden*.

I needed help—that is to say, I needed to know more.

I arranged to meet Henry for a pool game at Herman's. During an interval I asked him if he knew George F. Granberry. He was chalking his cue thoughtfully and said, "Funny, your asking me that," and went on with the game. When the set was over we paid up and withdrew to a corner and ordered our usual.

"I don't like to mention names. We'll call the party Longears. Choppers, under idleness all men and women become children again. Women cope with it better than men, but all men become babies. Look at me: when my Chief's away I have to fight it every minute. Fortunately, just now I'm busy. Edweena and I are exchanging letters and making plans. We're the Governors of the Servants' Ball at the end of the season and that takes a lot of hard work. . . . Longears belongs to a very large family. He could get a job any minute in the family's firm, but it's stuffed already with a dozen members of the same name, all of them brighter than he is. They don't want him. He doesn't need the money. Before the War there were scores of young and middle-aged men like him in New York and Newport, rich, and idle as tailors' dummies. In 1926 you can count 'em on one hand. When I arrived here he was already a divorced man—so maybe the blight had set in early. Everybody said he used to be intelligent and popular. For some reason he couldn't get into the War. He married again—a girl from the Wild West, like Tennessee or Buffalo. She has poor health. Nobody sees her much. Men like that take to drink or women or gambling. A few take to boasting, to setting themselves up as some kind of superior person—something special. Longears pretends that he's an inventor. He has a workshop out in Portsmouth—very secret, very important. Rumors—some say he's making bread out of seaweed or making gasoline out of manure. Anyway, he *hides* there. Some people say that he doesn't do anything more than play with electric trains or stick postage stamps into his collection. . . . Used to be a fine fellow. He was my Chief's best friend, but now my Chief just wags his head when he's mentioned."

"Was it the divorce that broke him up?"

"I wouldn't know. I think it's merely nothing-to-do. Idleness is dry rot. . . . He has a girl hidden in the bushes here somewhere— he's not the only one who does that, of course. . . . That's all I know."

At the next session I appeared with a satchel under my arm. Among the books it contained were three school editions of *Twelfth Night* and three of *As You Like It*. I had worked for hours on them, selecting scenes for group reading. "Good afternoon, ladies. Today we are going to try something new." I drew out the copies of *Twelfth Night*.

"Oh, Theophilus—not Shakespeare! *Please!*"

"You dislike his work?" I asked in hypocritical wonder. I began cramming the copies back into the satchel. "That surprises me, but you remember we agreed at our first meeting that we'd not read anything that bored you. Excuse me! My mistake is due to my inexperience. Hitherto I've tutored only boys and young men. After a short resistance I'd found that they take to Shakespeare enthusiastically. I've had them striding up and down my classroom pretending to be Romeo and Juliet and Shylock and Portia— eating it up! . . . I remember now how surprised I was when Mr. Granberry also said that he had always thought Shakespeare to be 'piffle.' Well, I have another novel here to try."

Myra was staring at me. "Wait a minute! . . . But his plays are so childish. All those girls dressing up in men's clothes. It's idiotic!"

"Yes, a few of them. But notice how Shakespeare has arranged it. The girls have to do so because they're destitute; their backs are against the wall. Viola is shipwrecked in a foreign country; Rosalind is exiled—thrown out into the wilderness; Imogen has been slandered in her husband's absence. Portia dresses like a lawyer to save the life of her husband's best friend. In those days a self-respecting girl couldn't go from door to door asking for a job. . . . Let's forget it! . . . But what girls they are: beautiful, brave, intelligent, resourceful! In addition, I've always felt they have a quality that I've found . . . a little . . . missing in you, Myra."

"What's that?"

"A humorous mind."

"A *what?*"

"I don't know exactly what I mean, but I get the impression that they've observed life so attentively—young though they are—that they don't shrink from the real; they're never crushed or shocked or at their wit's end. Even when the big catastrophe comes their minds are so deeply grounded that they can face it with humor and gaiety. When Rosalind is driven out into that dangerous wilderness she says to her cousin Celia:

> Now go we in content
> To liberty, and not to banishment.

I wish I'd heard Ellen Terry say that; and soon after Viola had lost her brother in that shipwreck someone asks her about her family and she—dressed as a boy and now called Cesario—says:

> I am all the daughters of my father's house,
> And all the brothers too.

I wish I'd heard Julia Marlowe say that."

Myra asked me harshly, "What good does it do you—this famous 'humorous mind'?"

"Shakespeare places these clear-eyed girls among a lot of people who are in an incorrect relation to the real. As a later author said, 'Most of the people in the world are fools and the rest of us are in great danger of contagion.' A humorous mind enables us to accommodate ourselves to their folly—and to our own.—Do you think there's something in that, Mrs. Cummings?"

"Oh, Mr. North, I think that's why nurses laugh when they're off duty. It helps us—like you might say—to survive."

Myra was staring at me without seeing me.

Mrs. Cummings asked, "Mrs. Granberry, can't we ask Mr. North to read to us a little out of Shakespeare?"

"Well . . . if it's not too long."

I put my hand tentatively into the satchel. "My idea was that we all take parts. I've underlined Myra's part in red, and Mrs. Cummings's in blue, and I'll read the rest."

"Oh," cried Mrs. Cummings, "I can't read poetry-English. I couldn't do that. You've got to excuse me."

"Cora, if that's the way Mr. North wants it, I suppose we must let him have his way."

"God bless my soul!"

"Now slowly, everybody—*slowly!*"

Within the week we had done scenes from those plays—and repeated them, switching roles—and the balcony scene from *Romeo and Juliet* and the trial scene from *The Merchant of Venice*. Mrs. Cummings astonished herself as Shylock. It was Myra who, at the end of each scene, said, "Now let's do it again!"

One afternoon Myra greeted me at the door with an air of suppressed excitement. "Theophilus, I asked my husband to come here at four-thirty. We're going to do the trial scene from *The Merchant of Venice* and I'm going to make him play Shylock. You be Antonio, I'll be Portia, and Cora will be everybody else. Let's rehearse it once before he comes. Cora, I want you to be splendid as the Duke."

"Oh, Mrs. Granberry!"

We put our hearts into it. *Myra had memorized her lines.*

A knock on the door: enter George F. Granberry II. Myra was silken. "George darling, we want you to help us. Please don't say no because it would make me very unhappy."

"What can I do?"

She put the open book in his hands. "George, you must read Shylock. Go very slowly and be very bloodthirsty. Sharpen the knife on your shoe. Mr. North is going to lean backward over that desk with his chest exposed and his hands tied behind him."

"Now, Myra, that's enough! I'm no actor."

"Oh, George! It's just a game. We'll do it twice so you'll get the hang of it, and *go slowly.*"

We started off haltingly, groping for our words on the page. As Shylock leaned over me, an ivory paper-cutter in his hand, he said under his voice, "North, I'd like to cut out your gizzard. Something's going on here that I don't like. You've fouled up the whole air around here."

"You engaged me to interest your wife in reading and especially in Shakespeare. I've done that and I'm ready to resign when you pay the three two-week bills I've sent you."

That took his breath away.

During the first rehearsal Myra had made a show of reading indifferently and stumbling over her words. On the second time around we played for all we were worth. Myra laid aside her book; at first she represented the young lawyer Balthasar with a slight playful swagger, but she grew in authority speech after speech.

George was caught up into the spirit of the thing. He roared for his "bond" and his pound of flesh. Again he leaned over me, savagely, knife in hand. Then something extraordinary took place.

PORTIA: *Do you confess the bond?*
ANTONIO: *I do.*
PORTIA: *Then must the Jew be merciful.*
SHYLOCK: *On what compulsion must I? Tell me that!*

Here George felt a hand rest on his shoulder and heard behind him a voice saying—gravely, earnestly, from some realm of maturity that had been long absent from his life:

PORTIA: *The quality of mercy is not strained,*
            It droppeth like the gentle rain . . .
            . . . We do pray for mercy;
            And that same prayer doth teach us all to render
            The deeds of mercy. . . .

George straightened up and threw down the ivory knife. He said confusedly, "Go on with your reading. I'll see you . . . another time," and he left the room.

We looked at one another surprised and a little guilty. Mrs. Cummings took up her sewing. "Mr. North, play-acting is a little too exciting for us all. I haven't said much about it, but Mrs. Granberry always stands up and moves about the room. I don't think the doctor would like that. We haven't had a talk-time lately. You told Mrs. Granberry you'd tell her sometime what it was like when you went to school in China."

I vowed that I'd send in my resignation that night—before I was fired—but I didn't and I wasn't. I was more than half in love with Myra. I was proud of her and proud of my work. A check arrived for me in Monday morning's mail. We began *Huckleberry Finn.* On Friday another surprising thing happened. I bicycled up to the portal of the house. I saw a young man of about twenty-four strolling on the lawn, smelling a long-stemmed rose. He was dressed in the height of fashion—straw hat, blazer of the Newport Yacht Club, flannels, and white shoes. He approached me and put out his hand.

"Mr. North, I believe. I am Caesar Nielson, the twin brother of Myra Granberry. *How* d'you do?"

Zounds! Holy cabooses! It was Myra.

God, how I hate transvestism! I shuddered; but never contradict a pregnant woman.

"Is your sister at home, Mr. Nielson?"

"We've ordered the car. We thought it would be nice to drive to Narragansett Pier and ask your friend Mademoiselle Desmoulins for a cup of tea."

"Sir, you forget that I am employed here to read English literature with Mrs. Granberry. I am only here under the conditions of my contract. Will you excuse me? I don't wish to be late for my appointment.—Would you like to join us?"

I looked up at the house and saw Mrs. Cummings and Carel, stricken, watching us from the drawing-room windows. Faces were similarly framed in many windows of the upper floors.

Myra came nearer to me and murmured, "Badgers fight to defend what they've got."

"Yes, but since nature made them small she made them clever. No well-conditioned badger or woman destroys her home to preserve it. Please precede me, Mr. Nielson."

She entered the house disturbed, but chin up. As I followed her through the hall Carel said to me in a low voice, "Mr. Granberry has been in the house for half an hour, sir. He returned by the coachhouse drive."

"Do you think he saw the show?"

"I'm sure he did, sir."

"Thank you, Carel."

"Thank you, sir."

I followed Myra and Mrs. Cummings into the morning room. "Myra, please change your clothes quickly. Mr. Granberry is in the house and will probably be here in a few minutes. He will probably dismiss Mrs. Cummings and me, and your next few months will be very dreary indeed."

"Shakespeare's girls did it."

"Please leave the door of your dressing room open two inches so that I can talk to you while you are changing your clothes.— Can you hear me?"

But we were too late. Mr. Granberry entered the room without knocking. "Myra!" he called. She appeared at the door, still Caesar Nielson. She returned his angry gaze unabashed.

"Pants!" he said, "PANTS!"

"I'm an emancipated woman like Miss Desmoulins."

"Mrs. Cummings, you are leaving the house as soon as you can pack. Mr. North, will you follow me into the library?"

I bowed low to the ladies, opening my eyes wide in smiling admiration.

In the library Mr. Granberry was seated behind the desk like a judge. I sat down and crossed my legs composedly.

"You broke your promise to me. You told my wife about Narragansett Pier."

"Your wife told me about Narragansett Pier. She had received two anonymous letters."

He blanched. "You should have told me that."

"I was engaged by you to be a reader of English literature, not a confidential friend of the family."

Silence.

"You're the biggest nuisance in town. Everybody's talking about the hell you kicked up among the Bosworths at 'Nine Gables.' And Heaven knows what's going on at the Wyckoff place. I'm sorry I called you in.—God, I hate Yale men!"

Silence.

"Mr. Granberry, I hate injustice and I think you do too."

"What's that got to do with it?"

"If you dismiss Mrs. Cummings as incompetent in her profession, by God, I shall write a letter to the doctor or to whatever agency sent her telling them what I found here."

"That's blackmail."

"No, that is a deposition in a suit for slander. Mrs. Cummings is obviously a superior trained nurse. In addition—as far as I can see—she has been your wife's only friend and support in a difficult time." I put a slight emphasis on the word "only."

Another silence.

He looked at me somberly. "What do you suggest I do?"

"I seldom offer advice, Mr. Granberry. I don't know enough."

"Stop hammering that 'Mr. Granberry.' Since we hate each other I suggest we use first names. I'm told that you are called Teddie."

"Thank you. I don't give advice, George, but I think it would help you if you just talked to me at random about the whole situation."

"God damn it, I can't live like a monk half a year *again,* just because my wife's under doctor's care. I know a pack of men who have someone like Denise in the woods. What did I do wrong? Denise was a friend of a friend of mine; he passed her over to me. Denise is a nice girl. The only trouble with her is that she cries half the time. French people have to go back to France every two years or they expire like fish on ice. She misses her mother, she says. She misses the smell of the Paris streets—imagine that! . . . All right, I know what you're thinking. I'll give her a pack of Granberry stock and send her back to Paris. But what the hell will I do here? *Play Shakespeare all day?* . . . Well, say something. Don't just sit there like an ox. Jesus!"

"I'm trying to get some ideas. Please go on talking a little longer, George."

Silence.

"You think I neglect Myra. I do and I know I do. Do you know why? I . . . I . . . How old are you?"

"Thirty."

"Married? Ever been married?"

"No."

"I can't stand being loved—loved?—worshiped! Overestimation freezes me. My mother overestimated me and I haven't said a sincere word to her since I was fifteen years old. And now Myra! She suffers and I know she suffers. I wasn't lying to you when I told you I loved her. Wasn't I right when I told you she was intelligent and all that?"

"Yes."

"And suffers all the time . . . four years of suffering and I'm the only person she gives a damn about. I can't stand it. I can't stand the responsibility. When I come into her presence I freeze. Teddie, can you understand that?"

"Can I ask you a question?"

"Go ahead. I'm numb anyway."

"George, what do you do in the laboratory all day?"

He rose, threw me an angry glance, sauntered about the room, then placed his hands on the lintel above the door into the hall and hung there—as boys with their excess energy do (and to hide their faces).

"Well," he said, "I'll tell you. The principal reason is to hide myself. To wait for something, to wait for things to get worse or to get better. 'What I do' is to play war-games. Since I was a boy I've played with tin soldiers. I wasn't able to get into war service because of some malfunction of the heart. . . . I have dozens of books; I do the Battle of the Marne, and the whole lot. . . . I do Napoleon's and Caesar's battles. . . . You're famous around here for keeping secrets, so please keep that secret."

Tears filled my eyes and I smiled. "And soon you'll have to face another ordeal. In about three years a little girl or a little boy is going to come into the room and say, 'Papa, I fell down and hurt myself. Look't, Papa, look't!' and someone else will love you. All love is overestimation."

"Make it a girl, professor; I couldn't stand a boy."

"I see your next step, George. Learn to accept love—with a smile, with a grin."

"Oh, God!"

"Can I be a fool and give a piece of advice?"

"Keep it short."

"Go down the hall into the morning room. Stand up straight in the door and say, 'I'm sending Mademoiselle Desmoulins back to France with a nice goodbye present.' Then go and get down on one knee by the chaise-longue and say, 'Forgive me, Myra.' Then look

Mrs. Cummings in the eye and say, 'Forgive me, Mrs. Cummings.' Women won't forgive us for ever and ever, but they love to forgive us when we ask them to."

"You mean that I should do that now?"

"Oh, yes—now.—And, by the way, ask her to dinner Thursday night at the Muenchinger-King."

He left the room.

As I went out the front door I shook hands with Carel. "This is the last time I shall be in this house. If you have an opportunity, could you express to Mrs. Granberry and Mrs. Cummings my admiration . . . and affection? Thank you, Carel."

"Thank you, sir."

Mino

At the bottom of Broadway, at a corner of Washington Square and across the street from Old Colony House, there stood a store that I visited daily. It sold newspapers, magazines, picture postcards, maps for tourists, toys for children, and even Butterick patterns. It was very Ninth City. It was run by one family, the Materas—father, mother, son, and daughter took turns serving the public. I was to learn that their name was far more complicated; when the parents emigrated to America they adopted the name of their birthplace to simplify the formalities at Ellis Island. They came from the desolate impoverished part of the instep of Italy's boot that the government of Rome and—as we are told in Carlo Levi's fine book *Cristo si è fermato a Eboli*—God forgot. The title does not mean that Christ stopped at Eboli to enjoy the environs, but that in despair He went no further.

I love Italians. My friendship with the Materas began with my attempts to ingratiate myself by speaking their language, however haltingly. I barely made myself understood. I then tried the Neapolitan dialect even more haltingly (yet how I relished it!), but the dialects of Lucania are impenetrable to the outsider. We conversed in English.

High among the glories of Italy are the mothers of Italy. Their whole self is delivered over to husband and children. Through sheer selflessness they become wonderful selves. Maternal love there has no element of possessiveness; it is a hearth-fire of astonished wonder, ever renewed, that those lives are bound up with their own. It can be just as dangerous for the growing girl and especially the growing boy as devouring maternal love—so often prevalent in other parts of the world—can be; for what young person can wish to break away from the warmth and support of all that devotion, laughter, and cooking?

Mamma had love and laughter to spare. I stopped in at the store daily to buy my New York paper, and pencils, ink, or other incidentals. I bowed to the parents with due deference and to the children with comradely liveliness and before long came within the orbit of Signora Carla's generous heart. The Materas were of a dark complexion (the Saracen invaders of Calabria). Rosa, twenty-four, seemed to be unaware that some might regard her as plain; helping her parents and brother was quite sufficient to fill her life with buoyancy. Benjy, twenty-two—when it was his turn to mind the store—sat cross-legged on a shelf beside the cash register. All spoke English, but all non-Italian names seemed equally unpronounceable to Signora Matera; the only ones she knew well (and revered) were "Presidente Vilson" and "Generale Perchin." Except very occasionally I am not going to attempt to reproduce the *signora's* pronunciation. After a certain time we cease to notice a valued foreigner's "accent"; the communications of friendship transcend the accidents of language.

One late afternoon I returned to the "Y" and was informed by the desk clerk that a lady was waiting for me in the little reception room off the lobby. What was my surprise to discover Signora Matera sitting majestically at ease, with a six-weeks-old clipping of my newspaper advertisement in her hand. I greeted her delightedly.

She was amazed. She waved the clipping. "*You . . .you* are Mr. Nort'?"

"Yes, *signora*. I thought you knew my name."

She repeated with heart-felt relief: "*You* are Mr. Nort'!"

"Yes, *cara signora*. What can I do for you?"

"I come for Benjamino and myself. Benjamino wants to take lessons with you. He wants to study Dante with you. He makes money; he can pay you very well. He wants to read Dante with you for eight hours—that is sixteen dollars. You *know* Benjamino?"

"Yes, indeed, I know Benjamino. I see him almost every day in your store and I often see him at the People's Library where he is surrounded by dozens of books. But, of course, we are not allowed to talk in the library. Tell me about him. Why is he always up in one place by the cash register?"

"You did not know he is a cripple? He has no feet."

"No, *signora,* I did not know that."

"When he was five he ran into a train and lost his feet."

Her memory of that terrible occasion was all in her eyes and I met it; but she had lived so many days since in wondering astonishment and love of her son that the grief had been transmuted into what she was about to tell me. "Benjy is a very bright boy. He wins prizes every week. He does all the puzzles in the papers. You know how many papers and magazines we have. He wins all the contests in the advertisements. Checks come in the mail every week, five dollars, ten dollars, once twenty dollars. He wins clocks, bicycles, big cases of dog food. He won a trip to Washington, D.C.; when he told them he was a cripple they sent him the money. But that is not all." She pointed to her forehead. "He is very smart. He makes up puzzles for the papers. Papers in Boston and New York pay him to send them puzzles—arithmetic puzzles, joke puzzles, chess puzzles. And now something new has happened. He has invented a new kind of puzzle. I do not understand it. He makes patterns of words that go up and down. *Sindacatos* want to buy them for the Sunday papers.—Why do they call them *sindacatos*, Mr. Nort'?"

"I don't know." (To her, *sindaco* meant a mayor or town magis-
trate.)

"How much schooling has he had, *signora?*"

"He went through grammar school—always top of his class. But
the High School has stone steps. He goes to school in his little
wagon, but he did not want the boys to carry him up and down
those big steps twenty times a day. The boys like him very much;
everybody loves Benjy. But he is very independent. Do you know
what he did? He wrote to the Department of Education at Providence to send him the lessons and examinations that they have
for students in hospitals—for TB students and paralyzed students.
And he passed High School, top of his class. They send him a
diploma with a note from the Governor!"

"Wonderful!"

"Yes, God is good to us!" she said and burst out laughing. She
had long steeled herself not to weep, but one has to do something.

"Does Benjamino want to go to college?"

"No. He says he can do studies by himself now."

"Why does he want to read Dante?"

"Mr. Nort', I think he has played a trick on me. I think he knew
all the time that you were the Mr. Nort' in this advertisement. I
think he liked the way you talked to him. He has many friends—
school friends, teachers, his priest; but he says they all talk to him
as if he were a cripple. I think he thought you knew he had no
feet, but you did not talk to him as if he were a cripple. The others
pat him on the back and make loud jokes. He says they don't talk
to him *natural*. Maybe you talked to him natural." She lowered her
voice. "Please do not tell him that you did *not* know he had this
trouble."

"I won't."

"Maybe he wants to learn what Dante says about people who've
had accidents—about why God sends accidents to some people and
not to other people."

"*Signora,* tell Benjamino that I am not a Dante scholar. The
study of Dante is a vast subject to which hundreds of men have

devoted a whole lifetime. Dante is full of theology—*full* of it. I know very little theology. I'd be ashamed. A brilliant boy like your son would ask me questions every minute that I couldn't answer."

Signora Matera looked stricken. I can't endure calling forth a stricken look on an Italian mother's face.

"*Signora,* what time do you all go to church on Sunday?"

"The seven o'clock Mass. We have to sell the Sunday papers at eight-thirty."

"I have a Sunday morning appointment at a quarter before eleven. Would it be inconvenient if I came and sat with Benjamino at nine o'clock?"

"*Grazie! Grazie!*"

"No lesson. No money. Just talk."

I was punctual. The store was filled with customers buying their Boston or Providence Sunday papers. Rosa slipped out of line and led me through the door connecting the store with the house. Finger on her lip, she pointed to the door of her brother's room. I knocked.

"Come in, please."

His room was as small and neat as a ship's cabin. He was sitting cross-legged on some pillows at the head of his bed. He was wearing a trim sea-captain's coat with silver buttons. Across his knees was a drawing-board; this was also his workroom. A carpenter had built shelves on three sides of the room, including those at his right and left within reach of his long arms. I saw dictionaries and other works of reference and piles of paper ruled with grid lines for the making of puzzles. Benjy was a very handsome fellow, his large head covered with curly brown hair and his face lit up by his Saracen-Italian eyes and the Matera smile. But for his accident he would have been an unusually tall man. His level gaze and deep bass voice gave the impression of his being older than he was. For me there was an armchair at the foot of the bed.

"*Buon giorno, Benjamino!*"

"*Buon giorno, professore!*"

"Are you disappointed that we aren't going to read Dante?" He made no answer, but continued smiling. "I thought of Dante yesterday morning. I drove out to Brenton's Point on my bicycle to see the sunrise. And

> *L'alba vinceva l'ora mattutina,*
> *che fuggía innanzi, sì che di lontano*
> *conobbi il tremolar della marina.*

Do you know where Dante says that?"

"At the beginning of the *Purgatorio*."

I was taken aback. "Benjamino, everybody around here calls you Benjy. That sounds a little too street-corner and ordinary for you. May I have your permission to call you Mino?" He nodded. "Do you know of anyone else who was called Mino?"

"Mino da Fiesole."

"What was 'Mino' probably short for in that case?"

"Maybe Giacomino—or Benjamino."

"Do you know what Benjamin means in Hebrew?"

" 'Son of the right hand.' "

"Mino, this is beginning to sound like a classroom examination. We must stop that. But I do want to go back to Dante for a moment. Did you ever take the trouble to learn any passages in Dante by heart?"

The reader may think this was reprehensible on my part, but one of the rewards of being a teacher is watching a brilliant student display his knowledge. It is like putting a promising young racehorse through his paces. A good student enjoys it.

Mino said, "Not very much—just the famous passages, like Paolo and Francesca or La Pia and some others."

"When Count Ugolino was locked up in the Tower of Famine with his sons and grandsons, without food, and days and days went by—what do you think that much-disputed verse means: *'Poscia, più che 'l dolor, potè il digiuno'?*" Mino gazed at me in silence. "How would you translate it?"

" 'Then . . . hunger . . . had more power than . . . grief.' "

"What do you think we are to understand?"

"He . . . ate them."

"Many distinguished scholars, especially in the last century, think it means 'I died of hunger which was even stronger than my grief.' What makes you think as you do?"

Suddenly his expression became one of passionate intensity. "Because the whole passage is full of *that*. The son says to his father, 'You gave us this flesh; now take it back!' And all the time he is talking—in all that ice at the bottom of Hell—he is gnawing the back of his enemy's neck."

"I think you're right, Mino. The nineteenth-century scholars refused to face the cruel truth. The *Divine Comedy* was translated in Cambridge, Massachusetts, by Charles Eliot Norton and again by Henry Wadsworth Longfellow—with notes—and by Thomas Carlyle's brother in London; they refused to see it as you do. It should teach us that Anglo-Saxons and Protestants have always misunderstood your country. They've wanted the sweetness without the iron—without the famous Italian *terribilità*. Evasion, shrinking from the whole of life. Haven't you found people pretending that you never had an accident?"

He gazed at me earnestly, but made no answer. I smiled. He smiled. I laughed. He laughed.

"Mino, what do you miss most because of the accident to your feet?"

"That I can't go to dances." He blushed. We both burst out laughing.

"If you'd lost your eyesight, what would you have missed most?"

He thought a minute and replied, "Seeing faces."

"Not reading?"

"There are substitutes for reading; there are no substitutes for not seeing faces."

"Damn it, Mino! Your mother was right. It's too bad about your feet, but you're certainly all right in the upper story."

Now, reader, I know what he wanted to talk about, you know

what he most wanted to talk about (at two dollars an hour), and I suspect that his mother knew what he most wanted to talk about —there had been a certain emphasis in her report of his complaint that the boys and men he knew did not talk to him "natural." By what appears to be a coincidence (but the older I grow, the less surprised I am by what are called coincidences) I came to this interview with Mino prepared—armed—with a certain amount of experience acquired five years previously.

The following recall of this experience in 1921 is no idle digression:

When I was discharged from the Army (having defended, un-opposed, this very same Narragansett Bay) I returned to continue my education; then I got a job teaching at the Raritan School in New Jersey. In those days at no great distance from the school there was a veterans' hospital for amputees and paraplegics. The hospital had a hard-worked staff of nurses and recreation directors. Ladies in the neighboring towns volunteered their services in the latter department—and stout-hearted ladies they were, for it is no easy thing to enter suddenly into a world of four hundred men, most of whom have lost one or more limbs. They played checkers and chess with the men; they gave lessons in the mandolin and guitar; they organized classes in watercolor painting, public speaking, amateur theatricals, and glee club singing. But the volunteer workers fell all too short. Those four hundred men had nothing to do for fifteen hours a day but to play cards, torment the nurses, and to conceal from one another their dread of the future that lay before them. Moreover there were few male volunteers; American men were back at home from war, hard at work, picking up their interrupted lives. And naturally no man would willingly enter that jungle of frantic wounded men unless he had himself been a soldier. So the superintendent of the hospital sent out word to the headmasters of the private schools in the nearby counties asking for ex-military volunteers to assist the recreation director. Transportation would be provided. A number of us from the Raritan

School (including T. T. North, corporal, Coast Artillery, retired) piled into a weapons-carrier and rattled off thirty miles to the hospital on Monday mornings and Friday afternoons.

"Gentlemen," said the recreation director, "a lot of these fellows think they want to learn journalism. They think they can earn a million dollars by selling their war experiences to the *Saturday Evening Post*. Some don't want to think about the War; they want to write and sell Wild West stories or cops-and-robbers stories. Most of them never got out of high school. They can't write a laundry list. . . . I'm dividing you volunteers into sections. Each of you has twelve men. They've signed up eagerly; you don't have to worry about that. Your classes are called Journalism and Writing for Money! They're eager enough, but let me prepare you for one thing: their attention gets tired easily. Arrange so that every fifteen minutes *they* have a chance to talk. Most of them are real nice fellows: you won't have any trouble with discipline. But they're haunted by fear of the future. If you finally get their confidence you'll get an earful. Now I'm going to talk frankly to you men: they think they can never get a girl to marry them; they're afraid they can't even get a whore to sleep with them. They think most of the outside world looks on them as sort of eunuchs. Most of them aren't, of course, but one of the effects of amputation is the fancy that they've been castrated. In one ward or another every night someone wakes up screaming in a nightmare *about that.* All they think about, really, is sex, sex, sex—and just as desperately: the prospect of being dependent all their lives on others. So every fifteen minutes take a conversation-break. Your real contribution here is to let them blow off steam. One more word: all day and most of the night they use foul language to one another—New York smut, Kentucky smut, Oklahoma smut, California smut. That's understandable, isn't it? We have a rule here; if they talk like that within the hearing of the nurses or the padres or you volunteers, they're penalized. They get their cigarette allowance cut or they can't get their daily swim in the pool or they can't go to the movie show. I wish you'd cooperate with us in this matter. You'll get their respect by being severe with them, not easy. Give them an assignment. Tell them you want an article or a story or a poem from each one of them when you return a week from today. Miss Warriner will now lead you to your tables in the gym. Thank you, gentlemen, for coming."

"Mino, I think it's great the way you struck out for yourself and are on the way to making yourself self-supporting—first solving the puzzles and then inventing new ones. Tell me how that happened?"

"I began doing them when I was about twelve. Schoolwork wasn't very hard so I used to read a lot. Rosa would bring me books from the library."

"What kind of books then?"

"I thought then that I'd be an astronomer, but I began that too early. I wasn't ready for the mathematics. I am now. Later I wanted to be a priest. Of course I couldn't, but I read a lot of theology and philosophy. I didn't understand all of it, but . . . that's when I learned a lot of Latin."

"Couldn't you find anyone to talk those things over with?"

"I like to figure things out by myself."

"Hell, you wanted to read Dante with me."

He blushed and murmured, "That's different . . . then I began doing puzzles to make money to buy books."

"Show me some puzzles that you've been making."

Most of the shelves within reach of his hand were like those in a linen closet. He drew out a sheaf of leaves; the puzzles were written with India ink on art paper. *"Opus elegantissimum, juvenis!"* I said. "Do you get a lot of pleasure out of this?"

"No. I get pleasure out of the money."

I lowered my voice. "I remember my first paycheck. It was like a kick in the pants. It's the beginning of manhood. Your mother told me you were inventing some new things."

"I have designs for three new games for adults. Do you know Mr. Aldeburg?"

"No."

"He's a lawyer in town. He's helping me take out patents for them. The whole field of puzzles and games is full of crooks. They're crazy for new ideas and they'd steal anything."

I leaned back. "Mino, what are the three most important things you want to do when the real money starts coming in?"

He reached toward another shelf and brought out a manufacturer's catalogue—hospital equipment, wheelchairs for invalids. He opened it and held a page toward me: a rolling chair, propelled by a motor, nickel-plated, with a detachable awning for protection against rain, snow, or sun—a beauty. Two hundred and seventy-five dollars.

I whistled. "And after that?"

Another catalogue. "I get fitted for some boots. They're attached to my legs above and below the knee by a lot of straps. I'd still have to use crutches, but my feet wouldn't swing. Through my legs I could put some of my weight on the ground. But I'd have to use some kind of cane to prevent my falling on my face. I think I could invent something after I'd got used to the boots."

Such was his mature control that he might have been talking about buying a car. But there was one element of confidence still lacking. I went right to the point. "And after that you want to rent your own apartment?"

"Yes," he said surprised.

"Where you can entertain your friends?"

"Yes," he said and looked at me sharply to see if I had guessed what was in his mind. I smiled and repeated my question, holding his glance. The courage ebbed out of him and his eyes fell away.

"Can I look over your books, Mino?"

"Sure."

I rose and turned to the shelves behind me. The books were all second-hand and appeared to have suffered long use—longer than his life. If he had bought them in Newport he must have ransacked the same second-hand stores that I had come to know when I was "excavating" the Fifth City. Maybe he had ordered them from the catalogues of such dealers in the larger cities. On the bottom shelf were the *Britannica* (eleventh), some atlases, star charts, and other large works of reference. The majority of the shelves were filled with works on astronomy and mathematics. I took down Newton's *Principia.* The margins were covered with notes in fine handwriting and in faded ink.

"Are these notes yours?"

"No, but they're very sharp."

"Where's your *Divina Commedia?*"

He pointed to two shelves within his reach: the *Summa,* Spinoza, the *Aeneid,* the *Pensées* of Pascal, Descartes . . .

"You read French?"

"Rosa's crazy about French. We play chess and go and parcheesi in French."

I had been thinking of Elbert Hughes. So there was another half-genius in Newport; maybe a genius. Maybe a late blooming of the Fifth City. I remembered having heard that in Concord, Massachusetts, almost a century before, groups used to devote an evening to reading aloud in Italian or Greek or German, or even in Sanskrit. In Berkeley, California, my mother used to read Italian aloud with Mrs. Day on one evening in the week and French with Mrs. Vincent on another. She attended German classes at the University (Professor Pinger), because we, her children, had learned some German in two successive German schools in China.

It was on the tip of my tongue to ask Mino if he had any wish to go to either of the two universities nearby. I saw that his rigorous independence not only forbade his relying on others to help him move about from place to place, but that his deprivation had shaped his mind toward becoming an autodidact. ("I like to figure things out by myself.") I remembered how the father of Pascal had come upon the young boy reading with delight the First Book of Euclid. The father had other plans for his son's education. He took away the volume, scarcely begun, and shut the boy in his room; but Pascal wrote the rest of the book himself, deducing the properties of the rectangle and the triangle, as a silkworm produces silk from his own entrails. But in the case of Mino I was saddened. In the twentieth century it is not possible to advance far as an autodidact in the vast fields of his interests. I had already known such solitary men—and in later years discovered others—who, having early repudiated formal education, were writing a *History of the Human Intelligence* or *The Sources of Moral Values*.

I sat down again. "Mino, have you seen any girls you like lately?"

He looked at me as though I'd struck him or ridiculed him. I continued looking at him and waited.

"No . . . I don't know any girls."

"Oh, yes you do! Your sister brings some of her friends here to see you." He couldn't or didn't deny it. "Didn't I see you talking to one of those assistant librarians in the magazine room at the People's Library?" He couldn't or didn't deny it.

At last he said, "They don't take me seriously."

"What do you mean, they don't take you seriously?"

"They talk for a minute, but they're in a hurry to get away."

"God damn it, what do you want them to do: start taking their clothes off?"

His hands were trembling. He put them under his buttocks and continued to stare at me. "No."

"You think they don't talk naturally to you. I'll bet you don't talk naturally to them. A fine-looking young man like you, with top-quality first-rate brains. I'll bet you play your cards wrong." There was a breathless silence. His panic was contagious, but I plunged on. "Sure, you have a handicap, but the handicap isn't as bad as you think it is. You build it up in your imagination. Be yourself, Mino! Lots of men with a handicap as bad as yours have settled down and got married and had kids. Do you want to know how I know this *personally?*"

"Yes."

I told him about the veterans' hospital. I ended up almost shouting, "Four hundred men in wheelchairs and wagons. And some of them still send me letters and cards. With photographs of their family—their own *new* family around them. Especially on Christmas cards. I haven't got any of them in Newport, but I'll send home for some to show you. But, Mino, understand this: they're older than you. Most of them were older than you when they were wounded. What the hell are you so impatient about? The trouble with you is that you're building up an anxiety about the years ahead; you've got 1936 and 1946 planted in your head as though they were tomorrow. And the other trouble with you is that you want the Big Passionate Bonfire right now. A man can't live without female companionship, you're damn right about that. But don't spoil it, don't ruin it by building up a lot of steam too early. Begin with friendship. Now listen: the Misses Laughlins' Scottish Tea Room is just eight doors from your father's door. Have you ever eaten there?" He shook his head. "Well, you're going to, you and Rosa. I'm inviting you and *some girl you know* to lunch with me next Saturday noon."

"I don't know any girl *well enough* to ask."

"Well, if you don't bring a girl to lunch on Saturday, I'll clam up on the whole matter. It'll always be a pleasure to me to come and call on you and talk about Sir Isaac Newton and Bishop Berkeley—I'm very sorry to see that you haven't got any of his works on your shelves—but I'll never open my damn mouth on the subject of girls again. We'll just pretend we're eunuchs. My idea was that you ask one girl this Saturday with the three of us—just to break the ice—and that the following Saturday you ask *another* girl, all by yourself. I guess you can afford it, can't you? They serve a very good seventy-five-cent blue-plate lunch. You were ready to throw away sixteen dollars on some lousy Dante lessons with me.— Then the following Saturday I'll give another party and you bring still a different girl."

A terrible struggle was going on within him. "The only girls I know . . . I know a little . . . are twin sisters."

"Great! Are they lively?"

"Yes."

"What's their name?"

"Avonzino—Filumena and Agnese."

"Which do you like better?"

"They're just the same."

"Well, Saturday you sit by Agnese and I'll bring a friend of mine to sit by Filumena. You know what Agnese means in Greek, don't you?" He made no sign. "It comes from *hagne*—'pure, chaste.' So put the damper on those lascivious ideas of yours. Keep calm. Just a pleasant get-together. Just talking about the weather and about those puzzles of yours. We'll give the girls a big thrill talking about your new inventions and patents. Is it a deal?" He nodded. "You aren't going to backslide, are you?" He shook his head. "Remember this: Lord Byron had to strap up his misshapen foot in complicated boots and half the girls in Europe were crying their eyes out for him. Put that in your pipe and smoke it. What does King Oedipus's name mean?"

"Swell-foot."

"And who did he marry?"

"His mother."

"And what was the name of that splendid daughter of his?"

"Antigone."

I burst out laughing. Mino managed a hesitant laugh. I continued, "I've got to go now. Shake hands, Mino. I'll see you next Sunday at this time; but *first* I'll see you next Saturday at twelve-thirty at the Scottish Tea Room. Wear just what you're wearing now and be ready to have a good time. Remember, you don't win the right kind of girls by dancing with them and playing tennis; you win them by being a fine honorable fellow with a lot of zzipp in your eyes, and enough money in the bank to feed the little Antigones and Ismenes and Polyneiceses and Eteocles. 'Nuff said."

Passing through the store I told Rosa about the Saturday engagement. "Will you come?"

"Oh, yes! Thank you."

"See that Mino gives the invitation to the Avonzino girls. He may need a little help from you, but leave as much of it to him as you can.—Signora Matera, you have the brightest boy on Aquidneck Island."

"Datt'a wot I tole you!" And she kissed me in the crowded store.

I shook hands with her husband. "Goodbye, Don Matteo!" (In southern Italy respected heads of families even in the working classes are addressed as "Don"—vestige of centuries of Spanish occupation.)

I reached a telephone and having called the Venable house asked to speak to the Baron.

"*Grüss Gott, Herr Baron!*"

"*Ach, der Herr Professor! Lobet den Herrn!*"

"Bodo, we had dinner in the Eighth City—remember?"

"I'll never forget it."

"How'd you like to have lunch in the Ninth City?"

"*Schön!* When?"

"Are you free next Saturday at twelve-thirty?"

"I can get free."

"You'll be my guest. You'll be enjoying the seventy-five-cent blue-plate lunch at the Scottish Tea Room on Lower Broadway at twelve-thirty *punkt*. Do you know where that is?"

"I've seen it. Will there be any police interference?"

"Bodo! The Ninth City is the most respectable of all the nine cities of Newport."

"Have you got another of your plans on your mind?"

"Yes. I'll give you a hint. You won't be the guest of honor. You won't even be a baron. The guest of honor is a twenty-two-year-old genius. He has no feet."

"What did you say?"

"A train ran over him when he was a baby. No feet. Like you, he reads the *Summa* and Spinoza and Descartes before breakfast— in the original. Bodo, if you had no feet, would it make you a little shy about meeting girls?"

"Ye-e-es. Maybe it would, a little."

"Well, there are going to be three charming Ninth City girls there. Don't dress too elegant, Mr. Stams. And no pinching, Mr. Stams."

"Gott hilf uns. Du bist ein verfluchter Kerl."

"Wiederschaun."

On Saturday morning I dropped in at the Tea Room and had a word or two with my esteemed and straight-backed friend Miss Ailsa Laughlin.

"There'll be six of us, Miss Ailsa. Can we have the round table in the corner?"

"We never hold reservations, Mr. North. You know that. Five minutes late and you must take your chances with the other guests."

"When I listen to you, Miss Ailsa, I have to close my eyes— just to listen to that Highland music."

"It's Lowland, Mr. North. It's Ayrshire. The Laughlins were neighbors of Robbie Burns."

"Music, perfect music. We'll be here exactly at twelve-thirty. What is being offered?"

"You know perfectly well that on Saturday noons in summer we have shepherd's pie."

"Ah, yes, *agneau en croûte.* Kindly convey my shy admiration to Miss Jeannie."

"She won't believe it, Mr. North. She thinks you're a fickle deceiver. You and Miss Flora Deland behaving scandalously in our house!"

We are all prompt, but the Materas were promptest. They arrived five minutes early so that we did not see Mino rise from his rolling chair, adjust his crutches, and swing himself into the Tea Room—Rosa's hand in the small of his back as leverage. I arrived just in time to seat them. Rosa was the kind of girl who appears more attractive at each successive meeting; happiness casts a spell. Mr. Stams and the Avonzino girls followed immediately. Filumena and Agnese were bafflingly identical and so beautiful that the world was enhanced by the duplication. They were enchantingly and even alarmingly dressed. Rosa, who sat at my right, informed me that they were wearing the dresses and hats which they had made themselves from a Butterick pattern, five years before, to serve as bridesmaids at an older sister's wedding. These were of tangerine organdy and they had "built" wide-brimmed hats of the same material, stretched on fine wire. When they went down a crowded street passers-by formed two hedge-rows to watch them. Each had embroidered the initial of her first name over her heart to help us to identify her. Agnese wore a wedding ring. Her name was Mrs. Robert O'Brien; her husband, a naval warrant officer, had been drowned at sea three years before.

I made the introductions. "We're all going to call one another by our Christian names. Beside me is Rosa; next is Bodo—he is from Austria; next is Agnese; next is Mino, who is Rosa's brother; next is Filumena. Bodo, will you repeat these names, please."

"They're all such beautiful names, except mine, that I'm ashamed. But we are Theophilus, Rosa, poor old Bodo, Agnese, Mino, Filumena."

He was applauded.

It was a warm day. We began the meal with a glass of Welch's grape juice with a "scoop" of lemon sherbet in it (ten cents extra). Two of my guests—Mino and Bodo—were intimidated, but the twins were raving beauties and knew that everything would be permitted them.

"Bodo," said Filumena, "I like your name. It sounds like the name of a very nice dog. And you look like a very nice dog."

"Oh, thank you!"

"Agnese, wouldn't it be nice if we could build a big kennel in our back yard and Bodo could live with us and keep naughty men away. Mamma would love you, Bodo, and feed you very well."

"And," said Agnese, "Filumena and I would make flower-chains to put around your neck and we'd go for walks on the Parade."

Bodo barked happily, nodding his head up and down.

Agnese continued, "But Mamma loves Mino best, so you mustn't be jealous, Bodo. Mamma loves Mino because he knows everything. She told him the date of her birth and he looked up at the ceiling a moment and said 'That was a Monday.' Papa asked him why a leap-year comes every four years and Mino made it as clear to him as two-times-two-makes-four."

I said, "Mino has given me permission to tell you a secret about him."

"Mino's going to get married!" cried Filumena.

"Of course, Mino's going to get married. So are we all, but Mino's too young yet. No, the secret is that he's getting out patents for some games he's invented and they're going to sweep the country like mahjong. They're going to be in every home like parcheesi and jackstraws and he's going to be very rich."

"Oh!" cried the girls.

"But you aren't going to forget us, are you, Mino?"

"No," said Mino, dazed.

"You aren't going to forget that we loved you before you were rich?"

"Another secret," I announced. "He's started inventing a practical boot so that he can climb mountains and go skating—and *dance!*"

Applause and cheers.

The shepherd's pie was delicious.

Agnese said to Mino, "And you're going to give Bodo some beautiful dog biscuits, and you're going to give Filumena a sewing machine that doesn't break down all the time?"

"And," continued Filumena, "you're going to give Agnese some singing lessons with Maestro del Valle, and you're going to give your sister a turquoise pin because she was born in July. What are you going to give Theophilus?"

"I know what I want," I said. "I want Mino to invite us all to lunch the first Saturday in August, 1927—the same place, the same people, the same things to eat, the same friendships."

Bodo said "Amen"; everybody said "Amen" and Mino added "I will."

Now we were eating prune whip. The conversation became less general. While I was talking to Rosa Bodo was asking Agnese about her interest in singing. All I was able to overhear was the name of Mozart. Bodo was suggesting to her a riddle that she was to put to Mino. He did not tell her the answer.

"Mino," she said, "you must answer this riddle: what connection is there between the names of our host today and the composer I love best, Mozart?"

Mino looked up at the ceiling a moment and then smiled. "*Theophilus* is one who loves God in Greek and *Amadeus* is one who loves God in Latin."

Applause and delighted wonder, especially mine.

"Bodo told me to ask you," she added modestly.

"And Mozart knew it well," added Bodo. "Sometimes he would sign his middle name in Greek or in Latin or in German. What would the German be, Mino?"

"I don't know much German, but . . . *liebe* . . . and *Gott*—oh, I have it: *Gottlieb*."

More applause. Miss Ailsa had been standing behind me. The Scots love learning.

Agnese addressed Mino again. "And does my name mean 'lamb'?"

Mino shot a glance at me, but turned back to her. "It could come from that, but many people think it comes from an earlier word, from the Greek *hagne* that means 'pure.' "

Tears started to her eyes. "Filumena, please kiss Mino on the forehead for me."

"Indeed, I will," said Filumena and did so.

We were all a little exhausted by these surprises and wonders and fell silent while the coffee was placed before us. (Five cents extra.)

Rosa whispered to me. "I think you know someone who's sitting over there in that corner."

"Hilary Jones!—Who's he with?"

"That's his wife. They've come together again. She's Italian, but she's not Roman Catholic. She's Italian and Jewish. She's Agnese's best friend too. We're all best friends. Her name's Rachele."

"How's Linda?"

"She's home with them. She's out of the hospital."

When my guests took their leave (Bodo whispering, "You should hear the conversation I'm accustomed to at luncheon!") I crossed and shook hands with Hill.

"Teddie, I'd like you to meet my wife, Rachele."

"Very happy to meet you, Mrs. Jones. How's Linda?"

"She's much better, much better. She's at home with us now."

We talked about Linda and Hill's summer job in the public playgrounds and about the Materas and the Avonzino sisters.

Finally, "I want to ask you a question, Hill—and you, Mrs. Jones. I trust you not to think it's just vulgar curiosity. I know that Agnese's husband was drowned at sea. There must be many such widows in Newport, as there are all up and down the coast of New England. But I feel that she carries some particular burden—some additional burden. Am I right?"

They looked at one another in a kind of dismay.

Hill said, "It was terrible. . . . Nobody talks about it."

"Forgive me. I'm sorry I asked."

"There's no reason you shouldn't know," said Rachele. "We all love her. Everybody loves her. You *do* see why everybody loves her, don't you?"

"Oh, yes."

"We all hope that *that* and her wonderful little boy and her singing—she sings beautifully, you know—will help her forget what happened. You tell Mr. North, Hilary."

"Please . . . you tell him, Rachele."

"He was on the crew of a submarine. It was way up in the north, like near Labrador. And the submarine struck a reef or something under the water and the machinery broke down. And the ice began to crush it. And the compartments got closed. They had air for a while, but they couldn't get into the galley. . . . They had nothing to eat."

We all looked at one another in silence.

"Airplanes were looking for them, of course. Then the ice moved away and they were found. Their bodies were brought back. Bobby's buried in the Naval Cemetery on the Base."

"Thank you.—I'm only free on Sunday afternoons. Can I call on you a week from tomorrow and see Linda?"

"Oh, yes. Please come to supper."

"Thank you, I can't stay to supper. Please write down your address, Hill. I'll look forward to seeing you all at four-thirty."

Throughout the following week I met one or other of the Materas every noon when I picked up my New York paper. Italians, all of us. On Sunday morning I called on Mino at nine.

"*Buon giorno, Mino.*"

"*Buon giorno, professore.*"

"Mino, I'm not going to ask you if you kept your promise to invite a girl to lunch yesterday. I don't want to hear a word about it. From now on that's your business. What shall we talk about today?"

He was smiling with a more than usual air of "a man who knows where he's going" and I was answered. Young people are eager to be made to talk about themselves and to hear themselves discussed, but there is a limit—as they approach twenty—beyond which they shrink from such talk. Their interest in themselves becomes all inward. So I asked, "What shall we talk about today?"

"*Professore,* will you tell me what a college education gives a man?"

I spoke of the value of being required to devote yourself to subjects that at first seem foreign to your interests; of the value of being thrown among young men and young women of your own age, many of whom are as eager as you are to get the best of it; of the possibility—it's only luck—of being brought into contact with born teachers, even with great teachers. I reminded him of Dante's request to his guide Virgil. "Give me the food for which you have already given me the appetite."

He was looking at me with urgent intensity. "Do you think I should go to college?"

"I'm not ready to answer that question. You are a very remarkable young man, Mino. It is very possible that you have outgrown what an American university could give you. You have the appetite and you know where to find the food. You have triumphed over one handicap and the handicap was spur to the triumph. It may well be that you will triumph over this other handicap—the lack of a formal higher education."

He lowered his voice and asked, "What do you think I lack most?"

I laughed and rose to go. "Mino, centuries ago a king in one of the countries near Greece had a daughter he loved very much. She seemed to be wasting away with some mysterious illness. So the old man journeyed to the great oracle at Delphi, bringing rich gifts, and asked the sibyl, 'What can I do to make my daughter well?' And the sibyl chewed the bay leaves and went into a trance and replied in verse, 'Teach her mathematics and music.' Well, you have the mathematics all right, but I miss in you that music."

"Music?"

"Oh, I don't mean what we call music. I mean the whole vast realm that's represented by the Muses. You have your Dante—but the *Divina Commedia* and the *Aeneid* are the only works that I've seen here that are inspired by the Muses."

He smiled at me, almost mischievously. "Wasn't Urania the Muse of astronomy?"

"Oh, yes. I forgot her; but I stick to my point."

He was silent a moment. "What do they do for us?"

I said briskly, "A school of the sympathies, of the emotions and passions, and of self-knowledge. Think it over. Mino, I can't come next Sunday morning, but I'd like to be here the Sunday after that. *Ave atque vale!*" At the door I turned and asked, "By the way, do Agnese's son and Rachele's Linda come to call on you here?"

"They come and see Rosa and my mother, but they don't come to see me."

"Do you know much about the death of Agnese's husband?"

"He was drowned at sea. That's all I know."

He was blushing. I guessed that he had invited Agnese to lunch on the day before. I waved my hand airily and said, "Cultivate the Muses! You are an Italian from Magná Graecia—you have probably lots of Greek blood in you also. Cultivate the Muses!"

In my Journal, from which I am refreshing my memory of these encounters, I find that I was assembling a "portrait" of Mino, as of so many others in these pages. I come upon a hastily written notation: "Mino's handicap involves restrictions I had not foreseen. Not only is he aware that people do not talk to him 'naturally,' he has never received visits from the young children of his sister's two best friends, and has probably not even seen them. The implication is that the children would be affected 'morbidly' by his accident. That consideration would not have arisen in Italy where the disfigured, the scrofulous, and the maimed are visible daily in the market-place—generally as beggars. Moreover, Mino seems not to have been told those details of Warrant Officer O'Brien's death that had so distressed the Hilary Joneses and that were rendering life all but unendurable to his widow. In America the tragic background of life is hidden in cupboards, even from those who have come most starkly face to face with it. Should I some day point this out to Mino?"

On the following Sunday afternoon I called on Linda and her parents, carrying a small old-fashioned bouquet nestling in a lace-paper frill. Hilary, reunited with his wife, had become family-proud, which is always an engaging thing to see. Rachele's family had come from the north of Italy, from the industrial region near Turin where girls of the working classes are brought up to enter the widening field of office workers and, when possible, to become schoolteachers. The little apartment was spotless and serious. Linda was still convalescent and a little wan, but delighted to receive company at tea. I was surprised to see what used to be called a "cottage piano" or a "yacht piano," lacking an octave at the upper range and an octave in the bass.

"Do you play, Rachele?"

She let her husband answer. "She plays very well. She's very popular at the boys' clubs' rallies. She sings too."

"Usually on Sunday afternoon Agnese drops in with her Johnny. You don't mind, do you?" asked Rachele.

"Oh, no," I said. "I liked the Avonzino twins at once. Will you and Agnese sing for me?"

"We do sing duets. We each take two lessons a month from Maestro del Valle and he made us promise to sing every time anyone seriously asks us to. Are you serious, Theophilus?"

"Am I!"

"Then you'll hear four of us. Our children have heard us practice so often at home that they know the music and sing with us. First we'll sing alone, then we'll sing again and they'll join in. Please act as though it were a perfectly natural thing. We don't want them to become self-conscious about it."

Presently Agnese arrived with Johnny O'Brien, also almost four. I'm sure Johnny was a firehouse of energy at home, but like most fatherless small boys he was intimidated by two full-grown men. He sat wide-eyed by his mother. Agnese, apart from her vivacious sister, was subdued also. We talked about the lunch at the Scottish Tea Room and the glowing picture I had painted of Mino's future. I assured them it was true. Agnese asked who Bodo was and what he "did." I told them. All girls like one surprise a day.

"Then it was shocking our talking about him as a dog."

"Oh, Agnese! You could see how pleased he was."

When we'd finished tea I asked the girls to sing to us. They exchanged a glance and Rachele went to the piano. Each mother turned to her child, put her finger to her lip and whispered, "Later." They sang Mendelssohn's "Oh, That We Two Were Maying." Mino should have heard that.

"Now we'll do it again."

The mothers sang softly; the children sang unabashed. I glanced at Hilary. So this was what he almost lost for Diana Bell!

Agnese said, "For a bazaar at my church we learned some parts of Pergolesi's *Stabat Mater*."

They sang two terzets of that; first alone, then with the children. Pergolesi should have heard that.

Newport is full of surprises. I was learning that perhaps the Ninth City is nearer to the Fifth—perhaps to the Second—than any of the others.

When we had taken our leave I walked to her house door with Agnese, hand in hand with Johnny.

"You have a beautiful voice, Agnese."

"Thank you."

"I think that Maestro del Valle must have ambitious plans for you."

"He does. He has offered to give me regular lessons without fees. With my pension and my daily job I could pay for them, but I have no ambition."

"No ambition," I repeated, meditatively.

"Have you ever suffered terribly, Theophilus?"

"No."

She murmured, "Johnny, music, and submission to the will of God . . . they . . . they hold me."

I ventured a very rash remark, still meditatively. "The War left behind many hundreds of thousands of young widows."

She answered quickly, "There are some aspects of my husband's death that I cannot talk about with anybody—not with Rosa or Rachele, not even with my mother or Filumena. Please, don't . . . say . . ."

"Look, Johnny, do you see what I see?"

"What?"

I pointed.

"A candy store?"

"Open on Sunday too! When I went to call on Linda I took her a present. I didn't know that you were going to be there. Come up to the window and see what you'd like."

It was what used to be called a "notions" store. In one corner of the window were toys—model planes, boats, and automobiles.

Johnny began pointing, jumping up and down. "Look! Look, Mr. North! There's a submarine, my daddy's submarine. Can I have that?"

I turned to Agnese. She gave me a harrowed glance of appeal and shook her head. "Johnny," I said, "today's Sunday. When I was a boy my father *never* let us buy toys on Sunday. Sunday we went to church, but no games and no toys." So I marched in and bought some chocolates. When we reached the Avonzino home, he said goodbye nicely and went into the house.

Agnese stood with one hand on the swinging gate. She said, "I think you have urged Benjy—I mean, Mino—to ask me to lunch?"

"Before I ever knew that the Avonzino sisters existed, I urged him to bring any girl or girls he knew to the Scottish Tea Room. I then urged him to bring any girl, preferably a different girl in order to widen his acquaintance, on the following Saturday. He said no word to me about inviting you."

"I have had to tell him that I cannot accept such invitations again. I admire Mino, as we all do; but weekly meetings in a public place like that are not suitable. . . . Theophilus, do not tell anyone what I am about to say: I am a very unhappy woman. I am not capable even of friendship. Everything is just play-acting. I shall be helped, I know"—and she pointed with forefinger from an otherwise motionless hand to the zenith—"but I must wait patiently for that."

"Please go on play-acting for Johnny's sake. I don't mean by going to lunches with Mino, but by seeing some of us in groups from time to time. I think Bodo is planning a kind of picnic, but his car can hold only four and I know he wants to see Mino and yourself again. . . ." She did not raise her eyes from the ground. I waited; finally I added, "I do not know your intolerable burden, Agnese; but I do know that you do not wish it to be a shadow on Johnny's life forever."

She looked at me, frightened; then said abruptly, "Thank you for walking home with us. Oh, yes, I am happy to meet Mino anywhere when there are others in the company." She put out her hand. "Goodbye."

"Goodbye, Agnese."

At seven o'clock I telephoned Bodo. You could always catch him dressing for some dinner party.

"Grüss Gott, Herr Baron."

"Grüss Gott in Ewigkeit."

"What time is your dinner engagement tonight?"

"Eight-fifteen. Why?"

"When could I meet you in the Muenchinger-King bar to lay a plan before you?"

"Is seven-thirty too soon?"

"See you then."

Diplomats are punctual. Bodo was wearing what we used to call in college his "glad rags." He was dining at the Naval War College with some visiting "brass," admirals of all nations—decorations (known to the lower ranks as "fruit salad") and everything. Quite a sight!

"What's your plan, old man?" he asked with happy expectation.

"Bodo, something very serious this time. I must talk fast. Do you know the Ugolino passage in Dante?"

"Naturally!"

"You remember Agnese? Her husband was lost in a submarine at sea." I told him the little I knew. "Maybe the men died of suffocation within a few days; maybe they lived on for a week without food. The boat was finally liberated from the ice. Do you suppose the Navy Department informed the widows and parents of the men of what they may have found?"

He thought a minute. "If it was appalling, I don't think they did."

"The possibilities haunt Agnese. They are robbing her of the will to live. She does not suspect that I know what is haunting her."

"Gott hilf uns!"

"She tells me that she is filled with thoughts that she cannot tell her sister, her best friends, or even her mother. When people say a thing like that it means that they are longing to tell them to someone. Mino has asked her to lunch several times since our party at the Scottish Tea Room. She tells me she cannot accept any more invitations from him *alone*. Don't you think Mino a fine fellow?"

"I certainly do."

"I want to give a sunset picnic at Brenton's Point next Sunday. Are you free to come between five and eight?"

"I am. It is one of my last days in Newport. They're giving a reception for me at nine-thirty. I can make it."

"I shall provide the champagne, the sandwiches, and the dessert. Will you, as a Knight of the Two-Headed Eagle, come with us and lend us your car? You and Agnese and Mino will sit in the front seat and I will sit in the rumble seat with the ice-bucket and the provisions. I don't want to appear to be host. Will you be the ostensible host?"

"No! For shame! I shall *be* the host. Now I too must talk fast. In my guest house there are always bottles of champagne in the ice-box. I shall bring along a little portable kitchen with a hot dish. Any Swiss can open a hotel with one day's notice; we Austrians can do it in a week. If it's raining or cold we can go to my guest house. You have supplied the idea—that's quite enough from you.—Now tell me your plan. What is the idea?"

"Oh, Bodo, don't ask me. It's only a hope."

"Oh! Oh!—Give me a hint."

"Do you know *Macbeth*?"

"I played in it at Eton. I was Macduff."

"Do you remember Macbeth's question to the doctor about Lady Macbeth's sleepwalking?"

"Wait!—*'Canst thou not . . . Pluck from the memory a rooted sorrow. . . .?*, and something about *'Cleanse the stuffed bosom of that perilous stuff Which weighs upon the heart?'* "

"Oh, Bodo!—That's what will win you Persis; that's what we must do for Agnese."

He stared at me. He whispered, "Persis too? Did her husband die in a submarine?"

"Only the happiness that is snatched from suffering is real; all the rest is merely what they call 'creature comforts.' "

"Who said *that*?"

"One of your Austrian poets—Grillparzer, I think."

"*Schön!*—I must run. Send me a note about where to pick up my guests and all that. *Ave atque vale.*"

The invitations were sent through Rosa and accepted. "Rosa, we would love to invite you and Filumena, too, but you know the size of his car." Rosa's eyes showed she understood—perhaps understood the whole stratagem. "Will you show me, Rosa, where you put your hand on Mino's back to help him in and out of doorways and cars?"

Her mother watched us laughing. "I do'no w'at you are tinking now, Signor Teofilo, but I no afraid."

The great day arrived. The weather was perfect. Mino was seated in the car by skilled hands. Agnese preferred to be picked up at the Materas' store, in order—I assumed—that her son's disappointment would not be enhanced by his longing to accompany her on an automobile ride. When we arrived at Brenton's Point that great hotel-man Baron Stams whisked out two portable service tables, spread them (with a flourish) with linen, and proceeded to uncork a bottle. Mino and Agnese remained in the car with trays on their laps while the other two cavaliers drew up beside them on folding chairs.

Mino said, "Now I can say that I've tasted champagne twice. I've tasted Asti Spumante at my brothers' weddings. The only time I had champagne before was at your wedding, Agnese."

"You were only fifteen then, Mino. I'm glad you did." She spoke like someone treading on ice. "My husband's family live in Albany, New York. They came and stayed at our house. They brought three bottles of champagne. . . . Do you remember Robert well, Mino?"

"I certainly do. His boat didn't come in to the Bay often, but he once asked me if I wanted to go on board and, of course, I was crazy to. But on that day there was a big storm blowing up and I couldn't have managed the ladders and the gangway. He told me he'd take me another time. He was my idol. My mother thought he was the handsomest man she'd ever seen—and the nicest."

Agnese looked about her distraught.

Bodo asked, "Did the Navy give him special leave for the wedding?"

"Oh, he'd saved up his shore leave. We went to New York. We saw everything. We took a different El and a different subway to the end of the line every day. Robert knew that I loved music, so we went to the opera three times." She turned to Mino and looked up into his face. "Of course, we had to sit way up high, but we could see and hear everything perfectly. And we went to the zoo and to Mass at St. Patrick's." There were tears in her eyes, but she added with a little laugh, "We went to Coney Island too. That was fun, Mino."

"Yes, Agnese."

"Yes . . . Theophilus, what is Bodo doing?"

Bodo was busy over a chafing-dish. "I'm cooking supper, Agnese. It won't be ready for a while so have another glass of champagne."

"I'm afraid that it'll make me tipsy."

"It's not very strong."

"Agnese," I asked, "has Maestro del Valle given you any songs that you can sing without piano accompaniment? You know he wants you to sing if anyone asks you seriously. I can promise you we're all serious."

"Well, there's an old Italian song. . . . Let me recall it a minute."

She put her hand over her eyes and then sang *"Caro mio Ben, Caro mio Ben,"* as purely as a swan gliding over the water. In the second verse she broke down. "I'm sorry I can't go on. That was one of the three songs he loved best. . . . Oh, Theophilus, oh, Bodo . . . he was such a good man! He was just a boy really and he loved life so much. Then that dreadful thing happened to him —under the ice, without food. I suppose they had water, didn't they? . . . but nothing to eat . . .''

Bodo started speaking, distinctly but without emphasis, his eyes on the work before him. "Agnese, during the War I lay in a ditch for four days without food. I was so wounded that I could not get up to look for water. I kept losing consciousness. When the doctors found me they said that I had died several times, but that I was smiling. You can be sure that the men in the boat— *with so little air*—lost consciousness. Air is more important than even food and water."

She stared at him startled, a gleam of hope. She put her hand to her throat and murmured, "No air. No air." Then she threw her arms about Mino; she laid her cheek on the lapel of his coat and sobbed, "Mino, comfort me! Comfort me!"

He put his arm around her and repeated, "Dear Agnese, beautiful Agnese . . . dear Agnese, brave Agnese . . .''

"Comfort me!"

Bodo and I stared at one another.

Suddenly Agnese collected herself, saying, "Forgive me, forgive me, everybody," and drew a handkerchief from her handbag.

Bodo said loudly, "Supper's ready."

Alice

During my earlier stay in Newport—at Fort Adams in 1918 and 1919—I had belonged to the Fourth City, that of the military and naval establishments. In this summer of 1926 there was little likelihood—nor did I seek any—that I would have any contact with those self-sufficient enclosures.

Yet I did come to know and delight in one very humble member-by-alliance of the United States Navy—Alice.

From time to time I am overcome by a longing for an Italian meal. I had received invitations to dinner at the homes of the Materas, the Avonzinos, and the Hilary Joneses, where I was promised an Italian meal; but the reader knows of my resolve to accept no invitations whatever. My life was so gregarious and fragmented that only a strict adherence to that rule could save me from something approaching breakdown. I ate alone. There were three restaurants in Newport purporting to be Italian, but like so many thousands in our country they offered sorry imitations of true Italian cooking. My favorite was "Mama Carlotta's" at One Mile Corner. There one was able to obtain, in a teacup, a home-grown wine popularly called "dago red." About once in two weeks I wheeled the mile to "Mama Carlotta's" and ordered the *mine-strone*, the *fettuccine con salsa*, and the bread; the bread was excellent.

This restaurant was across the road from one of the half-dozen entrances to the vast high-fenced Naval Base. It adjoined the many acres of barracks—six apartments to a house—in which lived the families of sailors many of whom worked at the Base, the majority of whom were often absent for many months at a time. Ulysses, King of Ithaca, was separated from his wife Penelope for twenty years—ten of them fighting on the plains before Troy, ten of them on the long voyage home. These men in Newport, their wives and children, lived in a densely crowded area of identical dwellings, identical streets, identical schools and playgrounds, and identical *conventions*. Since 1926 the area has grown many times in size, but with the increase of air travel home leave is granted more frequently and even the families are transported for a time to similar "compounds" in Hawaii, the Philippines, and elsewhere. In 1926 there were hundreds of "shore widows." Density of population increases irritability, lonesomeness, and a censorious view of the behavior of others, all exacerbated at that time by walled enclosure. Penelope's was a hard lot and she must have been surrounded by the wives of absent seamen, but at least, being a queen, not *every* moment of her daily life was exposed to the eyes of women as unhappy as herself.

Residents on the Naval Base were permitted to leave the enclosure at will, but they seldom ventured into the town of Newport —they had their own provision stores, their own theaters, club-houses, hospitals, doctors, and dentists. Civilian life did not interest and perhaps intimidated them. But they enjoyed escaping briefly from what they themselves called the "rabbit warren" and the "ghetto" to certain locations outside the walls. "Mama Car-lotta's" was one of a group of restaurants and licit bars at One Mile Corner that they felt to be theirs. It consisted of two large parallel rooms, the bar and the restaurant. The bar was always crowded with men, though there were tables for ladies (who never came singly); the restaurant at noon and evening was generally well filled. The naval families seldom spent money for meals away from home, but occasionally when parents and relatives arrived for a visit they were offered the treat of a meal off the Base. A warrant officer or a chief petty officer came here, out into the world, to celebrate an anniversary. It is proverbial among the other services that professional seamen, from admirals down, marry good-looking women, not conspicuously intelligent, and that they find them in our southern states. I was able to confirm this rash generalization over and over again, notably at "Mama Carlotta's."

Early one evening, soon after I had entered into possession of my apartment, I was enjoying a meal at "Mama Carlotta's." It was my custom to read a paper or even a book at table. The fact that I was alone and reading was sufficient to mark me a land-lubber. On this evening for reasons unknown I could not be served with wine and was drinking Bevo. I sat alone and exposed at a table for four, though the crowd was so great that the feminine portion of it had overflowed from the bar into the restaurant where it stood, two by two, glass in hand, engaged in animated conversation.

This chapter is about Alice. I never knew her married name. During the few hours I saw her I learned that she came from a large, often starving, family in the coal-mining region of West Virginia and that she had run away from home at the age of fifteen with a gentleman-friend. I shall not attempt to reproduce her accent nor to indicate fully the limitations of her education.

Alice and her friend Delia (from central Georgia) were standing, touching two of the empty chairs at my table. They were talking to be seen talking—not for my benefit only, but for the benefit of the public. Almost everyone in the room knew everyone else in the room and was keeping watch on everyone else in the room. As an author of a later day has said, "Hell is *they*." I have unusually sharp hearing and became aware of an alteration in their tone. They had lowered their voices and were debating whether it would be "out of place" to ask me if they could sit in the empty chairs at my table. Presently the elder, Delia, turned to me and asked with chilly impersonality if the seats were taken.

I half-rose and said, "No, indeed, ladies. Please sit down."

"Thank you."

I was to learn later that even my partially rising from my chair was positively exciting. In the circles where they moved men did not under any occasion rise to acknowledge the presence of a woman; that was what gentlemen did in the movies, hence the excitement. I resumed my reading and lit a pipe. They turned their chairs face to face and continued their conversation in their earlier manner. They were discussing the election of a friend to the chairmanship of a committee responsible for supervising a charity bingo tournament. I had the sensation of listening to a scene from one of those old-fashioned plays wherein—for the audience's benefit—two characters inform one another of events long known to each of them.

It went on for some time. Delia was pointing out that it was ridiculous that a certain Dora had been elected. Dora, in a former high office, had made a perfect mess of organizing a farewell tea-party for a couple transferred to Panama; and so on.

"She tries to make herself popular by telling fortunes from palm-reading. Do you know what she told Julia Hackman?"

"No." Some whispering. "Alice! You made that up!"

"Cross my heart to die."

"Why, that's *terrible!*" (Stage laughter.)

"She'll do anything to get talked about. She said there was a Peeping Tom outside her bathroom; she opened the window suddenly and threw a soapy wet sponge in his face—in his *eyes.*"

"Alice! That's not true."

"Delia, that's what she says. She'll say anything to get famous. That's the way she gets votes. Everybody knows her name."

I had now the opportunity to observe them surreptitiously.

Delia was the taller, dark and handsome, but discontented and even embittered; I took her to be about thirty. Alice was scarcely over five feet, about twenty-eight years old. She had a pretty, bird-like, pointed face, of a pallor that suggested ill-health. Under her hat some wisps of lusterless straw-colored hair could be seen. But all was rendered vivid by dark intelligent eyes and an almost breathless eagerness to extract enjoyment from life. Her drawbacks were two: her native intelligence led her into a constant irritation with those less quick of mind than herself; the other was an un-prepossessing figure which, like her pallor, was probably the result of malnutrition in childhood. In spite of the difference in their ages Alice exerted an ascendancy over her friend.

They emptied their glasses. Almost without raising my eyes I spoke to them in a low voice: "May I offer the ladies a glass of beer?"

Each stared into the other's face, frozen—as though they had heard something that *cannot be repeated*. Neither looked at me. Having established the audacity of my overture, Delia assumed the responsibility of answering me. Without smiling, she lowered her head and murmured, "That's very kind of you."

I arose and gave a barely audible order to the waiter and returned to my book.

Convention! Convention! That rigorous governor of every human assembly, from the Vatican to the orphanage sandpile, is particularly severe on "shore widows," for a sailor's advancement is also conditioned by his wife's behavior. We were being observed. We were under fire. Convention demanded that no smiles be exchanged. The important thing was to give no impression that we were enjoying ourselves—for envy plays a large part in censorious morality. When the glasses were placed before them the girls nodded slightly and resumed their conversation. But before I returned to my reading Alice's eyes met mine—those superb dark eyes in the body of that early-aging hedge-sparrow. Quicksilver began coursing through my veins.

After a few minutes I ostentatiously spilled some of my beer on the table—"I *beg* your pardon, ladies," I said, mopping up the beer with my handkerchief. "Excuse me. I'd better have my eyes examined. Have I spilled any on you?"

"No. No."

"I'd never forgive myself, if I'd spilled anything on your dresses." I pretended to dry the hem of my jacket.

"I have a scarf here," said Delia. "It's an old thing. Use it. It'll wash out easily."

"Thank you, thank you, ma'am," I said earnestly. "I shouldn't read in a place like this. It's bad for the eyes."

"Oh, yes," said Alice. "My father used to read all the time—at night, too. It was terrible."

"I'd better put my book away. I sure need my eyes every minute of the day."

We were solemn enough to satisfy the severest critics.

Alice asked, "Do you live in Newport?"

"Yes, ma'am. Seven years ago in the War I was stationed at Fort Adams. I liked the place and I came back here to find work. I work on the grounds of one of the places."

"On the grounds?"

"I'm a kind of handyman—furnaces, leaves, cleaning up the place—like that."

In the services "cleaning up the place" denotes a form of punishment that resembles chain-gang labor; but they had decided that I was a civilian and were merely confused. Delia asked, "Do you live at the place you work at?"

"No, I live alone in a little apartment just off Thames Street—not really alone because I have a big dog. My name is Teddie."

"A dog? Oh, I love dogs."

"We're not allowed to keep dogs on the Base."

I invented the dog. There's an American myth, diffused by the movies, that a man who keeps a *big* dog and smokes a pipe is all right. Things were going very fast. What had not yet been con-

veyed was which girl I liked best. Alice and I knew, but Delia
was not markedly bright.

"Would you ladies like to be my guests at the nine o'clock show
at the Opera House? After the show I could bring you back here
in a taxi."

"Oh, no . . . Thank you."

"It's far too late."

"Oh, no!"

I could swear on a pile of Bibles that Delia pushed her shoe
against Alice's and Alice pushed Delia's shoe according to some
prearranged code. Delia said, "You go, Alice. We could leave
here together and the gentleman could meet you later up the
street a ways."

Alice was horrified. "How could you think of such a thing,
Delia!"

"Well," said Delia, rather grandly, rising. "Thoughts are free.
I'm going to the little girls' room. Excuse me. I'll be back in a
minute."

Alice and I were left alone.

"I think you're from the South," I said with the first smile of
the evening. She did not smile; in fact, she glared at me. She put
her head forward and began speaking in a low voice, but very
distinctly. "Don't smile! In a few minutes I have to introduce you
to some of the girls. I'm going to pretend that you're a doctor, *so
be ready*—I'd better say that you're an old friend of my husband's.
Were you ever in Panama?"

"No."

"In Norfolk, Virginia?"

"No."

"Well, where have you been all your life? I'll say Norfolk. . . .
Delia can't go downtown because her husband's coming back
next week and she don't dare go anywhere. *Stop smiling!* This is a
serious conversation. *When Delia and I leave here you say goodbye
to us. Then five minutes later you go out through the kitchen
and then out the back door. Then go up the road—not down toward*

Newport—and I'll meet you where the streetcar stops opposite Ollie's Bakery."

These instructions were given me in a manner of being very angry at me. I began to get the idea. Whatever followed would be dangerous.

"When I say goodbye to you what do I call you?"

"Alice."

"What's your husband's first name?"

"George, of course."

"I see. My name's Dr. Cole."

Alice's face had become flushed through the exertion of her generalship and through exasperation at my stupidity.

Delia rejoined us. From time to time the girls had exchanged greetings with members of the audience. Alice now raised her voice. "Hello, Barbara, hello, Phoebe. I want you to meet Dr. Cole, an old friend of George's."

"Pleased to meet you."

"Pleased to meet you, Barbara—and you, Phoebe."

"Imagine, George told him, if he was in Newport to call me up. He did and Dr. Cole said he'd meet me here. Hello, Marion, I want you to meet Dr. Cole an old friend of George's. So Delia and I sat here trying to decide who looked like a doctor. Isn't that a sit-you-ation! Hello, Annabel, I want you to know Dr. Cole, an old friend of George's, just passing through town. He asked Delia and I to go to the movies with him, but of course we can't, it being so late and everything. He knew George at Norfolk before I did. George told me about this doctor he knew. Were you a doctor then, Teddie?"

"I was in my last year at Baltimore. I have cousins in Norfolk."

"Imagine that!" said Barbara and Marion.

"What a coincident!" said Phoebe.

"The world's a very small place," said Delia.

"Well, you'll want to talk over old times," said Barbara. "Happy to have know'd you, Doctor."

I had risen. The girls withdrew to talk it over.

"That'll go like a grass-fire," said Delia.

Alice rose. "Finish your beer, Delia. I'm going to put my hat straight."

Now Delia and I were alone.

"Alice tells me your husband will be in next week, Delia. Congratulations." Delia looked at me hard and waggled her hands. "How long has he been gone?"

"Seven months."

"Gee, it must be very exciting."

"You said it!"

"What ship is it?"

"Four destroyers . . . More'n two hundred men on 'em have homes right in this town."

"Have you children, Delia?"

"Three."

"Wonderful for them too."

"They've faced it before. I'm taking them to my mother's. She lives in Fall River. I'm lucky."

"I don't understand."

"Doctor, when the men get off the ship, we're down there waving. See? They kiss us and all that. And then we go home to wait for them. They go straight off to the Long Wharf."

"Oh."

"You can say that again."

I was learning things. Ulysses returned to his home in disguise. None of those tear-stained embraces. They get rip-roaring drunk on the Long Wharf. No sight for children. Reunions require more courage than partings. The institution of marriage was not designed by Heaven to accommodate long separations.

"Has Alice some children?"

"Alice—Alice and George?"

"Yes?"

(It is characteristic of communities like a naval base that their residents believe their customs and affairs are what the earth revolves about; anyone who does not know them is stupid.)

"Married for five years and no children. It's driving Alice wild."

"And George?"

"Says he thanks God it's that way and gets drunk."

"When does she expect George's return?"

"He's here now." I stared. "He got here a week ago. Stayed here three days. Then went up to Maine to help his father on the farm. He has three weeks' shore leave coming to him. He'll be back soon."

"Does everybody like George?"

Everything I said exasperated her. In certain walks of life the question of liking or not liking—short of downright villainy—does not arise. One's neighbors, including one's husband, are simply there—like the weather. They're what mathematicians call "given."

"George is all right. He drinks, but who doesn't?" She meant males. Men are expected to drink; it's manly. "If Alice goes to the movies with you, see that she gets back to the gate by one."

"What'd happen if she got back after one?" She gave me a look of exhausted patience. "Wives must often get back later when they've been visiting their parents—trains late and all that?"

"They don't kill you, if that's what you mean. But they remember it." That mighty word "they." "I don't think Alice has ever been out after eleven so they might overlook it. You ask a lot of questions."

"All I know about is the Coast Artillery. I don't know anything about the Navy."

"Well, the Navy's the best and don't you forget it."

"I'm sorry I've made you angry, Delia. I didn't mean to."

"I'm not angry," she said shortly. Then she looked me in the eye and said something between her lips that I couldn't understand.

"I didn't hear what you said."

"There's something that Alice wants more than anything in the world. Give it to her."

"What? . . . What?"

"A baby, of course."

I was thunderstruck. Then I was very agitated. "Did she tell you to say that to me?"

"Of course not. You don't know Alice."

"Has Alice led other men downtown for this?" I was so urgent that I struck her knee with my knee under the table.—I had pictures of troops and parades.

"Take your knee away!—She only made up her mind that she had to last week. The evening after George went to Maine Alice and I went to the Opera House to see a movie. She got talking to a man that sat next to her. They didn't like the movie and went out to get something to eat. She whispered to me not to wait for her. She told me later that the man had a boat tied up by the Yacht Club. She went along, but she wouldn't go aboard. She said that while she was walking Jesus told her the man was a bootlegger, a rum-runner, and that he'd tie her up and start the boat and she'd be in Cuba for weeks. She wouldn't walk up the gangway and when he began pulling her she screamed for the Shore Patrol. He let hold of her and she ran most of the way home."

"You swear you're telling the truth?"

"You're hurting my knee! Everybody's looking at us!"

"Swear!"

"Swear what?"

"That you're telling the truth."

"As God is my judge!"

"And Alice would have no idea that I knew any of this?"

"As God is my judge!"

I leaned back exhausted, then I leaned forward again. "Would George think it was his baby?"

"He'd be the proudest man on the Base."

Alice rejoined us. She had touched up her appearance considerably; there were sparks in the air.

"Well, Delia, it's *late*. We'd better be going. It's very nice to have met you, Dr. Cole. I'll tell George."

"Goodbye, girls. I'll write him."

"He'll be sorry to have missed you."

Each of these remarks was repeated several times. I gathered that shaking hands would have been excessive. Left alone, I ordered another beer, relit my pipe, and resumed reading. Others sat down at my table. When the moment came I obeyed Alice's instructions, though I had to steal around to the side of the restaurant to pick up my bicycle. Alice was waiting at the streetcar stop. She said, moving away from me and scarcely turning her head, "I'll sit in the front of the car. Don't you want to bicycle down to Washington Square?"

"No. At night they let you put the bike on the back platform."

"I don't want to go to the movies. I know a kind of quiet bar where we can talk. It's by the telegraph office. If I see anybody I know on the car, I'll tell them I'm going to the telegraph office to get a money order from my mother. You follow me down Thames Street about a block behind me."

"My apartment's not many blocks beyond the telegraph office. Couldn't we go there?"

"I didn't say we were going to your apartment! Where did you get that idea?"

"You said you liked dogs."

"The name of the bar is 'The Anchor.' While I'm in talking to the telegraph man you stand just inside the door of 'The Anchor.' Ladies can't go in there unless they're with a gentleman-friend." She looked at me fiercely. "This is all very dangerous, but I don't care."

"Aw, Alice, can't we go straight to my apartment? I have a little rye there."

"I told you! I haven't made up my mind yet."

The streetcar came rattling and squealing down the road. A very dignified Alice boarded it and advanced to the front seat. At the One Mile Corner stop she was joined by some friends, a chief petty officer and his wife.

"Alice darling, what are you doing?"

Alice launched into a long narrative filled with disasters and miracles. She held them spellbound. All passengers descended at Washington Square. She was overwhelmed with good fellowship. "I hope everything comes out all right. Good night, dear. Tell us all about it next time we see you."

Again I followed her instructions. Through the great window of the telegraph office I could see her telling another thrilling story to the night clerk. Finally she started toward me with determination, her heels clicking on the brick paving. Suddenly halfway across the street she was accosted by two reeling sailors. Alice managed to do three things at once: she signaled to me to go back into "The Anchor," she reversed her direction as though she had forgotten something in the telegraph office, and she dropped her handbag.

"Alice, you cutey! Wha' you doin' in the beeg city?"

"Alice, where's George? Where's old Georgie, the old skunk?"

"Oh my, I've lost my purse. Mr. Wilson, help me find my purse. I left it in the telegraph office, I know. Oh, isn't that terrible! I'll *die!* Mr. Westerveldt, help me find my purse."

"Here it *is.* Lookit! Now do I get a lil kiss—just a lil lil kiss?"

"Mr. Wilson! You never said a thing like that before. I won't tell George this time, but don't you ever say such a thing again. I had to hurry and send a postal money order off before *closing time.* Mr. Westerveldt, please . . . take . . . your . . . hand . . . away. I just saw the Shore Patrol following me down Thames Street. I think you'd better go up to Spring Street. It's after nine."

Thames Street was out of bounds to Navy seamen after nine. They took her advice and tumbled up the hill.

With set face she marched resolutely into "The Anchor," put her arm through mine—single women are not allowed in the taverns on the *north* side of Thames Street—and propelled me to the last booth at the back of the room. She sat against the wall and shrank to the size of a child. Between her teeth she muttered, "That was a close call. If they'd seen me with you, I don't know what would have happened."

I whispered, "What shall I order for you?"

Again I was to be regarded as an idiot child. She lowered her head and said, "A Rum Floater, of course."

"Alice, please understand I'm not a Navy man. I don't speak Navy language. Please don't be like Delia. I'm not stupid; I'm only ignorant. I haven't been to Norfolk or to Panama. I've been to lots more interesting places than those."

She looked surprised, but remained silent. Alice's silences were weighty; to borrow a schoolboy's expression, "You could hear the wheels go round." The Rum Floaters turned out to be rum in ginger ale, a combination I couldn't abide. She fell on hers like one famished.

"What was Panama like?"

"Hot . . . different."

"What were you doing in Norfolk?"

"I was a waitress in restaurants." She had turned morose. I waited for the rum to take effect. Looking straight before her she said, "I shouldn't have come. . . . You've been telling lies to me all night. You don't 'clean up places'; you live in them. You're one of those rich people. I know what you think of me, *Dr. Cole.*"

"*You* made me say I was a doctor. *You* made me say I was an old friend of your husband's. I'm not rich. I coach children to play tennis. You don't get much for that, I can tell you. Don't let's quarrel, Alice. I think you're a very bright girl and very attractive too. I think you've got knock-out eyes, for instance. You have a personality that sends out electric shocks all the time, like door-knobs when a storm's coming on. Alice, don't let's quarrel. Let's have another Rum Floater and then I'll take you back to the gate in a taxi. There are some taxis standing in the Square every hour of the day and night. Forget all that I said about going to my apartment. Damn it, I hope you and I are grown up enough just to be friends. I can see that you've got some trouble on your mind. Well, leave that trouble behind at the Base."

She had been looking at me fixedly.

"What are you looking at?"

"When I look at a man I try to figure out what movie star he looks like. I can almost always find it. You don't look like any I've seen. You're not very good-looking, you know. I don't say that to hurt your feelings; I just say it because it's true."

"I know I'm not good-looking, but you can't say I have a low-down mean face."

"No."

I got the barman's attention and put up two fingers.

I asked, "What movie star does your husband look like?"

She turned to me sharply. "I won't tell. He's a very good-looking man and a very good man."

"I didn't say he wasn't."

"He saved my life and I love him. I'm a very lucky girl.—Oh, it would have been awful if those men had seen me with you. I'd never have forgiven myself. I'd have just died, that's all."

"How do you mean—George saved your life?"

She gazed before her broodingly. "Norfolk is an awful town. It's worse than Newport. I got fired out of five restaurants. It was awful hard to keep a job. There were a million girls for every job. George was beginning to kind of court me. He'd come back to eat at the same table where I was serving. He'd leave twenty-five cents every time! . . . The men who ran the restaurants were always trying to take advantage of the girls; they'd act fresh in front of the customers. I didn't want George to see anything like that . . . and just when I'd given up *hope* he asked me to marry him. And he gave me twenty-five dollars to buy some nice things, because he had a brother there in the Service too. George knew that he'd write home about me. I owe everything to George." Suddenly she brushed my hand with hers. "I didn't mean to hurt your feelings with what I said a while ago. You haven't got a low-down mean face at all. Every now and then I *say* things— "

Suddenly Alice disappeared. She slid from our bench and crouched under the table. I looked about and saw that two sailors wearing the armband of the Shore Patrol had entered. They greeted a number of the guests affably and, leaning against the bar, discussed at length a certain fracas that had taken place the night before. The public joined in. The conversation threatened to be interminable. Soon I became aware that some little fingernails were scratching my ankles. I leaned over and brushed them away angrily. There are certain torments a man cannot put up with. I heard a giggle. Finally the Shore Patrol left "The Anchor." I whispered, "They're gone," and Alice hoisted herself onto the bench.

"Did you know them?"

"Know them!"

"Alice, you know everybody. You'd better make up your mind whether you'll let me take you back to the Base, or whether you'll come and see my apartment."

She looked at me without expression. "I don't like big dogs."

"I was lying to you. I haven't any dog at all. But I have a pretty nice little present for you." I had three younger sisters. Girls love presents, especially surprise presents.

"What is it?"

"I won't tell."

"Where did you get it?"

"At Atlantic City."

"Will you give me a hint?"

"It glows at night like a big glowworm. So when you're lonesome at night it'll be a comfort to you."

"Is it a Baby Jesus picture?"

"No."

"Oh!—It's one of those wrist-watches."

"I couldn't afford to give anyone a radium wrist-watch. . . . It's about the size of a pin-cushion. It's friendly."

"It's one of those things that keep papers from blowing away."

"Yes."

"You don't wear a wedding ring."

"In the part of the country I come from men don't wear them—only Catholic men wear them. I've never been married anyway."

"If I go to your apartment you won't act fresh or anything?"

It was my turn to look hard and blank. "Not unless someone scratches my ankles."

"I was just *tired* of sitting on the floor."

"Well, you could have said your prayers."

She was staring before her in deep thought. You could "hear the wheels go round." She leaned up against my shoulder and asked, "Is there a roundabout way to your house?"

"Yes. First, I'll pay the bill. Then you follow me."

We got there and crept up the outside staircase. I opened the door and turned on the light, saying, "Come in, Alice."

"Oh, it's big!"

I put the paperweight on the center table and sat down. Like a cat she circled the room inspecting everything within reach. Talking to herself in short admiring phrases. Finally she took up the paperweight—a view of the Atlantic City boardwalk, picked out with bits of mica, under an isinglass dome.

"Is this what you said I could have?" I nodded. "It doesn't . . . glow."

"It can't glow as long as there is one bit of sunlight or electric light around. Go into the bathroom, shut the door, turn out the light, keep your eyes closed for two minutes and then open them."

I waited. She came out, threw herself on my lap, and put her arms around my neck. "I'll never be lonesome any more." She put her lips against my ear and said something. I thought I heard what she said but I couldn't be certain. Her lips were too close; perhaps shyness muffled her speech. I thought I heard her say, "I want a baby." But I had to be sure. Holding her chin with one hand I moved my ears two inches from her lips and asked "What did you say?"

At that moment she heard something. Just as dogs hear sounds that we cannot hear, just as chickens (I had worked on farms as a boy) could see hawks approaching from a great distance, just so Alice heard something. She slid off my lap and pretended to be busy straightening her hair; she picked up her hat and—resourceful actress that she was—said sweetly, "Well, I'd better be going. It's getting late. . . . Did you really mean that I could keep this picture for my own?"

I sat motionless watching her play the scene.

Had I said anything to offend her? No.

Made a gesture? No.

A harbor sound? A street quarrel? My neighbors at Mrs. Keefe's?

In 1926 the invention known in my part of town as the "raddy-o" was present in an increasing number of homes. On a warm evening through open windows it diffused a web of music, oratory, and dramatic and comic dialogue. I had become habituated and deaf to this, and certainly Alice on the Base had become so also.

"You've been very sweet. I love your apartment. I love your kitchen."

I rose. "Well, if you must go, Alice, I'll follow you as far as the Square and pay your taxi-man to drop you at the gate. You don't want to meet any more of the thousand people you know."

"Don't you move *one inch*. The streetcars are still running. If I meet anybody I'll tell them I've been to the telegraph office."

"I could walk with you perfectly safely along Spring Street. It's darker and the Shore Patrol will have swept it up pretty well by now. Here, I'll wrap up the paperweight."

Mrs. Keefe had furnished my room according to her own taste which called for a wide selection of table runners, lace doilies, and silk table covers to support vases and so on. I picked up one of the latter and wrapped it around the gift. I opened the door. Alice was now very subdued and preceded me down the stairs.

Then I heard it—another music that had escaped my ears, but not hers. During the summer a small frame house near Mrs. Keefe's had been turned into "The Mission of the Holy Spirit," a fervent revivalist sect. A meeting was in progress. While working on farms in Kentucky and Southern California I had attended many camp-meetings of a similar kind and knew well some of their hymns, seldom heard in urban churches. Surely these hymns had been built into the lives of boys and girls growing up in rural West Virginia where the camp-meeting was the powerful center of the religious, social, and even "entertainment" life of the community. What Alice had heard was the hymn that precedes the "offering of one's life to Jesus": *"Yield not to temptation; Jesus is near."*

We turned up the hill to Spring Street. It was deserted and I stepped forward and walked beside her. She was weeping. I enclosed her tiny hand in mine.

"Life is hard, dear Alice."

"Teddie?"

"Yes."

"Do you believe in hell?"

"What do you mean by hell, Alice?"

"That we go to hell when we do bad things? When I was a girl I did a lot of bad things. When I was in Norfolk I had to do a lot of bad things. I had a baby but I haven't got it any more. It was before I knew George but I told him about it. Since I married George I haven't done a bad thing at all. Really, I haven't, Teddie. Like I told you, George saved my life."

"Has George ever struck you, Alice?"

She looked up at me quickly. "Do I have to tell the truth? Well, I will. He gets very drunk after he comes back from a long tour of duty and he does strike me. But I don't hate him for it. He has a reason. He knows that he . . . he can't make babies. He makes love, but no babies get to be born. Wouldn't that make you kind of upset?"

"Go on."

"Every now and then I thought I'd get a baby with another man without George's knowing about it. I don't think going to bed with another man once in a while is very important. . . . Even though it was a lie, it would make George very happy. He's a good man. If it made him feel good to be a father, that wouldn't be a very bad sin, would it? Like what they call in the Bible adult'ary. Sometimes, I think I'd go to hell for a long time if it would make George happy."

I turned her hand over and over in mine. We reached Washington Square. We crossed the street and sat down on a bench farthest from the street lights.

I said, "Alice, I'm ashamed of you."

She said quickly, "Why are you ashamed of me?"

"That *you*—who know that the heart of Jesus is as big as the whole world—you think that Jesus would send you to hell for a little sin that would make George happy or a little sin that you had to do to keep alive in a cruel city like Norfolk."

She put her head against my shoulder. "Don't be ashamed of me, Teddie. . . . Talk to me. . . . When I ran away from home my father wrote me that he never wanted to see me until I had a wedding ring on my finger. When I wrote him that I was married he changed his mind. He said he never wanted to see a hoor in his house."

I'm not going to put down here what I said to Alice almost fifty years ago. I reminded her of some words that Jesus said and maybe I invented some. And then I said, "I'm not going to say any more." Her hand in mine had become calmer. I could hear "the wheels going round."

She said, "Let's go over nearer to the street lights. I want to show you something."

We moved to another bench. She had taken something out of her handbag, but kept it hidden from me.

"Teddie, I always wear a chain and locket around my neck, but when I came out tonight with Delia I took it off. You can guess who gave it to me."

I looked at the picture in the locket. It had been taken several years before. A sailor about eighteen years old—the sailor who could have sat for any recruiting poster—was laughing into the camera; his arm was about Alice. I could imagine the occasion:

"Step up, ladies and gentlemen! Just twenty cents for the picture and a dollar for the locket and chain. You two there—you're only young once. Don't miss this opportunity."

I looked at it.

She looked at it.

Again she whispered in my ear. "I want a baby—for George."

We rose and walked back to my apartment. As we got near the stairs I said, "It's very important that George doesn't know. That's the whole point. Will Delia talk?"

"No."

"Can you be sure?"

"Yes. Delia knows how important that is. She's said so over and over again."

"Alice, I don't know your last name and you don't know mine. We must never meet again." She nodded. "Twice tonight you've had narrow escapes. You can go to 'Mama Carlotta's'; I'll never be there again."

Two hours later we returned to the Square. She peered around the corner as though we'd robbed a bank. She whispered, "The movie's over." She giggled.

I left her in a doorway and went up to a taxi. I asked the driver how much it cost to go to One Mile Corner.

"Fifty cents," he said.

I went back and put half a dollar and two dimes in her hand. "Where will you say you've been?"

"What do they call that place where they were singing hymns?"

I told her. "I'll stay here at this corner and see you off."

She kissed her finger tips and put them on my cheek. "I'd better not keep that picture of Atlantic City."

She gave it back to me. She took some steps toward the taxi, then returned to me and said, "I won't be lonesome at night any more, will I?"

Off she drove.

I thought suddenly, "Of course, all those twenty years Penelope had Telemachus growing up beside her."

"The Deer Park"

This chapter might also be called "The Shaman or *Le Médecin malgré lui*."

One day I found a note in my mailbox at the Post Office asking me to telephone a Mrs. Jens Skeel, such and such a number, on any day between three and four.

"Mrs. Skeel, this is Mr. North speaking."

"Good afternoon, Mr. North. Thank you for calling. Friends have spoken to me with much appreciation of your reading with students and adults. I was hoping that you could find time to read French with my daughter Elspeth and my son Arthur. Elspeth is a dear sweet intelligent girl of seventeen. We have had to take her out of school because she suffers from migraine. She misses school and particularly misses her courses in French literature. Both my children have been to school in Normandy and in Geneva. They speak and read French well. Both of them adore the *Fables* of La Fontaine and wish to read all of them with you. . . . Yes, we have several copies of them here. . . . The late morning would suit us very well. . . . Eleven to twelve-thirty, Mondays, Wednesdays, and Fridays—yes. May I send a car for you? . . . Oh,

you prefer to come by bicycle. . . . We live at 'The Deer Park'—
do you know it? . . . Good! May I tell the children that you will
be here tomorrow? . . . Thank you so much."

Everyone knew "The Deer Park." The father of the present
Mr. Skeel had been a Dane engaged in international shipping. He
had built this "Deer Park" not in imitation of the famous park in
Copenhagen, but in affectionate allusion to it. I had often dis-
mounted before the high iron grille enclosing a vast lawn that
ended in a low cliff above the sea. Under the glorious trees of
Newport I could catch glimpses of deer, rabbits, peacocks—alas,
for La Fontaine, no foxes, no wolves, not even a donkey.

I was met in the front hall by Mrs. Skeel. "Elegance" is too
brilliant a word for such perfection of presence. She was dressed
in gray silk; there were gray pearls about her neck and in her
ears. All was distinction and charm and something else—anguish
under high stoic control.

"You will find my daughter on the verandah. I think that
she would prefer that you introduce yourself.—Mr. North, if
at any time you see that she is suffering from fatigue, will you
find an excuse to draw the lesson to a close? Arthur will help
you."

Like mother, like daughter—though the anguish was partially
replaced by an extreme pallor. I addressed her in French.

"Mr. North, may I ask that we read in French? But it tires me
to speak in it." Her hand lightly indicated the left side of her
forehead. "Look! Here comes my brother."

I turned to see a boy of eleven scrambling up the cliff in the
distance. I had seen him often on the tennis courts, though he had
not been among my pupils. He was the lively freckled American
boy so often pictured on grocers' calendars to illustrate Whittier's
poem. He was called "Galloper," because his middle name was
Gallup and because he talked so rapidly and never walked when he
might run. He sped toward us and came to an abrupt halt. We
were introduced and shook hands gravely.

"Why, Galloper," I said, "we've met before."

"Yes, sir."

"Are you called by that name here too?"

"Yes, sir. Elspeth calls me that."

"I like it. May I call you so?"

"Yes, sir."

"Are you fond of the *Fables* also?"

"We're both very interested in animals. Galloper spends many hours watching a tidal pool. He's come to know some of the fish and shellfish and he's given them names. We talk over everything together."

"I'm very happy, Miss Skeel, that you wish to read the *Fables*. I haven't read them for some time, but I remember my admiration for them. They are small but somehow great, modest but perfect. We shall try and find out how La Fontaine manages that. But before we begin, kindly let me have a moment to become accustomed to this beautiful place—and to those friends I see there. Would it tire you if we took a short walk?"

She turned to the nurse who came toward her. "Miss Chalmers, may I take my morning walk now?"

"Yes, Miss Elspeth."

The deer enjoyed a pavilion at our right within a grove of trees; the rabbits resided in a village of hutches; the peacocks reigned in an aviary, a portion of which could protect them throughout the winter.

"Should we have some biscuits in our hands?"

"The caretaker feeds them several times a day. They don't expect anything from us. It's best that way."

The deer watched us approach, then slowly drew nearer. "It's best not to put out your hand until they've touched us first." Presently the deer were beside us and between us and before us and behind us. We were taking a walk together. Even the fawns who had been lying in the shade of a tree struggled to their feet and joined the procession. The older deer began brushing us—

bumping us, ever so slightly. "What they like most is to be talked
to. I think they live most in their eyes and ears and muzzles.
That's the most beautiful baby, Jacqueline. I remember when you
looked just like her. You must be careful that she doesn't fall
over the cliff, as you did. You remember the splints you had to
wear and how you hated them. . . . Oh, Monsieur Bayard, your
antlers are growing fast. They like it when you stroke their horns.
I think their horns itch when the velvet is growing on them. The
rabbits hope that we'll come over and visit them too. They stay
away from the deer. They don't like hoofs. *Oh, Figaro, how hand-*
some you are! The deer will leave us soon; they find the company of humans exhausting. . . . See, they are drifting away already. . . . It's terrible to see them on the Fourth of July. Of
course, no one has ever shot at them, but they carry some memory
of hunters in their blood—do you think that's possible? . . . It's
too early to see the rabbits play. When the moon's come up they
tear around as though they'd gone out of their mind."

"Mademoiselle, why do the deer push against us that way?"

"I think, maybe . . . Will you excuse me if I sit down for
a minute? Please sit down too. Galloper will tell you what we
think about that."

I had noticed that bamboo chairs with wide armrests, such as
I had known in China as a boy, were placed, two by two, at intervals on the lawn. We sat down. Galloper answered for his
sister. "We think that we must imagine their enemies. We have
a picture in the hall—"

"I think it's by Landseer."

"—of stags and does huddled together in a mass surrounded by
wolves. Before there were any men with guns on the earth, the
deers' enemies were wolves or maybe men with spears or
bludgeons. The deers must have lost some, but they defended
themselves that way—with a sort of wall of antlers. They don't
like to be patted or stroked; it's nearness they like to feel. That's
different from the rabbits. The hare has been thumping the ground
to warn the others that we are coming. But if there is no shelter

near, they 'freeze' wherever they are; they 'play dead.' They have enemies on the ground too, but they mostly fear hawks. But hawks hunt singly. Either way, the deer and the rabbits lose a few of their kind——"

"What I call 'hostages to fortune.' "

"But they do what they can for their kind."

Elspeth looked at me. "Do you think that there is something in that idea?"

I looked at her with a smile. "I'm your pupil. I want to hear what you say."

"Oh, I'm just beginning to try to think. I'm trying to understand why nature is so cruel and yet so wonderful. Galloper, tell Mr. North what you see in the tidal pool."

Galloper answered reluctantly. "It's a battle every day. It's . . . it's terrible."

"Mr. North," said Elspeth, "why must that be? Doesn't God love the world?"

"Yes, He surely does. But we must talk that over later."

"You won't forget?"

"No.—Mademoiselle, have you ever seen deer in their wild—I mean, their natural—state?"

"Oh, yes. My Aunt Benedikta has a camp in the Adirondacks. She's always asking us to visit her in the summer. There you can see deer and foxes and even bears. And there are no fences or cages at all. They're *free!* And so beautiful!"

"Are you going there this summer?"

"No . . . Father doesn't like us to go there. And besides, I'm not . . . I'm not very well."

"What are some of the other things about animals that you talk about together?"

"Yesterday we had a long talk about why nature placed the eyes of birds on the sides of their heads."

"And why," added Galloper, "so many animals' heads are bent to the ground."

"We love WHYS," said his sister.

"And what did you decide?"

Galloper, after a glance at his sister, released her from the effort of answering. "We knew that herbivorous animals had to keep their eyes on the plants beneath them and that the birds had to be alert for enemies on all sides of them; but we wondered why nature couldn't have worked out a better way—like the eyes of the Crustacea in my tidal pool."

"The difficulty of thinking," murmured his sister, "is that you have to think of so many things at once."

She had been carrying a copy of the *Fables*. It fell from the wide armrest of the chair. (Had she pushed it?) We both leaned over to pick it up from the ground. Our hands met and struggled for it a moment. She drew in her breath hastily and shut her eyes. When she opened them she looked into mine and said with unusual directness: "Galloper says that your pupils at the Casino say that you have electric hands."

I think I blushed furiously and was furious at myself for blushing. "That's absurd, of course. That doesn't mean anything."

Hell! Damnation!

Every once in a while it rains in Newport. Sometimes a shower would fall during those two early hours when I was coaching tennis at the Casino. I never had more than four pupils at a time; my other pupils would be playing against one another on courts nearby. And we would all run for shelter to one of the social rooms behind the spectators' gallery. My pupils, all between eight and fourteen, made a very pretty sight, dressed in spotless white, radiant with youth, delicately fostered, and expending their energy. They would gather about me, crying, "Mr. North, tell us some more about China!" or "Tell us some more stories like 'The Necklace' "—I had once held them hushed and dismayed by de Maupassant's story. The ever-watchful Bill Wentworth—himself a father and grandfather—knew well that children of that age love to sit on the floor. He would spread out some sail cloth about the "teacher's chair." Galloper had not been among my pupils, but he joined the circle and even some older players hesitantly drew up their chairs. It was there that I had first beheld Eloise Fenwick and it was for her dear eyes and ears that I had first retold Chaucer's story of "The Falcon." It was for Galloper that I told of Fabre's discovery of how a wasp paralyzes a grub or a caterpillar and then lays its egg upon it to nourish the future insect. Was it Rousseau who said the primary function of early education was to expand in children the faculty of wonder?

I felt no prompting to caress the children about me. I do not like to be touched myself, but children must pet and stroke and tease and even buffet any older person who has gained their confidence. When the shower was over there was a great dragging of me to return to the courts and a great dragging of me to stay and tell one more story because "the grass is still wet." And one child after another claimed to discover that I had " 'lectric" hands, that my hands gave off sparks. I took a severe attitude toward this. I forbade such remarks. "That's silly! I don't want to hear any more about that." Then one day things got out of bounds. In the tumultuous rush to the courts, Ada Nicols, aged nine, was flung to one side; striking her head against a post she lost consciousness. I leaned over her, parting her hair where the bruise seemed to be and repeating her name. She opened her eyes, then closed them again. The whole group was staring down at her anxiously. She pulled my hands to her forehead murmuring, "More! More!" She was smiling vacantly. Finally she said happily, "I'm hypmertized," and then, "I'm a angel." I picked her up and carried her to Bill Wentworth's office which was frequently called upon to serve as a first-aid station. From that hour I became a far sterner and more matter-of-fact coach. No more Uncle Theophilus's stories. No more mesmerism.

But Ada's story spread.

I have already told the reader in the first chapter of this book

that I knew I possessed a certain faculty and that I wished to
ignore it. I had often parted furious dogs; I could calm frantic
horses. During the War and elsewhere, in bars and taverns, I had
only to lay my hands on the shoulders of quarrelsome men and
to murmur a few words in order to establish peace. I take no
interest in the irrational, in the inexplicable. I am no mystic.
Besides, I had already learned that—whether it was a "real"
thing or not—it inevitably led me to a certain amount of imposture and quackery. The reader knows that I'm no stranger to
imposture, but I want to practice deceptions when I please to,
not when they're forced upon me. I want to engage in life in
the spirit of play, not in leading others by the nose, not in rendering others ridiculous in my own eyes.

And here this wretched business of my "electric hands" had
raised its head at "The Deer Park" in the presence of that rare and
suffering girl and that keenly intelligent boy.

HELL! DAMNATION!

For two afternoons we read the *Fables* and analyzed them by
the French method called *"l'explication de texte."* I stayed up
half the night doing my "homework" preparation for the sessions. I brought forward all the professional commonplaces: the
art with which homely speech is elevated to poetry; the energy
imparted by the insertion of short verses among the long (condemned by a number of La Fontaine's most distinguished contemporaries); the irony conveyed by the heroic alexandrines; the
redoubled simplicity when the poet closes the fable with its
edifying or instructive moral.

At my arrival for the third session I was met by Galloper who
told me that his sister was suffering from a migraine that day and
could not come downstairs.

"Well, Galloper, shall we have our class just the same?"

"Sir, when Elspeth isn't well . . . I can't keep my mind on
books and things. My mother told me to tell you that we'll pay
you as usual."

I looked at him hard. He was indeed in great distress.

"Galloper, would it be any relief to you if you gave me a half hour of your time now to show me your tidal pool?"

"Oh, yes, sir. Elspeth would like me to do that—sir." He looked back at the house calculatingly. "We have to go down the cliff behind the caretaker's house. Father's at home and he doesn't like me to be interested in the tidal pool. He . . . he wants me to go into the business, I mean his shipping business."

We took the roundabout way almost stealthily. On the descent I asked him, "Galloper, do you go to a military school?"

"No, sir."

"Then why do you feel that you must address me as 'sir' *every* time you speak to me?"

"Father likes me to do it to him. His father was a count in Denmark. He's not a count because he's an American; but he likes it when important people call him 'Count.' He wants Elspeth and me to be like his father and mother."

"Oh, so you must be very much a lady and a gentleman?"

"Oh, *yes,* s- s-"

"Do you ever have headaches? . . . No? . . . Forgive me asking so many questions. In a minute you're going to tell me all about this pool. Is your Aunt Benedikta very much a countess too?"

"Oh, no. She lets us do anything we want to do."

We knelt over the pool. We saw the anemones opening to welcome the incoming tide; we saw the crayfish lurking ominously in their caves. He showed me the marvels of protective coloration —the waterlogged sticks that were not sticks, the pebbles that were not pebbles. He showed me the fury with which tiny fish, when near their eggs, can fight off predators many times larger than themselves. I, too, was revived by the inflowing tide of wonders. My wonder included the small professor. At the half hour's close I asked him to accompany me to the front door. As we rose I said, "Thank you, sir. I haven't been so filled with the excitement of science since I read *The Voyage of the Beagle.*"

"We think that's the best book in the world."

As we crossed the lawn the deer gathered about us as though they had been waiting. They bumped me and even pushed me from side to side. I stopped and talked to them in French. Galloper stood apart and watched this. When we moved on he said, "They don't do that to me or even to their keeper—not so much. They only do it to you and to Elspeth. . . . They know you have galvanic hands."

"Galloper! Galloper! You're a scientist. You know there are no such things."

"Sir, there are a lot of mysteries in nature, aren't there?"

I made no reply. At the door I asked if he felt that his sister was improving. He looked up at me. He was fighting back tears. "They say she has to go to Boston for an operation soon."

I shook his hand in goodbye, then put my hand on his shoulder. "Yes . . . Yes . . . There are a lot of mysteries in nature. Thank you for reminding me of that." I leaned down and said, "You're going to see one. Your sister is going to get better.—Put this in your pipe and smoke it, Dr. Skeel: your sister has no trouble with her eyesight; and she can go down those verandah steps without losing her balance."

At the next session Elspeth seemed much improved. She volunteered to recite a *Fable* she had newly committed to memory. I cast a glance toward her brother to see if he had caught the significance of this achievement. He had.

She said, "Galloper, will you tell Mr. North what we decided yesterday to ask him?"

"My sister and I decided that we don't want to read any more of the *Fables*. . . . Oh, we like them very much; but we don't want them now. . . . We feel that they're not really about animals; they're about human beings and my sister has always had a strong feeling that animals should not be . . . ?"

He looked at her. She said, "—regarded as persons. We went through ten of the most famous *Fables* and underlined the places where La Fontaine seemed to have his eye really on the fox and the pigeon and the crow . . . and we didn't find very many. Oh, we admire him, but you told Galloper to read Fabre. And Mother ordered the books from New York and we think they're almost the best books we ever read."

There was a silence.

I said, with a gesture faintly implying withdrawal, "Well, you don't need me to read Fabre with you."

"Mr. North, we haven't been quite honest with you. Galloper persuaded Mother to invite you to read with us. Galloper wanted me to meet you. We wanted you just to come and talk with us. Won't you do that? We can pretend that we're reading La Fontaine."

I looked at them gravely, still with the attitude of one about to rise from his chair.

She added, bravely, "And he wanted you to put your hands on my head. He told me about Ada Nicols.—Almost all the time I have such pain. Will you put your hands on my forehead?"

Galloper was staring up at me with an even more intense urgency.

"Miss Elspeth, it is unsuitable that I put my hands on your head without permission from your nurse."

As before she beckoned to Miss Chalmers who came toward her. I arose and descended some steps of the verandah. I heard Miss Chalmers say something about . . . "most unladylike . . . cannot take the responsibility for such unsuitable behavior. . . . You are my patient and I do not wish you to be agitated. . . . Well, if you insist, you must ask your mother. If she asks me I must tell her that I emphatically disapprove. . . . I think these readings have been most harmful to you, Miss Elspeth."

Miss Chalmers withdrew, bristling with indignation. Galloper arose and entered the house. His absence was prolonged. I assumed that Mrs. Skeel was being told for the first time of the Ada Nicols incident. While we waited I asked Elspeth where she had

attended school and if she had enjoyed it. She named one of
the best-known girls' finishing schools.

"Every moment you had to remember what you were supposed
to do. It was like being in a cage; you were being trained to be
a lady. . . . It was like those horses that they teach to waltz. . . .
When I'm at Aunt Benedikta's camp in the Adirondacks, I can
see real deer in the wild. A deer jumping is one of the most
beautiful sights in the world—these deer have never really leaped
over anything. There's no room and no reason for their jumping,
is there? . . . Mr. North, do you ever have a nightmare about
being in prison?"

"Yes, I have. It's the worst dream a man can have."

"Next year my father wants me to do what they call 'come out
in society.' I think it's not a coming out but a going in. The girls
at school talked about the Christmas and Easter vacations—three
dances a night and tea-dances . . . and being stared at by a *wall*
of young men all the time. Don't you think that's like animals
in the zoo? Whenever I think about it my head begins to ache.
—And Father wants me to take the name 'Countess Skeel.' "

"Haven't you things to think about to drive away those nightmares?"

"I used to have music . . . and the books Galloper and I read
together, but . . ." She put her hand to her forehead.

"Miss Elspeth, I'm not going to wait for your mother's permission. Miss Chalmers lives in a very small cage. I'm going to put
my hand on your forehead," and I rose.

At that moment Galloper returned. He went directly to Miss
Chalmers with his message; then came to our table.

"Mother says you may place your hands on Elspeth's forehead
for a few minutes."

What to do?

Play the charlatan.

Elspeth shut her eyes and lowered her head.

I arose and said in a matter-of-fact tone, "Please, look toward the sky, Miss Elspeth, and keep your eyes open. Galloper, will you please place your hands on your sister's right forehead." I placed my hands lightly on her left forehead. I looked down into her open eyes and smiled. I did two things at once: I concentrated on forcing "some kind of energy" into my finger tips and I spoke to her as unemphatically as I could. "Look up at the cloud. . . . Try to feel the earth slowly turning under us. . . ." Her hands rose to my wrists. She could not keep her eyes open. She was smiling. She murmured, "Is this dying? Am I dying?"

"No. You are feeling the earth turning.—Now say anything that comes into your head. . . . Give me your right hand." I enclosed it between mine. "Say anything that comes into your head."

"Oh, *mon professeur*. Let us go away, the three of us. I have some money and some jewels that were given to me. Aunt Benedikta has a camp in the Adirondacks. She has asked me to come at any time. We would have to escape without anyone knowing. Galloper says he does not know how to arrange it, but you and he could together. If I am taken to Boston, they will kill me. I am not afraid to die, but I don't want to die in their way. Mr. North, I want to die in your way. Hasn't everyone a right to die in the way they choose?"

I stopped her by increasing the pressure above and below her hand. "You are going to Boston, but the operation is going to be postponed. Gradually your headaches are going to go away. You are going to spend the rest of the summer at your Aunt Benedikta's camp." Then I spoke in French, "Please say 'Yes, professor' very slowly. Remember—the clouds and the ocean and the trees are listening."

Slowly, *"Oui, monsieur le professeur!"* Then more loudly, *"Oui, monsieur le professeur!"*

We remained motionless for a full minute. An overpowering weakness invaded me. I doubted that my legs could carry me to the front door and to my bicycle. I withdrew my hands. I made a gesture to Galloper to stay where he was and I stumbled and swayed through the house. I caught a glimpse of Miss Chalmers on her feet staring at her patient. The butler and some servants were peering through the drawing-room window. Their heads turned toward me as I hurried by. I fell off my bicycle twice. I had difficulty keeping to the right side of the road.

A weekend elapsed. I rang the bell at "The Deer Park" on the following Monday morning at eleven. I was ready to resign, but I wanted to be dismissed. At the door the butler informed me that Mrs. Skeel wished to see me on the verandah. I bowed to her. She put out her hand, saying, "Will you please sit down, Mr. North?" I sat down and kept my eyes on her face.

"Mr. North, when I first telephoned you I was not quite honest with you. I did not tell you the whole truth. My daughter Elspeth is very ill. For several months we have driven her to Boston twice a month for consultations with Dr. Bosco—examinations and X-rays. The doctor fears that she has a tumor of the brain, but there are many aspects of the case that puzzle him. As you will have noticed she has no difficulty in speaking, though it pains her to raise her voice. She has no impairment in her vision or in her sense of balance. She suffers from lapses of memory but they can be attributed to her difficulty in sleeping and to the medication that she is given." Her hands were grasping the arms of her chair as though she were clinging to a raft. "Dr. Bosco has decided that he must perform a major operation on her brain next week. He wishes that she enter the hospital on Thursday. . . . My daughter feels that this is all unnecessary. She is convinced that you have the power to heal her. . . . Of course, the doctor's assistant could give her an injection and she could be transported to Boston . . . as . . . as she says, 'like a mummy.' She says that she would fight him 'like a dragon.' You can imagine how distressing that would be for the whole household."

I continued to listen gravely.

"Mr. North, I would like to make a request of you. I ask this not as an employer, but as the suffering mother of a suffering child. Elspeth says she will consent to go to Boston 'quietly,' if the operation is postponed for two weeks and if I can obtain your promise to visit her there twice."

"Certainly, ma'am, if the doctor permits it."

"Oh, thank you. I'm sure I can arrange it; I *must* arrange it. A car and chauffeur will be placed at your disposal on both days for your trip and return."

"That will not be necessary. I can find my way to Boston and to the door of the hospital. Please write down the hours when I am to call, the length of the visit, and enclose a letter which I am to present to the office of admission at the hospital. I shall send you a bill for whatever expenses I may incur, including the cost of the engagements I must cancel here. I do not wish any remuneration except those basic expenses. I think such an interview would be easiest for us if your son Arthur were present at the same time."

"Yes, you can be sure of that."

"Mrs. Skeel, since my visit last Friday has Miss Elspeth had a return of the migraine?"

"She was greatly improved. She said she slept 'like an angel' all night. Her appetite improved. But last night—Sunday night —the pain returned. It was terrible to see. I longed to telephone to you. But Miss Chalmers and our Newport doctor were here. They believe you to be the cause of the whole trouble. They forget that this happened over and over again before you ever came here. And her father was here. The Skeels, for generations, have known very little illness. I believe his suffering to be worse than mine, for I have grown up among many . . . such illnesses."

"Are we to have a class today?"

"She is sleeping. She is blessedly sleeping."

"When does she go to Boston?"

"Even if the operation is postponed—as I shall insist—she will leave here Thursday."

"Please tell Miss Elspeth, I shall be here Wednesday and that

I shall visit her in Boston at whatever hour you name. . . . Mrs. Skeel, do not hesitate to call on me any hour of the day or night. It is often hard to reach me by day, but I shall leave you here a schedule of telephone numbers where I can be reached. You and Miss Elspeth must have the courage to face those who resist my visits."

"Thank you."

"I wish to say one more word, ma'am. Arthur is a very remarkable young man."

"*Isn't he! Isn't he!*"

And for a moment we laughed, astonishing ourselves. At that moment a gentleman appeared at the door. There was no mistaking the former Count Jens Skeel of Skeel.

He said, "Mary, kindly go into the library. This foolishness has gone on long enough. This is the French tutor's last visit to this house. Will the French tutor kindly send me his bill as promptly as possible. Good morning, sir."

I smiled sunnily into his outraged face. "Thank you," I said nodding in the manner of a clerk who has been accorded a long-wished-for vacation. "Good afternoon, Mrs. Skeel. Kindly convey my deep regard to your children." Again I smiled at the master of the house, raising my hand in a manner of saying "Don't trouble to see me to the door. I know the way." Only an accomplished actor can be thrown out of a house and leave a room as though a favor had been conferred upon him—John Drew, say; Cyril Maude, William Gillette.

I was expecting a late telephone call that night, so I sat up reading. The call came at about one-thirty.

"Mr. North, you told me I might call you at any hour."

"Yes, indeed, Mrs. Skeel."

"Elspeth has been in great distress. She wishes to see you. Her father has given his permission."

I wheeled to the house. There seemed to be lights in every window. I was led to the sickroom. Servants in breathless dismay, but dressed as though it were high noon, could be seen lurking in shadows and behind half-open doors. Mrs. Skeel and a doctor were standing in the upper hall. I was introduced to him. He was very angry and shook my hand coldly.

"Dr. Egleston has given me permission to call you."

At a distance I saw Mr. Skeel, very handsome and furious. Mrs. Skeel opened a door a few inches and said, "Elspeth dear, Mr. North has called to ask how you are."

Elspeth was sitting up in bed. Her eyes were bright and fierce after what I presumed to be a prolonged battle with her father and the doctor. My smile included all the bystanders. There was no sign of Miss Chalmers.

"*Bonsoir, chère mademoiselle.*"

"*Bonsoir, monsieur le professeur.*"

I turned back and said in a matter-of-fact tone, "I would like Galloper to join us."

I knew that wherever he was he would hear me. He came forward quickly. Over his pajamas he was wearing a thick dressing-gown bearing the insignia of the school he attended. I let the onlookers see me take out my Ingersoll watch and place it on the bedside table. At a gesture from me Galloper opened wide the door into the hall and another into an inner room where Miss Chalmers was probably boiling.

"You have been in pain, Miss Elspeth?"

"Yes, a little. I don't let them give me those *things*."

I turned back to the door and said calmly, "Anyone may come in who wishes to. I shall be here five minutes. I only ask that no one come in bringing anger or fear."

Mrs. Skeel entered and took a chair at the foot of her daughter's bed. An elderly woman who had been turning the beads of a rosary in her hand—probably Elspeth's nurse since childhood—came in with an air of defying some order. She knelt in a corner of the room, still fingering her beads. I continued to smile about me as though this were a very usual call and as though I were an old friend of the family. Indeed, it was so unusual an occasion that the household servants gathered about the door, unrebuked. Several even entered the room and remained standing.

"Miss Elspeth, as I came up the Avenue on my bicycle, not a person could be seen. It was like a landscape on the moon. It was very beautiful. I was looking forward to seeing you. I was a little *exalté* and I heard myself singing an old song that you must surely know: '*Stone walls do not a prison make, Nor iron bars a cage.*' Those lines, written almost three hundred years ago, must have brought comfort to thousands of men and women—as they have done to me. Now I am going to talk to you in Chinese for a moment. You remember that I was brought up in China. I shall give you the translation too. "*Ee er san*"—with a downward, then upward glide—"*See. Gee—der—gaw*"—with a rising inflection. "*Hu*" (a descending note) "*li too bay. Nu chi fo n' yu*" and so on. The first seven words are all the Chinese I know. They mean: "one, two, three, four, chicken—egg—cake." "Mademoiselle, this means: 'All nature is one. Every living thing is closely related to every other living thing. Nature wishes every living thing to be a perfect example of its kind and to rejoice in the gift of life. That includes Galloper's fish and Jacqueline and Bayard and everybody here, including you and Galloper and me." Those were not the words of Confucius or Mencius, but a paraphrase of something remembered from Goethe.

I leaned forward and spoke to her in a low voice. "Let them drive you to Boston. The operation is going to be postponed and postponed. I am not only going to Boston to see you; I am going to see Dr. Bosco. Has he ever been here to see 'The Deer Park'?"

"Yes. Yes, he has."

"I shall tell him that you have been like a beautiful deer in the deer park, but that you want to be outside that iron fence. Your headaches are your protest against those bars. I shall tell Dr. Bosco to send you to your Aunt Benedikta's camp among those deer who have never known a cage."

"*Can* you do that?"

"Oh, yes."

"I know you can!—Will you come to see me there too?"

"I will try. But a man of thirty has cages and cages. Don't forget I shall see you more than once in Boston and for the rest of the summer I shall write you often. Now I have one minute left. I am going to put my hand on your forehead . . . and all the way home my thoughts will be on you, like a hand, and you will fall asleep."

There was a hush. . . . Sixty seconds of silence on the stage is a long time.

"*Dormez bien, mademoiselle.*"

"*Dormez bien, monsieur le professeur.*"

I may not have galvanic hands but I can put on a galvanic performance. This time I chose as my model that of Otis Skinner in *The Honor of the Family,* after Balzac's story. Moving toward the door I smiled commandingly on those within the room and outside it, on the tear-stained face of Mrs. Skeel, on the Greek chorus of awestricken servants, and on the angry and frustrated faces of Mr. Skeel, Dr. Egleston, and Miss Chalmers who had joined them. I gained two inches in height, a cylinder hat rose from my head at a jaunty angle. I carried a short riding-crop with which I thrashed the jamb of the door. I was all assurance to the degree of effrontery—Colonel Philippe Bridau.

"Good morning, ladies and gentlemen. Good morning, Galloper —Charles Darwin expects every man to do his duty."

"Yes, sir."

"Good morning, all." I called back into the sickroom, "Good morning, Miss Elspeth. '*Stone walls do not a prison make, nor iron bars a cage.*' Please say 'No, they don't!' "

Her voice rang out, "*Non, monsieur le professeur!*"

I advanced bowing to right and left and descended the staircase two steps at a time, singing the Soldiers' Chorus from *Faust.*

Hope is a projection of the imagination; so is despair. Despair all too readily embraces the ills it foresees; hope is an energy and arouses the mind to explore every possibility to combat them. On the bicycle ride to "The Deer Park"—through that mysterious landscape on the moon—*I had had an idea.*

It was arranged that I call at the hospital on the following Friday afternoon at four o'clock. I wrote Dr. Bosco, asking for a five-minute appointment to see him at that time to talk to him about his patient Miss Elspeth Skeel. I wrote that I had enjoyed many congenial talks with his great friend and colleague Dr. de Martel at the American Hospital at Neuilly near Paris. Dr. de Martel was another of the three greatest surgeons in the world. I had never met that eminent man, but hope leaps over obstacles. He had, however, performed an operation on a friend of mine, six days old. Besides, he was the son of the novelist "Gyp" (the Comtesse de Martel), a zestful writer with eyes wide open.

Dr. Bosco received me with a cordiality that immediately turned to professional impersonality. During the entire interview his secretary stood behind him, notebook in hand, open.

"What is your work, Mr. North?"

"I am tutor in English, French, German, and Latin; and children's tennis coach at the Newport Casino. I do not wish to waste your time, Doctor. Miss Skeel has confided to me that she dreads going to sleep because she is afflicted by nightmares of being caged. She is dying of cultural claustration."

"I beg your pardon?"

"She is an exceptional human being with a quick adventuring mind. But at every turn she is met by the tabus and vetoes of genteel society. Her father is her jailor. If I were talking again to your friend Dr. de Martel, I would say, 'Dr. de Martel, your brilliant mother wrote that story over and over again. She believed in the emancipation of young women.'"

"And so?"

"Dr. Bosco, may I make a request of you?"

"Be quick about it."

"Elspeth Skeel's Aunt Benedikta—the former Countess Skeel of Denmark—has a camp in the Adirondacks where the deer roam freely and even the foxes and bears come and go as they wish—and where even a girl of seventeen will never hear a brutal and a life-denying word." I bowed and smiled. "Good afternoon, Dr. Bosco. Good afternoon, ma'am."

I turned and left the room. Before the door closed I heard him say, "I'll be damned!"

A few minutes later I was led to Elspeth's room. She was sitting in a chair by the window overlooking the Charles River. Her mother was sitting beside her; her brother was standing by the bed. After the greetings Elspeth said, "Mother, tell Mr. North the good news."

"Mr. North, there is to be no operation after all. Dr. Bosco made the examination yesterday. He thinks the condition that alarmed us is clearing up of itself."

"Isn't that splendid! When are you returning to Newport?"

"We're not returning to Newport at all. I told Dr. Bosco about my sister-in-law's camp in the Adirondacks and he said, 'Just the place for her!'"

So all my play-acting and heroics and prevarication had not been necessary. But I had enjoyed them. Elspeth's smile as her eyes rested on mine were reward enough. It implied that we shared a secret.

There was nothing left to do but to talk small-talk: the Harvard students sculling on the river; the departure for the Adirondacks at the end of the week; the wonderful nurses (from Nova Scotia) —small-talk. My mind began to wander. For me small-talk is a wearisome cage.

A nurse appeared at the door. She asked, "Is a Mr. North here?" I made myself known.

"Dr. Bosco's secretary has called. He will be here in a few minutes. He wishes you to remain here until he comes."

"I shall be here, ma'am."

Zounds! What now?

Presently the doctor appeared. He gave no sign of having recognized me. He spoke to Mrs. Skeel. "Mrs. Skeel, I have been thinking over your daughter's case."

"Yes, Dr. Bosco?"

"I think it advisable that she be given a longer rest and change than this summer in the Adirondacks. I recommend that she spend eight to ten months abroad—in the mountains, if possible. Have you friends or relatives in the Swiss Alps or in the Tirol?"

"Why, Doctor, I could take her to an excellent school we know in Arosa. Would you like that, Elspeth?"

"Oh, yes, Mother." Her glance included me. "If you write letters to me there."

"Indeed, we shall, dear. And I shall send Arthur over to you for the Christmas holidays.—Dr. Bosco, could I ask you to write Mr. Skeel telling him that you strongly advise this plan?"

"I'll do that.—Good afternoon again, Mr. North."

"Good afternoon, Dr. Bosco."

"Mrs. Skeel, Mr. North deserves some kind of medal. He asked me for five minutes of my time. He called on me and finished his business in three minutes. That has never happened to me in my long experience. Mr. North, I telephoned my wife that you were a good friend of our friend Dr. de Martel. She is fonder of Thierry de Martel than she is of me. She asked me to bring you home to dinner tonight."

"Dr. Bosco, I told a lie. I have never met Dr. de Martel."

He looked around the room and shook his head in amazement.

"Well, come just the same. It won't be the first time we've had liars to dinner."

"But, Dr. Bosco, I'm afraid that I'd have nothing to say that could interest you."

"I'm accustomed to that. Kindly be waiting at the entrance to this building at six-thirty."

That stopped me. I had heard many stories of Dr. Bosco and I knew that I had received more than an invitation—a command.

When he had left the room, Mrs. Skeel said, "That's a great privilege, Mr. North."

Elspeth said, "He's very interested in you, *monsieur le professeur*. I told him about your hands and how you had driven my headaches away and how wonderful you had been about Ada Nicols, and how people said that you cured Dr. Bosworth of cancer. I think he wants to know what you *do*."

My eyes popped out of my head with horror, with shame. HELL AND DAMNATION! . . . I had to get out of the building. I had to get by myself and think. I toyed with the idea of throwing myself into the Charles River. (It's too shallow; besides I'm an expert swimmer.) I hastily shook hands with the Skeels, thanking them, et cetera, and wishing them many happy days in the Adirondacks. To Galloper I whispered, "Someday you'll be a great doctor; start learning now how to give orders like that."

"Yes, sir."

I walked the streets of Boston for two and a half hours. At six-thirty I was waiting as directed. An unpretentious car drove up to the curb. A man of fifty, more resembling a janitor than a chauffeur, alighted and crossing the pavement asked me if I was Mr. North.

"Yes. I'd like to sit up in front with you, if you don't mind. My name's Ted North."

"Glad to know you. I'm Fred Spence."

"Where are we going, Mr. Spence?"

"To Dr. Bosco's house in Brookline."

"Dr. Bosco's gone home already?"

"On Friday afternoons he don't operate. He takes his students around the building and shows them his patients. Then I call for him at five and take him home. On Friday nights he likes a guest or two for dinner. Mrs. Bosco says she never knows what he'll bring home." That "what" implied stray dogs or alley cats.

"Mr. Spence, I wasn't invited to dinner. I was ordered. Dr. Bosco likes to give orders, doesn't he?"

"Yes. You get used to it. The doctor's a very moody man. I take him to the hospital at eight-thirty and I take him home at six-thirty. Some days he don't say a word the whole time. Other days he don't stop talking about how everything's in bad shape and everybody's stupid. Been like that since he came home from the War. He likes his guests to go home at ten, because he has to write everything down in his diary."

"Mr. Spence, I've got to take a train from South Station at ten-thirty. How'd I get there?"

"Dr. Bosco's arranged for me to drive you to Newport or to anywhere you want to go."

"To Newport!—I'll be very obliged to you, if you'll drive me to South Station after dinner."

Entering the house I was met by Mrs. Bosco—of generous proportions, gracious, but somehow impassive.

"Dr. Bosco would like you to join him in his study. He is making you one of his famous Old-Fashioned cocktails. He doesn't drink them himself, but he likes to make them for others. I hope you aren't hungry, because the doctor doesn't like to sit down to dinner until a quarter before eight."

In the afternoon, in his white coat, he had the head of a lean Roman senator; in a dark suit his features were more delicate and ascetic—the vicar-general of a religious order, perhaps. He shook hands in silence and returned to the matter that was occupying him. He was making me an Old-Fashioned. I got an impression of a crucible, a mortar and pestle, some vials—Paracelsus making an alchemical brew. He was totally absorbed. I was not asked if I wished an Old-Fashioned nor was I asked to sit down.

"Try that," he said finally. It was indeed rich and strange. He turned and sat down—with a plan in his head, as though conversation were also a totally occupying discipline.

"Mr. North, why did you represent yourself as a friend of Dr. de Martel?"

"I felt that it was urgent that I have a few minutes of your time. I felt that you should know *one* of the reasons for Miss Skeel's migraines—a reason that no one in the family was in a position to tell you. I felt that a great doctor would want to know every aspect of the case. I have since learned that you had already recommended her removal from her home and that my call on you was unnecessary."

"No. It opened my eyes to the part that her father was playing in her depressed condition." He passed his hand wearily over his eyes. "In my field of work we often tend to overlook the emotional elements that enter into a problem that faces us. We pride ourselves on being scientists and we do not see how science can come to grips with such things as emotions. . . . Apparently *that* is an aspect of these problems that you have interested yourself in." I pretended not to have heard him, but there was no evading any step in the conversation that Dr. Bosco had planned to pursue. "You *do* engage in healing?"

"No. No, Dr. Bosco. I have never made claim to any capacity for healing. Some *children* have talked some nonsense about my having 'electric hands.' I hate it. I don't want to have anything to do with it."

He gazed at me fixedly for a moment. "I am told that you enabled Dr. Bosworth to leave his house for the first time in ten years."

"Please change the subject, Doctor. I just talked common sense to him."

He repeated thoughtfully, "Common sense, common sense.— And this story about a girl Ada—Ada somebody—who struck her head against a post?"

"Doctor, I'm a fraud. I'm a quack. But when a person is suffering right under your eyes what do you do? You do what you can."

"*And what is it that you do?* You hypnotized her?"

"I never saw a person hypnotized. I don't know what it is. I merely talked soothingly to her and stroked the bruise. Then I carried her to the superintendent of the Casino who has a lot of experience in first-aid. There was no real concussion. She came back to class two days later."

"If I ask Mrs. Bosco to join us, will you tell us the full story of Dr. Bosworth's recovery? There's still half an hour before dinner."

"There are some homely vulgar details connected with it."

"Mrs. Bosco is used to such details from me."

"I am a guest in your house," I said discouragedly. "I shall try to do what you wish me to do."

He refreshed my glass and left the room. I heard him calling, "Lucinda! Lucinda!" (It was not an invitation but an order.) Mrs. Bosco slipped into the room and sat by the door. The doctor sat at his desk.

"All right," I said to myself, "I'll give him the works." I gave him the background of the Death Watch, my first interview with Mrs. Bosworth, our readings in Bishop Berkeley, my increasing awareness of a "house of listening ears," the family's efforts to persuade him that he was condemned and going crazy, my trip to Providence disguised as a truck driver, the attempt on my life.

Toward the end of the story Dr. Bosco had covered his face with his hands, but not in boredom. When I had finished, he said, "No one tells me anything. . . . I am the specialist who is called in at the end of the game."

A servant appeared at the door. Mrs. Bosco said, "Dinner is ready."

Dinner was delicious. The doctor was silent. Mrs. Bosco asked me, "Mr. North, would it bore you to tell us the story of your life and interests?"

I spared them nothing—Wisconsin, China, California, Oberlin College, Yale, the American Academy in Rome, the school in New Jersey, then Newport. I mentioned some of my interests and ambitions (omitting the *shaman*).

"Lucinda, I shall ask Mr. North to join me in my study for coffee."

It was a quarter before ten.

"Mr. North, at the close of the summer I wish you to come to Boston. I am appointing you to be one of my secretaries. You will accompany me on my rounds. I shall tell each patient that I have full confidence in you. You will visit them regularly. You will report to me on each patient's intimate life-story, and on any strains he or she may be living under. Get to know them by their first names. I have seldom known a patient by his or her Christian name. What is yours?"

"Theophilus."

"Ah, yes, I remember. That is a beautiful name. It carries connotations that were once real to me; I wish they were today. Are you returning to Newport tonight?"

"Yes, Doctor."

"I have arranged that Fred Spence will drive you there." (It was an order.) "Here is a five-dollar bill you will give him at the end of the journey. It will make you feel more comfortable about the trip. Do not answer now about the proposal I have laid before you. Think it over. Let me hear from you by a week from today. Thank you for coming to dinner."

I said good night to Mrs. Bosco in the hall. "Thank you for coming and for bringing those soothing hands with you. The doctor's not often as patient as he's been tonight."

I slept all the way home. At Mrs. Keefe's door I gave Fred Spence the honorarium and climbed up my stairs. Three days later I wrote Dr. Bosco—with many expressions of regard—that my return to Europe in the autumn would prevent my accepting the position that he had offered me. I thought the whole damnable *shaman* business was at an end, but ten days later I found myself in a mess of trouble.

I rejoiced in my apartment, but I was seldom there. My daily work became more and more difficult and I spent many evenings at the People's Library preparing for my classes. At midnight I found notes under my door from my good landlady: "*Three ladies and a gentleman called for you. I let them wait for you until ten in my sitting-room, but I had to ask them to go home at ten. They did not wish to leave their names and addresses. Mrs. Doris Keefe.*" On another night, the same message speaking of eight people. "*I cannot have more than five strangers waiting in my sitting-room. I told them they must go away. Mrs. Doris Keefe.*"

Finally on a Thursday evening I was at home and received a telephone call from Joe ("Holy Joe"), the supervisor at the Y.M.C.A. "Ted, what's going on? There are twelve people—mostly old women—waiting for you in the visitors' room. I told them you didn't live here any more. I couldn't tell them your new address because you never gave it to me. . . . There are some more coming in the door now. What are you doing—running an employment agency? Please come over and send them away and tell them not to come back again. There've been a few every night, but tonight beats everything. This is a young men's Christian association, not an old ladies' home. Come on over and drive the cattle out."

I hurried over. The crowd now overflowed the visitors' room. I recognized some of the faces—servants from "Nine Gables" and from "The Deer Park" and even from "Mrs. Cranston's." I started shaking hands.

"Oh, Mr. North, I suffer from rheumatism something terrible."

"Oh, Mr. North, my back hurts so I can't sleep nights, not what you'd call sleep."

"Mr. North, look at my hand! It takes me an hour to open it in the morning."

"Ladies and gentlemen, I am not a doctor. I don't know the first thing about medicine. I must ask you to consult a regular practicing physician."

The wails mounted:

"Oh, sir, they take your money and do nothing for you."

"Mr. North, put your hand on my knee. God will reward you."

"Sir, my feet. It's agony to go a step."

I had spent a part of my childhood in China and was no stranger to the unfathomable misery in the world. What could I do? First, I must clear the lobby. I rested my hand here and there; I grasped an ankle or two; I drew my hand firmly down some spines. I gave particular attention to the napes of necks. I made a point of *hurting* my patients (they yelped, but were instantly convinced that that was the "real thing"). Gently propelling them to the front door, I planted the heels of my hands on some foreheads, murmuring the opening lines of the *Aeneid*. Then I said, "This is the last time I can see you. Do not come back again. You *must* see your own doctors. Good night, and God bless you all."

I returned to my own address and dispersed a group that had gathered there.

I dreaded the following Sunday night and had reason to. I made my way to the "Y" and from afar I could see that they had all come back and brought others; a line extended from lobby to sidewalk. I called them all together and held a meeting in the middle of the street. "Ladies and gentlemen, there's nothing I can do for you. I'm as ill as you are. Every bone in my body aches. Let us shake hands and say good night." I hurried back to Mrs. Keefe's house where another crowd had gathered. I dismissed them with the same words. Mrs. Keefe was watching us from a window. When the strangers had gone she unlocked the front door to me.

"Oh, Mr. North, I can't stand this much longer. When I lock the door they wander around the house knocking on the window-panes like beggars I've shut out in a snow storm. Here is a letter for you that was brought by hand."

"Dear Mr. North, it would give me much pleasure to see you this evening at ten-thirty, your sincere friend, Amelia Cranston."

At ten-thirty I hurried to Spring Street. The rooms were emptying quickly. Finally no one was there but Mrs. Cranston, Mr. Griffin, and Mrs. Grant, her principal assistant in running the house. I sat down by Mrs. Cranston who appeared to be unusually large, genial, and happily disposed.

"Thank you for coming, Mr. North."

"Forgive me for being absent so long. My schedule gets heavier every week."

"So I have been informed . . . bicycling up and down the Avenue at two in the morning and feeding the wild animals, I presume." Mrs. Cranston enjoyed giving evidence that she knew everything. "Mrs. Grant, will you kindly tell Jimmy to bring the refreshments I set aside in the icebox." We were served the gin-fizzes I had come to recognize as a mark of some special occasion. She lowered her voice. "You are in trouble, Mr. North?"

"Yes, I am, ma'am. Thank you for your letter."

"Well, you have become a very famous man *in certain quarters*. My visitors Thursday night and tonight talked of little else. Somehow or other you put new life in Dr. Bosworth and now he's bounding about the country like a lad of fifty. Somehow or other you brought relief to Miss Skeel's headaches. Servants watch their employers very closely, Mr. North. How many patients were waiting for you tonight?"

"Over twenty-five in one place and a dozen in the other."

"Next week the waiting line will stretch around the block."

"Help me, Mrs. Cranston. I love Newport. I want to stay until the end of the summer. I haven't got 'electric hands.' I'm a fake and a fraud. That first night I couldn't *drive* them out of the building. You should have seen their eyes: It's better to be a fake and a fraud than to be . . . brutal. I didn't do them any harm, did I?"

"Put your hands down on the table, palms upward."

She passed five finger tips over them lightly, took a sip from her glass, and said, "I always knew you had something."

I hastily hid my hands under the table. She went on speaking evenly with her calm smile: "Mr. North, even the happiest and healthiest of women—and there are very few of us—have one corner of their mind that is filled with a constant dread of illness. Dread. Even when they're not thinking about it, they're thinking about it. This is not true of most men—you think you'll live forever. Do you think you'll live forever, Mr. North?"

"No, ma'am," I said, smiling. "I'll say, 'I've warmed both hands before the fire of life; It sinks and I am ready to depart.' But I'd like to have seen Edweena before I departed."

She looked at me in surprise. "It's funny your saying that. Edweena's back from her cruise. She's been in New York a week, making arrangements for her fall season there. Henry Simmons has been to New York to bring her back here. I'm expecting them tonight. Edweena knows all about you."

"About *me?!*"

"Oh, yes. I wrote her all about your problem a week ago. She answered at once. It's Edweena who's had the idea about how you can get free of this mess you're in. It's Henry Simmons and I who have arranged it at this end." She took up an envelope from the table before her and waved it before my nose as you'd wave a bone before a dog.

"Oh, Mrs. Cranston!"

"But let's say one more word about your new situation in Newport. Women never put their full confidence in doctors. Women are both religious and superstitious. They want nothing less than a miracle. You are the latest miracle man. There are many *masseurs* and manipulators and faith-healers in this town. They have licenses and they take money for their services. Your fame rests on the fact that you take no fees. That inspires a confidence that no doctor can inspire. If you pay a doctor you buy the right to criticize him as though he were any other huckster. But everybody knows that you can't buy miracles and that's why you are a miracle man. There is no sign that Dr. Bosworth or the Skeels gave you an automobile or even a gold watch—and yet look what you did for them! *You still go about on a bicycle!*"

I didn't like this talk. My eyes were fixed on the envelope. My tongue was hanging out of my mouth for that bone. I knew that Mrs. Cranston was teasing me, perhaps punishing me—for not having called on her for help earlier, for having been absent from "Mrs. Cranston's" so long.

I got down on one knee. "Please forgive me, Mrs. Cranston, for having been away so long. I'm indebted to you for so much."

She laughed and put her hand on mine for a moment. Well-conditioned women love to pardon when they're asked. "In this envelope is a document. It's not official, but it *looks* official. It has a ribbon and some sealing-wax and is on the stationery of a health organization that has long since been absorbed by others." She took it out and laid it before me:

To whom it may concern: Mr. T. Theophilus North, resident in Newport, Rhode Island, has no license to provide medical service of any kind or manner unless the patient appears before him with the written permission of a physician duly registered in this city. Office of the Superintendent of Health, this day the —— of August, 1926.

"Oh, Mrs. Cranston!"

"Wait, there is another document in this envelope."

Mr. T. Theophilus North, resident in Newport, Rhode Island, is hereby given permission to make one visit, not lasting longer than thirty minutes, to Miss Liselotte Müller, resident at —— Spring Street, and to furnish her such aid and comfort as seems fitting to him.

This was signed by an esteemed physician in the city and bore the date of the previous day.

I stared at her.

"Miss Müller lives here now?"

"Could you see her now? This building is really three buildings. The third and fourth floors of the building on this side have been fitted out to be an infirmary for very old women. They have spent their lifetimes in domestic service and many of them have been well provided for by their former employers. Most of them cannot negotiate even one flight of stairs, but they have a terrace where they can sun themselves in good weather and social rooms for all weather. You will see sights and smell smells that will distress you, but you have told us of your experiences in China and you are prepared for such things." Here I heard her short snort-like laugh. "You have accepted the truth that much of life is difficult and that the last years are particularly so. You are not a green boy, Mr. North. Few men pay calls in that infirmary—occasionally a doctor, a priest, a pastor, or a relative. It is a rule of the house that during such calls the door into the sickroom is left ajar. I am sending you upstairs with my assistant and friend, Mrs. Grant."

I asked in a low voice, "Will you tell me something about Miss Müller?"

"Tante Liselotte was born in Germany. She was the eleventh child of a pastor and was brought to this country at the age of seventeen by an employment agency. She has been the nanny in one of the most respected houses here and in New York for three generations. She has bathed and dressed all those children, spent the entire day with them, paddled and powdered and wiped their little bottoms. I have selected her for your visit because she was kind and helpful to me when I was young, lonesome, and frightened. She has outlived all the members of her family abroad who would take any interest in her. She has been much loved in her station, but she is a strict rigid woman and has made few friends except myself. She is sound of mind; she can see and hear; but she is racked by rheumatic pains. I believe them to be excruciating because she is not a complaining woman."

"And if I fail, Mrs. Cranston?"

She ignored the question. She went on: "I suspect that your fame has preceded you upstairs. The guests in this house have many friends in the infirmary. News of miracles travels fast. . . . Mrs. Grant, I should like you to meet Mr. North."

"How do you do, Mr. North?"

"I think we shall be speaking German tonight, Mrs. Grant. Do you understand German?"

"Oh, no. Not a word."

"Mrs. Cranston, after these meetings I am sometimes very weak. If Henry Simmons returns before I come down, will you ask him to wait for me and walk home with me?"

"Oh, yes—I think both Edweena and Henry Simmons will be here. Your visit to Tante Liselotte is also Edweena's wish."

I was staggered.

Again I was to learn: happy is the man who is aided by what folklore calls "the wise women." That is a lesson of the *Odyssey.* "Then the gray-eyed Athene appeared to Odysseus in the guise of a servant and he knew her not, and she spoke unto him. . . ."

I followed Mrs. Grant upstairs. The women I passed on the landings and in the corridors lowered their eyes and shrank against the walls. On the third and fourth floors all wore identical "wrappers" in gray and white stripes. Mrs. Grant knocked at a half-open door and said, "Tante Liselotte, Mr. North has come to call on you," then she sat down in a corner, folded her hands, and lowered her eyes.

"Guten Abend, Fräulein Müller."

"Guten Abend, Herr Doktor."

Tante Liselotte appeared to be a skeleton, but her large brown eyes were bright. She seemed barely able to turn her head. She wore a knitted cap and a comforter over her shoulders. The linen and the entire room were spotless. I continued in German. "I am neither a doctor nor a pastor—merely a friend of Mrs. Cranston and of Edweena." I had no idea what I was going to say. I made my mind go blank. "May I ask where you were born, Tante Liselotte?"

"Near Stuttgart, sir."

"Ah!" I said with delighted surprise. "A Swabian!" I knew nothing about the region except that Schiller was born there. "In a moment I want to look at all these photographs on the walls. Forgive me if I put my hands on yours." I took her infinitely delicate right hand between mine and rested all three on the counterpane. I began to concentrate all the energy I could assemble.

"I speak German so badly, but what a wonderful language it is! Aren't *Leiden* and *Liebe* and *Sehnsucht* more beautiful words than 'sufferings' and 'love' and 'longing'?" I repeated the German words slowly. Tremors were passing through her hand. "And your name *Liselotte* for Elizabeth-Charlotte! And the diminutives: *Mütterchen, Kindlein, Engelein.*" I felt prompted to push our three hands all but imperceptibly toward her knee. Her eyes were wide, staring at the wall opposite her. She was breathing deeply. Her chin was twitching. "I think of the German hymns I know through Bach's music: '*Ach, Gott, wie manches Herzeleid*' and '*Halt' im Gedächtnis Jesum Christ.*' '*Gleich wie der Regen und Schnee vom Himmel fällt . . .*' They can translate the words, they cannot translate what we hear who love the language." I remembered and recited others. I was trembling because I was recalling Bach's music which so often has something multitudinous about it—like waves and generations.

I was aware of much tiptoeing in the corridor but at first no whispering. A large group was gathering outside the door. I suspect that the custom of lowering lights at such a late hour had been set aside because of my visit. I gently withdrew my hands, rose, and started on a tour of the room; pausing before the pictures. I stood before two silhouettes—probably a hundred years old—her parents. I glanced at her and nodded. Her eyes were following me. A faded blue snapshot of Tante Liselotte seated beween two perambulators in Central Park. In every photograph—first as a happy young woman with a square plain face, then as a woman in middle age, inclining to stoutness—she was dressed in a uniform that resembles what we in this country know as the garb of a deaconess, surmounted by a bonnet tied under her chin with a wide muslin band. On her feet she wore stout "hygienic" shoes that had undoubtedly aroused discreet laughter throughout her long life:

Tante Liselotte in an old-world "bath chair" with children at her feet—in faded ink "Ostende, 1880";

A large party on the deck of a yacht gathered about the German Kaiser and the Kaiserin; at the edge of the picture stood Tante Liselotte with a baby in her arms and her young charges beside her. As though talking to myself I said, "Their Imperial Majesties have graciously requested that I present to them Miss Liselotte Müller, a much valued member of our household"—"Kiel, 1890";

Tante Liselotte on the Cliff Walk in Newport, always with children;

A wedding picture, bride and groom and Liselotte, "Love to Nana, from Bertie and Marianne—June, 1909." I said aloud to myself in English, "You were present at my father's wedding too, weren't you, Tante Liselotte?"

Photographs in the nursery. "Nana, can we go hunting for shells today?" "Nana, I'm sorry I was naughty about the overshoes this morning. . . ." "Nana, when we go to bed will you tell us the story about the carpet that flies in the air?"

All my movements were slow. My eyes returned to hers at each improvisation. I went back to my chair and placed our three hands against her knee. She shut her eyes but suddenly opened them wide in great alarm or wonder.

The throng that had gathered in the corridor was filling the doorway. There was a sound now of sighing and groans and the chittering of bats. An old woman on crutches lost her balance and fell face downward on the floor. I paid no attention. Mrs. Grant came forward and lifted the woman from the floor and with the help of others led her from the room. During the disturbance another woman, not a patient, had entered the room and had sat down in Mrs. Grant's chair. Tante Liselotte drew her hand from between mine and beckoned me to lean nearer to her. In German she said, "I want to die. . . . Why does God not let me die?"

"Oh, Tante Liselotte, you know the old hymn and Bach's music for it, *'Gottes Zeit ist die allerbeste Zeit.'* "

She repeated the words. *"Ja . . . Ja . . . Ich bin müde. Danke, junger Mann."*

I rose with effort. I looked about, drowsy with fatigue, for Mrs.

Grant. My eyes fell on the woman who had taken her place—on one of the nine faces dearest to me that I have known in my life, though I was to know her such a short time. She rose smiling.

I said, "Edweena," and the tears rolled down my face.

"Theophilus," she said, "you go downstairs. I will stay here a little longer. Henry is waiting for you. Can you find the way?"

As I leaned against the door I heard Edweena ask, "Where is the pain, dear Tante?"

"There is none . . . none."

I wanted to reach the staircase, but my way was barred. I could scarcely keep my eyes open; I longed to lie down on the floor. I slowly walked as through a field of wheat. I had to unfasten hands from my sleeves, from the hem of my coat, even from my ankles. On the flight of stairs between the second and third floors I sat down on a step, leaned my head against the wall, and fell asleep. I don't know how long I slept, but I woke much refreshed and found Edweena sitting beside me. She had taken hold of my hand.

"Do you feel better?"

"Oh, yes."

"It's nearly midnight. They'll be hunting for us. We'd better go downstairs. Can you walk all right? Are you yourself?"

"Yes. I think I had a long nap. I'm all rested."

On the second-floor landing, under a light on the ceiling where we could see each other's face, she said, "Can you bear a bit of good news?"

"Yes, Edweena."

"About five minutes after you left, Tante Liselotte died."

I smiled, I started to say, "I killed her," but Edweena put her hand on my mouth. "I understand a little German," she said. " 'Ich bin müde. Danke, junger Mann.' "

Together we entered the front rooms on the ground floor.

"Well, you've been quite a while," said Mrs. Cranston. "Mrs. Grant has told me about the ending. You've performed your last miracle, Dr. North."

"I'll walk you home, cully," said Henry.

I said good night to the ladies. As I was going out the door, Mrs. Cranston called, "Mr. North, you've forgotten your envelope."

I returned and took it. I bowed and said, "And thank you, ladies."

On the way home, buoyed up by good old Henry and by the consciousness of having made a new friend in Edweena, I recalled a theory that I had long held and tested and played with—the theory of the Constellations: a man should have three masculine friends older than himself, three of about his own age, and three younger. And he should have three older women friends, three of his own age, and three younger. These twice-nine friends I call his Constellation.

Similarly, a woman should have her Constellation.

These friendships have nothing to do with passionate love. Love as a passion is a wonderful thing but it has its own laws and its own histories. Nor do they have anything to do with the relationships within the family which have their own laws and their own histories.

Seldom—perhaps never—are all eighteen roles filled at the same time. Vacancies occur; some live for years—or for a lifetime—with only one older or younger friend, or with none.

What a deep satisfaction we feel when a vacant place is filled, as it was by Edweena that night. ("Then felt I like some watcher of the skies When a new planet swims into his ken.")

During those months in Newport I found one sound older friend, Bill Wentworth; two friends of my own age, Henry and Bodo; two younger friends, Mino and Galloper; two older women, Mrs. Cranston and (though meeting seldom) Signora Matera; two women of about my own age, Edweena and Persis; two younger women, Eloise and Elspeth.

But we must remember that we also play a part in the Constellations of others—which is a partial replacement in our own. I was certainly a younger friend necessary to Dr. Bosworth, though so self-centered a man could never meet the need of an older friend for me. "Rip" Vanwinkle and even George Granberry were ghosts of their former selves (the test is laughter; their resources for laughter were spent or quenched). I hope I was an older friend in Charles Fenwick's Constellation, but he was struggling to arrive at his rightful age and the struggle left him with little to give in the free exchanges of friendship.

Of course, this is only a fanciful theory of mine—not to be taken too literally, nor to be dismissed hastily. . . .

At the end of the summer I met Galloper at the Casino. We shook hands solemnly as usual.

"Have you got a minute to sit down over here in the spectators' gallery, Galloper?"

"Yes, Mr. North."

"How's the family?"

"They're all very well."

"When do your mother and sister leave for Europe?"

"Day after tomorrow."

"Please tell them I wish them a happy voyage."

"I will."

Comfortable pauses.

"You don't end every sentence with 'sir' any more, do you?"

He looked at me with what I had come to know as his "interior smile." "I told my father that American boys call their father 'Dad' or 'Papa.' "

"*Did* you? Was he very angry?"

"He threw his hands up in the air and said that the world was going to pieces. . . . I call him 'sir' the first thing in the morning, but most of the time I call him 'Dad.' "

"He'll come to like it."

Comfortable silences.

"Have you decided what you're going to be in life?"

"I'm going to be a doctor. . . . Mr. North, do you think Dr. Bosco will still be teaching when I get to medical school?"

"Why not? He's not an old man at all. And you're a sharp

student. You'll skip a class or two. I see where a fellow graduated from Harvard the other day at the age of nineteen. . . . So you're going to be a brain surgeon, eh? . . .

"Well, that's one of the most difficult professions in the world —hard on the body, on the mind, and on the spirit. . . . You come home tired at night after a couple of four- or five-hour operations hanging between life and death. . . .

"Marry a calm girl. See that she doesn't laugh outside, but inside, as you do. . . . Many great brain surgeons have a hobby to escape into when the burden gets too great—like music or collecting books about the early history of medicine. . . .

"Many great surgeons have to set up a kind of wall between themselves and the patients. To shield their hearts. See if you can change that. Put your face near to the patients when you talk to them. Pat them lightly on the elbow or the shoulder and smile. You're going down into the valley of death together, see what I mean? . . .

"Many a great Dr. Sawbones—do you mind the word?"

"No."

"Many a Dr. Sawbones tends to withdraw into himself. To save his energy. They become domineering or eccentric—always a sign of an inner loneliness. Pick out a few friends—men and women, of all ages. You won't have much time to give them, but that doesn't matter. Dr. Bosco's best friend lives in France. He only sees him once in every three or four years, at congresses. They steal away and have a choice and expensive dinner together. Great surgeons tend to be great gourmets. After half an hour they discover that they're laughing together.—Well, I have to go now."

We shook hands solemnly.

"Keep well, Galloper."

"You, too, Mr. North."

Bodo and Persis

This chapter might also be called "Nine Gables—Part Two," but it has seemed advisable to place it here among these later chapters. It is therefore out of its chronological order. The events recounted here took place after the drive with Dr. Bosworth and Persis to Bishop Berkeley's "Whitehall" (when I explained that Bodo was not a fortune hunter but was himself a fortune) and before my last visit to "Nine Gables" (and that smashing ultimatum from Mrs. Bosworth: "Father, either that monster leaves this house or I do!").

I have not yet entered into possession of my apartment. I am still living at the Y.M.C.A.

I had no classes on Monday nights. After supper in town on a certain Monday evening I returned to the "Y" at about eight. The desk clerk gave me a letter which I saw resting in my pigeonhole. Standing at the desk I opened and read it. *"Dear Mr. North, I often take a late drive. I hope you will not be too tired to join me tomorrow night when you've finished reading with my grandfather. You can place your bicycle in the back seat of my car and*

*I can return you later to your door. There is something urgent I
should tell you. This needs no answer. I shall be at the door of
'Nine Gables' when you leave. Sincerely yours, Persis Tennyson."*
I put the letter in my pocket and was starting upstairs when the
desk clerk said, "Mr. North, there's a gentleman over there who's
been waiting to see you."

I turned and saw Bodo coming toward me. I had never seen his
face stern and taut before. We shook hands.

"Grüss Gott, Herr Baron."

"Lobet den Herrn in der Ewigkeit," he replied unsmilingly.
"Theophilus, I've come to say goodbye. Have you time to talk for
an hour? I want to get a little bit drunk."

"I'm ready."

"I left my car up at the corner. I have two flasks of *Schnapps*."
I followed him. "Where are we going?"

"To Doheney's, down at the Public Beach. We need ice.
Schnapps is best when it's very cold."

We started off. He said, "I shall never come to Newport again,
if I can help it."

"When do you go?"

"The Venables are giving a small dinner for me tomorrow
night. When the guests are gone, I'll start driving to Washington
and shall drive all night."

His unhappiness was like a weight and a presence in the car.
I remained silent. Doheney's was a "straight" bar, that is to say
no illegal liquor was sold there. The curtains at the windows were
not drawn. Guests could bring their own. It was as friendly as Mr.
Doheney himself and it was almost empty. We sat at a table by an
open window and ordered two teacups and a small pail of ice. We
embedded the flasks and the teacups in the ice.

Bodo said, "Danny, we're going for a walk on the beach while
the stuff gets cold."

"Yes, Mr. Stams."

We went out, crossed the road, and started walking toward the
bathing pavilion—shut up for the night—our feet sinking in the

sand. I followed like a familiar dog. Bodo ascended the steps and stood with his back against one of the pillars on the verandah. "Sit down, Theophilus; I want to think aloud for a few minutes."

I obeyed and waited. Something awesome was going on in Bodo.

It is a universally held opinion of our day that full-grown men do not shed tears. I'm quite a weeper myself, but I'm not a sobber. I weep at music and at books and I weep at the movies. I never sob. I have told in Chapter 7 how Elbert Hughes—who was not a full-grown man—cried like a baby and how exasperating it was. At college I had a friend who was about to be dismissed from the university for having published a plagiarized story in the undergraduate magazine of which I was an editor. His father was a clergyman. The scandal and disgrace would be overwhelming and would shatter his life. Perhaps I shall tell that story some day. The spectacle of his abasement was all the more devastating because he had been innocent of any intention to deceive. When I was at Fort Adams I knew a soldier, drafted from his farm in Kentucky. He had never been farther from his dirt-floor cabin, from his parents and his eight brothers and sisters than a visit to the nearest county seat. ("Till I was drafted I'd never wore a pair of shoes except on Sunday; my brother and I took turns wearing the shoes to church.") Sobbing of homesickness. At the American Academy in Rome I cut down a friend who had been trying to hang himself in the shower because he had contracted a venereal disease—sobbing of rage.

There's a vast amount of suffering in the world—a small, but important, part of it, unnecessary.

Bodo's condition was something else. It was soundless, motionless, and tearless. Even in that diffused starlight I could see that his jaws were clenched and white; his gaze was not fixed on me nor on the wall behind me. It was turned inward. Here was my best friend—well, with Henry Simmons my best friend—in extremity. That starts a fellow thinking.

At last he spoke. "I called at 'Nine Gables' this afternoon to say goodbye. I had the foolish notion that I might—just possibly might—ask Persis to be my wife. She showed a little more animation than usual, but we're all relieved when someone who bores us to death comes to say goodbye. Her grandfather, however, showed a real interest in me for the first time; wanted to talk about philosophy and philosophers; wouldn't let me go. . . . I don't understand her. . . . I can understand a woman not liking me, but I can't understand a total absence of any reaction whatever—just politeness, just evasive good manners. . . . We've spent so many hours together. We've been thrown at one another—by Mrs. Venable and Mrs. Bosworth and half a dozen others. We have *had* to make talk. Of course, I've asked her out to dinner, but there's no place on this island to go to dinner except the damned Muenchinger-King and she says that she doesn't like dining in public places. So we make talk at formal dinners. Each time, I'm knocked over by the fact that she's not only a very beautiful woman, but a superior one. She knows all about music and art and even *Austria*. She speaks three languages. She's reading all the time. She dances like Adeline Genée—I'm told that she sings beautifully. What's more, my instinct tells me that she has great capacity for life and love . . . and life. I love her. I love her. But she gives me no sign of recognizing that I am a living, breathing, possibly loving, human being. All that talk and nothing catches fire. You know how I like children and *children like me.* I turn the conversation to her three-year-old son, but even then nothing catches fire. . . . Sometimes I wish she showed annoyance, or downright dislike; I wish she'd snub me. I look around the dinner tables; she's the same with every man. . . . Perhaps she's grieving for her husband—but she's out of mourning; perhaps she's in love with someone else; perhaps she's in love with you. Don't interrupt yet! So I'm leaving Newport forever. I'm erasing Persis from my mind and heart. I'm renouncing something that I was never offered. Let's go see if the *Schnapps* is cold."

We returned to our table. He lifted a flask and the cups out of the pail and poured. We exchanged a hearty *"Zum Wohl!"* and drank.

"Old man, I've wanted for a long while to clear up something between us. When I told you at Flora Deland's that I was a fortune hunter you must have thought that I was a contemptible skunk, as they say over here. Now don't answer me until you hear my story. In fact, before we part you're going to talk to me tough and straight. This is the situation: I am the head of my family. My father was aged and broken by the War. My older brother went off to Argentina and is selling automobiles. He has renounced his title and taken Argentine citizenship to help him in his business. He has a family of his own and cannot send back much money to the *Schloss* and my parents don't want him to. My mother's a wonderful manager. During the summer and especially during the winter she takes in paying guests. More and more people are interested in the winter sports resorts nearby. But it's hard work and the profits are small. The castle needs repairs all the time—roof, drainage, heating. Try and imagine all that. I have three sisters—angels every one of them. They have no *dots* and I must and will see them married comfortably and happily in their own class. Legally, the castle is mine; morally, the family is mine. —*Zum Wohl, Bruder!"*

"*Zum Wohl, Bodl!"*

"I shall marry within a year. In Washington young women are pushed at me all the time—attractive, charming girls, with visible *pecunia.* I've selected two, either one of whom I could come to love and whom I could make happy. I'm old for marriage. I want to have children who will know my parents; I want my parents to know my children. I want a *home. . . .* For two years I've been having a love-affair with a married woman who wants to divorce her husband and marry me; but I can't take her to my parents— she's had two husbands already. She's very accomplished and for the first year she was delightful, but now she cries most of the time. Beside I'm tired of little hotels in the country and signing idiotic names. And something more—I'm a Catholic; I'd . . . I'd like to try harder . . . to be a good Catholic."

Here for the first time tears appeared in my friend's eyes.

"Zum Wohl, Alter."

"Zum Wohl, Bursche."

"So within a year I shall be married to a girl with a fortune. Can I call that an act of filial duty or am I still a skunk?"

"I am a Protestant, Bodo. My father and my ancestors went about grandly telling others where their duty lay. I hope that will never be said of me."

He threw back his head, laughing. "God in Heaven, what fun talking is—maybe I mean unloading."

"Are you drunk or can we get back to the subject of Persis? I have no right to call her that, but I shall while talking to you."

"Yes, oh yes! But what is there left to say about her?"

I put my elbows on the table, clasped my hands, and looked him in the eye gravely.

"Bodo, don't laugh at what I'm about to say. It's a hypothetical case, but I'm trying to make a point of urgent importance."

He sat up straight and returned my gaze, somewhat disturbed. "Go on! What's on your mind?"

"Suppose—just *suppose*—that two and a half years ago there had been a hushed-up scandal in your Foreign Affairs Office. Some secret documents had disappeared and it was thought that someone in the Foreign Office had sold them to the enemy. And suppose that a shadow of suspicion rested on you, just a shadow. There was of course a very thorough inquiry and you were completely cleared. The heads of the government departments went out of their way to invite you to the most important functions. The Foreign Secretary seated you beside him at a very high council or two. You were ostentatiously declared innocent. There was no trial, because there were no charges—but there was *talk*. A retired diplomat once told me that the two worst cities that he'd served in, for gossip and malicious tongues, were Dublin and Vienna. Everything damaging about you—real or imagined—was kept alive decade after decade. You'd be a 'man under a cloud,' wouldn't you?"

"Why are you asking me these questions?"

"What would you do about it?"

"Ignore it."

"Are you sure? You have a very delicate sense of honor. Your wife and children would also learn that there was a faint bad odor connected with the family. You know how people talk. 'There was more to that matter than met the eye.' 'The Stams are so well connected that they could hush anything up!' "

"Theophilus, what are you driving at?"

"Maybe Persis Tennyson is a 'woman under a cloud.' You know and I know and God knows that she could not have been capable of anything dishonorable. But as Shakespeare says somewhere, 'Be thou as . . . pure as snow, thou shalt not escape calumny.' "

Bodo arose, glared at me with something between fury and despair. He strode about the room; he opened the door onto the road as though to fill his lungs with fresh air. Then he returned and flung himself into his chair. His eyes resting on me had now taken on the air of a trapped animal.

"I'm not trying to torment you, Bodo. I'm trying to think of some way that you and I can help that splendid unhappy young woman locked up in that 'Nine Gables,' that spiteful, loveless house. . . . Isn't that just the way a woman of impeccable feeling would behave toward any man she respected—maybe loved—who approached her as a suitor; she wouldn't want to bring a suspicion of malodor into his family. Think of your mother!"

He was now looking at me with a terrible intensity.

I went on brutally: "You know that her husband killed himself?"

"All I know is that he was a crazy gambler. He shot himself over some debts."

"That's all I know. We must know more. But we do know that the town is busy with hateful gossip. 'There's more in that case than meets the eye.' 'The Bosworths have enough money to hush anything up.' "

"Oh, Theophilus! What can we do?"

I pulled the letter out of my pocket and laid it before him.

"I know the urgent thing she wants to talk to me about. She wants to warn me that there are Bosworths who are planning to do me harm. I know that already. But maybe what she wants to do is to tell me the story of her husband's death—the true full story—so that I'll put it in circulation. Take heart and hope, old Bodo. We know that Mrs. Venable admires and loves her. Mrs. Venable looks upon herself as the guardian of correct behavior on Aquidneck Island. Mrs. Venable must know all the facts. She does everything she can to shield and protect Persis. But it's possible that Mrs. Venable hasn't enough imagination to see that it's not enough to take Persis under her wing. There may be some details relative to Archer Tennyson. She thinks that silence is the best defense; *but it isn't*. . . . Bodo, I have a hard day tomorrow. I must ask you to drive me home. Can I propose something?"

"Yes, of course."

"What time is your dinner over tomorrow night when you start driving for Washington?"

"Oh—about eleven-thirty, I should think."

"Could you postpone your departure for two hours? Persis will drop me at my door at about one-thirty. Could you be waiting in your car up around the corner? I may have the *facts* to tell you. We'll have something to go on. Don't you think that to rescue a damsel from injustice is one of the noblest jobs a young man can have?"

"Yes! Yes!"

"Well, you fall asleep in the car. I hope to have something for you to think about as you drive through the night."

At my door I said, "We're sure that Archer Tennyson didn't

kill himself because of any imperfection in his wife's behavior, aren't we?"

"Yes! Yes, we are!"

"Well, take heart! Take hope!—What were Goethe's dying words?"

"Mehr Licht! Mehr Licht!"

"What we're looking for is more light. Thanks for the *Schnapps.* See you tomorrow night."

The next day held a crowded schedule. I hadn't come to New-port to work so hard, but I checked up fourteen dollars before supper. Then I took a short nap and wheeled out to "Nine Gables" for my ten-thirty appointment.

Since the alarming improvement in his health Dr. Bosworth had felt the need of some refreshment during the evening. This took the form of a French *tisane* and biscuits (I declined with thanks) that Mrs. Turner brought to him at about eleven-thirty. It did not escape me that these interruptions in our work were designed to afford an occasion for desultory conversation. My employer was longing to talk. We were now reading (for reasons best known to ourselves alone) Henri Bergson's *Deux sources de la morale et de la religion* when Mrs. Turner arrived with her tray.

What followed was something more than a conversation: it was a military foray, a diplomatic maneuver, with some of the character of a chess game. I had noticed earlier that he had tardily concealed an *aide-mémoire,* an "agenda," such as he had drawn up so often in his career. I put myself on the alert.

"Mr. North, September is the most beautiful month in the year in Newport. I hope you are not planning to leave the island then, as so many do." Silence. "I would be very sorry to hear it. I would miss you very much."

"Thank you, Dr. Bosworth," et cetera, et cetera.

"Moreover, I have some projects involving yourself that could most profitably occupy you here. I wish to employ you on the planning staff of our Academy. You have a quick apprehension and grasp that would be invaluable to me." I bowed my head slightly and remained silent. "During the winter months my circle of friends narrows. Now that I am able to drive about there is much that I can explore—*we* could explore—in this part of New England. It is a great joy to me that my granddaughter takes pleasure in these drives also. I have begun to share with her some aspects of what I call my 'Athens-in-Newport.'" (Silence.) "Mrs. Tennyson strikes some people as a 'reserved' person. She is, but I assure you that she is a woman of marked intelligence and wide culture. She is also an accomplished musician—did you know that?"

"No, Dr. Bosworth."

"On winter nights, I shall hear much fine music. Does music appeal to you, Mr. North?"

"Yes, sir."

"Oh, yes. Up to the time of her husband's tragic death she continued to take lessons of the best teachers in New York and abroad. Since that unhappy occasion she refuses to sing for my guests or for Mrs. Venable's. Had you heard of the unfortunate circumstances of Mr. Tennyson's death?"

"I know only that he took his own life, Mr. Bosworth."

"Archer Tennyson was a very popular man. He derived great enjoyment from living. But there was also in him, perhaps, an element of eccentricity. The whole unhappy business is best forgotten." He lowered his voice and added significantly, "On winter evenings the three of us could make rapid progress on the design for our Academy."

The game of chess was being played very rapidly and recklessly. There was no need of any subtlety on my part. I advanced my black knight boldly.

"Sir, do you think that Mrs. Tennyson has put out of her mind any intention of marrying again?"

"Oh, Mr. North, she is a superior woman. What younger men are there around here—or even in New York!—who could interest her? We have a few yachtsmen; we have a few of that type that is called 'the life of the party'—tiresome quips and gossip. She now refuses her Aunt Helen's invitation to join her for a few weeks in the winter season. She refuses all those opportunities to attend concerts and the theater. She has turned in upon herself. She lives only for her small son, for her reading and her music —and, I am happy to say, for her devoted kindness to me." Again he lowered his voice. "She is all I have—Persis and the Academy. Her Aunt Sarah has lost all patience with her and I am at my wit's end. I would be happy if she married anyone, *wherever* he came from."

"She must have many admirers, Dr. Bosworth. She's an exceptionally beautiful and charming woman."

"Isn't she?" He advanced his white queen the length of the board, again lowering his voice. "And, of course, very well off."

"*Is she?*" I asked with surprise.

"Her father left her a large fortune and her husband another."

I sighed. "But if the lady gives no sign of encouragement, there's not anything a gentleman can do. I have the impression that Baron Stams is most deeply and sincerely interested in Mrs. Tennyson."

"Oh, I've thought of that. Especially since you opened my eyes to his excellent qualities. He called on us here to say good-bye yesterday. I've never been so mistaken in a man in my life . . . and such interesting connections! Did you know that his mother's sister is a marchioness in England?" I did not know this and shook my head. "It was she who put him through Eton College, as they say. To think that he knows so much about philosophy and philosophers. If he were a little older I could consider appointing him Director of our Academy. But I must tell you something: Persis became quite cross with me—quite firm

—when I spoke of him, last night, with high commendation. I couldn't understand it. Then I remembered that there have been a number of disappointments among our friends in the matter of international marriages—especially with European aristocrats. My daughter Sarah had a most unhappy time—perfectly nice fellow, but couldn't keep his eyes open. I don't think a foreigner would be very welcome, Mr. North."

This foolishness had gone on long enough. I brought my rooks and bishops forward. I spoke lightly, "I wouldn't know anything about such obstacles, Dr. Bosworth. I'm just a Wisconsin peasant." It was my turn to lower my voice. "I have been engaged to be married for some time, but I must tell you in confidence that I am slowly and painfully dissolving that engagement. A young man cannot be too careful. Even in my walk of life a man would hesitate to marry a woman whose former husband took his life in her presence."

Dr. Bosworth gasped like a harpooned whale. "It wasn't in Persis's presence! It was on a ship. He shot himself in the head on the top deck of a ship. I told you he was *eccentric*. He was eccentric. He enjoyed playing with firearms. No reproach was brought up against dear Persis." The tears were pouring down his face. "Ask anyone, Mr. North. Ask Mrs. Venable—ask anyone . . . some insane person sent around those anonymous letters —wicked letters. I think they broke my dear child's heart."

"A very tragic situation, sir."

"Oh, Mr. North, that's what life is—tragic. I am almost eighty years old. I look about me. For thirty years I served my country, not without recognition. My domestic life was all that a man would wish for. And then one misfortune followed upon another. I won't go into details. What is life?" He grasped the lapel of my jacket. "What is life? Can you see why I wish to found an Academy of Philosophers? Why are we placed on this earth?" He began drying his eyes and cheeks with an enormous handkerchief. "How rich this book of Bergson's is! . . . Alas, time is passing and there is so much to read!"

There was a knock at the door.

Persis entered, gloved and veiled for motoring. "Grandfather, it is a quarter past midnight. You should be in bed."

"We've been having a very good talk, dear Persis. I shall not go to sleep easily."

"Mr. North, I was wondering if you were in the mood for a short drive before retiring. I can deliver you at your door. The night air has a wonderful way of clearing the head after a difficult day."

"That's very kind of you, Mrs. Tennyson. I would enjoy it very much."

I said good night to Dr. Bosworth, and Persis and I started down the long hall. I have described "Nine Gables" as "the house of listening ears." Mrs. Bosworth emerged from one of the sitting rooms. "Persis, it is most unsuitable for you to drive at this hour. Say good night to Mr. North. He must be tired. Good night, Mr. North."

Persis said, "Get a good rest, Aunt Sally. Climb in, Mr. North."

"Persis! Did you hear what I said?"

"I am twenty-eight years old, Aunt Sally. Mr. North has spent forty hours in learned talk with Grandfather and can be regarded as an established friend of the family. Get a good rest, Aunt Sally."

"Twenty-eight years old! And so little sense of what is fitting!"

Persis started the motor and waved her hand. We were off.

The reader may remember from the opening chapter of this book that I was somewhat afflicted by the "Charles Marlow complex"—not, fortunately, to the extent of Oliver Goldsmith's hero. I did not stammer and blush and keep my eyes lowered in the presence of nice well-brought-up young women, but Persis Tennyson certainly presented the image (the lily, the swan) of what most intimidated me. I suffered that ambivalence which I had read was at the heart of every complex; I admired her enormously and wished I were many miles away. I was rattled; I floundered; I talked too much and too little.

She drove slowly. "I thought we'd go and sit on the sea wall by the Budlong place," she said.

"At the end of the day I'm usually too tired to drive anywhere. But I don't need much sleep. I get up early and ride out there to see the sun rise. It's still quite dark, of course. At first the police used to think I was on some nefarious business and would follow me. Gradually they came to see that I was merely eccentric and now we wave our hands at one another."

"I often take a late drive at this hour and the same thing happens to me. The police still feel they must keep an eye on me. But I've never been out at dawn. What's it like?"

"It's overwhelming."

She repeated the word softly and reflectively.

"Mr. North, what magic did you use to bring about such a change in my grandfather's health?"

"No magic at all, ma'am. I saw that Dr. Bosworth was under some kind of pressure. I've been under pressure too. Gradually we discovered that we shared a number of enthusiasms. Enthusiasms lift a man out of himself. We both grew younger. That's all."

She murmured, "I think there must have been more to it than that. . . . We feel deeply indebted to you. My grandfather and I would like to give you a present. We have been wondering what you would like. We wondered if you would like a car?" I did not answer. "Or the copy of *Alciphron* that Bishop Berkeley presented to Jonathan Swift? It was written at 'Whitehall.'"

I was disappointed. I concealed my bitter disappointment under a show of effusive thanks and some friendly laughter. "Many thanks to you both for your kind intention," et cetera, et cetera. "I try to live with as few possessions as possible. Like the Chinese a bowl of rice . . . like the ancient Greeks a few figs and olives." I laughed at the absurdity of it, but I had also indicated a firmness in my refusal.

"But, surely, some token of our gratitude?"

The privileged of this world are not accustomed to take no for an answer.

"Mrs. Tennyson, you did not invite me to join you on this ride to talk about presents but to give me an urgent message. I think I know what that is: There are some persons in and near 'Nine Gables' who wish me *out*."

"Yes. Yes. And I am sorry to say that there is something more than that. They are working on a plan to do you harm. There are some very rare first editions on the shelves behind my grandfather's chair. I overheard a plan to remove them gradually and replace them with later editions of the same works. These last years you are the only person who has come into the house who would realize their value. Their idea is that the suspicion will fall on you."

I laughed. "Thrilling!" I said.

"I anticipated their project and substituted the volumes. The originals are in my jewel safe. If some unpleasant talk starts up about you I shall produce them.—Why did you say 'thrilling'?"

"Because *they* are coming into the open. *They* are beginning to make mistakes. I thank you for removing those volumes, but even if you hadn't, I'd have enjoyed the showdown. I'm not a fighting man, Mrs. Tennyson, but I hate slander and malicious gossip—don't you?"

"Oh, I do. *How* I do! People talk—people talk hatefully. Oh, dear Mr. North, tell me how a person can defend himself."

"Here we are at the Budlong place.—Let's get out and sit on the sea wall."

"Don't forget what you were about to tell me."

"No."

"You will find a lap robe in the back seat to throw over the stone parapet."

An untended field of wild roses was at our back. The flowers were entering their decline and the perfume was heady. Our faces were swept by the beams of the lighthouses; our ears were lulled by the dull booming and wailing and tinkling of the buoys. Above us the sky was like a jeweled navigators' chart. It was here that a few afternoons before Bodo had brought Agnese and Mino and me to his picnic.

As usual there were a number of cars in which were couples younger than ourselves.

"You advise me to resign from the work at 'Nine Gables'?"

"You have brought us that great benefit. All that is left for you is the danger of certain persons' ill will."

"You inherit it—conspicuously."

"Oh, it doesn't matter about me. I can bear it."

"With that spitefulness? You have your small boy to think of. Excuse my question, but why have you continued to live in that house?"

How calm she was! "Two reasons: I love my grandfather and he loves me—insofar as he can love anyone. And—where would I go? I hate New York. Europe? I have no wish to go to Europe for a while. My mother left my father long ago—before his death —and has been living in Paris and at Capri with a man to whom she is not married. She seldom writes letters to any of us. Mr. North, I often think that a large part of my life is over. I am an old widow-lady living only for my son and grandfather. The humiliations I am sometimes subjected to and the boredom of the social life do not touch me. They merely age me. . . . You were going to tell me how to get the better of malicious tongues. Did you mean it?"

"Yes . . . Since we are talking about matters that concern you closely, may I—just for this hour—call you Persis?"

"Oh, yes."

I took a deep breath. "Have you reason to believe that in some quarters you have been the object of slander?"

She lowered her head then abruptly raised it. "Yes, I know I am."

"I have no idea what these people are saying. I have never heard any reference to you that was not in terms of admiration and respect. I was told that your husband took his own life, alone, on the top deck of a ship at sea. I assume that malicious interpretations were circulated about that tragic event. I am convinced that nothing discreditable could ever be attributed to you. You asked me how one would go about defending oneself against slander. My first principle would be to state all the facts—the truth. If there is someone involved whom you feel you must shield, then one must resort to other measures. Is there such a person involved in this case?"

"No. No."

"Persis, do you wish to drop the whole subject and talk of other things?"

"No, Theophilus. I have no one to talk to. Please let me tell you the story."

I looked up at the stars for a moment. "I don't like secrets—unhappy family secrets. If you place me under an oath not to repeat a word of this, I must ask you *not* to tell it to me."

She lowered her voice. "But, Theophilus, I want all those talkers and letter-writers and . . . to know the simple truth. I loved my husband, but in a moment of utter thoughtlessness—of madness really—he left me under a cloud of suspicion. You can tell the story to anyone, if you thought it would do any good."

I folded my hands on my lap. In the diffused starlight she could see the welcoming smile on my face. "Begin," I said.

"When I left school I was, as they say, 'presented to society.' Dances, balls, tea-dances, debutante parties. I fell deeply and truly in love with a young man, Archer Tennyson. He had not been in the War because he had had tuberculosis as a boy and the doctors wouldn't pass him. I think that was at the bottom of it all. We were married. We were happy. Only one thing disturbed me; he was reckless and at first I admired him for it. He drove his car at great speeds. On shipboard once he waited until after midnight to climb the masts. The captain rebuked him for it in the ship's bulletin. I gradually came to see that he was a compulsive gambler—not only for money; that, too, but that did not matter—for life itself. He gambled with his life—skiing, motorboat racing, mountain-climbing. When we were in the Swiss Alps he would descend only the most dangerous *pistes*. He took up lugeing which was fairly new then: toboggan descents between walls of packed ice. One day when my attention was distracted he picked up our one-year-old baby, placed him between his knees, and started off. I saw then for the first time what was in his mind: he wanted to raise the stake in his duel with death; he wanted to place what was nearest and dearest to him in the balance. First he had always wanted me beside him in the car or in the boat; now he wanted the baby too. I used to dread the approach of summer because each year he tried to break his record driving from New York to Newport. He broke everyone's record driving to Palm Beach, but I wouldn't go in the car with him. And all the time he betted on everything—horses, football games, Presidential elections. He'd sit in his club window on Fifth Avenue and bet on the types of automobiles that happened to pass. All his friends begged him to take a position in his father's brokerage office, but he couldn't sit still that long. Finally he began taking flying lessons. I don't know if wives go down on their knees to their husbands any more, but I did. I did more than that—I told him that if he went up in the air alone, I would never give him another child. He was so astonished that he *did* give up flying."

She paused and showed uncertainty. I said, "Continue, please."

"He was not seriously a drinking man, but he spent a great deal of time in bars where he could play the role of daredevil and—I'm sorry to say—could swagger. The story is almost over."

"May I interrupt a moment? I don't want the story hurried. I want to know what was going on in your mind during those years."

"In me? I knew that in a way he was a sick man. I loved him still, but I pitied him. But I was afraid. Do you see that he needed an audience for all this show of daring and risk? I had the front seat at the show; a large part of it—but not all of it—was to impress me. A wife can't scold all the time. I did not want to put a gulf between us. . . . He thought of it as courage; I thought of it as foolishness and . . . cruelty to me. One night we were standing on the deck of a ship going to Europe and we saw another ship approaching us in the opposite direction. We had been told that we would pass close to our sister-ship. He said, 'Wouldn't it be glorious if I dived in and swam over to her?' He kicked off his dancing pumps and started to undress. I slapped him hard—very hard—on one cheek and then on the other. He was so shocked that he froze. I said, 'Archer, I did not slap you. Your son did. Learn to be a father.' He slowly pulled up his trousers. He picked up his jacket from the deck. Those were not words that came to me at that moment. They were words I had said over and over to myself on sleepless nights. There were more: 'I have loved you more than you love me. You love defying death more than you love me. You are killing my love for you.' I shouldn't have been weeping but I was, terribly. He put his arms around me and said, 'It's just games, Persis. It's fun. I'll stop whatever I'm doing any time you say.' . . . Now I'll finish my story. It was bound to happen that he'd meet someone with the same madness, someone even madder. It was two days later. Of course, he met him in the bar. It was a War veteran with a wild look in his eye. I sat with them for an hour or two while that man crushed my husband with the narrow escapes he'd been through in combat. What fun it had been, and all that! A storm was rising. The barman announced that the bar was closing, but they gave him money to keep it open. I kept trying to persuade Archer to come to bed, but he had to keep up with this man, drink for drink. This other man's wife had gone to bed and finally, in despair, I went to bed, too. Archer was found on the top deck with a revolver in his hand and a bullet through his head. . . . There was an inquiry and an inquest. . . . I testified that on several evenings my husband and this Major Michaelis had talked about Russian roulette, as though it were a joke. But nothing of that came out in the serious newspapers and very little, as far as I know, even in 'sensational' papers. My grandfather was greatly respected. He knew personally the publishers of the better papers. The incident was briefly reported in the inside pages. Even then I begged my grandfather to see that my testimony was published; but the Michaelises also belong to those old families that move heaven and earth to keep their names out of the papers. And it was that silence that's done me so much harm. It was closed with the verdict that my husband had committed suicide in a state of depression. I had no one to advise me or help me—least of all the Bosworth family. Mrs. Venable has been a dear and close friend to me since I was a child. She joined the family in soothing me: 'If we don't say anything it will soon be forgotten.' She knows the Michaelises. She stays with cousins near them in Maryland. She knows the stories about him down there—that the neighborhood complains of his carrying on revolver practice at three in the morning and bullying the men at his country club about Russian roulette. . . ."

"Mrs. Venable *knows* this? Really knows it?"

"She confided it to my grandfather and to my Aunt Sally—to comfort them, I suppose."

I strode up and down before her. "Why didn't she *confide* it to everybody—to her famous Tuesday 'at homes'? . . . Oh, I hate the cliquishness and the timidity of your so-called privileged class. She hates unpleasantness. She hates to be associated with anything unpleasant, is that it?"

"Theophilus, I'm sorry I told you the whole story. Let's forget it. I'm under a cloud. There's nothing that can be done about it now. It's too late."

"Oh, no, it's not. Where are the Michaelises now?"

"The Major's in a sanatorium in Chevy Chase. I suppose Mrs. Michaelis is in their home nearby in Maryland."

"Persis, Mrs. Venable is a kind woman at heart, isn't she?"

"Oh, very."

"Heaven knows she's influential and likes being influential. Can you explain to me why she hasn't used her kindness and her knowledge and her sense of justice to clear up this fog about you long ago?"

Persis did not answer at once. "You don't know Newport, Theophilus. You don't know what they call the 'Old Guard' here. In those houses nothing disturbing, nothing unpleasant, may ever be mentioned. Even the grave illness or death of old friends can be alluded to only in a whisper and a pressure of the hand when saying goodbye."

"Cotton wool. Cotton wool.—Someone told me that she invites the heart of the 'Old Guard' to luncheon every Thursday. Some people call it 'The Sanhedrin' or 'The Druids' Circle'—is that so?—Are you in it?"

"Oh, I'm not old enough."

I hurled an empty beer bottle into the sea. "Persis!"

"Yes?"

"We need an ambassador to persuade Mrs. Venable and 'The Sanhedrin' that it's their responsibility and their Christian duty to tell *everybody* what undoubtedly happened on that ship. . . . They should do it for your *son's* sake." She must often have thought of that for she clasped her hands tightly to conceal their trembling. "I think our ambassador should be a man—one for whom Mrs. Venable has a particular regard and who has the authority of an acknowledged social position. I have come to know the Baron Stams much better. He is a man of far solider character than you and your grandfather first believed, and let me assure you he hates injustice like the devil. For parts of two summers he has been Mrs. Venable's house guest. Have you observed that she has a real esteem and affection for him?"

She murmured, "Yes."

"Moreover, he has a very real and deep admiration for you. Do you give me permission to tell him the whole story and to urge him to be this ambassador?—But you don't like him."

"Don't . . . don't say that! Now you understand why I had to be so cold and impersonal. I was under a cloud. Don't talk about it. . . . Do—do what you think best."

"He was leaving Newport today. He is staying over. He will have half an hour talk with Mrs. Venable tomorrow morning. You should hear him talk when he's on fire with a subject. It's late. I must ask you to drive me home. I'll drive as far as my door."

I picked up the lap robe and held open the right front door of the car for her. The starlight fell on the face she turned toward me. She was smiling. She murmured, "I am not accustomed to the agitations of hope." I drove slowly, taking neither the longest nor the shortest way home. A police car discreetly followed the great heiress into the town, then turned off.

Her shoulder rested against mine. She said, "Theophilus, I made you cross earlier this evening when I suggested a choice of presents from Grandfather and from myself as an expression of our appreciation. Will you explain that to me?"

"You mean it?"

"Yes."

"Well, as this is to be a soothing little lecture I shall address you as Mrs. Tennyson. Let me explain, Mrs. Tennyson, that each of us is conditioned by our upbringing. I am a member of the middle class—in fact, of the middle of the middle classes—from the middle of the country. We are doctors, parsons, teachers, small-town newspaper editors, two-room lawyers. When I was a boy each house had a horse and buggy and our mothers were assisted in running the house by a 'hired girl.' All the sons and many of the daughters went to college. In that world no one ever received— and, of course, never gave—elaborate presents. Such presents were obscurely felt to be humiliating—perhaps I should say, ridiculous. If a boy wanted a bicycle or a typewriter he earned the money for it by delivering the *Saturday Evening Post* from door to door or by cutting his neighbors' lawns. Our fathers paid for our education, but for those incidentals so necessary at college—such as a 'tuxedo' or trips to dances at the girls' colleges—we worked during the summer on farms or waited on table at summer hotels."

"Did nothing unpleasant ever happen in the middle classes?"

"Oh, yes. People are the same everywhere. But some environments are more stabilizing than others."

"Are you telling me all this to explain to me why you were displeased about the present we wished to make you?"

"No." I turned to her with a smile. "No. I'm thinking about your son Frederick."

"Frederick?"

"In 1918 a woman who worked on Bellevue Avenue—and whom I think you know well—said to me, 'Rich boys never really grow up—or seldom.' "

"Oh, that's . . . superficial. That's not true."

"Have you heard Bodo describe his home—his father and mother and sisters? Provincial nobility. Where the castle is part farmhouse—where the servants have stayed with them generation after generation. Now they take in paying guests. Everybody is busy all day. Austrian music and laughter in the evening. Mrs. Tennyson, what an environment for a fatherless boy!"

"Did he send you to tell me these things?"

"No—on the contrary. He told me he was leaving Newport in despair and that he would never again put foot on this island if he could help it."

We had arrived at my door. I lifted my bicycle from the back seat. She walked around the car to take her place in the driver's seat. She put out her hand to me, saying, "Until that cloud of suspicion is lifted I have no word to say. Thank you for coming with me on this drive. Thank you for listening to my story. Is one permitted to exchange a friendly kiss in the middle class?"

"If no one is looking," I said and kissed her slowly on the cheek. She returned it, as to Ohio born.

Presently I joined Bodo. He had not fallen asleep, but leaped from his car.

"Bodo, could you possibly stay in Newport until tomorrow noon?"

"I have already received permission."

"Could you possibly have a private conversation with Mrs. Venable tomorrow morning?"

"We always have Viennese chocolate together at ten-thirty."

I told him the whole story, and ended up with the job which was now on his shoulders. "Can you do that?"

"I've got to and, by God, I'll succeed—but, Theophilus, you idiot, we still don't know if Persis can love me."

"I can vouch for it."

"How? . . . How? . . . How?"

"Don't ask me! I *know*. And one thing more: You will be back in Newport on August twenty-ninth."

"I can't.—Why? . . . What for? How do you know?"

"Your Chief will send you. And bring an engagement ring with you. You've found your Frau Baronin."

"You're driving me crazy."

"I'll write you. Get a good rest. Don't forget to say your prayers. I'm dog-tired. Good night."

I walked back to my door. I had had an inspiration. Edweena would help me find the way.

Edweena

When in Tante Liselotte's room my eyes fell on Edweena and the tears rolled down my cheeks, my relief sprang not only from seeing a replacement; I was also seeing an old and loved friend. I *knew* Edweena—I had known her in 1918 as Toinette and as Mrs. Wills. During all the weeks at Mrs. Cranston's when she had been referred to so often—Henry's fiancée and Mrs. Cranston's "star boarder" in the garden apartment—she had never gone under any other name than Edweena. Yet I knew at once that my old friend must be the long-expected Edweena.

This is how I had come to know her:

In the fall of 1918 I was twenty-one years old, a soldier stationed at Fort Adams in Newport. On my advancement to the grade of corporal I was given a seven-day leave to return to my home to show my new-won stripe to my parents, to my sisters, and to the public. (My brother was overseas.) I returned to my station via New York and embarked on a boat of the Fall River Line for Newport. Old-timers still remember those boats with

sighs of deep feeling. They offered all that one could imagine of
luxury and romance. Most of the cabins opened on the deck by a
door faced with wooden slats that could be shifted to temper the
air. We had seen such accommodations in the motion-pictures.
We could imagine that at any moment there would be a tap at the
door, we would open it to confront a beautiful heavily veiled
woman whispering imploringly, "Please let me in and hide me. I
am being pursued." Ah! We were traveling under blackout. Dim
blue lights indicated the entrances to the interior of the vessel. I
stayed up on deck for an hour, barely distinguishing the Statue
of Liberty, the outlines of Long Island's coast, and perhaps the
lofty joy-rides of Coney Island. All the while I was aware by a
prickling down my spine that our progress was being observed
through the periscopes of enemy submarines—baleful crocodiles
below the surface of the water—yet knowing that we were not
sufficiently important game to induce them to reveal their presence.
Finally I entered the hull of the boat, which consisted of a vast
brightly lit dining saloon, a bar, and a series of social rooms where
all was carved wood, polished brass, and velvet drapery—the
Arabian Nights. I went to the bar and ordered a Bevo. I noticed
that other passengers were refreshing themselves from flasks carried in their hip pockets. (I was not then a drinking man unless
opportunity arose, having solemnly taken the Pledge of life-long
abstinence at the age of eight under the deeply moved eyes of my
father and an official of the Temperance League in Madison, Wisconsin.) I sat down to dinner, hovered over by stately waiters in
white coats and gloves. I denied myself the "Terrapin Baltimore"
and ordered dishes from the less expensive items on the menu.
The dinner cost me half a week's pay, but it was worth it. A
soldier's pay was weightless. The government provided all his
necessities; a portion was automatically deducted and sent to his
loved ones; he was under the impression that the end of the War
was, like his middle age, unimaginably remote. I had been told
that the boat was completely filled. It would reach Fall River at
about nine when passengers for Boston and the north would dis-

embark. Those with tickets for Newport had to go ashore at six in the morning. I was in no hurry to go to bed and having finished my blueberry pie *à la mode* I returned to one of the many tables near the bar and ordered another near-beer.

At the table next to mine was an elegantly dressed couple quarreling. The chair of the woman was back to back with mine. At that time—to counteract the routine of my work at the Fort— I was assiduously keeping my Journal and was already composing an account of this trip in my mind. I have no compunction about overhearing conversations in public places and this one I could not fail to overhear without moving to another table.

The man may have been drinking, but his articulation was precise. I had the impression that he was "beside himself," he was crazy. His wife, sitting very straight, was attempting to make her remarks both soothing and admonitory. She was at the end of her tether.

"You've been at the back of it all for years. You've been trying to put them against me the whole time."

"Edgar!"

"All this talk about my having ulcers. I haven't got ulcers. You've been trying to poison me. You're in cahoots with the whole family."

"Edgar! The few times I've seen your mother and brothers during the last three years have always been in your presence."

"You *telephone* them. When I leave the house you telephone them by the hour." Et cetera. "*You* got me blackballed at that damned club."

"I don't know how a woman could do that."

"You're sly. You could do anything."

"You lost your temper at Mr. Cleveland himself. The vice-president of the club—in front of everybody.—Please go to bed and get some rest. We have to get off this boat in seven hours. I'll sit here quietly for a while and slip into the cabin when you're asleep." A woman had approached them. "You can go to bed, Toinette. I shan't need you until the ship whistles for landing."

Apparently Toinette lingered. There was a shade of insistence in her voice. "I have some sewing to do, madam. The light is better here. I shall be sitting by the bandstand for an hour. I heard them say there might be some bad weather tonight. I shall be in Cabin 77, if you should need me."

The man said, "That's right, Toinette. Tell the whole boat your cabin number."

"Tomorrow, Edgar, I shall ask you to apologize to Toinette. You forget that you were brought up to be a gentleman—and the son of Senator Montgomery!"

"Women's voices! Women's voices! Insinuations, innuendoes! Nagging! I can't stand any more. You can sit here quietly until the boat sinks. I'm going to bed and I'm going to lock the door. I'll put your dressing-case in the corridor. You can bunk with Toinette."

"Toinette, here's my key to the cabin. Will you kindly pack my necessaries in my dressing-case.—Edgar, please remain at this table until Toinette has collected my things. I shall not say a word."

"Where's that waiter? I want to pay the bill. Waiter! Waiter!— What are you doing with my purse?"

"If I'm to arrange for another cabin I shall need some money. I'm your wife. I shall pay your bill here too."

"Stop! How much are you taking?"

"I may have to bribe the purser for a cabin."

Edgar Montgomery rose and strolled moodily the length of the saloon. I caught a glimpse of his dark tormented face. He had what we used to call a "weeping willow" mustache. He peered into the card room and the coffee rooms (scarlet damask and gilt mirrors).

Toinette returned with the dressing-case. I turned and saw her descending the great staircase. She was dressed in what I assumed to be a French maid's uniform for street-wear in winter. It was a jacket and skirt in the severest dark-blue wool, probably to be worn under a long swinging cape. It was close-fitting and the edges were "piped" (is that right?) in black braid. If you have an eye for simplicity, it was exceedingly elegant. But what smote me was her carriage. At the age of twenty-one I had no wide experience in such matters, but I had seen "La Argentina" and her company dance in San Francisco when I was sixteen and had saved up my money in the New Haven years to see Spanish dancing—what I called to myself the "spine of steel" of Spanish women, the "walk of the tigress," the "touch-me-not" arrogance of the dancer relative to her partner. Toinette came down those stairs not only without lowering her eyes to her feet, without lowering her eyes below the level of the horizontal regard. Zowie! Olé!! What deportment! She soon passed out of my line of vision.

"Madam," she said in a low voice, "I'd be very happy if you used my cabin. It's not for long and I've often sat up the night."

"I wouldn't think of it, Toinette. Will you sit here by the dressing-case while I go down to the purser's office? The trip was a mistake. Both the doctor and I thought he was so much better. Toinette, don't give a thought to me. You go to bed when you're ready."

Mr. Montgomery made as though to approach them, then changed his mind and ascended the great staircase. Apparently a number of the cabins had doors that opened on the gallery as well as on the deck. He entered his and shut the door resolutely.

Toinette whispered something into his wife's ear.

"That's all right, Toinette. I did as the doctor told me. I emptied the *things* and put some blank cartridges in the chambers."

Mrs. Montgomery sat in silence for a moment. She then turned and looked briefly at me as I did at her. A very handsome woman. After a pause she turned again and said, "Sergeant, have you a cabin to yourself?"

"Yes, madam," I said, rising to military attention.

"I'll give you thirty dollars for it."

"Madam, I'll clear out at once and give you the key, but I'll take no money for it. I'll get my gear and be back in a moment."

"Stop! I won't accept it."

She left the hall, descending the steps to the purser's office. I turned and saw Toinette's full face for the first time—a fascinating triangular face of what I took to be some Mediterranean origin, dark eyes, dark lashes, and an air of mock gravity over the distressing situation that had brought us together.

"Madam," I said. "If I give you the key to my cabin, I think she'd accept yours. I have some friends on the boat. They're sitting up all night and have asked me to play cards with them. I've often sat up all night playing cards."

"Corporal, we must let these people work things out in their own way."

"It's hard to believe that Mr. Montgomery is a grown-up man."

"Rich boys never really grow up—or seldom."

I started. I'd been warned strongly for years against making generalizations. I was ready to weigh Toinette's.

"Madam, what was that I heard about guns?"

"May I ask your name, sir?"

"North, Theodore North."

"My name is Mrs. Wills. May I take you into my confidence, Mr. North?"

"Yes, madam."

"Mr. Montgomery has always played with guns. Though I have never heard of his firing one except at cardboard targets. He thinks he has enemies. He keeps a revolver always in the drawer by his bedside table. All rich boys do. Mr. Montgomery has little nervous breakdowns from time to time. Mrs. Montgomery was advised by his doctor last week to substitute blank cartridges for real bullets. They're almost noiseless—just cork and feathers, I think. He's a little disturbed tonight—that's the way we put it. If Mrs. Montgomery insists on sitting up all night, I shall sit up too."

I said firmly, "I'll sit up too. Excuse me, Mrs. Wills—what do you think will happen?"

"Well, I know he's not going to sleep. Maybe in half an hour he's going to come to his senses and be ashamed of himself for throwing his wife out of his cabin. Anyway, he'll come out to see the effect of his big noise. Sooner or later he'll break down—

tears, apologies.—They're dependent, men like that. He'll consent to take a *piqûre*. Do you know what a *piqûre* is?"

"A puncture—I mean, an injection."

"All those words have soothing names around here. We call it a little sleeping-aid."

"Who gives it to him?"

"Mrs. Montgomery, mostly."

"It must be an exciting life for you, madam."

"Not any more. I've given Mr. Montgomery notice that I'm leaving in two weeks. While we were in New York I arranged for some new work."

"I'm going to sit here where I can see him come out of that door on the balcony. If he's as what you call disturbed as that, we may see some action. I wish you'd sit where you could see it too and where I could catch your eye."

"I will. You're a planner, aren't you, Corporal?"

"I never thought of it that way, ma'am. Perhaps I am. *Now* I am when I see you mixed up in a thing like this. Even dummy bullets can cause a bit of trouble."

I couldn't take my eyes off her and our eyes were constantly meeting with little sparks of recognition. I sent up a trial kite. "Mr. Wills must be glad that you're resigning from an unpleasant situation like this."

"Mr. Wills? That's another piece of business I did in New York this last week. I put my husband on a ship for England. He was homesick for London. He didn't like America and took to drinking. The mistakes we make don't really hurt us, Corporal, when we understand every inch of the ground."

I was losing my distrust of generalizations.

Mrs. Montgomery reappeared. It was apparent that her inquiries had been fruitless. I again offered her my key. "There are all-night card games at Fort Adams every Saturday night. I've often joined them."

She looked at me directly. "Would you like to play cards?"

"Very much. There are some friends of mine in the next room.

If Mrs. Wills would play with us we'd only need one of them."

"I don't play cards, Corporal North," said Toinette.

"There are two soldiers there that play well and would appreciate playing with a lady."

"Corporal, my name is Mrs. Montgomery. My husband has had many things to worry him lately. When I find that he's moody I often leave him alone to rest."

"I'll get the cards and the men, Mrs. Montgomery. We'd better play bridge for low stakes. When men return from leave they generally have very little money in their pockets."

What was in my mind was that they might take her over the barrel.

"You're very kind, Corporal."

The men I selected were eager to play with a lady. I dug into my uniform and pulled out two ten-dollar bills. "Low stakes, fellas—just to pass the time. Lady's husband's a little off his head but not dangerous.—Mrs. Montgomery, this is Sergeant Major Norman Sykes. He was wounded overseas and has been sent back to build up cadres over here. This is Corporal Wilkins. He's a librarian in Terre Haute, Indiana."

With no apparent effort on my part I seated myself in direct view of the Montgomery cabin. I placed Mrs. Montgomery at my left. By turning her head Mrs. Montgomery could see her cabin door; as far as I was aware she did not glance at it once. She was charming; so was the sergeant. Wilkins ran off to find a cleaner pack of cards.

"From what state do you come, Sergeant Major Sykes?"

"I'm a Tennessee wildcat, ma'am. I had only a short lick of schooling, but I was reading the Bible at six. I'm in the Army for life. I got a bit of steel in my shoulder, but the Army's found work for me to do. I've got three little wildcats of my own. Young children take a lot of feeding, as you may know, ma'am. . . . I had the good fortune to marry the brightest, prettiest schoolteacher in Tennessee."

"I think the good fortune was equally divided, Sergeant."

"That was very pleasant-spoken, ma'am. We have a good number of Montgomerys in Tennessee and I've noticed they're all pleasant-spoken."

"That is not always true of the Montgomerys of Newport, I'm sorry to say."

"Well," said the sergeant soothingly, "civil manners come hard to some folks."

"How true!"

Wilkins returned with fresh cards and we were soon engrossed in tense play. From time to time I exchanged glances with Toinette. She was engaged—or perhaps pretended to be—in mending or altering a skirt.

Neither of us missed the moment at which Mr. Montgomery stepped out of his cabin onto the gallery. He had changed into a burgundy-colored velveteen smoking jacket. He gazed down for a few moments on the congenial foursome. Nothing irritates a bully like seeing others having a good time without him. There's a generalization for you. I could swear that Mrs. Montgomery was aware of his presence also. She raised her voice and said, "Three no trumps! Sergeant, we must pull ourselves together."

"Ma'am," he said, "I'm a slow warmer-upper. We'll take their shirts yet. Pardon the expression."

Mr. Montgomery slowly passed along the balcony and as slowly descended the great staircase. He crossed to the bar and ordered a set-up, reached into one pocket, then the other, and brought out a flask. He poured from its contents into his glass which he carried to a table. He sat down, facing us directly, and gazed at us somberly.

To myself I said, "He's going to goof."

The majority of the passengers had dispersed to their cabins, but there was a large group of intermittently noisy drinkers at the bar. Eight strokes of the ship's bell were clearly audible.

"Midnight," said the sergeant.

"Midnight," said I.

I glanced at Toinette. Still smiling she performed an odd bit of pantomime. She leaned toward the right as though she were about to fall out of her chair and then dropped her piece of sewing from her right hand to the floor. I got the idea at once.

"It's your play, Corporal North," said Mrs. Montgomery.

The game continued for a few moments. Then slowly Mr. Montgomery's hand went to his right pocket. His wife rose. "Excuse me, gentlemen, I must speak to my husband."

At that moment he fired. A wad of cork struck my right shoulder and fell on the table before me.

I fell off my chair and lay dead on the floor.

"Edgar!" cried Mrs. Montgomery.

"Corporal!" cried Toinette and rushed to my side. "He's wounded! Corporal! Corporal! Can you hear me?"

Mr. Montgomery was panting. He doubled up, retching. The sergeant strode over to him and tore the gun out of his hand; he cocked it and dropped the cartridges on the table.

"Duds!" he said, "goddamned DUDS!"

Toinette was slapping my cheeks. "Corporal, can you hear me?"

I sat up. "I guess it was just the shock, ma'am," I said, blissfully.

The barman's chin hung like a swinging satchel. The noisy revelers had observed nothing.

Mrs. Montgomery leaned over her husband. "Edgar, you're tired. We're both tired. It's been a very pleasant trip, hasn't it?— but *wearing*. You've been simply splendid. Now I think you might have a very small sleeping-aid. We'll have forgotten all about it by tomorrow. Say good night to all these friends. Barman, will five dollars cover my husband's bill? Here, Sergeant, take this for my share in our losses; if it's too big, give the rest to your church."

Mr. Montgomery had raised his head and was peering about him. "What happened, Martha? Was anybody hurt?"

"Corporal North, will you take Mr. Montgomery's other arm?

I can carry the dressing-case, Toinette. I won't need you. Edgar, don't stop for the flask now. Let's leave it for these gentlemen who kindly asked me to join their game."

Mr. Montgomery didn't want the help of my arm. "Please go away from me, sir. . . . Martha, *what happened?*"

"You and your schoolboy jokes! You made us laugh. . . . Turn right, Edgar. . . . No, the next door. Good night, gentlemen. Thank you all."

"I don't want his gun," said the sergeant, "or his liquor neither. I took the Pledge."

"So did I," said the corporal.

"I'll give them to him in the morning," said Toinette, dropping them into her sewing bag.

The corporal swept up the dummies and said to the sergeant, "Let's get out of here before they start asking questions."

The barman must have pressed a button summoning the night watchman. The two approached the table where Toinette and I were sitting.

"What was that fracas that was goin' on over here?"

"Oh, you mean *that!*" I said laughing. "One of the passengers played a schoolboy's joke. Had a black bat made of rubber. Tried to scare the ladies.—Barman, can I have two soda-water set-ups?"

"Every night something crazy," said the watchman and left.

So there we sat, face to face, over that table, looking into each other's eyes. I can go out of my mind about a pair of fine eyes. Mrs. Wills's were unusual in several ways. Firstly there was a slight "cast"—so mistakenly called a "flaw"—in her right eye; in the second place you couldn't tell what color they were; thirdly, they were deep and calm and amused. When I go swimming in a pair of eyes I am not fully master of what I may say.

"Please, what color are your eyes?"

"Some people say they're blue in the morning and hazel at night."

My attention is almost as consumedly drawn to hands. I was to learn later that Toinette was five years older than I. I now saw

that her hands gave evidence that in earlier life they had been
engaged in hard manual labor—scullery work, maybe—probably
accompanied by malnutrition and harsh treatment. She had suffered and in all other aspects of her mind (and body) she had
surmounted those trials; she had come through. To the eyes of
friendship and love the coarseness of her hands had become
spiritualized. She did not attempt to hide them.

"Excuse me asking questions.—Are you English?"

"I think so. I was found."

"Found?"

"Yes, found in a basket."

I was so filled up with delight that I laughed at the good
fortune. "Do you have any idea—?"

"Theodore, do come to your senses. I was less than a week old.
Do you know Soho?"

"It's a part of London where there are foreign restaurants and
where artists live. I've never been there." I was bewildered. I
could see the orphanage; I could see the scullery. Like Henry
Simmons she had risen from the hardest stratum of London life,
but—unlike Henry—her accent had been consciously schooled. She
spoke the English of a "lady" with the faint suggestion of speaking
a foreign language. (My conjecture was an apprenticeship in a
hairdresser's establishment, perhaps in the theater . . . she had
known what it was to be a protégée here and there—just long
enough to confirm her outstanding trait of independence; a quick
learner.)

A fine gold wire was strung between our eyes and some kind of
energy was passing back and forth. Our hands were clasped before
us on the table as though we were good children at school. But
my hands were moving toward hers—without pushing, as on a
Ouija board.

"I think I'm part Jewish and part Irish."

Again I overflowed with laughter. "That's a great situation for
an orphan; you get all the good of it without having to listen to

the advice." The golden wire went zingazingaling. "The blight of family life is advice." Who was making generalizations now? "Can I ask what new work you're going into?"

"I'm going to open a shop in New York—and maybe in Newport later. Things for ladies to wear, not dresses, not hats, but just pretty things. It will be a great success." She did not stress the word "great"; it would be a great success and that was that. I learned that mark of maturity from her, then and there.

"What are you going to call it?"

My finger tips had reached one of her knuckles.

"I don't know. I'm going to change my name. Maybe I'll choose a simple name like Jenny. Everything in the shop is going to be simple but perfect. Maybe for the first weeks nobody will buy anything, but they'll come back and look again."

She lifted her glass to her lips. Then put her hand back on the table where it had been touching mine.

"What do you do, Mr. North?"

"I'm a college student. When the War's over I'm going back to college."

"What do you study most?"

"Languages."

"You have nice friends. Are many of the men at Fort Adams like that?"

"Yes. For one reason or another the Army hasn't given us orders to go overseas. My eyes are all right, but they're just below the grade for overseas duty."

By now the fingers of my right hand were intertwined with those of her left. What with eyes and hands, I was finding myself again.

She asked, "After you've learned those languages what are you going to do?"

She seized my restless hand firmly, flattened it on the table, and laid her hand over it to keep it still.

"In New York day before yesterday I had a narrow escape.

A cousin of my mother's is in the business of importing silk from China. Big office. Typist girls tiptoeing around like whipped mice. He offered me a job when I graduate. He says the War is going to end in a month, so I'd graduate in 1920. He's a Scotchman and doesn't say a word he doesn't mean. He promised me that I'd be making five thousand dollars a year in five years. I wrestled with temptation for three minutes flat. Then I thanked him properly and got out. On the street I frightened the New Yorkers by shouting, 'AN OFFICE! AN OFFICE!!' *No*, I can make money without sitting in a chair for forty years."

"Theodore, not so loud!"

"I'm going to be an actor or a detective or an explorer or a wild animal tamer. I can always make money. What I want to see is a million faces. I want to *read* a million faces."

"Sh—sh!"

I lowered my voice. "I guess I've read a million and so have you."

She was laughing interiorly.

"But you're a new face, Miss Jenny. If a man travels enough he'll run into the Bay of Naples or Mount Chimborazo or something. He'll run into a surprise like Mr. Edgar Montgomery . . . or a great surprise like Miss Jenny," and I leaned down and kissed her hand. I kissed it again and again.

The barman called out, "The bar's closing in about five minutes, ladies and gentlemen. We don't want that kind of business in here, soldier. You heard me say 'ladies and gentlemen' and I meant it."

I rose grandly and said, "Barman, I don't like your tone of voice. This lady and I have been married for three years. I wish you to apologize to my wife at once or I shall report you to Mr. Pendleton, passenger agent of this line and my own cousin."

Even the revelers heard this.

The barman said, "I didn't mean no offense, ma'am, but I'm ready to tell Mr. Pendleton or anybody else that wherever your husband is, some peculiar things start to happen. He laid out dead here just twenty minutes ago."

Mrs. Wills said, "Thank you, barman. Surely, you know that soldiers must be given consideration on the short leave that's given them before they cross the sea to offer their lives for us."

The revelers applauded.

She rose, glass in hand, and said splendidly, "My husband is a very distinguished man. He speaks twelve languages better than he speaks English."

More applause. I put my arm around my dear wife and shouted, "Iroquois! Choctaw!"

"Eskimo!" she cried.

"Jabberwocky!"

"Mulligatawny!"

There were cries of "Give 'em a drink!" . . . "Sprekkenzy Doysh?" . . . "Me likee Chinee girl, she likee me!"

Flushed with success, we sat down—the picture of conjugal love and pride.

Suddenly, however, world events took the matter out of our hands. The night watchman appeared at the head of the staircase, wearing a sou'wester and swinging a hurricane lantern. He had heard town-criers as a boy and put his whole soul into it. "Ladies and gentlemen, quiet please! Word has just come over the wireless that the War has come to an end. The Arnstiss—the Armystiss—what they call it!—has been signed. The skipper has tole me to tell you in the saloon, but not to wake anybody up that's gone to bed. There's high seas runnin' and the boat will be delayed, maybe, dockin' at Newport and Fall River.—Tommy, the skipper says the Line offers a free drink to anybody that's sittin' up. I gotta go down to the engine room."

All hell broke loose. The revelers began hurling crockery about the hall. Cuspidors are too heavy to hurl, but they can be rolled on their rims for quite a distance. The card-players poured into the saloon.

"Jenny," I said.

"What?"

"Jenny, let's not separate."

"I didn't hear what you said."

"Yes, you did! Yes, you did!"

"Why, where did you ever get such an idea!"

"Jenny!"

"Well, we don't see a war come to an end every day. In about ten minutes come down to Cabin 77. I have an alarm clock set for five-thirty."

I whirled her about. When I restored her to the floor, she went downstairs to the cabins reserved for servants; I went upstairs and packed my gear.

"Charmes d'amour, qui saurait vous peindre?" as Benjamin Constant wrote on setting out to describe a similar encounter. "Enchantments of love, what artist can picture you?" The generosity of the woman, the bold tenderness of the grown man—the fathomless gratitude to nature for its revelation of itself, yet with some reminder that death is the end of all, death accepted, death united with life in the chain of being from the primal sea to the ultimate cold. *"Charmes d'amour, qui saurait vous peindre?"*

She must have turned off the alarm clock instantaneously for it did not wake me. When I woke at the ship's whistle she had taken all her possessions and was gone. On the mirror was written with soap, "Don't change." I dressed and was about to leave the cabin when I turned back and flung myself on the bed again and buried my head in the pillow, alone and not alone.

I was among the last to disembark. From the gangplank a strange sight met my eyes. There was a great bonfire in Washington Square. Hundreds of men and women and children, hastily dressed, in a tumult of distraught dogs, were dancing about it. "The War's over! The War's over!" Everyone in the Ninth City was hugging and kissing everyone else, particularly the few service men who were disembarking or who had come to the center of the town. Maybe I was hugged and kissed by the Materas and the Avonzinos and by Mrs. Keefe, and the Wentworths and Dr.

Addison, but this was November, 1918, and I knew only seven civilians in all the Nine Cities. The apparatus of the Newport Fire Department was dashing up and down in the streets in an ecstasy of uselessness. In the little park where Alice and I were to see each other for the last time, sporadic religious revivals and scandalous orgies were contaminating each other. Nicolaidis's All Night Café, having run out of coffee and frankfurter buns, was jammed and was being looted by enraged customers. Reader, it was gorgeous!

No, I was not the last to leave the boat. I saw Mr. Montgomery, having aged thirty years in a few hours, unsteady on his legs, being met by his doctor, his valet, and two chauffeurs. His wife took her place beside him looking very fine indeed in sables. The second car was so filled with luggage that Toinette had to sit on the valet's knees.

I disentangled myself from the embraces of a grateful populace and started my walk to Fort Adams under the dawn's early light, only two miles, but the longest trek I remember ever having taken. At reveille about ninety percent of the soldiers were absent without leave.

That was the famous "False Armistice."

All discipline broke down. During the intervening days before the end of the War was officially declared, the Headquarters Company had time to run up *pro forma* papers for the soldiers' separation from the service and I had time to obtain my travel orders and to brace myself for endless peace and the serious business of living. I made no attempt to get in touch with the Montgomery household which I assumed to be in as chaotic a condition as that about me.

So it was that—almost eight years later—it was not Toinette, not Jenny, but Mrs. Edweena Wills who followed me downstairs from Tante Liselotte's room and found me asleep against the wall between the second and third floors.

The summer was drawing to a close. Many of my "pupils" were
occupied with plans for the fall and our lessons drew to a close. I
welcomed the increase in my free time. I spent long contented
hours in my apartment bringing my Journal up to date, filling in
"portraits" of the persons I had known—pages which refreshed
my memory and on which I am now drawing so many years later
in the composition of this book. I had worked very hard and the
"professor" experienced little difficulty in refusing invitations from
his former "pupils," however kindly intended.

I saw Edweena and Henry almost every day. They were engaged
to be married as soon as Mr. Wills in far-off London had drunk
himself to death on the allowance his wife continued to send him.
I loved Edweena and I loved Henry and I'm proud to say they
loved me. Never for a moment, in company or alone, did Edweena
and I make any reference to having met previously. Even Mrs.
Cranston, whom little escaped, had no inkling of it. Edweena
had prospered. Her shops, first in New York, then in Newport,
were a great success. She had selected and trained assistants and
presently handed the management over to them, because a more
satisfying and even more remunerative career opened up for her.
No name could be found for it, but she was delighted when (from
my fund of "twelve languages") I offered and explained to her
the words *arbitrix elegantiarum*, "The woman who dispenses the
laws of good taste," as Petronius Arbiter did at the Emperor
Nero's court. She continued to insist that she was a lady's maid,
but she turned down all invitations to serve as maid to any one
lady; how far that designation falls short of the role she played
in New York and Newport. No ball, no dinner of great occasion
was imaginable without Edweena's presence in the *boudoir* reserved for the ladies. Many guests brought their own maid with
them, but no guest was completely sure of her presented self until
Edweena had approved of it. It was her sternly upheld doctrine
of *nothing too much* that had changed the modes of dress. She
proffered counsel only when she was asked for it; many a dame,
supremely sure of herself in Chicago or Cleveland or even in New

York, would start down the great staircase like a galleon in full sail, only to discover that confidence was ebbing step by step, and would remount the stairs. Insecurity as to how one looks can be a torment, particularly in a time of transition; the baroque was passing into the classic. Edweena had not created the new; she had felt the shifting tide "in her bones" and rode the wave.

Edweena was more than a judge of what was fitting, however. She was a refuge and a comforter and a source of encouragement to old and young; she knew or divined everything: incipient hysterics, rages, domestic jars, feuds, confrontations of a man's wife and his mistress, the terror of brides introduced into this scene for the first time. ("If you feel tired at any time, Mrs. Duryea, come up and sit by me for a while.") Before long her career extended itself. She was invited into homes to plan trousseaus for marriage or mourning. She was engaged by women to advise them on their entire wardrobe. She enjoyed the work; the remuneration was considerable, but the basis of her contentment was her love for Henry and her friendship with Amelia Cranston.

This is the Edweena I encountered in the middle of August. I was now able to be a more frequent guest at Mrs. Cranston's in the late evening. Edweena served tea every afternoon at four-thirty in the "garden apartment" and I was duly reproached when I failed to appear. Edweena loved conversation. Often we were joined by Mrs. Cranston when her duties permitted. After dispensing tea Edweena would stretch out on the long sofa, her shoulder resting against Henry's—Henry sitting straight and proud.

I remained reticent about my encounters on the Avenue. I had little doubt that Mrs. Cranston had received partial accounts of my involvements with the Bosworths, the Granberrys, the Vanwinkles, perhaps—as she had had of my involvement with the Skeels. But she respected my silence. Then when I was beginning to feel that my summer tasks were coming to an end I was confronted with the nearest and weightiest of them all: the matter of Persis and Bodo.

What had I meant when I said to Bodo, "You will be back in

Newport on August twenty-ninth"? I don't know. That's the kind
of irrational impulse to which I am prone. I knew that something had to be done quickly and if it had to be done, it could be
done.

From the moment Bodo left Newport my imagination began
groping for a solution; it continued to grope even while I slept.
I have said before that both despair and hope invoke the imagination. In response to hope the imagination is aroused to picture every
possible issue, to try every door, to fit together even the most
heterogeneous pieces in the puzzle. After the solution has been
found it is difficult to recall the steps taken—so many of them are
just below the level of consciousness. I began to feel that somewhere there must be public confirmation of Major Michaelis's obsession with Russian roulette. I began to be visited with images of
Bodo's return to Newport to create a *divertissement* at the Servants'
Ball in Mrs. Venable's own cottage. I began to see that in some
way, somehow, Edweena could help me.

The very day after Bodo left I appeared punctually at the "garden apartment" for tea.

"We're going to have a visitor today, Teddie. . . . Yes, a most
respected one—Chief of Police Diefendorf. Mrs. Cranston and I
have a little matter to discuss with him. Poor helpless women
though we are, we have been able to be of real service to the
Chief on a number of occasions and, of course, he's been many
times of service to us."

"Edweena, my love, before you returned from shipwrecks and
sharks I took the liberty of telling my old pal of what a wonderful
detective you were."

Indeed, he had. It was a blood-warming story.

Servants live in terror of being unjustly dismissed from a situation without a letter of recommendation. This usually takes the
form of being charged with having stolen objects of value. As
the reader knows I shrink from making a generalization, but when
I do it's a bold one: persons endowed with enormous inherited

wealth tend to be more than a little unbalanced. So would you or I. They know they are marginal citizens—a very small portion of the inhabitants of this industrious or idle, mostly starving, often much-enduring, often rebellious world. They are haunted by the dread that what destiny, chance, or God has given them, destiny, chance, or God may as mysteriously withdraw. They are burdened by the problem of their merits. They assume (often with reason, often with none) that they are the object of envy (one of the uglier sins), of hatred, or of ridicule. They herd together for company. They know that something is wrong, but who began it? Where will it end? Hysteria lurks under the surface.

Masters and servants live under one roof in a close symbiosis, a forced intimacy. A woman's jewels (*precious* stones) are the outward and visible symbol that someone loves her, even if it's only God. A number of the ladies on Bellevue Avenue no longer trusted the safes in their own bedrooms. They had what Edweena called "the squirrel complex." When they returned from a ball they hid their emeralds and their diamonds in old stockings or behind picture frames or in electric light sconces and *then forgot where they'd hidden them.* (There's something in one of Professor Freud's books about that.) The next morning they'd be frantic. They'd give orders that every servant in the house be present in the dining room at ten o'clock. "A thing I value very much for association's sake has disappeared. You are to remain in this room while the housekeeper and I search through your rooms. If it is not found by us or restored by one of you—by noon today—every one of you except Watson, Wilson, Bates, Miles, and the kitchen staff will be dismissed without a letter of recommendation. While I am gone now you may sit down." In some cases the lady called up the police, but most of the ladies regarded the police as bumbling yokels. One of the suspected criminals would creep out of the dining room and call up the police. But the police could do no more than ring the doorbell and ask permission to enter. Chief Diefendorf then telephoned "Miss Edweena" who was permitted to enter and who, with transcendental tact, was permitted to join the searching party. Four times out of five she found the missing object very soon, but pretended for a whole half hour— to save the poor woman's face—that the case was hopeless. In many ways the Chief was deeply indebted to Edweena and treated her with an old-world admiring deference, as he did Mrs. Cranston.

Edweena lowered her voice to tell me that this expected visit of the Chief did not have to do with a supposed theft but with another problem that appears from time to time in this Seventh City. "It concerns a housemaid Bridget Trehan who is being persecuted by the master of the house where she is employed. She has resigned from her position, but the Chief and I have ways of extorting from her former mistress—who is furious—an excellent letter of recommendation!"

"Golly," I said in awe. We both nodded. "Edweena, can I ask you what your plans are for the Servants' Ball this year?"

"You know in general what it's like, don't you?"

"I only know that Mrs. Venable lends her ballroom for the occasion and that you and Henry are chairwoman and chairman of the committee. And I know that you and Henry made the rule two years ago that no one of the summer colony can come and look down on you from the balcony as they used to."

"Teddie, I have no plans. I have no ideas. We're all tired of fancy-dress balls. We've had enough pirates and gypsy flower girls. We've had enough of the 'Gay Nineties' and the gas-lit era. There are fewer and fewer young people among the domestic servants. We all have a good time, but we need a fresh idea. Couldn't you think up some idea, Teddie?"

Heaven sent me an idea. I pretended to be reluctant. "Well, I haven't an idea . . . but I have a dream. The trouble with your ball and many of the balls I hear about is that the same people step out on the same floor with the same people they stepped out with the last time. In Vienna the most enjoyable ball is called the 'Fiaker Ball'—the ball for the cabmen of the city. And the people from the highest society enjoy going to it and they all mingle together. . . . My dream is this: that you begin gradually and invite two guests of honor from Bellevue Avenue—a young man and a young woman—good-looking and charming and particularly admired for their friendly appreciation of servants. Honor them and they will feel honored. Tactfully make it clear to them that you would be much pleased if they wore their most elegant ballroom dress."

"Teddie, you're crazy. Would they want to come? Why?"

"Because that's the kind of persons they are. They've long wanted to know the servants better. I know just such a gentleman who often comes to dinner at a house where I have a pupil. My pupil and I aren't in the dining room, but I can hear him when he arrives at the front door chat with the man who takes his coat. I can hear him exchanging comradely greetings with all the staff. He's never accepted a barrier between employer and employee."

"Who is it, Teddie?"

"I know a young lady who dines twice a week at the very house where you're holding your ball. The household staff has known her since she was a child. She calls them all by name and asks after their relatives. Edweena, she knows you well and loves you. She doesn't call you 'Miss Edweena'—at least not to me; she calls you affectionately 'Edweena.' Who—together with you—is the most attractive woman on Aquidneck Island?"

"Who is it, Teddie? Teddie, you're like a child blowing soap-bubbles. Whoever they are, they wouldn't think of accepting the invitation. Henry, ask Teddie who he has in mind."

"Teddie, speak up. Who do you have in mind?"

"Baron Stams and Persis Tennyson."

Henry stared at me for a moment, then he struck the table. "God help me, he's right! I thought he meant Colonel Vanwinkle, but his wife wouldn't let him come, and I thought he meant young Mrs. Granberry, but she's expecting a baby. I don't think the Baron

and Mrs. Tennyson would come, but that's the most happy-barmy
dream I ever heard."

"Do you give me permission to sound them out or must you
consult your committee?"

"Oh, we're the committee," said Edweena. "You should remember that servants—as individuals or as a class—have very little experience in taking the initiative. They're glad to leave all of that
to us. But, Teddie, isn't Persis—whom I love dearly and whom I
practically introduced into society—isn't dear Persis a ghost of herself since that tragic death of her husband?"

Mrs. Cranston had slipped into the room some time before,
refusing tea, and had been listening to us.

"Mrs. Cranston, have I your permission to break a rule of the
house and to name names while telling a story? The lady in question expressly asked me to tell the truth about something that had
been unwisely hushed up."

"Mr. North, I trust you."

I told them of Archer Tennyson's desperate compulsions and of
their unhappy consequence. When I had finished they were silent
a moment.

"So that's what happened!" said Mrs. Cranston.

"Oh, the unhappy child!" said Edweena rising. "She'll receive
no proposals of marriage except from the wrong kind of man. Mrs.
Cranston, I want to see Chief Diefendorf. I think there's something that can be done about this."

"Edweena, you forget. He'll be here in a minute when he can
get away from his office."

And he knocked on the door. There were sedate greetings on all
sides. He refused tea, but was given permission to smoke. He
conferred with the two ladies about the Bridget Trehan matter and
arrived at a satisfactory procedure.

"Chief, are you in a hurry or might we consult you on a matter
we think you should know?"

"I'm completely at your disposal."

"Chief, Mr. North has come across some very interesting light on the tragic death of Mr. Archer Tennyson. He wants you to know about it because you're so resourceful and because you helped him so splendidly once before. Mr. North, will *you* tell the Chief what you learned?"

I told him the whole story. I made a point of talking quickly but very distinctly. At the end I said, "I wish Miss Edweena would now point out to you the consequences of that game of Russian roulette as they affect the life of Mr. Tennyson's widow."

She did so. He thought a moment and then said, "May I do what I would do if the whole thing had happened to my own daughter?"

"We hope you will, Chief."

"May I use your telephone? . . . I shall make a long-distance telephone call using the code number reserved for the police. The rest of you can go on talking or remain silent, as you wish."

First he called his own office. "Lieutenant, Chevy Chase, Maryland, is on the border of the District of Columbia. Will you find for me the nearest station-house to Chevy Chase, its telephone number, and the name of the Chief of Police?" He took out his notebook and jotted down the information given him. He then called the distant number. He gave his own name, office, and code number. "Chief, I'm sorry to call you so late in the afternoon. I hope I have not caused you inconvenience. . . . A problem that has arisen in Newport requires my asking you what you can tell me of Major James Michaelis." The conversation continued for almost ten minutes. Chief Diefendorf continued writing in his notebook. "Thank you again, Chief Ericson, and forgive me for intruding on you at this hour. If you will send me as much of that material as was rendered available for the public record, I shall be very indebted to you. Good evening, sir."

Chief Diefendorf was very pleased with himself—and with reason.

"Ladies and gentlemen, two years ago Major Michaelis was asked to resign from the Chevy Chase Country Club, popularly known as the 'golf club of Presidents.' He had brandished a re-

volver in the billiard room and attempted to induce a number of
the club members to engage in a game of Russian roulette with him.
His resignation was also required of him by the Army and Navy
Club in Washington. He was obviously becoming more and more
unbalanced. He comes of an influential family and no reference
to this appeared in the Washington papers. Last year his wife
instituted a suit for divorce. She was interviewed by the reporter
of a Takoma Park paper published near her home. Among the
grounds for her suit she specifically mentioned her husband's
obsession with that desperate game. Official and unofficial copies
of that material will be in my hands in a few days. I hope that
will take a load off Mrs. Tennyson's mind."

"Yes, and take her out of Coventry, Chief," said Edweena.

Three mornings later I telephoned "Nine Gables" and asked
Willis, who answered, if I might speak to Mrs. Tennyson.

"Mrs. Tennyson is seldom here in the morning, sir. She is in her
own cottage beyond the greenhouses." He gave me the telephone
number.

"Thank you, Willis."

I had frequented "Nine Gables" all those weeks without learning that Persis had a residence of her own. She retained an apartment at her grandfather's and spent much time there but even more
with her son and his nurse and her books and her piano in her
own cottage, "The Larches." This was merely another example of
the stifling reticence that Mrs. Bosworth had introduced into her
father's home. No words were wasted that could convey any
intimation of a family existence. Coventry, indeed.

"Good morning, Mrs. Tennyson."

"Good morning, Theophilus."

"This morning I am leaving some documents at your door.
Might I call on you this afternoon about five to discuss them?"

"Yes, indeed. Will you give me a hint as to what I may find in
them?"

"Is Frederick well?"

"Oh, yes—very well."

"Some day he will be glad to know that there is official evidence that his father did not take his own life in a fit of depression but in one of foolish but hopeful high spirits."

"Ah! . . ."

At five o'clock I drove my bicycle to her door. "The Larches" was built in the style of "Nine Gables" and was often referred to as the "little cottage." Diminutives were constantly misapplied in Newport. The door was open and Persis came forward to greet me. Again she was wearing a linen dress, this time in crocus yellow. There was a string of pale amber beads around her neck. My expression involuntarily expressed my admiration. She was accustomed to such expressions of admiration and met them with a light disculpatory smile—as much as to say "I can't help it." Her small son peered at me from behind her and fled—a sturdy young citizen with enormous eyes.

"Frederick's shy. He'll lurk about and gradually try to make friends with you later. . . . Let us have a cup of tea first and then discuss the surprising material you left at my door."

I was led into a large sitting room with tall windows open to the sea air. I had often seen them when passing on the Cliff Walk. Two elderly maids were busying themselves with the tea urn, the sandwiches, and the cake.

"Mr. North, this is Miss Karen Jensen and Miss Zabett Jensen."

I bowed. "Good afternoon, good afternoon."

"Good afternoon, sir."

"Your name is very well known in this house, Mr. North."

"I think I have had the pleasure of meeting the Miss Jensens at Mrs. Cranston's."

"Yes, sir. We have had that pleasure."

As Mrs. Cranston had said, I was a very famous person "in certain circles."

When the tea things had been cleared away Persis asked, "Please tell me what I am to think about these clippings and documents."

"Mrs. Tennyson, you will soon become aware that the climate that surrounds you is undergoing a change. Those who enjoyed—*enjoyed*—putting a malicious interpretation on your situation at the time of your husband's death must find some other victim for their spite. You are no longer a woman who drove her husband to desperation; you are a woman whose husband was imprudent in the choice of his friends. Mrs. Venable has received a copy of these papers; Miss Edweena, who is in and out of many cottages these days and who has always been your devoted champion, is *hard at work clearing the air*. You are in the situation of many women a century and a half ago whose husbands were killed in duels over foolish quarrels about racehorses or card games. Do you feel that the climate is changing within yourself?"

"Oh, yes, Theophilus, but I can scarcely believe it. I must have time."

"Let us not talk about it any more," I laughed. "We can be certain that a considerable number of people are talking about it at this very moment. There is something else I want to talk to you about. But first!" I rose. "I am incapable of seeing music on a music rack without wanting to know what has been studied or played."

I walked over to the piano and saw Busoni's transcriptions of six Bach organ chorale preludes. I glanced at her. With her same "disculpatory" smile she said, "My grandfather's very fond of Bach. For the coming winter evenings I've been preparing these for him."

"There is very little good music on the island of Aquidneck. I'm starved for it. Could you *try* these on me?"

"Oh, yes, if you wish it."

She was indeed accomplished. She was ready for Schloss Stams. The music blew away spite and condescending self-righteousness and the presumed shelter of worldly gratifications. . . . She set ringing the carillon of "*In Dir ist Freude*"; she found voice for the humility of *"Wenn wir in höchsten Nöten sein."* Frederick crept back into the room and sat down under the piano.

When she ceased playing she rose and said, "Frederick, I'm going into the garden to pick some flowers for Granddaddy. Don't let Mr. North go away while I'm gone," and she left the room.

I rose hesitantly from my chair. "Did your mother say she wanted me to go away, Frederick?"

"No!" he said loudly, coming out from under the piano. "No . . . you *stay!*"

"Then we must play the piano," I answered in a conspiratorial manner. "You sit here on the bench and we'll play church bells. You play this note softly, like this." I put his finger on the C below middle C and showed him how to repeat it slowly, softly, and on count. I put my foot on the damper pedal and I released the overtones of the note, including the dissonances in the higher registers. Then I reached over and played the C in the bass. This is an old musical parlor-trick. The novice has the sensation of playing many notes and of filling the air with Sunday morning chimes. "Now a little louder, Frederick." He looked up at me with awe and wonder. What did that Frenchman say? "The basis of the education of the very young is the expansion of the sense of wonder." There is also an element of fright in awe. His eyes fell on his mother standing motionless at the door. He ran to her, crying, "Mama, I'm making piano!" He'd had enough of that disturbing Mr. North and fled upstairs to his nurse.

Persis advanced smiling. "The Pied Piper of Hamelin!" she said. "I just invented that visit to the garden. Frederick doesn't have an opportunity to see many gentleman callers in this house.— What else did you want to discuss with me?"

"A notion.—I have become a close friend of Edweena Wills and Henry Simmons. Just now because of Edweena's delayed return from that almost disastrous cruise in the Caribbean they are very busy with their plans for the Servants' Ball. They've engaged the Cranston High School Band again. They've sold many cards already, but they're searching for a novel idea that will make the thing take on new life. I suggested they invite some guests of honor, beginning with the Chief of Police and six gallant young members of his force and Chief Dallas and six gallant young fire-fighters. They certainly are public servants."

"What a good idea!"

"Then I told them about Vienna's famous 'Fiaker Ball' where all levels of society mingle happily together. Then it occurred to us to begin gradually with an idea like this: to invite a young gentle-man and a young lady of the summer colony—the best-looking, the most charming, and particularly those who had shown them-selves most appreciative of the servant community. They didn't have much confidence about this, but they took a straw vote in their committee for such a gentleman and the votes were unanimous: Baron Stams. Have you noticed how his beautiful manners include *everyone?*"

"Indeed, I have."

"Well, I sounded him out. Did he feel it was beneath his dignity to be such a guest, or did he think it would bore him? On the con-trary! He said he'd long wanted to meet the staff at Mrs. Venable's, *socially,* and the staff at "Nine Gables" and at Mrs. Amis-Jones's and those other houses where he's dined so often. But he didn't see how he could get away. His Chief couldn't spare him from the embassy. Edweena laughed at that. Edweena and Mrs. Venable are not only valued friends but are often fellow-workers on pro-jects that make Newport a congenial place for those who both work and play here. She is sure that she has only to suggest that she call the Ambassador. 'Dear Ambassador, could I ask a small favor of Your Excellency? We wish to institute a sort of Fiaker Ball here. Could you lend us Baron Stams who has been chosen as the most popular guest of the summer season? Vienna-in-Newport, that kind of thing?' Don't you think that could be done?"

"It's a charming idea."

"Then the committee cast votes for the young lady guest of honor. They chose you."

"Me? . . . *Me?* But that's impossible. I hardly go out to dinner at all! They don't know I exist."

"Persis, you know better than I do that the domestic servants in Newport seldom change from year to year. They are like a silent spellbound audience watching the brilliant world they serve. How often you 'great folk' are astonished at all they know. They have long memories and deep sympathies, as well as deep resentments. The misfortune that happened to you happened to them also. They remember you in your happiest years—so few years ago. They remember that you and Mr. Tennyson won the cup for the best dancers at the benefit ball for the Newport Hospital. But most of all they remember your graciousness—you may have seemed removed and impersonal to your fellow-guests, but you were never impersonal to *them*."

She put her hands to her cheeks. "But I'd disappoint them so. I can understand their admiring Bodo, but as I told you, I'm just a dreary old widow-lady 'under a shadow.' "

"Well," I said sadly, "I told them it was doubtful that you would wish to accept their invitation; that your Aunt Sarah would feel that you were *degrading* yourself, and all—"

"*No! No! Never!*"

"May I present their ideas a little further? The grand march is set for midnight. Henry and Edweena would advance down the center of the hall to a march by John Philip Sousa, followed by the members of the committee, two by two. Then Chief Diefendorf and his six gallant men and Chief Dallas and his six gallant men in their dashing uniforms. Then you and Bodo in your finest clothes, smiling to right and left. When you reached the head of the line Henry would raise his staff (with all those ribbons) as a signal to the band which would start playing softly the 'Blue Danube Waltz.' You two would make a tour of the room dancing. Then the band would fall silent; Miss Watrous would take her place at the piano and you two would encircle the room first with the polonaise, then the polka, then the varsovienne, dancing like angels. Then the band would come in again with the 'Blue Danube

Waltz' and you two would pick a succession of partners from right and left. Finally you would bow to the assembly, shake hands with Henry and Edweena—and then you could go home. . . . No one would ever forget it."

There were tears in my eyes. I am never so happy as when I'm inventing. Bodo had not yet heard a word of this. The Ambassador had not yet received the request.

Just sheer soap-bubbles.

Just sheer kite-flying.

But that's what finally happened.

Edweena and Henry and Frederick and I were invited to attend one morning a dress rehearsal of those dances at "The Larches." Persis wore a many-layered dress of pale green tulle that billowed about her in the waltz ("as danced in Vienna"), although dresses of that sort were not in fashion in 1926. After the close of the rehearsal and after the Master and Mistress of Ceremonies had praised the dancers, Edweena and Henry sat on in silence for a moment.

Henry said, "Edweena, my love, that show could have gone on at the Queen's Jubilee in the Crystal Palace, I swear it could."

Frederick was practicing the polka all around the room. He fell down and hurt himself. Bodo returned, picked him up in his arms, and carried him upstairs to his nurse—as one accustomed.

As we rose to go, Henry said, "Now, Teddie, old Choppers, couldn't you tell a little lie just once and say that you were a servant? We'll give you a card and let you into the show tomorrow night."

"Oh, no, Henry. You made the rule: There are those who go in the front door of the house and those who don't. I can picture you all in my mind's eye and shall do so many times."

We were standing on the gravel path before the cottage.

Edweena said, "I think you're trying to say something, Teddie."

I raised my eyes to Edweena's. (It was true; they were more blue than hazel in the morning.)

I said hesitantly, "I always find it hard to say goodbye."
"So do I," said Edweena and kissed me.
Henry and I shook hands in silence.

The Servants' Ball

For some weeks I had felt intimations of autumn in the air. Some of the leaves of Newport's glorious trees were changing color and falling. I found myself murmuring the words of Glaukos in the *Iliad: "Even as are the generations of leaves so are those of men; the wind scatters the leaves on the earth and the forest buds put forth more when spring comes around; so of the generations of men one puts forth and another ceases."* The summer of 1926 was coming to an end. I had called at Mr. Dexter's garage and had paid the two final installments on my bicycle, up to and including the last day of my stay. In addition I had bought from him a jalopy at a price somewhat higher than I had paid for "Hard-hearted Hannah"—who in the meantime had been restored to further usefulness and was watching this transaction.

"I only use her myself," said Mr. Dexter. "I know what to do. Did you want to say a few words to her?"

"No, Mr. Dexter. I'm not so light-headed as I was."

"I heard you had some troubles. Everything gets around in Newport."

"Yes. True or false, it gets around."

"I heard you had a theory that Newport was like Troy—nine cities. When I was a boy our baseball team was called the Trojans."

"Did you mostly win or lose, Mr. Dexter?"

"We won mostly. In boys' schools Trojans were always the favorite team because in the story they didn't win. Boys are like that."

"What years were those?"

"Ninety-six, ninety-seven. All of us took Latin and some of us took Greek. . . . When would you like to pick up your car?"

"After supper next Thursday night. If you could give me the key now I could drive off without disturbing you."

"Now, professor, this isn't a new car and it isn't an expensive car; but it'll give you a lot of miles if you handle it right. I'd like to go on a short drive with you and give you some pointers."

"That's very good of you. I'll be here at eight and turn in my bicycle. Then we can drive to Mrs. Keefe's and pick up my baggage and go for that ride. Will you put in a big can of gasoline, because I'll be driving to Connecticut all night."

So on the night of the Servants' Ball I took Mrs. Keefe and her daughter-in-law to the "Chicken Dinner Church Sociable" at the Unitarian Church. I saw many new faces and was introduced to their owners. Unitarian faces are pleasant reading. Mrs. Keefe and I had become good friends, New England-fashion, and no moving words were necessary at our leave-taking. I finished my packing, stowed my baggage by the front gate, and bicycled down to Mr. Dexter's garage.

Lessons began at once. He showed me how to start and how to stop; how to back as smoothly as nodding to a neighbor; how to save gas, how to spare the brakes and the batteries. As in violin-playing there are secrets you can learn only from a master. When we had returned to his garage, I paid for the additional gasoline and put it in the car.

"You must be in a hurry to be off, professor."

"No. I have nothing to do until a few minutes before mid-night when I want to pass under the windows of Mrs. Venable's house to hear the grand march at the Servants' Ball."

"Since my wife's death I have a second home down here up in the loft. Could we sit there and have a little old Jamaica rum while you're waiting?"

I'm not a drinking man but I can take it or leave it. So we climbed the stairs to the attic. It was filled with portions of dis-mantled automobiles, but he had partitioned off a neat clean little three-room apartment with a big desk, a stove, some comfortable chairs, and some well-filled bookshelves. My host brought some water to the boil, added the rum, some cinnamon sticks, and half an orange. He filled our mugs and I settled down for an hour of New England taciturnity. I resolved to hold my tongue. I wanted to hear more from him. I had to wait for it.

"Have there been any more cities at Troy since the nine that Schliemann found?"

"Seems not. He found a scrubby village called Hissarlik and that's all there is still. You'd think it might have prospered being only four miles from the mouth of the Dardanelles, but it didn't. Probably no underground water left."

Silence. Wonderful rum.

"Started me thinking about what changes might take place here—give a hundred or a thousand years. . . . Likely the English language would be almost unrecognizable. . . . The horse is almost extinct already; they're thinking about pulling up the train tracks to Providence. . . ." He flapped his arms. "People will come and go on wings like umbrellas." He passed his hand over his brow. "A thousand years is a long time. Likely we'll be a different color. . . . We can expect earthquakes, cold, wars, invasions . . . pesti-lences. . . . Do ideas like that trouble you?"

"Mr. Dexter, after I graduated from college I went to Rome for a year to study archaeology. Our professor took us out into the country for a few days to teach us how to dig. We dug and dug. After a while we struck what was once a much traveled road over two thousand years ago—ruts, milestones, shrines. A million people must have passed that way . . . laughing . . . worrying . . . planning . . . grieving. I've never been the same since. It freed me from the oppression of vast numbers and vast distances and big philosophical questions beyond my grasp. I'm content to cultivate half an acre at a time."

He got up and walked the length of the room and back. Then he picked up the jug from the stove and refilled our mugs. He said, "I went to Brown University for two years before I came back here and got in the livery stable business." He pointed to his bookshelves. "I've read Homer and Herodotus and Suetonius— and still do. Written between twenty-eight hundred and eighteen hundred years ago. Mr. North, *one* thing hasn't changed much— *people!*" He picked up a book on his desk and put it down again. "Cervantes, 1605. They're walking up and down Thames Street— as you say—'laughing and worrying.' There'll be some more Newports before we slump into a Hissarlik.—Could we change the subject, Mr. North? I'm not yet freed from the oppression of time. After forty we get kind of time-ridden around here."

"Sir, I came to this island a little over four months ago. You were the first person I met. You may remember how light-headed I was, but underneath I was exhausted, cynical, and aimless. The summer of 1926 has done a lot for me. I'm going on to some other place that may be unrecognizable three hundred years from now. There'll be people in it, though at this moment I don't know a soul there. Thank you for reminding me that in all times and places we find much the same sort of people. Mr. Dexter, will you do a favor for me? Do you know the Materas? . . . and the Wentworths? Well, I'm a coward about saying goodbye. When you meet them will you tell them that among my last thoughts on leaving Newport was to send them my grateful affection?"

"I'll do that."

"Five persons that I love will be at the Servants' Ball tonight. They got the message already. Tonight, sir, will be among my happy memories." I rose and held out my hand.

"Mr. North, before I shake your hand I have a confession to make. I buy old cars, as you know. My young brother cleans them up. Some weeks we get four or five. He's a careless soul; he dumps old things he finds under the seats, in the linings, under the rug— all kinds of things—in a barrel for me to sift out later. Sometimes I don't get to look at it for weeks. About six weeks ago I found a sort of story. No name on it; no place mentioned except Trenton, New Jersey. The license on your car was New Hampshire. After talking to you tonight I think that story was by you."

I had turned scarlet. He reached down to a lower drawer in his desk and pulled out a long entry from my Journal—the account of an adventure I'd had with a shoemaker's daughter in Trenton. I nodded and he handed it over to me.

"Will you accept my apology, Mr. North?"

"Oh, it's of no importance. Just some scribbling to pass the time."

We looked at one another in silence.

"You made what happened pretty vivid, Mr. North. I'd say you had a knack for that kind of thing. Have you ever thought of trying to be a writer?" I shook my head. "I'll see you down to your car."

"Good night, Josiah, and thank you."

"Drive carefully, Theophilus."

I didn't wait under the trees outside Mrs. Venable's cottage to hear the Sousa march and the "Blue Danube Waltz."

Imagination draws on memory. Memory and imagination combined can stage a Servants' Ball or even write a book, if that's what they want to do.